Note for Librarians: A cataloguing record for this book is available from Library and Archives Canada at www.collectionscanada.ca/amicus/index-e.html
ISBN 1-4120-8626-4

Cover art by Chitra Bhatt
Back cover photograph by Trushar Joshi

*Printed on paper with minimum 30% recycled fibre.*
*Trafford's print shop runs on "green energy" from solar, wind and other environmentally-friendly power sources.*

# TRAFFORD
**PUBLISHING**™
*Offices in Canada, USA, Ireland and UK*

**Book sales for North America and international:**
Trafford Publishing, 6E–2333 Government St.,
Victoria, BC  V8T 4P4  CANADA
phone 250 383 6864 (toll-free 1 888 232 4444)
fax 250 383 6804; email to orders@trafford.com
**Book sales in Europe:**
Trafford Publishing (UK) Limited, 9 Park End Street, 2nd Floor
Oxford, UK  OX1 1HH  UNITED KINGDOM
phone +44 (0)1865 722 113 (local rate 0845 230 9601)
facsimile +44 (0)1865 722 868; info.uk@trafford.com
**Order online at:**
trafford.com/06-0382
10  9  8  7  6  5  4  3

To Coral,

# Follow the Cowherd Boy

A novel by

## J.A.Joshi

Much love !

Zarna

aka J. A. Joshi

Aug 8th 2015

# Acknowledgements

My teachers, who initiated me into the mysteries of the written word. Mira, who taught me her own special brand of heroism. My parents who taught me everything else.

My brother and my sisters, without whose help this book might have remained unfinished for years. The brats, who bounced into my room when I was writing and insisted they were not disturbing me.

Dipti, Jas, Raksha, Iain and Chitra, my dear mates, who read the book, told me they loved it, gave me lots of helpful comments and found all my typos and spelling mistakes (well, most of them).

The Maharaj of Panch Ganga Ghat, a descendant of Ramanand Acharya's disciplic line, who graciously gave me all he could, despite my terrible Hindi, in order to help me write this book.

Pujya Shri Rameshbhai Oza, the one from whom I first heard this story when I was fifteen years old. What a storyteller.

The two who inspire me, you know who you are. I couldn't write without seeing your faces every day.

—

And Arjun said to Krishna:

Bowing down and prostrating my body before Thee,
Adorable Lord, I seek Thy grace. Bear with me,
O Lord, as a father to his son, as a friend to his friend,
as a lover to his beloved.

Bhagavad Gita 11.44

# 1

# Wound

*1543, Merta*

The conch shell sounded, like the mountain's deep call to the sky, and Mira knew they had entered the palace. She ran to her sun-spotted balcony and strained against the holes of the carved marble screen, trying to see the crowd outside.

*

*Two days before…*

Mira twirled her way through the dance, striving to ignore the excited voices beneath her balcony.

Her ankle bells sang out chum chum across the marble floor and her long satin skirt flared around her. Her back poised as a peacock's tail, Mira moved her arms in the intricate motions, chanting the beat under her breath.

Outside, the people of Merta were preparing for her wedding. They were decorating the city with flowers and banners and designing rangoli patterns on the ground with colored powders. They sang songs of the legendary lovers, Sita and Rama, Parvati and Shiv.

Mira loved someone but he wasn't the man her father had chosen for her.

A sudden dizziness took her and she stopped. Her stomach rolled. Hand over mouth, Mira ran into her dressing room and vomited in the basin. Shivering, she sat on the stone floor.

"I won't marry Bapu Sa's choice," she said aloud. "I won't marry anyone but Krishna."

Her maid Lalita had come running into the room and was now wiping Mira's face with a wet cloth.

"Come and rest. All will be well, Jiji," Lalita said, her young brow muddled with a frown.

With slow movements, the maid helped Mira up and led her into the bedroom.

Mira took a deep breath. "Has he arrived?"

Lalita shook her head.

"He won't come, you know." Mira lay on the bed.

"Of course he will. He's your father."

"He won't come. He knows I don't want to marry the yuvraj."

"Shhhh...try to sleep."

"What day is it?"

"Shunivar."

"How many days left?"

Lalita sighed. "Two."

"See? He won't come."

Lalita was silent and Mira turned away, closing her eyes.

She dreamed of her grandfather. He was pulling a screaming eight-year-old Mira from her mother's room.

Kusum's dead, she heard people say. She's gone to the lord's house.

She didn't believe it but Shamal, her elder brother, told her it was true.

Mira turned to Krishna but he was silent. She thought that Krishna was sad and that was why he wouldn't speak. She decided she wouldn't speak either.

For months, even after she was brought with Lalita from Chaukari to the capital fort of her grandfather's kingdom, she didn't speak.

Why speak when there was no one to reply?

Mira jerked awake.

"Jiji?" Lalita said from beside her. "You have a fever."

Mira turned her aching head. "Is it late?"

Lalita nodded.

"Don't worry about me, Lalita. Go to sleep."

"Don't be silly, I'll rest when your fever's broken."

Mira gulped the water Lalita held to her lips. She lay down, panting.

"Has he come yet?"

Lalita was silent.

"Why does he hate me so?"

"He doesn't hate you, Jiji. You mustn't say such things."

"Then why do this to me?"

"He's a Rana. He's doing what's best for his people."

"His people," Mira repeated. "My people."

She remembered a lesson her father had given her and Shamal when they'd been little:

"A king is bound to serve his people just as his people are bound to serve him," Ratan had said. "His life belongs to his subjects and he must be prepared to sacrifice everything for them."

Her father lived by those teachings. He'd ridden out many times to protect his people from neighboring Rajputs and the Moghuls and the Afghans.

Mira's aunt had said this marriage alliance was for the people. But if this marriage was for the people, why didn't her father come?

He didn't come because it wasn't for the people. He just wanted to rid himself of Mira.

She remembered how her father used to tickle her with his beard and set her on the front of his saddle when he went riding. He took her to see the villagers on festival days and smiled when she'd kissed his cheek.

Now he didn't see her, or talk to her, or care what she thought.

He didn't even let Shamal visit her. No, Shamal remained in Chaukari learning how to fight and rule and lead.

Mira used to play with her brother, pretending that she was kidnapped by villains and he was rescuing her. His friends, Ranjeet and Raagav, joined them and together the four of them ran through the village lanes of Chaukari until the dark hours of the night.

Shamal wrote letters to Mira in the capital, asking why she was sent away and why they said she didn't speak.

When Mira wrote back, she didn't answer his questions. Even though he was two years older than her, she couldn't tell him her secret. If she did, he might hate her too.

Mira had hoped that her father might soften and come for her. He didn't and she remained under the care of her aunt and uncle.

Her eldest cousin Jaimal was distant, more concerned with weapons training than a young motherless girl.

It was her young cousins who were her comfort. With them, Mira learned to play again as she had played with Shamal and Ranjeet and Raagav. She learned to speak once again and when they asked what she was dreaming of when she thrashed about in her sleep, Mira told them she was dreaming of Krishna.

They told her he would come for her. They said he had to love her as she loved him.

Now she was thirteen and about to be married to the crown prince of Merwar.

Krishna hadn't come for her yet.

Mira awoke to full daylight and the muffled sound of thumping.

Lalita was slumped over the side of the mattress, asleep.

Careful not to wake her, Mira slid out from under the sheets. Her legs trembled with weakness so she filled a cup with water and gulped it down. There was fruit next to the bed and she ate some grapes, feeling the juices squirt around her mouth.

Feeling better, she went into her sitting room, trying to find the source of the noise. Beneath her balcony, all the people who'd been working in the gardens were gone. The parrots perched in the trees were silent and even the peacocks had folded their tails.

Mira went to the front door of her suite and peered out, but there was no one there either. She walked back inside rubbing her empty stomach, her skin bare without her veil. Where was everybody? She went to the balcony again and looked out through the tiny holes in the marble screen.

The city looked breathtaking with the gold and red banners of Merta floating in the air, flags raised on every rooftop.

The thumping was louder now.

Mira looked around, trying to see where the sound was coming from. What day was it? She tried to remember but wasn't even sure when she'd fallen asleep. She had a vague memory of having a fever.

"Jiji, your father didn't come."

Lalita was crying into her hands, her thin shoulders shaking, and Mira went to comfort the maid.

"What's happened, Lalita? Where is everybody? What day is it?"

"It's Somvar."

Somvar? But that meant she'd been ill for two days!

The thumping was much louder now and when Lalita was silent, Mira recognized the sound as the beat of drums. There was a procession going through the city.

A procession...

Mira gripped Lalita's shoulders. "What are those drums for?"

The maid just wept.

Mira shook her. "Lalita?"

"It's them, Jiji. The barat procession. Yuvraj Bhoj."

Mira almost couldn't speak. "My groom?"

When Lalita nodded, Mira backed away, wrapping her arms around herself.

"I told you Bapu Sa wouldn't come."

The conch shell sounded.

# 2

# Blood

The crowd was shielded by the east wing of the palace but Mira could hear the surge as the procession entered the courtyard in waves of cheering and dancing.

The scriptures gave her the right to refuse. Hadn't Draupadi refused to marry Karna? Krishna said a woman's wedding garland was hers to place around whomever she wished.

Mira tried to still her heaving shoulders. She went to her couch, an ancient piece of carved rosewood, her mother's favorite sitting place. She stroked the back of it, feeling its coolness, its smoothness. Her mother had promised Lord Krishna as her husband.

But if she didn't wed Bhoj, her aunt and uncle would be so angry. They were depending on this marriage to strengthen Merta's influence.

And what about her grandfather, Rao Duda? Her aunti Kirti said he was ill and that was why Mira couldn't visit him. If she refused to marry and her grandfather had already given his word to the groom's family, the Sisodias, it would humiliate him.

The marble beneath her feet began to thrum with vibrations as the celebrators made their way through the palace.

Her people had worked so hard to make everything perfect, she thought. This marriage would make their country strong.

But Merta was strong. This alliance with Merwar wasn't necessary. Mira could run away.

And go where? she thought, hugging herself, her stomach hollow from nausea. If her mother were alive, this wouldn't be happening.

Her father would disown her if she ran away. And what about her brother? Would Shamal be proud that she'd disgraced the Rathore clan?

No Rathore had ever run away before. Her family was renowned for its courage. If she ran away, people would say she was a coward not worthy of her ancestors.

Shuddering, she lowered herself to the couch.

Perhaps she could go to Bhoj and ask him not to marry her.

No, you fool! Mira screamed in her mind. No warrior of Rajput blood was going to turn back just because she asked him to. He was probably like her cousin Jaimal and used to ordering everybody around. If she told Bhoj she didn't want him, he'd become angry. He'd might marry her anyway and then what? Mira had heard that some men beat their wives.

She'd been educated in the love arts, as all princesses were. She knew what would happen on her wedding night. This faceless man would touch her. A man who was not Krishna would make love to her.

Mira closed her eyes against the horror. What should I do, Ma Sa?

She couldn't run away.

She couldn't ask Bhoj to turn back.

She couldn't make her father stop the wedding and she couldn't go to her sick grandfather.

In her mind's eye, Mira saw Krishna, his body relaxed and strong, smiling as he watched her. He had such a beautiful smile.

How could she stop this wedding?

Lalita was kneeling before her, helpless.

Mira caught her maid's hands and squeezed them. Suddenly, she was ashamed of herself for her cowardice when poor Lalita had been through so much more pain than she.

The drums were muffled now as the barat made its way through the palace to the guest wing.

Mira hadn't seen any of her relatives in days. It suddenly struck her as odd. What were they doing? Why had they left her alone all this time?

"Lalita, will you go and see the procession for me, and find out what is happening?"

Lalita nodded and wiped her long nose with her veil. She went out with her shoulders bent.

Mira went into her dressing room and splashed her face with cold water. Her skin dripping, she heard singers parading through the gardens, glorifying their prince and his bloodline, the brave Sisodia Rajputs of Merwar. They sang of heroic ancestors, legendary Maharana Ratan and his wife Padmini, who sacrificed themselves for the honor of their clan. Their family ruled Chittore and Kumbalgarh, great fortresses that had never surrendered, that stood for centuries as proud monuments of Merwar's history.

Mira thought of her father Ratan, her mother Kusum, her grandfather Rao Duda. She too had a great bloodline.

The conch sounded again and she knew that her aunt was performing the aarti rite to Bhoj, waving lamps around his face to ward the evil eye away. She imagined her uncle, bear-like with his flat feet and long arms, offering solicitations to the groom and his relatives, taking them through the halls, showing off the palace.

She felt the air around her begin to cool. Soon it would be night and then morning and then the wedding.

The sound of giggling came from the doorway and Mira turned to see a crowd of her aunt's maids.

"There you are, Raj Kumari!" said the creaking voice of Kirti's head dasi, Shakti. She hobbled over. "We've been looking everywhere for you!"

Is that why I've seen no one for two days? Mira wondered, wanting to shriek at them.

Laughing, the maids surrounded Mira.

"Come, we've work to do," said Shakti. "But what have you done to your face? It's all blotchy!" She took hold of Mira's chin and tilted her head from side to side.

When Mira had first come to the capital, there were some, like Shakti, who had taken Mira's silence as a sign of stupidity. Even now, five years later, they treated her like an imbecile and it was habit for her to endure it. Her aunt had never noticed, or perhaps had never cared.

"It'll take hours to repair," Shakti said, shaking her head at Mira's reddened skin.

Lalita entered the dressing room, her dark cheeks flushed.

"Looks like you've seen Bhoj," one of the maids snickered. "He has that effect on women."

Mira ducked her head to hide her disgust. Was he a philanderer then?

"You should be grateful, Raj Kumari," another dasi, Kamini, said. "Not many ladies are blessed with such a handsome husband."

"And so gracious!" Shakti said. "There were none too low for him to speak to. Come," she said to the younger maids, "we've work to do if we're to make the princess worthy of him. And why are you not wearing your veil?" she asked Mira, steering her towards the bath pond.

Mira endured in silence. What else could she do?

Someone untied the strings that bound her blouse and slipped it off, then pushed her onto the massage bed.

Shakti was ordering hot water and towels and massage oils and cleansing pastes with milk and honey.

Lalita came forward with a damp cloth, patting the tender skin around Mira's eyes. She leaned down. "Your father has arrived."

Mira's eyes widened and she almost leaped from the bed. Her father had finally come? He'd not abandoned her after all?

Lalita clasped her hand, speaking low. "I have his permission to take you to him."

Mira's heart erupted, like a stone had burst into a flower. Her father had come!

There was still time!

"Raj Kumari Mira is to visit Rana Ratan in one hour," Lalita was saying to the others.

One hour! Mira wailed inside. How can I wait that long?

"She cannot leave now!" Shakti shrieked. "We've so much work to do before tomorrow's wedding."

There won't be a wedding, Mira wanted to say, her chest bubbling and her head dizzy with relief.

"Those are her father's orders," said Lalita, her voice cool.

Despite herself, Mira smiled as she heard Shakti muttering about the waste of time. Her father would save her, Mira thought to herself.

The maids worked quickly as they stirred cooling sandalwood paste with honey and smeared it over Mira's skin.

She fidgeted, twitching her nose and mouth, waiting for them to finish the tedious scrubbing.

They sat her down in the bathing pond, rinsing her with warm goats milk, then rose water.

Relieved, Mira stood and let the dasis pat dry her pink gold body.

They rubbed in a mint cream for coolness and she bit back her groan. Hurry up! she thought.

"The redness in her face is going, thank the Devtas," Shakti said.

They took out fresh clothes of dawn pink satin.

Mira longed to scratch where the fabric itched her waist but remained still as Lalita bound the strings tight across her back.

At first, the skirt looked too long but she must have grown recently because the garment fitted her perfectly. When she walked, the material flowed out before her, making it look as if she was gliding through pink water. Satisfied but with no time to dwell on it, she looked at Lalita and tapped her feet, waiting for them to bring her veil.

"The color is a good choice," Shakti said. "It makes her complexion passable."

"Raj Kumari Mira," Lalita said in the coldest voice imaginable, "is considered the most beautiful girl in Merta, Merwar, and Amber combined!"

Really? Mira thought, diverted for the moment. Did Krishna think she was beautiful too?

Shakti waved her hand. "What would you know? You're not much older than her yourself. Raj Kumari Mira is not fair skinned enough to be a true beauty and you shouldn't tell her so or she'll develop an unbecoming ego."

"Jiji is a great beauty. Why else do you think a man like Yuvraj Bhoj wants to marry her?" Lalita snapped.

Oh no, not him, Mira thought. "Is it time to go?" she asked, stepping forward.

It was a moment before Lalita blinked. "I think so."

Glaring at Lalita, Shakti fastened Mira's earrings and bangles before picking up a bowl beside her. "Close your eyes, Raj Kumari."

Frantic now, Mira barely restrained her scream of impatience and let the maid apply the kajol, drawing the thick black paste around her eyes with a little brush.

Someone fasted a pink gauze veil around her body, then lifted the edge over her hair and fastened it with a hair jewel so that it draped diagonally over her bare back.

Mira took a deep breath and looked at Lalita. "Come."

"Hurry back," Shakti snapped. "Her elders will be here soon to supervise the henna painting of her hands."

Lalita gave a haughty nod before turning away.

As soon as they were out of Shakti's sight, Mira broke into a run.

She heard Lalita gasp behind her, trying to keep up as Mira turned a corner.

Panting, Mira whirled around. "Quickly!"

A guard on duty was standing a short distance away, trying to look as if he hadn't noticed what the princess was doing.

Lalita skidded into view. "Jiji, stop!"

Mira glared. "We have to hurry!"

"I know but you must use restraint. And I must show you a different path so that you do not bump into the wedding party!"

Now that she'd stopped, Mira heard once more the tumultuous sounds that were resounding through the palace. She could hear the distant clash of cymbals and thunder of drums. The ground vibrated.

Gritting her teeth, Mira tried to walk as she should, following the directions Lalita was murmuring behind her. People were now in sight, laughing and bowing and then hurrying around her as they went to perform their duties.

Passing corridors, Mira saw flower petals strewn on the floor and knew that Bhoj must have come down here in his tour of the palace.

She went up a set of stairs and spied massive double doors of carved rosewood. Finally! she thought.

Though only Rao Duda's second son, Ratan was a powerful influence in Merta. His quarters were huge, matched only by the king's suite. Ratan spent little time in the capital but no other dared lay claim to his rooms.

Bhima, her father's mountainous bodyguard, was standing outside the door with his arms crossed.

It had been years since she'd seen him and she strained to smile for him.

He gave her a tender look and opened the doors. "Your father is in his receiving room, Raj Kumari," he said, his voice deep and melodious.

But his receiving room is for ambassadors, she thought, panicked. It was too late. The rosewood doors closed behind her.

"Stay here," she said to Lalita who was twitching with nerves.

Mira's hands were shaking. Why did they have to start shaking now? She gripped her skirts and went through the door on the left into his receiving room.

A tall man stood at the window, his figure illuminated by night lamps. He'd removed his turban and the ends of his black hair gleamed on his shoulders. He didn't turn.

She wanted to call out to him but her throat was too tight. She walked a few paces into the room, taking a deep breath.

Ratan didn't turn.

He was leaner than she remembered, harder, the lines of his back still as if carved from stone.

She took another step forward and noticed how the ground vibrated.

He still didn't turn.

Why doesn't he face me? Mira wondered, searching the lines of his back in the severe cut of his purple kurta.

He was watching the crowd below, his windows overlooking the front courtyard of the palace.

The acrobats and dancers had gathered together here, competing with each other to get the greatest applause from the crowd. Servants were lighting bonfires and torches, and men with drums slung over their shoulders beat out a wild rhythm as they twisted and jumped over the flames, their knees bent, their torsos low to the ground.

Her father watched them, his feet planted to the floor like the roots of a tree.

He looked so alone.

Mira forgot her nerves and went forward, touching his back with her fingertips. "Bapu Sa?"

If anything, he became more clenched. He looked at her, his brown eyes meeting hers.

"Putri," he said, and kissed her forehead.

She almost cried, she was so glad he still loved her. Suddenly, it didn't matter that she hadn't seen him for years. She smiled, leaning in to him.

He didn't smile back. "You look like your mother."

She opened her mouth, but didn't know what to say. He'd said that as if he regretted it.

He turned back to the crowds below.

Why was he being this way? she wondered, blinking back her tears.

Slowly, he reached out and closed the shutters of his windows, blotting out the sight of the revelers and muffling the roar of celebration. The floor still trembled.

"So," he said. "Tomorrow is your wedding day."

She hid her shaking hands in the folds of her skirt.

"Bapu Sa, did you get the messages I sent?" She cursed herself for sounding so small and young. She had to be grown up if she was to persuade him.

He didn't reply.

"Bapu Sa?" she said, trying to make her voice firm. "I need to tell you something."

"I know. You're afraid. But you mustn't be," he said. "A daughter must marry and it is a father's duty to provide a suitable groom."

Mira opened her mouth but he held up his hand, silencing her.

"You've known of these negotiations for a long time."

She pulled herself together. "Bapu Sa, I cannot marry him."

He looked at her and she quaked, seeing the same stern expression she'd seen when her mother, Kusum, died.

"Royal marriages are never about just two people, Mira. They are about nations."

"I don't want to ruin this alliance," she whispered, then wanted to kick herself for being so weak. "But is there no other way?"

He frowned. "This is the best way."

Yet not the only way, she thought. Her next words came out in a rush. "It would be wrong for me to marry this prince when I love another."

His frown turned into a black scowl. "What?"

"Krishna," she stuttered.

He towered over her, glaring. "Who is this Krishna?"

"Shri Krishna, Bapu Sa!" she cried.

"Who?" He sounded taken aback.

"Shri Krishna," she whispered.

There was a moment of blank silence. Then: "Lord Shri Krishna? Bhagwan Krishna?"

She nodded.

He looked like someone had pulled off his beard. "Mira, are you still holding on to these dreams? Still, after all this time?"

Her tears fell, streaking her kajol. "What else have I to hold on to?"

His moustache bunched out, as if refuting what she said. He touched a kajol trail on her cheek, then looked down at his black fingertip. "Mira, don't you realize it's impossible?"

"Why?"

"Because he's not real."

She glared at her father.

"Of course *he* is real," Ratan was impatient. "But what you want isn't possible. I cannot just allow you to do whatever you wish. What of our people? Our country?"

She rubbed her eyes, smudging more kajol over her cheekbones. "But Ma Sa gave him to me!"

There was a pause. She looked up, and for a split second, saw Bapu Sa's face crumple. Then her stern father returned, his brows drawn tight over his forehead. He took her hand and led her to a seat.

"Putri, I thought you'd ceased these childish games."

She hiccupped.

"You've been gently bred and sheltered. I couldn't bear for you to be exposed to the ugliness of the world so I sent you here, to the capital, where it was safe."

She was confused. He'd sent her here to protect her?

"Perhaps I should have visited you more often, supervised you more. But I–" he looked away.

She searched his face. Wouldn't she have been safe in Chaukari? What was the need to send her away? And if he'd regretted it, why hadn't he sent for her?

"Other things held my attention," he finished, clearing his voice. He looked back at her. "You know that our country, indeed the whole of this land of Bharat, is threatened by Moghul and Afghan invaders."

She nodded. "I remember you telling me we were too strong for them."

"Yes. We've fought them for years." He gazed down at a jagged scar on his hand.

She'd never seen that particular scar; it must be recent. She took his hand in hers to examine it.

"We're not so strong anymore, putri."

She rubbed the mark on his skin, their hands gold on gold, just like so long ago. "What do you mean?"

"We're weak. If we were attacked now, I doubt we could withstand them."

"But our army–"

"We've no army left, Mira."

She dropped his hand.

"Our last battle was two weeks ago. My forces were destroyed. There aren't enough troops here in the capital or in any of the rest of our kingdom to replace them."

She shook her head. "Then why aren't we overrun?"

"Because we managed to destroy a great deal of their army as they destroyed ours. We were able to force them back, but if they regroup…"

She gaped at Ratan like an idiot, her mouth working but nothing coming out.

"Many kingdoms around us have fallen. The horrors they've endured, I cannot even speak of it." His look was grim. "You know that your own dasi Lalita was a victim, Mira, so you cannot pretend there hasn't already been pain. Suffice to say that the enemy does not see women and children as innocent."

She put her hand to her throat, knowing what he said was true. Years ago, when Mira had been a baby, Lalita had lost her family to a Moghul raid. She'd survived because her mother had hidden her in a large water pot and told her to be very quiet. However, Lalita had never forgotten the screams of her mother and aunts as she'd crouched in the water with her fist stuffed in her mouth, knowing that her father and uncles and brothers were already dead.

Ratan had found Lalita and brought her to Chaukari to be his daughter's playmate, and later, her maid.

He continued, his voice cold.

"Those who survive are forced to practice the religion of the enemy. Hindu mandirs are destroyed or desecrated and turned into houses of worship for their own faith."

She couldn't breath. What did he mean, "those who survive"? And who would be so evil as to destroy a temple?

"There are Rajput kingdoms that talk of surrendering."

"They cannot!" she cried.

He seized her shoulders. "Merwar is the only one that doesn't. That is why this marriage between our two kingdoms is so crucial! We need Merwar's help."

Mira couldn't breathe. She couldn't believe Merta had no army. So many could be killed, even the women and children. Her own little cousins might be hurt.

She pulled away from Ratan, rising to her feet. Her family could die, she thought. Her people could become slaves.

Walking around the room, Krishna's face flickered in her mind.

She ran back to her father. "Is there no other way?"

He gave her a grim smile. "Who would ally themselves to a kingdom with no army for no reason other than friendship? No, Mira, a royal marriage is the only way."

"But why me?" she asked, kneeling. "Why not one of my sisters?" She had so many cousins.

"They want only you." He ran a knuckle down her cheek. "Your beauty and talents are known to most of Bharat. Many kingdoms have asked for your hand, but I knew only Bhoj was worthy of you. And the advantage to our people was of utmost importance." He stroked her head, his hand tender.

Ratan gazed down at her, seeing through her face to someone else. "So like your mother," he whispered.

She wept at his feet, for him, for her, for her mother, for her people.

"And there is no other way?"

He was silent.

She laid her head upon his knee, just as she'd done as a little girl.

There is no other way, she told herself.

# 3

# Vow

That night, Mira didn't sleep.

Lying in her bed, her eyes hot and dry and open, she willed herself to accept.

The sounds of music died down just before midnight. The fort rested.

She sat up and drew back the gauze drapes that protected her from insects. Somewhere in this royal mahel, she thought, the yuvraj is lying in bed. Perhaps he's thinking of me.

No, she thought, why would he think of me? I'm just the means.

Cool night air touched her bare stomach. She swung her legs off the bed and stood, her blue cotton skirt slipping off the satin bed like water over rose petals. She listened for sounds of life.

There was nothing but peaceful silence. Peace that depended on her.

She walked out to her balcony. Through the holes in the marble screen, she gazed at the sky. The stars are constant, she thought. I cannot be as they are, I cannot be constant.

She bent her head back, searching the sky for something to comfort her. She arched her back, backwards, backwards, praying for the strength to bend backwards some more. She lay on the cold stone, staring at the stars, praying for the strength to bend.

In a few hours, it would be dawn. She had only a few more hours.

There were muffled voices behind her and Mira almost screamed. Why couldn't they leave her alone for just a few hours?

Give me the strength to bend, she thought, her prayers drifting up through the holes.

Inside, Shakti and Kamini were muttering and pointing at the empty bed.

"I must bathe now," Mira said.

They jumped and turned, scowling at her.

Shakti stepped forward. "We wondered where you were. Your dasi Lalita has readied the altar for your morning worship."

"Good." Mira went in. She bathed and dressed in simple clothes of white threaded with gold, then entered her sitting room and went to where her altar stood on the eastern side of the room.

The deity she worshipped had been given to her in her eighth year. A sage had come to Chaukari to visit Mira's pregnant mother and had left this behind. Kusum, on her deathbed, had given it to Mira.

The deity stood upon a raised altar of marble and gold, covered by a carved dome. Mira's tutor, Purohitji, had taught her that the dome symbolized the circular universe in which the lord stood supreme.

Mira had spent a long time wondering how the lord could be here with her and everywhere else at the same time. Then Purohitji had explained that the lord was the base of the universe, present in everything, animate or inanimate. Thus, he was with her and in her. He was in the trees, the birds, the animals, the ground she walked upon. He was in the sky, the clouds, the stars. He was the taste of water. He was her breath. And yet to please his devotees, he also appeared before them in a charming form.

She clung to Purohitji's teachings. She was never alone because her lord was with her.

Mira lit a lamp, illuminating the altar and turning her deity to golden blue. She rang the bell, as her mother had taught her, informing the world that her lord had awoken. The ting ting made Mira smile and she knew this moment was precious.

She touched her forehead to the floor before him.

In the dressing room, she heard Kamini snapping at another maid for measuring the oils wrong and Mira squeezed her eyes against the scream of frustration that swelled in her throat.

Try to ignore it, she thought. Think only of this, your puja.

Rising, she looked at his feet, delicately crossed at the ankles. She looked up his blue body. Blue like a thundercloud. Blue like those moments of silence before the sky lightened and the birds sang.

Some more maids ran past her into the dressing room but she refused to turn and see what was happening.

She raised her gaze to his face, his eyes. Dark, blooming lotuses, they reminded Mira of everything she would lose when she betrayed

Krishna. Many times, she'd asked Lalita to paint her eyes the way her lord's eyes were painted.

A peacock feather graced his crown, its rainbow hues deep and jewel-like. His arms were lifted in flute-playing pose and his palms were pink like cows' tongues.

Her mother had followed his music through the gates of paradise. Mira longed to hear his flute for she knew it wouldn't tell her to be a princess.

It would tell her to cut her bonds and be free.

She felt cool air against the hollow of her neck.

Bend backwards, it said.

Behind her, she heard Shakti and Kamini walking about, directing the rest of the maids with her trousseau.

Why couldn't they be quiet just this once? Couldn't they see she was performing puja?

She began her prayers, chanting the self-purifying mantras. Soon I will not be worthy, she thought. No! Don't think of that. Think only of the lord.

She bathed Him in bowls of milk, yogurt, honey, sugar, and ghee. This was panchaamrut, the five nectars. Her mother had explained that they symbolized love, devotion, trust, faith, and patience. Bless me with these virtues, my lord, she prayed, I will need them.

The thought of another man touching her rose like a monster ready to strike. She realized she was crying when a tear fell into the water she was using to bathe him. She called for a fresh bowl.

Soon, I will be as impure as this water, she thought. But I mustn't think of that.

Lalita appeared with fresh water but Mira didn't look at her. She mustn't look at anything right now but her lord.

She chose white and gold clothing for him, with accompanying earrings, necklace and crown topped with a peacock feather. She adorned his feet with leaves from the sacred Tulsi plant, the lord's most beloved devotee. Show me the mercy you showed to Tulsi, she prayed. Let me always feel you with me.

She applied a sandalwood paste tilak to his forehead, two thin vertical lines joined together just between the brows. The heady scent lingered on her fingertips, even after she washed the paste off.

Krishna loved sandalwood.

She strung a garland of jasmine flowers and placed it around his neck. Every day for years, she'd prayed that Krishna would take her away, but not now.

Behind, Mira heard Shakti crowing over the jewels Mira's in-laws had sent. Gritting her teeth, Mira tried to block out the nauseating sounds. Concentrate on your lord, she told herself.

She offered fruits and saffron-spiced milk.

Kusum had told her to always eat food that had been offered to the lord. He was the true master of everything and thus to take something without offering it to him first was a crime.

Next to her sat a tray that contained five unlit lamps, incense, flowers, water and a conch shell. She lit the lamps and incense and lifted the tray to circle it around the lord in the ancient rite of aarti.

There was splashing and giggling in the dressing room as the maids cleaned and readied it for later.

Mira gripped the aarti tray harder. Concentrate, she told herself. Don't think of what they're doing.

The lamps were the light, the truth, as the lord was the light, the truth, she recited in her mind, words that Purohitji had told her long ago. Performing the aarti, a devotee reminded himself to live in that light.

There was a clatter and a crash as someone dropped a pot. Shakti's screeches filled the chambers.

Live in that light, Mira thought. Live in that light. Live in that light.

She watched the lamps reflect the flames in her lord's eyes and realized that, married to Bhoj or not, she would always look for that light. She set down the tray and waved the heat of the lamps over her lord with her right hand. She passed her hands over the flames once more, her fingers slipping through the yellow heat, then smoothed her warmed hands over her heart and her eyes, drawing the light within.

Something touched her head. She sat up and felt with her hand. It was a single jasmine flower, fallen from his garland onto the parting of her hair.

Krishna, her lord, had blessed her.

*

Mira didn't know what happened for most of that morning.

She had vague impressions of Kirti and her uncle Vikramdev performing a puja to Ganesh, the Lord of Prosperity, and Gauri, the Goddess of Marital Bliss. She remembered lots of hands. It must have been her aunts and cousins rubbing the beautifying piti on her, a paste of sandalwood, turmeric, saffron, chickpea, and athar, a heady perfume.

Then Mira was sitting in her bath, her maids pouring milk and water over her and singing marriage songs.

As they drew her wedding garments on, Mira thought of how she should've worn them for Krishna before she shook herself and set her jaw. There was no use in thinking that way.

But her mother had made these garments, ready for when she gave her daughter away. Mira closed her eyes, seeing her mother, sewing and smiling.

Someone massaged Mira's hair with scented oils before weaving it into an elaborate arrangement. White jasmine was threaded through the design like vines and a damini was fastened along her hair parting so that the end ruby dangled over her brow.

They painted kajol around her eyes, then a vermillion bindi on her forehead, elaborating the design with white and red dots above her eyebrows.

Necklace upon necklace was poured around her throat and she struggled to keep her back upright against the weight. She had never worn so many jewels at one time.

How will I walk like this? she wondered.

They slipped gold armlets on, followed by thick jewel studded bracelets on her wrists. Kung kung sounds echoed her every movement. A hoop ring was slipped through the pierced hole on her left nostril.

A bride's nose ring symbolized her virginity, Kusum had told Mira. It was to be removed by her husband on the night of their first union.

Mira told herself that she would remove the nose ring before Bhoj entered the bedchamber. She wouldn't let him remove it.

"Putri," Kirti said from her lounging pose on the couch.

Mira dug her ruby toe ring into the rug beneath her. Don't call me daughter, she thought. My mother would never have done this to me.

"The auspicious hour draws near, putri."

Mira gazed at the ground and didn't turn.

Kirti came to stand in front of her. She smiled and touched her fingers to Mira's cheek. "Beautiful. Bring the mirror," she said to Shakti.

The glass had been covered before Mira had begun dressing but now the maids brought it before her. A dasi pulled off the cover from behind.

Mira gawked.

Her clothes were stunning. The gold threaded through the silk skirt shaped it so that the material skimmed over to her hips and thighs, outlining them. The extra paneling on the bottom half made the skirt swish outwards like a fish tail.

Her red silk blouse, drawn so tight over her breasts, was like the fruit on top of the flower. She looked more like a woman than ever before.

They were taking her to Bhoj like this? Like a ripe fruit? No, she couldn't go! They had to get her another blouse, another skirt. The veil was too thin over her back! Everyone could see her skin. Everyone could see—everything!

"Come, it is time," Kirti said.

"No, I—"

"Wait, Raniji." Kamini held up two gold anklets, covered in so many bells that Mira thought they'd deafen her. A dasi lifted the hem of her skirt and Kamini fastened the anklets. "Now she is ready."

Mira was about to scream that she couldn't go like this when an eruption of giggling made her look to the door.

A swarm of female relatives came into the room.

Mira swallowed a sob. "Kaki Sa, I can't—"

"Nervous?" It was another aunt, a tall, slender lady married to one of Mira's uncles. "Don't worry. You won't mind being married to Bhoj. And I can't see him being annoyed either!"

The women giggled and giggled.

"There will be heaven for them when they reach Chittore!" one of Mira's married cousins said.

No, Mira moaned in her head.

"Ah, young love."

How will I bear it? Mira thought.

Her relatives surrounded her and somehow, everyone managed to grab her. Someone clasped her shoulder, her waist, her hip. Her little cousins were clutching at her skirts, the wide panels at the bottom allowing them to dance two steps before her as they pulled her along.

She dug her heels into the rug but it was no use.

They pulled her forward.

She'd worried about the weight of her jewelry but the force with which her family propelled her was formidable. It was almost as if she flew to Bhoj.

Her suite, the hallway, the small courtyard outside her rooms, the eastern wing—everything went by in the blur of red mist that was her veil and tears. The grand courtyard was just beyond it, where weddings, ceremonies, and fire sacrifices, yagnas, were performed.

Mira's crowd stopped just shy of the doorway.

Kirti sent Lalita to ask if the bride should enter.

Mira stood in the shadows, imprisoned by her relatives.

Hundreds stood in the open light of the courtyard. These were just some of the people she was to save. They were strong and proud, the mens' moustaches waxed, the ladies' attire glittering. All were speaking in loud voices, their excitement rising with every minute.

Mira could hear the ladies singing wedding songs of Sita and Rama. Rama was Krishna's incarnation as a great king.

"The bride is Sita, glowing and blissful,
"The groom is Rama, noble and sure.
"The two are lovers of lifetimes divine,
"Bound by the ties of eternal love.
"Oh Mother, give our Sita fortune,
"Oh Mother, save her from the jealous eye.
"Oh Mother, grant her children many,
"And let her hold her Lord Rama's love."

Mira felt faint with shame. This was not her lord or her "eternal love"! She would be tied to Bhoj for a lifetime, joined before the holy fire, bound by irrevocable Vedic mantras.

She was making a mockery of the vedas! And she wasn't only lying to herself and Krishna, she was lying to Bhoj. She was dishonoring an innocent man.

Forgive me! she pleaded, only she didn't know to whom she was pleading; there were so many she was betraying.

The light in the doorway was blocked by a crowd of women. They were relatives from nearby provinces and they surrounded Mira.

"All of you bless my niece so that her married life may be fruitful," Kirti said.

The elders nodded.

"Saubhagyavati Bhavah," great-great-aunt Sandhya croaked. She lifted her wrinkled hand in blessing and kissed Mira's forehead.

Mira wondered what she would do with this blessing of good fortune.

"Putravati Bhavah," great-great-aunt Shama said, touching Mira's cheek.

Mira blinked, horrified at the thought of bearing Bhoj's children.

Lalita returned and gave Mira a numb look. "They're calling for the bride."

A shiver of excitement swept through the women.

Mira dug her nails into her palms. There is no other way, she told herself.

The ladies swept her into the light.

Banyan trees were garlanded with flowers and fountains splashed water into marble ponds. Banners decorated pillars, flags adorned arches and everything fluttered in the breeze.

The voices of her family faded. The song and the music faded. The splashing of the fountains faded. All Mira could hear were the anklets on her own two feet, chum chumming along their pathway to Bhoj, each step louder than the last.

I can't do this, she thought, stopping.

Her father's crumpled face flashed in her mind. I *must*, she told herself and forced her feet forward.

Somewhere along her path, the crowd fell away and only Kirti and the elders remained. They walked with her into the mandap, a square space defined by four pillars, centered with the sacrificial fire. This was where Bhoj waited for her.

The four pillars represented the four corners of the universe, the four directions, the four principles of life, dharma, arth, kaam, and moksha. Purohitji had taught her that. She focused on this teaching and tried to block out the person she knew was sitting opposite, blocked from her vision by a red sheet.

The priests sat at her right, guiding the ceremony.

"When the bride sits, the people see her willingness to marry and the groom is permitted to see her," Girija Shankar Purohitji said.

Mira glanced at him, her old tutor, and he winked at her.

Kirti gently forced her into her seat and the sheet was lowered.

Mira felt Bhoj's gaze but couldn't look up.

The priests, led by Girija Shankar, recited the mantras, invoking the demi-gods.

Mira was told to stand and trembling, she obeyed. She lifted the flower garland held out to her on a tray and almost laughed. The garland had jasmine flowers in it.

She moved to the head of the holy yagna fire and Bhoj moved to stand before her. She turned her face to the side, unable to look at him but raised her hands anyway and placed the garland around his neck.

Large hands, fair and strong with blunt fingernails, placed a matching garland over her head. The sweet scent engulfed her and she pictured Krishna as she'd dressed him this morning, in white and gold.

She stepped back and found her father, Rana Ratan, at her side.

Ratan took her right hand and placed it in Bhoj's, palm up. He recited mantras that said he gave his daughter in marriage and poured water over their hands, showing his people that this union was pure. He placed a Tulsi leaf in Mira's palm, telling her to be loyal and loving as Tulsi.

The ancient chants vibrated through Mira's body, leaving her shaken and raw.

Bhoj recited slokas, promising her love, protection, children, his voice deep and steady.

She wanted to snatch her hand away but was paralyzed, her father looming behind her.

Mira and Bhoj bowed before the fire and the end of her red gauze veil was tied to his cream satin pitambar and blessed.

Despite the flames, she was cold, her right arm aching where it was supported by Bhoj.

"It's time to circle the fire," Purohitji said.

Mira felt something edge down her left hand. It was wet and warm and she realized it was blood from where her nails had cut into her palm. How could she be marrying this man?

"But it's me," whispered someone into her ear.

Shivering, she looked down to see blue hands, pink at the palm. She looked up and saw a peacock feather crown.

A thrill ran through her. A burst of heat exploded in her stomach.

He held out a hand and she laced her fingers through his warmth, following him around the yagna kund.

Her people showered flowers on her and she felt them as the first drops of monsoon rain. She basked in the softness as she walked upon a carpet of petals.

The bride and groom made the four circles.

First for dharma, the righteous path. Let me be steady in my dharma to you, Mira prayed. Second for arth, the acquisition of wealth. Let my people never suffer from hunger, my lord. Third for kaam, the pleasures of the flesh. Let me always be faithful to you.

The couple stopped after the third circle so that Mira could take the lead.

Fourth for moksha, the way to salvation.

Purohitji explained to the onlookers that in the path to salvation, the wife had the first right. It was she who must lead her husband to their divine home.

Let it be so for me, my lord, Mira prayed.

"The groom must mark his wife with vermillion," Purohitji said.

She looked up and lost herself in blooming lotus eyes. She waited as his hand drew near, lifting up her damini ruby. She felt the red vermillion powder fall onto her hair parting.

The priests blew conch shells, like mountains calling the sky.

Mira blinked.

Dark blue eyes gazed down at her. This man was fair, and his eyes tilted up. He didn't wear a peacock feather on his turban.

Bhoj smiled at her, his look gentle.

Where was Krishna? Mira thought, staring at the stranger.

She could feel the crowd's gaze upon her and glanced around. Bapu Sa was watching her with grave pride. Her bear-like uncle Vikramdev was rubbing his hands. Kirti's face was flushed with the wedding's success.

Hadn't any of them seen Krishna?

Girija Shankar Purohitji was smiling, his eyes sad.

Why was her old tutor sad?

The flowers showered and showered as she waited for Krishna to reappear.

He didn't.

She realized that she'd been cheated. She looked down to where blood still dripped off her fingers, mingling with the petals on the floor.

I married only you, Krishna, she thought. I can accept no other husband.

She felt Bhoj step closer to her and she bowed her head.

In her defeat, she smiled.

# 4

# Curse

Vikram Sisodia showered the couple with flowers. He beamed and laughed just like everyone else.

Like Bhoj, he was blue-eyed and fair skinned. He also had curly shoulder-length hair and a straight nose that flared at the nostrils. He also possessed a warrior's build of powerful muscles and long legs. Perhaps he was a bit shorter than Bhoj but many women had told him that his lips were fuller and his eyelashes were thicker. They said his beauty was less ostentatious.

Still, it was Bhoj who was adored. Noble, honorable Bhoj. Destined to be a ruler.

Vikram's lip curled upwards before he remembered where he was and he smiled. He threw petals as he watched Bhoj apply the vermillion to Mira's forehead.

He was happy for his cousin, truly happy. How could he not be? Bhoj was like a brother to him. Bhoj *was* a brother to him.

It was Bhoj who had rubbed his back when Vikram awoke screaming for his dead mother. Bhoj who had embraced him when Vikram had cried for his parents. Bhoj who had protected Vikram's honor by never telling a soul.

Vikram threw petals and studied Bhoj's bride.

She was still half a child, of course, but in a few years, she would be breathtaking. She had an odd sort of complexion that made all fair women seem pale and uninteresting. She glowed. The rubies at her throat and red of her veil made her look so hot, she was like a part of the yagna flames she circled. Entrancing. Burning.

He watched the way her wedding clothes clung to her as she

walked. Flickering like flames. She had a remarkable body for a thirteen year old. Not at all boy-like. She was even lovelier than some courtesans Vikram knew.

Bhoj always got the best things. Now he'd even managed to snag the most sought-after bride in the land. There were kings everywhere who were furious because Bhoj had married Mira before they could.

Vikram was the firstborn, the eldest of his cousins, yet it was Bhoj who was yuvraj. Vikram was still unmarried, yet it was Bhoj who married Mira.

Vikram's lips began to twitch again. He needed to distract himself but had run out of petals. He looked around.

His aunt Gauri was standing next to him.

"My brother Bhoj is most fortunate, is he not, Kaki Sa?" he asked.

"Yes, my son is so happy. And he should be for I've never seen a girl so radiant. Did you see the way she smiled as they circled the fire? And the way he looked at her when he applied the vermillion? My boy is in love."

Vikram chuckled. "Only you would dare to call Bhoj a boy."

Gauri laughed. "A mother has a right to call her son whatever she wishes."

He felt an odd sort of violence rise in him as he watched her smile at Bhoj.

His aunt Gauri had brought him up after his parents performed johar, his father falling in battle, his mother taking her own life.

He smiled. "And what are your next plans for him?"

"Only that he be happy with his wife," she said.

And our kingdoms be protected, he added in his mind. Wasn't that what everyone wanted? This alliance with Merta, and all her technical expertise, would strengthen Merwar's manpower. It was a brilliant match.

He looked across the mandap to where the Merta camp stood.

Ratan and Vikramdev stood behind Bhoj and Mira. They were both powerful men, one the father of the bride, the other her uncle, Yuvraj of Merta.

Ratan was stern, his arms crossed as he watched his daughter marry. Triumph flared in his eyes. Of course Ratan would be feeling triumphant. He'd just negotiated a deal that would bring him an army almost as large as his previous one. Merta was saved. The Afghans would never dare attack now, when two great Rajput clans had united.

It was a good job he was in charge. His older brother wasn't the most effective of rulers.

Vikramdev was shifting his feet and rubbing his stomach as if he was hungry. He probably was. No one ate before a wedding. Thankfully, there'd be a feast soon, once all the wedding rites had been completed.

Next to Vikramdev stood his wife Kirti, looking like a tired broodmare from all her miscarriages.

Rao Duda watched from his throne on the dais. Now there was a legend. The very name Duda stood for courage and patriotism. His policies had led to an enduring peace between the Rathores and Sisodias. His bold negotiations, risky but successful, had earned him the respect of his enemies. Even Sangavat, Bhoj's father, never tired of talking about Duda's fearlessness.

Rao Duda looked like a shriveled mango. He was too old and sick to govern his kingdom now.

Vikram smirked.

Even legends got old.

He felt someone's gaze on his back and turned around.

There was a youth watching Vikram from the back of the crowd, his eyes shadowed, as if he'd not slept for days. The boy was distanced from the others, as if he wasn't one of them. His color and height reminded Vikram of Ratan. This must be Shamal, Ratan's son.

Shamal turned from Vikram to look back at the wedding couple.

Vikram also looked back to Bhoj and Mira.

Mira was smiling, her head bent.

Vikram glanced at Shamal.

Shamal was watching Mira, his face grim.

Vikram looked to the mandap again to see if there was something he'd missed. He could see nothing different. Mira and Bhoj were bending to touch Ratan's feet and receive his blessings.

Vikram looked back at Shamal but the youth had disappeared. There was no sign of him in the courtyard.

Why was Shamal upset at his sister's wedding? He'd looked, well...defeated.

\*

Vikram retired to his guest room, sleepy from too much food.

After the wedding, the Rathores had led the Sisodias to the dining hall and Vikram had been stunned by its beauty. The windows were made of colored glass designed into portraits of peacocks. There were carved arches and pillars twenty feet tall. There were reams of vibrant red carpet and mounds of satin pillows. Yuvraj Vikramdev gave the word and an incomparable feast was brought out by dozens of servants bearing enormous platters. Almost anything that a person could want was available.

Except meat, of course. The Rathores were vegetarians.

Still, Vikram wasn't going to complain. He'd happily be a vegetarian for a month if food like that was served every day.

Vikram reached the door of his room and smiled at two young maids who passed him.

They giggled and ran off.

He smirked. Bhoj wasn't the only attractive man in the world.

He went inside and reclined upon a green upholstered sofa, kicking off his shoes. A soft cough made him rear upwards, his dagger at the ready.

"Forgive me, Kumar, it's only I."

Vikram whipped about to see a small wizened man in a white turban. He sheathed his dagger. "You're lucky I didn't throw my weapon, Koirala. It was close."

Koirala bowed. "Forgive me, Kumar. I've been waiting here for several hours."

Vikram rubbed his hand over his eyes and stood. He went to the entrance to see if anyone was outside his rooms.

There was no one.

He closed the doors.

Koirala took a few short steps towards Vikram but remained far from the light.

"So, you've brought me news." Vikram went back to the couch and sat down, pointing Koirala to the seat opposite, shadowed from the windows.

Koirala bowed and sat, his skinny frame taking less than a third of the seat.

"Well?"

"I did as you bid me, Kumar, though the Shah in Delhi isn't an easy man to spy on. His court is full of rivalries and factions. Many are supporters of Humayun the Moghul but follow the Shah because he's too powerful to cross."

"Well, the Shah of the Afghans did send Humayun fleeing to the mountains around Kabul. The Moghuls are right to be afraid."

"But you're not?" the wily spy asked.

Vikram smiled, the corner of his curled moustache touching the apple of his cheek. "I'm a Rajput."

"Indeed," Koirala bowed.

Vikram arched an eyebrow. "The Shah...how does he rule?"

"He plays the factions against each other. While they fight, he holds power unchallenged."

"Shrewd man."

"Very shrewd, Kumar."

"What of my message?"

"After some days, I left the city and then re-entered in a different guise. I went to him as your ambassador and gave him your message."

"And?"

"He considered it for many days. I don't believe he discussed it with his ministers. He's too clever to give a prospective ally to those that may depose him."

"Of course."

"When he summoned me again, he said your proposal was a worthy one but that he must meet with you first."

"To perhaps kill or ransom me?"

"It's possible but I believe he'll keep you alive. He knows that he needs a Rajput's help if he's to defeat Merwar, the most powerful Rajput kingdom in all Bharat."

"Is he an honorable man?"

Koirala smirked. "As honorable as you or I."

Vikram felt a pang he didn't understand and therefore ignored. "Do you believe he'll keep his end of the bargain?"

"I believe you'll find ways to make certain he does."

"That's true. Any other news?"

"Nothing else, Kumar. Only that the women of his court are talented. He gave me some while I was his guest."

"I'm glad you enjoyed yourself in the course of fulfilling your duty."

"Yes. Thank you, Kumar, for your indulgence."

Vikram laughed. "Take a day's rest, enjoy the wedding festivities. Then return to Delhi. Tell him I'll send word of when I can visit." He leaned back against the couch. "You may go now."

Koirala stood and bowed. "I am ever in your service."

Vikram watched the malnourished man leave.

Koirala was a homeless wandering criminal condemned to the noose whom Vikram had released from Chittore's dungeon. He'd seen the man's cunning and quick tongue, and found a way to pardon him. Now he had himself a loyal and clever servant, never hesitant to take care of the uglier sides of politics. After all, the man had been imprisoned for murder.

The first step in Vikram's plan was complete. Now he must find a way to arrive in Delhi in secret.

His dear cousin Bhoj would soon realize that life was not so perfect after all.

*

It had been two days of singing and dancing since Mira's wedding.

She'd never imagined she could hate dancing so much.

Lalita said that Rana Ratan and Yuvraj Vikramdev were finalizing the marriage contract with the Sisodias. Then Merta would be safe.

Mira hadn't seen Bhoj since the wedding.

Today, Guru Mata Indumati would visit Mira. Indumati was Purohitji's wife, the eldest and most revered of the Brahmin women.

When Mira had received the message this morning, she'd felt such relief. At last, here was one person who wouldn't babble about Mira's good fortune.

Everyone went to Guru Mata for blessings but she rarely visited them. Surely, she must be coming to Mira now because she had something important to say.

"Guru Mata Indumati graces the chamber," Lalita announced from the doorway.

Everyone jumped to their feet, their chattering silenced.

Guru Mata entered wearing a white cotton sari with a red border at the hem. She was short, with a thin torso and wide hips. Her hair, white as cows' milk, had been rolled into a fat bun at the base of her neck. Her eyebrows were bleached white with age. Her skin had been fair in her youth and was even more so now. Almost everything about her was white.

Except her eyes. Her eyes were dark, unfaded by time.

Indumati hobbled into the room, leaning on a staff for support.

Mira bent to touch Guru Mata's feet.

"Saubhagyavati Bhavah," Indumati said. She touched her hand to Mira's head.

Mira stood. "Guru Mata," she couldn't control the breathlessness in her voice. She motioned behind her. "Please, be seated." She put her hand under Indumati's arm to assist her to the couch.

A dasi appeared at Mira's elbow, holding a tray.

Mira took it and knelt. The tray contained a drying cloth and a pot of water sprinkled with rose petals. She slid the tray underneath

Indumati's dry, callused feet and poured the warm water over them, rubbing her toes, hoping to ease some of Guru Mata's discomfort.

She slid the tray out and handed it to a dasi, then used the end of her veil to dry Indumati's feet.

"Why do you not use the drying cloth?" Indumati said.

Mira looked up. "My mother always taught me to use my veil."

Indumati smiled. "That does sound like her."

The dasi took away the unused drying cloth and the empty pot.

Mira settled herself at Guru Mata's feet.

Indumati was accompanied by other priestly ladies and they were attended by Mira's elders.

Mira didn't call for refreshments because these priests' wives chose not to compromise their standards of purity by eating the food of royalty. Mira agreed. The rich food of the palace made her so sleepy.

The Brahmin women blessed the ladies that served them and everyone settled down, the royal ladies seated on the floor, the priests' wives taking the seats, the maids crowded in the doorways.

"Mira, I am here to tell you a story," Indumati said.

Mira felt the others exchange looks behind her.

"There was once a princess called Vrinda. She was beautiful and cultured and a great devotee of Lord Vishnu."

Oh, she was going to talk about Vrinda, Mira thought. Purohitji had taught Mira this story and explained that Vishnu was Krishna's other form as the cosmic Father. He had many residences, one of which was at the bottom of the cosmic ocean. There, he reclined upon a bed formed from the lord of serpents, Shesh Naag.

Shesh had an infinite number of heads that hung over Vishnu like an umbrella, covering his dark blue body.

Lakshmi, Vishnu's consort and the Mother of Fortune, sat upon the bed next to Vishnu, her beauty ageless.

Mira had seen this image many times. Her mother had painted it often.

Vishnu had four arms. In one hand, he held a conch, spreading the eternal word 'AUM' throughout the universe. In another, he held a chakra, a fierce spinning disk that protected his devotees from danger. In the third, he held a mace to punish the evil-doers. In the last, he held a single lotus flower, sending a message of divine love to every soul.

Mira realized that Indumati was speaking again.

"Vrinda married a demon king called Jalandar and she was devoted to him. He also loved her and yet despite his love, he was a demon, and everywhere in his dominion his subjects suffered. Vrinda tried to make him see his errors but this lost her his favor. He went on terrible wars of conquest and soon enslaved the entire planet."

Mira always felt a tug in her chest when she thought of Vrinda, alone, abandoned by her husband. And this was a husband who'd told Vrinda he loved her. Mira looked up at Indumati, wondering why she'd chosen this tale when Mira knew it so well already.

"Vrinda tried so many times to prevent him from waging war. Jalandar punished her by cutting out her tongue and imprisoning her. He even took her deity of Vishnu away so that she couldn't worship, for he considered Vishnu his greatest enemy."

There was an outburst of muttering around the room, all the ladies venting their anger at the king's treatment of his gentle wife.

It was that part that horrified Mira the most. What sort of man would hurt his wife so much and then separate her from her god? Who could be that cruel as to leave her with nothing? And what fool would consider Vishnu an enemy?

"Jalandar went off on campaigns, leaving Vrinda to languish in her cell. Yet by a miracle, her deity appeared in front of her and when her tears fell onto the deities feet, her tongue was restored. When she sang her prayers, the door of her prison was opened and she went back to her palace, cradling her deity in her hands."

The ladies gasped, even though they had heard this story a thousand times. It was the magic of knowing that Vrinda's devotion had been victorious.

Indumati went on, her voice firm and slow. "Jalandar's greedy eyes had turned to the celestial realms of the demi-gods. He waged such wars in the heavens that they shook the universe. The demi-gods unleashed their divine weapons of fire and ice and yet he could not be defeated. Even Indra himself, the king of the demi-gods, could not slay the demon. The terrified celestials retreated into the upper realms of Brahmaloka and asked the all-knowing Father Brahma why it was that this demon could not be killed."

Purohitji had told Mira about Brahma, the first-created being in the universe, created by Vishnu to create.

Mira drew swirling patterns on the marble floor with her fingers. She knew why the demon king couldn't be killed.

"Brahma revealed that the source of Jalandar's invincibility was Vrinda. She was a faithful wife who, despite her husband's cruelty, spent her entire days in prayer. She prayed to Vishnu, the preserver and master of this universe, to protect the life of her husband. It was the purity and strength of her prayers that shielded Jalandar. As long as

Vrinda was faithful to the demon, Vishnu would allow no harm to come to him."

It was the aspiration of every female to be as strong as Vrinda, Mira thought. Her own mother had said so. Vrinda's faith had wielded such power that even Vishnu had to bow before her wishes.

Mira prayed that she could have that fortitude. She prayed that she would always be faithful.

"The demi-gods despaired of victory and feared that the demon king would conquer the entire universe. But Father Brahma showed them a way. He told them that the demi-gods were also devotees and thus Vishnu was bound to protect them. So Indra, with his court, ascended to the higher realm of Vaikuntha, one of Vishnu's abodes, and prayed for deliverance."

Indumati drew a deep breath. "Vishnu was in a dilemma. He had to protect the universe from evil, and yet Vrinda was his devotee, a beloved devotee. He had to honor her faith in him."

Mira bowed her head. There were so many who loved the lord, how could he help all of them? On one hand was the preservation of the universe while on the other, it was the prayer of one dear devotee.

Mira stiffened her spine. There was only one solution: a sacrifice had to be made. It was ethical. It was just. It was the only way.

That was what Indumati was telling her, Mira realized.

"Then Indra made a proposal. When Vrinda was in prayer, her husband was protected. So when her husband next went to war, she must not pray. Surya, the sun deity, asked how this could be done. How could they keep a devotee from prayer? To do so would be a great sin."

Indumati's expression was grave. "The demi-gods looked at each other, the answer forming as one in their minds. Maya: illusion. The devotee must be distracted by the illusion of her own desires."

Mira frowned, a pain forming between her eyebrows. Please let that never happen to me, Krishna. Please, never blind me with maya.

"But who should be sent to distract her? Vayu, the wind deity, asked. Vishnu told the demi-gods that Vrinda was his devotee so he would go to her. The only way Vrinda could be distracted from prayer would be to convince her that her husband was not at war but safe at home with her."

Mira's lips trembled. It was a bitter fate that the lord should be forced to deceive his own devotee.

"The only way to convince her would be to go to her in her husband's form. Then it would be possible to break her faith to the king. But Vishnu was aware that he would also break Vrinda's heart."

There has to be justice in whatever the lord does, Mira insisted to herself. He wouldn't do this to Vrinda without reason.

"Indra and Jalandar met on the battlefield, Indra with his legions of demi-gods, Jalandar with his hoards of demon soldiers. Vishnu took Jalandar's form and went to Vrinda in the palace who was overjoyed that her husband had returned to her. She danced and sang and enjoyed pleasure with him. Vishnu, for shame at his fraud, couldn't speak a word. Indra's war waged for days and nights as he fought to overcome the powerful Jalandar. And when Indra had wielded every weapon and spent all of his arms, he took up his divine arrow, a gift to him from Brahma."

Guru Mata paused and looked about the room. "He spoke the sacred mantra that unleashed the weapon and the arrow hit Jalandar with such force that his head shot off and fell many leagues back down to earth. It landed in the palace, in Vrinda's own garden."

Guru Mata looked at Mira. "Vrinda was sitting in that garden with Vishnu when she saw her husband's head on the ground. She realized she'd been cheated and demanded to know who had violated her chastity. Vishnu appeared before her."

Mira blinked away her tears. She too had been cheated.

"Seeing her own beloved lord, in whom she had placed her faith and her trust, Vrinda was furious. She could not believe that Vishnu would so humiliate her. She accused him of treachery, of vice, of everything that was cruel and hateful."

No, Mira moaned in her mind. He was only doing what was right, Vrinda.

"Vrinda cursed Vishnu that he would become stone. The lord of the universe, not to be bound by any curse, honored his devotee by turning to stone in that moment." Guru Mata turned to the others to explain. "Vishnu is above and beyond the beings of this universe, he is the foundation; he is the never-ending life, present in every moment; he is time itself. He cannot be controlled by anyone's curse. But for those who love him, he chooses to become controllable. If his devotees are angered and they curse him, he honors their curse as if he were an ordinary mortal. Because if he didn't, people would say there is no strength in love. Vishnu bowed before Vrinda and became stone to show the world that in the hands of his devotee, he is obedient."

Mira nodded slowly. It was just like when Krishna allowed Yashoda, his foster mother, to tie him up as a punishment for his pranks, even though Krishna couldn't be tied with any rope.

"Out of the stone grew a beautiful plant with delicate green leaves.

The demi-gods appeared before Vrinda and pleaded for their lord's release. In the throes of the bitterest anger, she refused. Then Lakshmi appeared and pleaded to have her husband returned to her. She reasoned with Vrinda, telling her that this was no ordinary man Vrinda could keep imprisoned. This was the lord who upheld the balance of the universe. He always acted for the good of his creation. She begged for Vishnu and Vrinda, knowing what it was to love one's husband, was merciful."

Mira closed her eyes. Krishna, please give me Vrinda's strength. How will I bear my separation from you?

Around her, she heard people sniffing and wiping their noses. Vrinda had set the standard of wifehood for all womankind. Who didn't want to be like her?

"Vrinda released the curse. Vishnu stood and she fell at his feet, weeping. After years of worshipping him, she was now granted with his presence, only to be overwhelmed by his betrayal. She told him that he was her lord, her god, her master and yet he could not go unpunished for his crime. She cursed him that he would be separated from his wife by a demon, just the way she was separated from her husband by deceit. She told him that he must also bear this pain.

"Vishnu accepted her justice."

Mira was awed by the tale of Vrinda, a lady who'd passed judgment on Vishnu.

"That is why, when the lord descended to earth as Rama and his beloved descended as Sita, Sita was kidnapped by the demon Ravan. Rama was separated from his wife for thirteen months before he could fight the demon to rescue her.

"Vishnu also granted Vrinda a boon. He told her that he would accept her as his wife, for she'd proven herself worthy. He declared her to be a pure devotee, such as had never been seen before. Vishnu would be adored in his form of the sacred Shalingram, the black stone that Vrinda had turned him into. He told her that she would be worshipped alongside him as the holy Tulsi plant that had grown out of the stone. And he promised her that he would accept no offerings from devotees unless they came accompanied by a Tulsi leaf. In this way, Vishnu and his beloved Vrinda would be united forever."

Mira suddenly realized why Vishnu deceived his devotee. If he hadn't, how would the world have known of her power? Of her greatness? And how would she have become his wife? He did it so that he and Vrinda could be united. He did it to show the world true love.

A tear ran down Indumati's face as she finished her tale. "On hearing his promise, Vrinda touched her forehead to his feet. At that moment, her soul left her body and split in two. Half merged into Vishnu and the other half entered the ground, emerging as the Tulsi plant. In this way, Vrinda lives for eternity with her true husband, Vishnu."

There was a long deep pause. Every woman in the room took a moment to collect herself.

Guru Mata reached down and lifted Mira's chin with her fingers.

"You understand me, Mira."

"Yes, Guru Mata," Mira whispered, "I understand."

# 5

# Whispers

Uda sat at her bedroom window, listening to the people celebrating in the gardens.

Her brother Bhoj was married and the people were preparing for the arrival of the new bride. They were more excited today than they'd ever been for Uda's wedding.

The stone pillars and arches of the buildings were being decorated with garlands of flowers and leaves. The roads leading to the Raj Mahel were sprinkled with colored powders so that the bride would be charmed by the blue, pink and yellow streets. The main road that led to the front of the palace was being carpeted with marigolds.

Uda couldn't see all of this but she knew it was happening because she'd ordered it. She was in charge of the city's preparation.

It had been Bhoj's wish that she be given this task.

His first wish had been that she attend his wedding but when that wasn't possible, he decided that she be given this honor instead.

Uda smiled. She knew that Bhoj would dance all the way to Chittore. He would dance and dance until someone, probably Vikram, told him to sit in his chariot and act with some dignity. And he would because he listened to Vikram. Mostly. But when they entered the capital and he saw all his people cheering for him, he wouldn't be able to resist jumping down again and dancing with them.

That was her brother.

Uda remembered her own wedding: the terror of the new household, the strangers who surrounded her. She'd feared doing anything wrong, feared not being beautiful or graceful enough. She'd feared not touching her elders' feet in the correct manner, lest they declare her inadequate. She'd feared so much. The only thing she forgot to fear was her husband.

He died two years after their marriage.

She'd not had the chance to bear children.

In the end, it wasn't beauty or grace or inadequacy that had been her downfall. It was her bad fortune. She'd been the shadow over her husband's life. She'd doomed him. That was what her mother-in-law had shouted at her, why the women of her husband's family shunned her.

She clenched her hands in her lap as she thought of her loss three years ago. Raj Kumari Uda, widowed at eighteen years of age. Her wifehood had ended and she'd been sent back to her parents.

They hadn't wanted her either. They only allowed her back into their household because society expected it.

At twenty-one years of age, unwanted, unlucky, she was avoided by others lest her shadow fall upon them.

Dressed in white, her head shorn, Uda retired to her rooms.

But Bhoj visited her. He adored his elder sister, always thinking of her as just a slightly smaller, female version of himself.

And she adored him.

His presence made others visit her, for Bhoj was followed in all matters. He asked her advice and called for music and rich food.

She took pleasure in watching his happiness but she refused to dance or sing. She refused the rich food. Uda acted with restraint at all times for she feared the tongue of society. A widow wasn't favored with its indulgence.

She turned to the crowd of maids behind her.

They didn't even bother to hide their dislike. All knew why Uda hadn't gone to the wedding. Just as a barren female was not invited to the ceremony of a pregnant woman, a widow was not invited to a wedding.

Uda arched a brow, reminding them that widow or not, she was still a royal lady.

"Tell the manservants to put the banners up in the great hall and–" she held out two huge baskets that had sat next to her, "take these flags and give them to the heralds."

Two maids picked up the baskets and left.

"How is the production of the vastra coming along in the tailoring quarters?"

A bored-looking maid with a plump face stepped forward. "Mandvi says she's almost ready. Just twenty more pairs to complete."

"Good. Make sure that baskets of vastra are kept in the storage rooms by the doors. When the barat enters the palace, hand out a pair to each subject."

"Ji, Raj Kumari," the dasi intoned as she turned to leave.

"I haven't finished yet," Uda said, her words clipped.

The dasi paused and turned back.

"A son of the House of Merwar has taken a wife. Our people must receive gifts that befit the occasion. No one must go without. Equally, no one must take more than their share…" She stared hard at the maid. Things were known to go missing in the heat of a celebration, but it wouldn't happen on Uda's watch.

The maid shifted her eyes from left to right. She shuffled her feet. "Of–of course, Raj Kumari," she said.

"Go." Uda turned to the next maid, a shrunken old lady who didn't look strong enough to lift a cup of water. "Gita, bring me the chests so that I may choose the gifts for the palace servants." Gita's bones groaned as she walked away.

Uda would've liked to go to the treasury herself and spare her old nurse Gita the trouble but she couldn't leave her quarters. A widow didn't wander around a palace, especially on happy occasions.

A little maid in sky blue came running up. "Raj Kumari, there is a messenger at your door."

"I'm coming, Janki," Uda said. She rose and went into her outer room to greet a messenger who looked like a walking dust cloud.

"What is the news?"

"Maharana wants to inform you that the barat will enter the city gates by nightfall. He wishes for everything to be ready by that time."

These were the first words that her father had spoken to her in years and they were through a messenger, Uda thought. "Everything is ready. You may return and tell him that the people are most anxious to see their new daughter-in-law. Ask the barat to make haste."

The messenger bowed his way out of the room.

Uda went back inside. "Bring me a report from the rasoiya immediately," she said to Janki. "You," she said to another, "send a message to Raj Purohit–the barat will be here by nightfall so he must please be ready with his priests to bless the bride and groom."

The Sisodia Raj Purohit had returned from Merta ahead of the wedding party so that he could arrange the rites for welcoming the new daughter-in-law of Merwar.

The two dasis scurried away.

Uda sat down at her window seat, looking out at the people. She curled her hands into fists, trying to still their trembling. If anything went wrong…no, it wouldn't. She hoped her parents were happy with her efforts.

"Send the best musicians and dancers to the front gates to play," Uda said to one of the dasis. She sent the remaining dasis to inform the other family members of Bhoj's imminent arrival.

She waited in her room, alone.

Before long, a dasi called Lakshmi appeared holding bundles of flower garlands of various designs, needing approval before they were hung in the bridal suite. An elder dasi called Savitri appeared with different incense samples for Uda to decide which one would be lit for the nuptial night.

Uda thought of the rose incense she'd fallen asleep to that first night in her in-laws' house. She chose sandalwood for Mira.

Gita entered, directing several manservants to place the treasury chests by the window seat.

Uda picked out the jewelry that would be gifted to each member of the household as befitted their status, noting everything down in lists.

The rasioya's report came. He needed more wood for the cooking fires.

Uda sent men with dry logs from the palace temple supplies.

There were more messages.

Raj Purohit wanted to know exactly when the barat was arriving so that he could work out an auspicious time for the bride to enter her new home.

Uda replied that she didn't know the exact time. She would let him know as soon as she found out.

Some of the musicians were offended because people weren't making enough room for their instruments.

Uda sent a maid to pacify them.

The dancers, long suffering, were rehearsing in the gatekeeper's house next to their posts by the palace road.

Uda sent a maid with special mint drinks for them.

Gita returned when Uda was alone once more. "I overheard some rumors."

Uda stiffened because she knew what Gita was going to say.

"The family isn't happy you were given this responsibility."

Of course. Why should an unwanted dependent be honored with great duties? Uda thought.

"But don't worry. You've Bhoj's support so they can do nothing."

Yes, they can do nothing, Uda thought. Nothing except curse my very name to Narak.

Dusk was fast approaching.

Uda sent a maid to check that the nightmen had lit the sconces along the roads so that the barat would be illuminated as it proceeded through the city.

Another dust-ball messenger appeared, and Uda sent a dasi running to Raj Purohitji with the news that he must proceed to the gates with all speed.

Just as another messenger arrived, the piercing call of a conch shell was heard. In the distance, bugles were blown like the trumpeting of elephants.

Queen Gauri appeared in Uda's doorway. She must have traveled ahead of the procession to welcome the bride into the palace.

"Uda, I will take over the arrangements now."

Uda frowned and moved forward to greet her mother. "But Bhoj told me–"

"He told you to be in charge while we were gone. Now we've returned, so I'll take over." Gauri stepped back and walked out just as Uda bent to touch her feet.

Uda stared after her, her fingertips still touching the floor where her mother's feet had been. My own mother doesn't want my touch, she thought.

She went back to her window to listen to the dancing and singing. She imagined the flowers on the road being disturbed and hoped the people didn't dance too vigorously.

It was best that her mother had taken over, she told herself. Now the family wouldn't be angry. Uda's short period of importance was over.

Durga, her mother's most trusted maid, entered with several manservants behind her. "We need to take the treasury chests, Raj Kumari," she said. "Maharani wishes to inspect what you have selected."

"Of course," Uda said. She motioned behind her to where the chests were placed beside her long lists.

The men hefted them out of the room.

Gita entered, looking even more shrunken than usual.

"You're tired," Uda said to her. She helped her old nurse into a seat. "I made you do too much today. Forgive me."

"There is nothing to forgive," Gita muttered.

"No, I shouldn't have pushed you. It was just that I wanted everything to be perfect. And you're the only one I trust not to do things wrong just to make me look a fool."

Gita sighed. "I know." She rose and went into Uda's dressing room and came back with a lamp to light the lamp-stands around the room.

"It will be some hours before the procession arrives at the palace. Bapu Sa will want it to be quite a spectacle," Uda said.

"Hmmm."

"Gita, I know you're tired. Go and rest."

Gita set the last lamp down. "Well, if you insist."

"I do."

Gita left the room through the servants' door.

Uda stood at the window. She knew where the procession was just by the cheering of the crowds. Now they must be passing Bhim Kund, she thought, picturing the huge foot-shaped lake that, legend told, was the footprint of the great hero Bhim.

The last rays of day disappeared from the sky as the sounding of bugles grew louder. Now they must be passing the Jain Mahavir mandir, she thought.

The drums were harder. The leaves on the trees outside her window quivered.

Now she could hear the softer sounds of flutes and bells below the drumming. They must be near the palace. She leaned close to her window screen, straining to see as far to the right as possible.

She couldn't see anything, of course. The procession was obscured by gardens and buildings and everything else.

The sounds remained the same for over an hour. Uda thought that the barat must be at the palace gates, waiting for the auspicious time before entering.

Conch calls, deep and pure, sailed over the fort.

Mira and Bhoj had entered the palace.

The sounds of revelry slowly became muffled as the barat passed inside.

Uda stepped back into her room. Sitting on her couch, she examined the lines of destiny etched into her palms.

After an hour, thrum thrum sounds started coming from her floor. Surprised, she tilted her head to listen more closely.

Her mother would have first taken Mira to the Kula Devi, the family goddess, then to the gurus and elders to be blessed, then to the great hall for a feast in her honor, then to the bridal suite. None of those places were anywhere near Uda's rooms. So why were those thrum thrum sounds so close?

They must be beginning the feast in the great hall by now, Uda thought. Of course, if Mira felt the churning nausea that Uda had felt on her own wedding night, she would eat almost nothing.

Uda prayed to Kula Devi to grant her brother happiness.

The thrum thrum was even deeper.

She frowned, wondering if perhaps Bhoj was bringing Mira to her. No, her mother wouldn't allow that tonight. In a few days perhaps, once Mira had settled in, but not tonight.

Bugles were blown so nearby that Uda jumped out of her seat. Oh no, she thought, turning to face the door.

Bhoj entered with a female dressed in red. There was no one else from the family with him. He came forward.

"Didi, this is my wife."

Uda couldn't think of a thing to say. She was stunned that he'd ignored the whole family's displeasure and come to her. Now Uda would be punished.

The bride dropped in one graceful movement to touch Uda's feet.

Bhoj also bent for her blessings.

Uda's face softened and she smiled. She lifted her hand in blessing. "Saubhagyavati bhavah," she said to Mira. "Kirtimaan bhavah," she said to Bhoj, blessing him with fame.

They rose and Uda embraced the girl, her bony frame awkward against the girl's softer curves. When they pulled apart, Mira kept her gaze lowered, allowing Uda to study her features.

It was a delicate face, with a teardrop chin and thick eyelashes that made the girl's huge eyes seem even bigger, curving and slanting like the perfection of a painting.

And Bhoj had brought her here, on her wedding night, to be blessed by a widow? What was he thinking?

Uda frowned at him.

Ignoring it, he put his arm around Uda's shoulders and kissed her cheek. "That blessing isn't enough for my bride, Didi. You can do better than that."

He always managed to disarm her, Uda thought, the tension easing from her shoulders. She turned back to Mira.

"The whole of Bharat has heard of your beauty, sister-in-law, and now we Sisodias may say it belongs to us. I bless you that you will make your husband happy and be loved by your in-laws. May your wifehood be an example to society and your name remembered by all women."

Mira's gaze was lowered but somehow, Uda thought she flinched.

I've distressed her, Uda thought. Why can I never do anything right? "You must go now, the feast will be waiting."

"Come with us," Bhoj said.

"You know that is impossible, my brother." Uda turned to Mira. "It will be your duty to make him see sense. He shouldn't have brought you here as it is."

Mira looked up. She saw Uda's white sari, her shorn hair, her bare forehead.

"Why shouldn't he have brought me here? I was anxious to meet you, Didi."

Uda blinked. How kind...

She kissed Mira's forehead. "Go now," she told Bhoj.

They left, Mira's ankle bells chum chumming away.

Uda sat down, shaken.

Now there would be talk. People would say that Uda had put the evil eye on Mira.

She had to explain to Bhoj that he couldn't flaunt the traditions of society.

Though Mira's words had been welcome, she also had to abide by Sisodia rules or she would suffer Uda's fate. She had to follow the regulations of society.

Uda didn't know what she would do, but she had to do something to protect her brother's bride.

*

In the early hours of the morning, Mira was escorted by her new relatives through the palace.

She tread upon petals for miles. It seemed there was no end to them. The scent of rose clung to her, sickening her with its suffocating fumes, like she was captured in the midst of a giant bud.

She swallowed her bile and tried not to breathe in.

"Not long now, bahu," Bhoj's mother told her.

There was an outburst of giggling from the women around her.

Mira wanted to scream and focused on clenching her fists instead. Why couldn't they stop it?

This would be the last time she was just Mira, pure and untouched.

She tried to concentrate on the blue carpet beneath her feet, feeling the way her toes sank into the fibers with each step. She looked around, trying so hard to be distracted by her surroundings.

She was walking down a cavernous corridor. On her right were walls hung with paintings and tapestries. She saw scenes of Krishna frolicking in the woods with the Gopis, his milkmaid lovers.

On her left were marble pillars that continued on down the corridor like trees along a road. The pillars were carved with the figures of dancing demi-gods and goddesses. An enclosed garden was beyond, where fountains hummed a faint tinkling sound and plants swayed in the cool night breeze.

They turned onto a path that led into the garden and walked through it to the other side of the enclosure, where they climbed a sweeping staircase.

Mira's heart was banging so hard it felt like an eagle, flapping its wings, each flap taking her higher, making her more lightheaded than ever.

At the top of the stairs, they stood on a balcony, opposite a pair of polished rosewood doors. Mira saw that the balcony encircled the garden beneath, and that on the other side was a pair of matching rosewood doors.

"Here we are, bahu, your new rooms. I hope they please you."

The door opened and Mira, in a panic, inhaled.

She smelled sandalwood. Krishna, you *are* with me, she thought, and the flapping eagle in her chest eased.

She walked in, her mother-in-law's arms around her.

It was so dark, Mira thought. Why hadn't someone lit the lamps?

In the darkness, they passed under an archway, a room, then another archway.

There was a blaze of light. Mira blinked hard. Squinting, she looked at what had blinded her.

One huge bed was before her, surrounded by hundreds of ghee lamps. There were lamps sitting on the ground around the bed. There were lamps on the tables beside the bed. There were lamps lit on lampstands at the bed posts. Lamps, lamps everywhere.

Mira swallowed her bile. Krishna, I can't do this, she thought. The bed sheets were purple satin, sprinkled with rose petals. Mira almost cried.

"Come, bahu, we will help you remove some of your jewelry," the queen said, steering Mira towards a doorway at the side.

Mira was relieved to see that her dressing room was lit in the normal fashion of lamps placed in moderate quantities in strategic corners so they lit the whole room.

The walls were painted light pink and in the middle of the room was a huge marble pond for her to bathe in. There was a mirror and a dressing table to one side, a massage table on the other and carved chests along the walls.

Mira sat on the chair before the dressing table.

The ladies went to work unfastening Mira's jewels, flinging them down on the table. Rope after rope of gold was unraveled. Mira's bridal rings and heavy bracelets were removed. Her damini was pulled away and her toe rings slid off.

Mira stared at the pile of jewels sitting before her on the table. Why didn't she feel any lighter?

For all the jewelry in front of her, they left a great deal on because a bride never appeared before her husband unornamented. Especially tonight.

Mira still wore her mangalsutra, a black beaded gold necklace that was the sign of a married woman. She wore her belt and her glass bangles. She wore her earrings and her anklets. With her damini removed, the red vermillion at her hair parting was visible.

"Perfect," Gauri declared. She motioned the women out with a flick of her hand. "We will leave you now, bahu."

Mira wanted to reach out and grab them but was paralyzed from the neck down. The sound of giggling echoed off the walls and Mira was alone with her jewelry and that monstrous bed.

Soon Bhoj would arrive.

Now what do I do? she thought, looking around the room. There was only one exit she could see.

She walked towards the bedroom, her heart hammering so hard it almost cracked her ribs open. So many lamps! How would she sleep with all of those lamps? They were making her hot, her veil sticking to the small of her back.

Of course, she wasn't expected to sleep tonight.

Kirti had told her to do whatever Bhoj wanted to do.

Mira backed away, stumbling through the archway into what must have been a sitting room but it was so dark, she couldn't tell.

Krishna, I'm afraid, she thought.

She put her hands out and walked forward, hoping to come in contact with a chair.

Her hands collided with a warm, hard, silk covered abdomen.

She gasped.

"It's only me," came a deep rumble.

She felt the vibrations of it beneath her fingers. She snatched her hands away.

There was a pause.

Say something, you fool, she told herself. "I'm sorry, I didn't see you. It's so dark in here." Idiot! she screamed in her mind. Now he'll take you to where the lights are!

"I can see light up ahead," he pointed behind her. "Let's go in there."

Before she had a chance to reply, he walked passed her into the bedroom. Helpless, she followed. To her horror, he walked straight up to the bed and sat down on it, looking like a god surrounded by stars.

He looked back at her. "Will you sit here with me?"

Mira felt sick. She forced herself to step towards him. Do your duty, she told herself. She sat down, her back wooden. The softness of the bed sucked her down and she struggled to sit straight.

He reached out and took her trembling hand in his.

She bit down on her tongue, straining to keep from crying out.

He rubbed her hand between his, encasing her cold sweaty palm, warming her.

She had to do something! "M–may I speak?"

"My wife may speak whenever she pleases."

Mira lost the words she had been thinking of. She searched for new ones. "I–I have to t–tell you something."

"Yes?"

She closed her eyes and rushed into battle. "I never wanted to marry. I–I only did it to protect my people."

There was a pause.

"You must have married for that reason also," she said.

"Actually, my family has been asking for you for five years. I was glad when your father agreed."

Taken aback, Mira struggled to respond. "Well…it was best for both our kingdoms."

"I was hoping it'd be best for the two of us," he said.

Mira was just about to snatch her hand away when he slipped his fingers in to mingle with hers, feeling her tender knuckles.

Her mouth went dry. "I really didn't want to marry. I was given to Krishna when I was very young and I've only ever wanted to serve him."

"Yes, I know. Your grandfather told us all about your devotion."

"He did?" She stared at Bhoj, watching the way his moustache curled into his cheek as he smiled. It looked so soft, that moustache.

"I understand, my lady," he said.

"You do?"

"Yes. I'm a stranger and your husband. It is understandable that you're nervous. That's why I'll wait."

"Wait?"

"Of course. You're only thirteen, while I am six years your senior. It's best that you have a chance to adjust."

Mira was mute.

"For the sake of politics, you came to Merwar earlier than planned. But I'm glad. Now we can know each other at leisure."

Know each other? What did that mean?

He touched her bottom lip with his fingertip. "I'll sleep in my own suite tonight. It's just across the courtyard. If you have any problems, send for me."

Mira's heart deflated as she watched him stand up. She sagged onto the bed.

"We'll be great friends, you and I. I'll be the best of husbands."

He doesn't understand, she thought. Say something!

Bhoj stepped away from the bed.

Quick, say something!

"Oh, I forgot." He came back towards her, reaching out his hand.

She froze.

He slipped off her hoop nose-ring. "I couldn't leave without doing that," he said, grinning.

She stared at it, stricken.

Still grinning, he straightened. "You're very tired. Go to sleep."

Mira watched him stride away with her nose ring, disappearing into the darkness of the outer room. She heard a door in the distance open and close.

Her shoulders stooped, she went back to the dressing room to remove the rest of her jewelry, her jerking hands pulling at the pearls in her hair when they wouldn't come free straight away. She was almost going to remove the last necklace about her neck when she stopped.

It was her mangalsutra. A wife never removed her mangalsutra. Mira collapsed on to the table, shaking, her head resting on her arms.

What if he comes back? she wondered, trembling.

No, he wouldn't, she suddenly thought. He said he wouldn't.

The reality of it hit her. She was free! "Thank you, Krishna," she whispered, rising, staring at her reflection in the mirror.

Relief made her lightheaded and she twirled about the room, flinging her hands out. Maybe Bhoj won't ever come back, she thought. If I don't draw attention to myself, maybe he won't notice me for a long time. Maybe he won't notice me at all.

Mira pulled out the pins that secured her veil to her head. The red gauze floated to the ground. She rifled through a chest of garments and pulled out a plain yellow blouse and petticoat and changed into them, tying the strings loosely at her back as she went into the bedroom.

Now that Mira didn't have to share the bed with Bhoj, she realized how magical it looked. The lamps cast orange twinkles on the purple satin and even the roses didn't suffocate. They seemed sweet and soft.

She spent several minutes blowing out the lights before crawling into bed. She closed her eyes, lingering between waking and sleeping. Then she was falling.

Mira jerked, reaching out to grab on to something.

She sat up covered in sweat.

He'll have to notice me sometime, Krishna, she thought. And then what will I do?

# 6

# Threats

Ratan sat upon his chariot, surveying the vast plains of his province.

Merta was largely flat, covered in fields of sarsau and jeeru, its two main spice exports. Sanchar, a black rock salt, was also a specialty.

Marble was the main building material, mined out of the rocky ground. Black, white, grey, pink, green, almost any color of marble could be obtained.

The earth here wasn't like the rest of Bharat. This earth was red.

His father had said it was stained from the blood of its patriots.

There weren't many forests here, just scattered khejadis, short trees with winding branches and tiny yellow-green leaves.

Enemies couldn't hide behind the small khejadi trees.

His company was approaching his fort in Chaukari village and his people came out of their mud houses to line the dirt roads. They bowed before him. The women were dressed in bright reds and oranges, their forearms covered with silver bracelets and their upper arms covered with white glass bangles. The men were dressed in white dhotis stained by dust and sweat. Their turbans were white, shielding them from the early summer sun.

"Rana Ratan ki jai!" they cried.

Children were running up to his chariot and he reached down to pat their heads. Fathers at the back were picking up their smaller children so they could see. More people were coming in from the fields, joining in the cheer.

"Rana Ratan ki jai!"

He told his charioteer to halt and the people hushed.

Ratan stood. "Your daughter Mira has married. I ask you to bless her with the greatest fortune." She has saved you all, he thought.

The women raised their hands in blessing.

The men raised their fists and gave up the call. "Raj Kumari Mira ki jai! Raj Kumari Mira ki jai!"

The gates, tall as elephants and constructed of solid teak, were hauled open.

The guards on the watch saluted him and his company marched into the outer bailey.

Ratan dismissed his men and continued on into the fortress, passing under a spiked portcullis and down a paved road, waving to his people as they came to stand alongside the road. He passed through a smaller gate and his charioteer pulled up before the palace.

His household was waiting to greet him.

Shamal was missing from the crowd. He'd left the capital as soon as the wedding was over whilst Ratan had stayed for several days to finalize the details.

Ratan kept a strict hold over himself, smiling and embracing his people. He went up to his quarters and bathed, then summoned his ministers.

They came to his receiving chamber and bid him felicitations on the nuptials of his daughter.

He thanked them.

They sat, quiet at last.

"What news from the capital, my lord?" Bharadwaj, Chaukari's chief minister, asked.

Ratan tapped the wooden arms of his throne. "The Maharana of Merwar has given five regiments to my brother. Another six will be arriving here within the week."

A sigh of relief ran through the room.

"And within the next two weeks, he'll have sent us a great force."

"It is happy news." Bharadwaj said, looking away.

Ratan nodded, even as a vision of Mira crying at his feet came before his eyes.

Bharadwaj was still looking away.

Then Ratan noted that all his ministers were avoiding his eyes. His Royal Herald Vyas was grinding his square jaw and staring out the window. Long-faced General Somnath was staring at the floor. Just a moment ago they'd all been full of congratulations!

He turned to his village ambassadors. "What news from the districts?"

Sanjay, a small man who was Chief Ambassador spoke but didn't look up. "The mukhyas are anxious. Some are saying that the alliance won't change anything."

"We cannot go to war yet," General Deva snapped, his wiry grey hair quivering. "Our last battle cost us dearly."

"Our only consolation was that we killed just as many, if not more, of them," said Somnath, nodding.

"My lord," Head Treasurer Acharya spoke up. "There's one way to increase confidence in the people without using our forces."

Ratan knew what Acharya was going to say, just as he knew it couldn't be done.

"We could make a trade alliance with the Shah."

The room erupted around Ratan.

He watched them snarl at each other for a moment before raising his hand. "Go on, Acharya."•

The other ministers closed their mouths.

Acharya's grey eyes met Ratan's. "My lord, trading kingdoms rarely invade each other. It would restore the people's confidence as well as make us all rich."

"We already are rich," Vyas said, his nostrils flaring.

Why is Vyas so angry? Ratan wondered. It is not his usual way. Studying Vyas, Ratan then noticed that his eyes had dark circles and looked hollow, as if he were tormented.

"It would violate our pact with Merwar," Somnath said.

"A trade alliance would be as good as giving them our land!" Deva leaned forward. "They will steal into our borders under the guise of merchants and build their forces within our own territory."

Vyas slapped his knee. "We could never trust them to keep their word! They have already shown their true nature."

There was a pause. No one was meeting Ratan's gaze.

"What do I not know?" Each word he spoke was precise and quiet.

It was clear that no one wanted to give him bad news.

"Has Sher Shah dared attack my people again?"

Bharadwaj rested his hand on his thigh. "There was an incident in the east district."

"What incident?"

"The village of Lingeshwar was destroyed."

Ratan stared at his minister and friend.

"How many survived?" Inside, Ratan was kicking things. Outside, he was utter stillness. Lingeshwar's population had been three hundred. Three hundred of his people.

Bharadwaj looked towards Vyas. "Only their chief, Mukhya

Narsingh," he said. "They gutted all seven of his sons in front of him."

Ratan gripped the arm of his throne like it was the Shah's head. Vyas's youngest daughter was married to one of Narsingh's sons. But Ratan sensed there was more.

Somnath's jaw clenched. "The younger women were taken."

Ratan's mind went blank and he looked, helpless, at Vyas.

"The children also," Somnath said.

Ratan choked on his own breath. "Is there any hope of recovering them?"

"Kumar Shamal took out two brigades. They followed the trail. It led to corpses."

Ratan felt an incredible weight descend on his chest, like an elephant was sitting on him. He'd left to give his daughter away and now three hundred of his people were dead.

He rose, fighting the weight. "Tell me everything," he said, moving to stand behind his throne.

"From the evidence of the tracks, there must have been a mass rape." Sanjay swallowed. "Then the women were killed or they killed themselves, which is most likely what happened. We took priests to perform the last rites for them."

"And the children?" Ratan whispered.

"We think they've been taken to Sher Shah's court."

"Perhaps as hostages," Acharya said.

Vyas glowered. "There's been no ransom message. The boys were taken to swell their own population as they've lost so many men. And young girls are always an asset."

"But our children won't fight us!" Raghu said. He was one of Ratan's best diplomats and second in command at Chaukari's fort.

"They will if they're turned into Muslims." Deva replied, his look grim.

Everyone looked sickened.

Ratan tried to think rationally, logically, swatting at the elephant that bore down on him. "When did this occur?"

"Two days ago," Bharadwaj said. "We sent you a message but you must have left the capital before it reached you."

Two days ago. If he'd had sufficient forces by then, this wouldn't have happened. Lingeshwar was close to the eastern border. He had to send reinforcements there now. But what if it was a diversionary tactic? Destroy a village in the east and then attack from the west? He looked at his generals. "Deploy our new forces equally to the east, west and northern borders. Let no strangers in, I don't care what they're trading."

They nodded, looking relieved to have some orders.

"I'll go to Lingeshwar myself to inspect the site. Where is Mukhya Narsingh?"

"He's here in the palace. I put him in the west wing," Raghu said.

"I'll go to him in one hour. You and Vyas will join me."

Raghu and Vyas nodded.

"Tonight, there'll be prayers for our dead. Bharadwaj, ask the priests to preside over the ceremony in the assembly hall. All our subjects are invited."

Bharadwaj nodded.

"And Vyas, hand your duties over to one of your deputies for a week."

Vyas looked to protest so Ratan held up his hand. "My friend, please do not make me seem heartless by working. It is your right to be with your family at this time."

There was a pause.

"Where is my son?" Ratan asked the room.

"He returned from Lingeshwar an hour before you arrived," Bharadwaj said. "He's with his men in the barracks."

Ratan felt Shamal's pain. Lingeshwar must have been a horrifying sight.

A short time later the ministers filed out.

Ratan held himself rigid as they left.

General Somnath was the last to leave. As he passed, he put his hand on Ratan's shoulder. "There was nothing you could've done to save them."

Ratan looked at him.

"By the time the news reached us, the village was lost." Somnath pressed Ratan's shoulder and was gone.

"Bapu Sa."

At the sound of Shamal's voice, so cool and normal, Ratan turned.

Shamal bent to touch his father's feet.

Ratan sighed.

"So you know about Lingeshwar," Shamal said, rising, his tone detached as though he couldn't quite believe his own words.

"Yes."

Shamal ran his hand along the back of a chair. "It would seem that my sister's wedding has had no effect on the enemy's aggression."

Ratan felt so tired. "That's not true. We now have an army again."

"If anything, it looks like the wedding instigated this attack."

"Putra, you know why this wedding had to be," he said.

Shamal was silent.

Ratan took his turban off and ran his hand through his hair. Just this morning he had seen three grey strands at his each of temples.

"Yes, I know," said Shamal. "But Mira is so innocent." He slammed his hand down against the back of the chair and it fell off, clattering to the floor. "Now she's been sacrificed." It sounded like there was a tree growing in the pit of Shamal's stomach and with every word he said, a new branch sprang forth to pain him.

Ratan reached out to him. "I'm not as cruel as that. The Sisodias are a noble family, descended from the Surya dynasty. Bhoj is a good man." He felt like he was repeating the same words over and over again.

"And what happens when Bhoj realizes she'll never care for him? What then?" Shamal turned to face Ratan.

"It won't come to that. She'll adjust."

"Bapu Sa, you know that's not true!" Shamal kicked the broken chair back. "Mira isn't like other girls. She can only love one and that is Krishna. She'll never give him up."

It was like talking to Mira all over again.

Ratan stood. "No, Shamal! Mira knows her responsibility to me and to her people."

"Of course she does, or she would never have married," Shamal shook his head. "Still, her heart lies only with Krishna. And why should it not? He's the only one who doesn't use her or leave her or reject her."

Ratan stared at his son. "Is that what you think?"

Shamal was silent.

"Is that was *she* thinks?" When Shamal still didn't reply, Ratan turned away. "I thought it best if she were away from here, from me. You know I didn't deal well with your mother's death."

Shamal stood near his father.

"And Mira looks so much like Kusum. So much! Every time I saw her it was like looking at your mother. I thought I'd go mad."

"Bapu Sa..."

"What else could I have done?" He looked at his son.

Shamal put his hand on Ratan's shoulder. "Nothing, Bapu Sa."

Ratan put his hand over Shamal's. "You must help me. You and Mira are my strength."

"I am with you until death." Shamal's expression hardened. "But always, I will remember that I couldn't help her. When she needed me, I could do nothing." He turned to leave. "I don't know what'll happen when the Sisodias turn on her."

"Shamal–"

"You must rest, Bapu Sa. Lord Raghu told me you're meeting Mukhya Narsingh soon. You must comfort him for he is broken. And Vyas grieves for his daughter."

"Yes."

Alone, Ratan sank onto his throne, trying to breath despite the elephant on his chest.

*

Mira awoke to see Lalita standing over her.

Her maid had finally arrived, bearing the remainder of Mira's dowry and wedding gifts. These included the rest of her clothes, chests of jewelry and gold plate, tributes from the territory that now belonged to her.

Her father had given her villages that lay on Merta's southern border.

"Their combined income is three hundred thousand rupees a year," he'd told her. "It's not included in the marriage contract so it doesn't belong to your in-laws. You may use it as you see fit."

Mira had traveled separately from her dowry. There'd been three caravans in all, each caravan on a different route with decoys so that spies wouldn't be able to determine which carried the princess.

Mira's caravan had traveled the fastest, the second had arrived yesterday. The last, the one that Lalita was in, had arrived in the early hours of this morning.

Lalita looked like she'd climbed the Himalayas. Her eyes were black holes. "Your mother-in-law is calling for you, Jiji."

"Maharani Gauri?"

"Ji. She wishes you to be ready in one and a half hours."

Mira stretched, the purple satin bedsheet sliding over the skin of her stomach and falling to the ground.

"You must hurry."

"I'm coming, I'm coming," she said, slipping out of bed. Her head felt foggy, like she was sitting in a cloud and couldn't feel the earth beneath her. Remnants of strange dreams floated across her mind.

She bathed and dressed and performed her puja.

Lalita was fastening Mira's earrings when Gauri glided in and Mira stood, folding her palms.

"Bahu, you look beautiful. I trust you are rested?"

"Ji." Mira bent to touch her mother-in-law's feet.

Gauri patted her head. "Good. I gave you all of yesterday to recover from your journey. Today is your first tour of the mahel and I want you to pay attention."

Mira told Lalita to remain behind and rest.

Gauri, careful to keep Mira from prying eyes, surrounded her with a guard of four maids. She introduced them as Durga, Lakshmi, Savitri and a little one named Janki.

Mira was used to being squashed by maids so didn't dwell on the suffocation.

They passed through the women's quarters, the west wing, and the guest quarters in the south wing.

Mira walked through so many draped archways and pillared halls that her eyes started to ache and her head spin. This mahel was even bigger than the palace in Merta.

"This wing was built by Maharana Ratan I for his queen, the famous Padmini," Gauri informed Mira. "And here is the entrance to a tunnel that leads to Lake Gow Mukh, the fort's natural spring and source of water. Maharani Padmini used this tunnel to go to Gow Mukh for her bath. The spring is next to the Gopeshwar Shiv temple. Bhoj likes to do Shiv puja there."

Gauri moved on to another window. She told Mira that through there one could see the Kirti Stumbh, a colossal tower Maharana Kumbh had built to commemorate his victory over the Moghul Babur. She pointed to the right. "That palace over there was built by Maharana Kumbh also."

Gauri pointed to the left. "Bhoj likes to train in that field over there."

Mira wished the queen would stop mentioning Bhoj.

"And if you look just beyond that, you can see the elephants bathing in their pond. Bhoj loves to watch them playing."

They came to the north wing. This was where the main kitchen and dining hall were. This was where Mira had sat, mute and ill, two nights ago at her wedding feast.

Gauri took her up three flights to observe the activity of the kitchen from above.

As Gauri pointed out the cooks and their names, Mira leaned forward to look out the portal window.

This kitchen was much the same as the great kitchen in Merta. The huge room had been divided into sections, one for bread, one for fruit and vegetables, one for legumes, and one for dairy. Each section was divided into sub-sections. The bread was divided into kneading, rolling, and cooking. The legume and vegetable sections, the largest, were divided into chopping, grinding, frying and stewing. All sections had their own supply of herbs, spices, milk, ghee and oil. Each was equipped with fires and huge cooking pots.

"Bhoj is very fond of milk sweets. You must make sure he has these in every meal."

Mira ground her teeth.

"He's fond of pickles and rich sauces but not too much oil. He prefers ghee. And he likes red chilies more than green. And never give him sweet pickles. He hates them."

Mira didn't know how much more she could take. The man she'd met on her wedding night didn't sound like the finicky man Gauri was describing.

She saw there were two other sections in the corner that she'd not noticed. They were removed from the rest by a wall and she leaned over to see what was going on.

She stared.

In one section, a wriggling fish was being taken out of a crate. It was slapped onto a great rock slab and with one stroke of a knife, beheaded.

Mira gasped to see the fish flop back on the table, dead.

In the other section, huge skinned animals, their flesh red and white, were being cut up with massive knives. From their size and shape, Mira guessed them to be goats or pigs.

She seized the window frame, unable to look away.

One cook was grinding meat in a huge mortar and pink paste was falling out the bottom into a wide bucket.

A sudden roiling feeling gripped Mira's belly. She heaved and put her hand to her mouth to stop the bile from escaping.

"Bahu? What's wrong?"

Mira swallowed, trying to control the spasms. "Meat is eaten here?" she gasped.

Gauri stood over her. "Of course. Warriors need meat to sustain them." Her voice was sharp. "Did you think we Sisodias were spinach eaters?"

Mira tried hard to push back the tears that burned her eyes.

"You've been sheltered, bahu, but you will learn." Gauri, conciliatory now, reached out her hand to rub Mira's back.

Mira straightened before Gauri could touch her. Had there been meat at her wedding feast? How could she have not seen it?

She backed away from the window. "Where do we go next?"

Gauri smiled. "Now we go to the granaries."

For the next hour, Mira walked behind her, hearing about granary inspections and grain distribution.

She was taken to the laundry department, and introduced to the head tailor, a man named Chitrasen. She wondered if Chitrasen ate animal flesh.

Visions of meat paste plopping into a bucket kept coming back to her. What poor helpless animal had that flesh come from?

Gauri took her into the Yagna Hall, next to the women's wing. It was the centre of religious activity in the household. Today, the sacrificial fires were unlit and the atmosphere was solemn. They passed through the sacred hall and came to another room.

The maids stopped at the doorway.

Gauri went inside and Mira followed. She saw that this room was almost as large as the Yagna Hall. It contained no furniture except a mattress that was placed next to the altar where a goddess stood. A huge woven rug covered the central part of the room.

Mira had come here on her first night in Chittore.

Of course she knew some families ate meat, she thought. She just hadn't expected to marry into one of them. That was, if her marriage could be called a marriage.

Did her father know? The thought stabbed at her. Had he given her to Bhoj, knowing that Bhoj ate meat? Perhaps he'd not thought of it. Where was the time for him to consider such things?

Gauri advanced into the room, heading for the altar.

Mira followed her.

"This is Kali Mata, the goddess Durga's fearsome form. Her main temple isn't far from here, built on the highest point of this mountain. We keep an image of her here because she is our Kula Devi, our family's protectress and benefactor. It will be your duty to offer prayers to her every day."

Mira stared at the Kula Devi whose black face was so serene. Her eyes were large and saw deep into a person's soul. Her seven hands were raised high, wielding weapons to destroy the wicked. Her eighth hand was raised in blessing, showing her devotees that though she looked ferocious, they need not fear her.

Does Kali Mata know her children eat meat? Mira wondered. She must. How can she tolerate it?

Gauri took Mira's hand and steered her towards the altar. "Bow to your Kula Devi."

Pulled to her knees, Mira looked from Kali Mata to Gauri who'd started whispering prayers.

Mira folded her palms. Kali Mata, please give me the strength to follow Krishna, she prayed. Please show me what is right.

Kali or Durga was the devoted wife of Lord Shiv. She was the mother of strength. She appeared to avenge herself on the demons that harmed her children. Surely she would protect Mira from this madness.

"When you do your bahu bhojan, your bride's feast, in two days, you'll be cooking with Kali Mata's prasad."

Mira frowned. "But food only becomes prasad after it's been offered to the deity. It means blessing. How can I cook *with* prasad?"

Gauri's white teeth gleamed in the light of Kali Mata's lamps. "It is the custom in our family for our bahu to cook her first feast using the meat of Kali Mata's sacrifice."

For a moment, Mira couldn't speak. "You want me to c–cook a sacrifice?"

The queen frowned as if she didn't understand why Mira was so upset.

Mira turned to the goddess. "Mata, you must stop this!"

Gauri touched her arm. "What are you talking about?"

Mira pulled away. "I cannot cook meat."

"Oh!" Gauri's eyes widened and she laughed, taking hold of Mira's arm again. "Of course you don't know how to cook meat but you mustn't worry. I'll teach you."

"You don't understand!" Mira struggled to keep her voice low.

Gauri frowned.

"I cannot cook meat. It's evil and against the vedas."

Gauri put her hands on her hips. "Insolent girl! This is our family tradition!"

Mira looked away. "I'm sorry, Maharani. I didn't wish to insult you."

Gauri relaxed. "Well, you must learn to speak with some restraint. You're no longer at your father's house."

"Ji." Mira whispered, a pang of homesickness assailing her. In Merta, she'd never have been ordered to cook meat.

"For a moment, I wondered if you had any breeding at all, shouting like that."

Mira bit her tongue to stay silent.

"You mustn't worry about the meat. It's easy once you understand how to cook it. The first rule is to–"

"But Maharani–"

"It's tradition."

How could they have such a barbaric tradition?

"You'll do as you're told, bahu."

What would Krishna say if he saw her cooking some poor slaughtered animal? He'd spent the first eleven years of his time on earth living in the forests of Vrindavan. He cared for the animals, he loved and protected them.

"Let us plan the menu." Gauri pulled Mira towards the door.

The animals were his creatures, all of them. If Mira cooked them, he would despise her.

"Raj Purohit will likely sacrifice a goat so we can think about the spices for that."

A sweet little goat? How could they be insulting their own Kula Devi by offering her such a sacrifice? The vedas described offering grains into the holy fire, not flesh to the cold sword!

"You mustn't worry, bahu. You must try to forget what you've been taught and adopt the Sisodia way of life." Gauri smiled as if she were granting a boon.

*Forget the scriptures?*

"Our Sisodia elders know what is best and you will adjust."

But the scriptures are older than anyone, Mira thought.

"I cannot do it, Maharani."

"What?"

Mira heard the impatience in Gauri's voice. She swallowed but couldn't stop now. "I cannot."

Gauri was glaring at Mira. "You'll do what I tell you. I'm your mother-in-law!"

"But it's wrong–"

Gauri's soft palm slammed into Mira's face, causing her to stumble and fall. It was lucky there was a carpet or she would have fallen hard onto the marble floor.

No one had hit her in a long time.

"If you don't obey me, everyone will shun you!"

Mira clutched her face. "If I do obey you, I'll shun myself."

With a gasp, Gauri hauled Mira up and pulled her out of the room. "Dasi!"

Durga appeared out of the shadows, gawking at the way the queen was treating Mira.

"Take bahu back to her rooms and make sure she stays there!"

Durga looked behind her and the other maids appeared. They surrounded Mira and shooed her along the corridor.

The drapes at the pillars flapped in the wind.

Mira kept her hand to her cheek. She did not want everyone to see that she'd been hit. What would her father say if he found out Gauri had hit her?

She went into her bedroom, leaving the maids in her front chamber.

Mira paced, trembling. What had she done?

Had she ruined the alliance? What if the Sisodias sent her back to Merta? Her father would be so angry with her.

Then Mira stamped her foot. It was his fault anyway! If he hadn't married her to Bhoj, none of this would be happening.

She went into the dressing room and sat down before the mirror. Her cheek was red and swollen. She'd never looked so ugly. Mira soaked a cloth in the bowl of water and pressed it to her face.

Would Bhoj come to punish her? she wondered, trembling.

He was strong. She'd seen his muscles. If he hit her, it'd hurt more than her face hurt now. And she'd planned that he would forget her and not even notice she was there!

Mira looked towards the door. She had no one to protect her. If only her brother Shamal were here.

# 7

# The Path

The day passed in silence.

When food came, it was vegetarian. Mira ate alone in her sitting room.

The next day was the same.

The third day, she couldn't stand it anymore.

No one stopped her when she walked out of her rooms.

Savitri, Lakshmi and Janki had been permanently assigned to her. They, along with Lalita, followed Mira through the mahel, carrying plates of flower garlands and sweets.

Savitri was the eldest, her gait slow and frail, forcing Mira to walk in a sedate manner. Janki was the youngest, still a girl at ten years old, smooth skinned and slim as a fresh young lemon tree. Lakshmi was in-between, not young, not old—modest, quiet, plain.

Mira wondered how much she could trust these new maids of hers. They were from Gauri after all and were probably spies.

Gauri had pointed out the marble landmark of the Kumbh-Shyam mandir, a great Vishnu temple, and Mira had decided to go there.

Today was Ekadasi, the eleventh day of the lunar fortnight. All devotees were fasting from grains because on this day, it was said that Kal Yuga, Chaos himself, entered the grains and caused havoc in the minds of any who ate them. Thus devotees took refuge in fasting and prayers, for only the supreme lord could protect someone from his own mind.

Mira needed to know there were other devotees in this city. She needed to know she wasn't alone.

Her mother had said to always be with the devotees, that they would give her strength.

In Merta, Purohitji had been Mira's support. He'd explained why her brother was so far from her and why her mother had died. He'd told her not to grieve for Krishna was with her.

But in Merwar there was no Girija Shankar Purohitji. The Sisodia Raj Purohit sacrificed animals!

Mira reached the entrance of the women's wing. A palanquin was waiting as Janki had ordered.

Mira wished she could walk to the temple because she needed to stretch her legs but she was in enough trouble without traipsing around the city, unescorted by her husband or guard. She descended into the box.

The palanquin lifted.

She saw that her bearers were heading towards a gate at the far end of the garden. It must be a shortcut.

They passed through the gate, her maids walking beside her.

The guards bowed their heads as she passed.

The gauze nets around the opening of her palanquin prevented any from observing her while allowing her to see as much as she wished.

The route took Mira through the main part of the city. Great buildings were everywhere and Mira watched as important looking people bustled about. Dust wafted around, sent up by the many feet that trod the roads. Garment shops lined the street and Mira saw the shopkeepers calling out to customers to come see their wares. Women carried baskets of fruit on their heads to sell.

There were many mandirs. Some were big, some were small, and all were popular.

Mira spotted the high orange flag of the Kumbh-Shyam mandir in the distance. Her bearers turned the corner and went down another lane, this one full of shops selling vermillion and colored powders for puja, vastra, mini thrones for little deities. Mira saw huge peacock feather fans and had an urge to tell Lalita to go buy one for Krishna at home.

She decided against it. It was best that she take darshan at the temple and return to the palace. Bhoj may be making his way to punish her even now. What would he say if she wasn't there?

Perhaps she shouldn't have left the palace.

The palanquin was set down.

Mira looked out her window and saw a monument of grey marble, cool and bright in the afternoon sun. The mandir looked wider than it was tall but Mira suspected the dimensions were a perfect square. In the architecture scriptures, a square was considered to be the supreme shape. It was auspicious, symmetrical in every way. She knew this because her cousin Jaimal loved architecture and had even discussed some of his own designs with her, when he'd had nothing else to do.

Her maids gathered around the opening to shield Mira as she came out.

The roar of the city smacked her ears. Odd that it hadn't seemed nearly so loud inside her palanquin.

Now she could hear the chaos as people shouted at each other, stomping about. Bells rang from somewhere, probably another mandir. Cows mooed, kicking up the dust. Carts creaked and groaned, rolling by.

There was a smaller temple to the right of the main one. The courtyard was paved with the same grey marble slabs as the mandir. There were sitafar trees behind the temples, squat and gnarled, the spiky green fruit hanging off the branches.

A little white cow walked up to Mira. It stared at her with lotus eyes, blooming like Krishna's.

His cows were so precious.

Mira took a plate of flowers from Lakshmi and showered the cow with petals. She gestured to Lalita. "Give me one sweet."

Lalita handed her a piece of fudge.

Mira placed it on the ground before the cow.

It leaned down and bit it, its soft lips barely grazing the dust.

Mira touched its hoof. "Gai Mata ki jai," she whispered.

The cow nodded and wandered off.

There was a crowd of men standing at the foot of the steps. They parted to make way for the Raj Kumari.

The devotees won't come near me, Mira realized. They'll stay away because of my rank. I should turn back.

At least try, a voice inside her urged. Mira climbed the steps. Up ahead, she saw a crowd of devotees jostling up and down for a better view. She rang the bell above her, telling Krishna that she'd arrived.

A murmur at her right spread around the room and people were turning to look at her.

Mira swallowed, feeling her cheeks burning with heat. There was no turning back now. She straightened her shoulders and walked towards the altar.

The crowd of devotees parted, retreating behind the carved pillars.

She wished they wouldn't. She didn't want to claim the best view simply because she was a princess. She wanted to be part of the crowd, fighting for a glimpse of the altar. Why should they move for her? Was Bhagwan only for the privileged?

Krishna, make me one of them.

She touched her head to the floor before the deity.

It was Vishnu, the beautiful four-armed savior. He was dressed in a yellow dhoti, made of cotton so he wouldn't feel hot. His black marble torso was dressed with blue vastra, a thin slip of material that hung over his shoulders. A single Tulsi leaf covered his heart.

Mira was conscious of the devotees watching her from behind. She saw a bare patch of floor to the left. "Let's sit," she told her maids.

As she sat, the crowd edged back to the altar for darshan. She nodded to her maids to give their trays of flowers and sweets to the priest for offering. When they got up to do this, Mira looked around.

Behind sat an old grandmother immersed in meditation, her creaky body rooted to the ground, silent mantras passing over her prayer beads. There was also a little boy, singing a prayer and clapping his hands in unsteady rhythm.

Mira smiled at him through her veil and he was close enough to see it and smile back.

Soon, most of the devotees sat down. A group of women started singing a bhajan.

Despite the crowd, it didn't feel hot in that cool marble temple.

Her maids returned.

Lakshmi held out a milk sweet as prasad.

"Did you distribute the rest?"

"Ji, Bahu Rani," Lakshmi said.

Mira knotted the sweet in a corner of her veil for later. A princess didn't eat before people who weren't her family.

Lalita held out manjira, two mini cymbals attached together with a string. "Take this, Jiji."

Mira was wide-eyed. "I'm not even supposed to be here and you want me to sing?" she whispered. "What about my status?"

Lalita smiled in mischief. "There's no law against singing in public. And I know what you want. These people don't know you yet but once they hear your voice...you sing like the celestial Gandharvas, Jiji."

Mira smiled back. "Only you say such things."

"It's the truth."

Mira looked about the mandir once more. There were so many people here. She'd only ever sung before her family, her grandfather especially.

"It's the only way to get what you want. There's nothing shameful in singing a bhajan for the lord."

Mira gazed down at the manjira, so small in Lalita's palm. She was in trouble anyway and Bhoj might lock her away as punishment. This was her one chance to be with the devotees. She grasped the manjira, locking the string around her fingers so the cymbals wouldn't hang loose.

Lalita took out several more and gave them to the other maids.

After a moment, Mira nodded at them and they played their manjiras, shing shinging sounds emanating from their hands. She led them in a gentle song of praise, her voice so low that the words didn't go beyond her group.

The little boy moved over to Lalita and whispered something in her ear.

Lalita leaned over. "He wants you to sing louder."

Mira smiled at him and her voice went up a notch.

He skipped back to his place.

The others in the temple were growing quiet, their own songs fading as they listened to the princess.

Mira faltered for a second, doubt assailing her. Then she remembered the boy and persevered. At least he liked her.

Some devotees stood, raising their arms above their heads, dancing to her words.

Mira faltered again in surprise before her voice grew stronger, soaring over the heads of the vaishnavs, the devotees of Vishnu.

Devotees were gazing at her in wonder, rising to join the others in dance.

They like me! Mira thought. Heady with success, she rose.

Her maids were appalled, their horror written on their faces like the scriptures.

Mira didn't care: for once in so long, she felt like she was with her mother again. She raised her voice and swayed.

Lalita jumped up to shield her, and the others followed, human shields playing manjiras.

Mira danced, her step light, graceful, free. Her voice flew to the top of the dome and came back down, swooping over the crowd.

The devotees joined her in the song, singing after her and swaying.

The old grandmother was laughing and weeping, her arms reaching up to Vishnu.

The little boy took Mira's manjira, shing shinging as he danced to his unsteady rhythm.

Mira raised her arms and moved from side to side, singing.

Blue hands, pink at the palm, slid around her waist.

Mira gasped, her arms coming down on top of his.

Lotus blooming eyes, so dark and soft, gazed into hers.

She gazed back and danced with him in the midst of the crowd.

Her wedding bangles kunged and her anklets chummed. The white jasmine in her hair came loose and the petals scattered the marble floor.

He smiled at her, his teeth gleaming like cow's milk.

She laughed, moving her hips beneath his palms. She raised her hand to touch his face.

The magic of his smile was blinked away.

He was gone.

Mira stopped dancing, her song silenced. She looked around, but he wasn't there.

She felt sweat in the small of her back making her veil stick to her skin. She felt weak, as if his hands on her body had held her upright and now alone she would collapse.

Her maids stood around, clutching their manjiras, anxious looks on their faces.

The devotees were staring at her, wondering at her sudden silence, wondering at her dancing, wondering at her singing at all.

She turned and the crowd parted to let her through. This time she was glad for it.

How could he just leave like that? She tripped down the steps, not daring to look at the people around her.

Her maids huffed to catch up.

Mira realized how fast she was walking. She stopped and waited for Lalita.

It's not fair! she wailed inside. Why must she always care about what everyone thought? Yet even as she raged, Mira knew she shouldn't have danced. Gauri would be furious and who knew what Bhoj would do?

But how could *they* ever understand?

Her four guardians caught up. From the way they were looking at each other, they thought she was mad. Lalita looked stunned.

"It's my fault, Jiji. I'll tell Yuvraj it was my fault," Lalita babbled.

Mira shook her head. I must go back to the palace, she thought, dragging her feet. It was my fault, all my fault.

A cheer lifted her head.

There was a crowd of people gathered outside the mandir compound. They were sitting in the shade of a saal tree, facing a saffron-clad man. The man was sitting in lotus position on the raised seat of earth that was always built around shade giving trees.

It's a sanyaasi, Mira thought, a thrill making her stomach flutter.

"Come, we should go," Savitri said.

Mira had had enough of people telling her what to do. "I want to listen to him. We'll sit at the back."

All four of them gaped at her.

"But–we have to go," Savitri said. "Bahu Rani, I'm thinking of your best interests–"

"I know. I also know I was very foolish in the mandir. And I know that I'll be punished. But if I go back now, Maharani will lock me away forever and then I'll never have the chance to come here again."

Savitri looked glum. She sighed and studied the crowd, then pointed to the farthest corner, where the shade would grow long as the sun set. "That seems like the best place," she said.

"Then come," Mira led the way, not quite believing she was doing this. She was only giving Gauri more weapons against her, yet the thought of going straight back to the palace and Bhoj after dancing with Krishna was unbearable.

Her fingers curled into her palm. She wanted Krishna with her so much!

Perhaps this sage would be like her old tutor, Girija Shankar, kind and understanding.

Mira came to the corner of the crowd and sat down, her dasis sitting around her. She pulled her purple veil further down over her face, hoping to make her maids, and perhaps herself, feel a bit easier with her modesty. She looked up at the sage.

The sanyaasi was pale, his eyes faded and sightless. He clasped the staff of a renunciate. A water bowl was placed at his side and a disciple sat behind him.

"Many believe that bhakti, the path of devotion, is easy." His voice was mellow and rich, like butter. "They believe that all one must do is worship and this will attain the lord. Yet that isn't true."

Mira frowned. What else could she do but worship Krishna?

"To truly please him, you must please his servants. It's like a stranger who comes to a village. He asks the woman who owns the guesthouse if he may stay there, but she refuses because he is dirty and poor. He doesn't deserve to be in her guesthouse. Then he sees her child playing and he compliments her on her beautiful, clever, well-bred child. Immediately, the woman allows the man to stay because he has pleased her by complimenting her child. The lord is like that woman. He may refuse a direct request from you because you have many faults such as greed and anger and hate. But if you serve the holy men and the sages, his very dear children, he will accept you. Because you have pleased him."

"Maharaj, how do we serve the sages?" a red turban at the front asked.

"The best way is to serve your guru," he said. "A guru is an enlightened soul who is your spiritual master. He guides you on the path to Krishna. And you must serve him with full faith and follow all his orders. This pleases the lord more than anything. Your guru is your best friend in the world, apart from Krishna himself. Your guru knows your past, present and future and helps you on the way to success."

Mira was staring at the sage's faded eyes, thinking about having her own guru. She had Girija Shankar Purohit but he was a family priest. He didn't initiate disciples like a guru.

"Many times, your guru will come to you. Or, he may summon you. He knows who you are and what your character is. He knows everything about you because he is the lord's intimate servant. A guru is a divine personality who descends to enlighten us. He inspires love and knowledge."

Who could my guru be? Will I ever find him?

"We often find our gurus in situations we'd never expect. They're very clever. They never reveal their divine personalities unless they wish to. Instead, they find ways to disguise themselves, sometimes descending into bodies of low caste or pretended ignorance."

Purohitji never pretended ignorance. And he was a Brahmin, not low caste. But he was very clever, she thought. He always knew the answers.

"How do we know when we've found our guru, Maharaj?" a yellow turban asked.

"If he wishes it, you'll know him on sight. A guru is merciful and rewards his disciples with knowledge."

Purohitji is merciful, she thought. He would have told me if he was my guru. So where is my true spiritual master?

Mira clasped her hands together. Oh, please Gurudev, let me find you, wherever you are.

"Bahu Rani?"

The whisper buzzed in her ear. She tried to flick it away.

"Bahu Rani? We must leave," Savitri said.

Mira waved her hand impatiently. Why wouldn't these silly maids be quiet? She wanted to know how to recognize her guru.

"Bahu Rani, we must go now. It's starting to get dark."

Mira frowned at Savitri.

"If I don't take you back to the palace now, I'll be punished."

That snapped Mira out of her trance. She nodded and stood, walking back to her palanquin to be carried back into the seclusion of her quarters.

*

Ravi Das dropped a stiff piece of brown leather in the clay bowl and poured water over it. He watched the water soak in, then crouched, withdrawing the leather every few minutes to beat its stiffness out with a hammer.

Squatting, he looked more like a pile of oddly shaped sticks than a real person. His curly hair bounced with every bang, like downward-growing banyan branches blowing in the wind. It was the color of rock salt, black and white and brown. His face was unlined, his skin glowed dark and supple. He had wide cheekbones that were held up by a rock salt beard.

Acids writhed around his stomach and jumped up his throat but he swallowed them back down.

Ravi crouched to pour some water into a battered pan. He placed the pan on the stove fire and added the leather he'd just been hammering. He picked up another piece of leather from the side, swiping it with a loofah, up and down, up and down.

The leather smoothed and stretched, smoothed and stretched.

In his mind's eye, he saw a Blue Boy, wearing a yellow turban topped with a peacock feather, twirling a flute in his hands.

The loofah in Ravi's hand fell at the Boy's blue lotus feet.

The Blue Boy smiled at Ravi.

Ravi smiled back.

"Your disciple is looking for you." The voice was deep and light, cool and soft.

"Yes, my lord, I've heard her."

"You must summon her."

"Yes, Gopal."

"Make haste. She'll need you before long."

Ravi almost fell into the fire. Blinking, he turned around and around, but Gopal was gone. He rubbed the blur from his eyes. "My lord?" he whispered to the empty room.

Ravi coughed down the lump in his throat. Then he coughed again. Looking down, he realized the loofah had fallen into the fire and he was coughing on the smoke.

He pulled it out and beat at it with his hands but it was useless. Most of it had burned away.

What did it matter? he thought, throwing it to the ground.

"I must send a message," he thought aloud. "Now."

"Another vision, Ravi?"

There was a man sniggering in the doorway.

Ravi picked up his burned loofah, trying to tear off the useless bits.

Mahendra spotted it. "Can't you even look after your tools? What was it this time? Did the Almighty drop in on you again?" He tip-toed his large bulk into the room, doing his best to avoid touching his surroundings.

"If you don't like where I live, you can always leave, Bhaiya."

"Hmph! I came to give you this but you won't appreciate it." Mahendra held out a package.

Ravi removed the leather from the water and hammered hard. Just when he had orders to fulfill, Mahendra had to show up.

Mahendra loomed over Ravi's shoulder. "Don't hammer so hard. It needs to be soaked more."

Ravi kept his mouth shut because arguing always encouraged his brother.

Mahendra looked about, his moustache curling at the single cramped room.

"Why is it that we brothers are both cobblers, yet I live in comfort and you live like this?"

Ravi didn't answer. He'd heard the question many times before.

"It's a disgrace."

Ravi moved over to his altar where a clay image of Rama stood, molded by Ravi himself. He took the cup of water he'd placed there for Rama and gulped it down. The acid in his stomach subsided.

"Doesn't it upset you that your wife and son live in my house?"

Ravi put the cup down with a thud. "I'm glad they're not living in poverty."

"Have you never once considered their feelings?"

"Lona is happy that I'm surrendered to my lord. She told me so."

"My dear brother, you are naïve. No wife wants to lose her husband. Every day she sends you food but you never touch it."

"You know I can't accept it."

Mahendra held out the package. "Take it. You haven't eaten in four days!"

"No." Ravi walked back to the stove.

The loofah was still smoking.

"Bhaiya, you know I'm renounced from worldly possessions. I don't accept gifts."

Mahendra made an exasperated sound.

Ravi knew what Mahendra was thinking. He'd thought this way for fifty-five years, ever since their father, Santokh Das, had made Ravi live in the dilapidated hut that stood at the edge of his land.

Ravi had never impressed his father. He was never able to concentrate when being instructed in cobblery because he was remembering a holy man he'd met or a passage in the scriptures.

His father had tried everything to bring Ravi back to the real world. He cajoled, beat, and starved his son. He married a ten-year-old Ravi to a ten-year-old Lona. He shouted that holy men and scriptures were for Brahmins and priests, not cobblers.

But Ravi had to ask *why* the scriptures were only for priests, and *why* ordinary people had to be ignorant.

Outraged, Santokh condemned his son to live forever outside the family home, agreeing to take Ravi back only if he apologized for his cheek.

Facing the terror of the outside world and with a young wife to support, Ravi was ready to relent.

But then a holy man visited Ravi's hut. He urged Ravi to continue his pursuit of spiritual knowledge, telling him about his past lives and why he'd been born into this body.

The holy man's name was Ramanand Acharya and he was Ravi's guru.

The first few years, the young couple barely ate, living on what Ravi made selling shoes. His mother sent food but Ravi refused it.

Lona wasted away and Ravi's resolve wasted with her but she protested when he told her to eat. She wouldn't eat if he didn't.

Lona kept her pregnancy from him for four months, starving herself, secretly starving their child also, because she didn't want the strain on him to worsen.

When he found out, he forced her to eat his mother's food, too angry and helpless to do anything else.

Lona gave birth to a son, Vijay.

Santokh took Lona and Vijay back into his household and Ravi was overjoyed to see his family cared for. But he didn't follow them there. The only time he entered his father's house again was when his mother died and then a few years later, when death claimed his father also.

For the rest of the time, he relied only on his Lord Rama. Hunger was the theme of his life, a habitual gnaw that he learned to accept.

"If only you stopped giving shoes away to beggars, you would eat at least a meal a day."

Ravi frowned at his brother. "I cannot take money from sages. They need shoes also."

"Then take some income from our land! You know it's there for you."

"No."

Mahendra thrust the packet under Ravi's nose. "Take it."

The fragrance of fresh rice wafted up into Ravi's nostrils and the bile in his stomach reacted eagerly, swishing and swashing back and forth.

Ravi stumbled and almost fell into the fire again.

"Stop this foolishness, Ravi! You need food."

"I cannot. Go now Mahendra, I must finish this pair of shoes." Ravi picked up the small patch of loofah and used it to scrape at the leather strip.

Mahendra watched for a few minutes, then tip-toed out. He left the package on the floor.

Ravi dropped what he was holding.

He turned his back on the package and went to his altar. He sat, crossing his thin legs before Lord Rama. His back straight, Ravi deepened his breath, in and out, in and out.

He meditated on the point between his eyes. His third eye appeared and he watched it spin, the violet flashes spinning faster and faster as his awareness strengthened. He told the eye to search.

It flew off, sweeping over of the lush green fields of his home in Kashi, and the fair creamy waters of the holy Ganga river. It swooped down over forests and glided over villages. It rushed over the desert plains and jumped over hilltops.

It came to a solitary mountain of red and yellow and green, sitting in the midst of a grand valley. The eye circled the mountain, going higher with every turn, finally bursting through a pair of huge gates. It whooshed down crowded city streets, careered through rowdy markets and buzzed over flower gardens. It hovered over a temple that shined pinkish-grey in the late evening sun. Circling the temple, it spotted a crowd sitting under a saal tree. It saw a saffron-clad sage. It saw a purple veil.

Ravi looked at the young girl sitting at the back of the crowd, attentive to the sage. She seemed lost, even though four tense ladies sat with her.

He stepped around the maids and whispered in her ear. "Listen to the wise man for he speaks the truth."

The girl clasped her hands together in renewed concentration.

He whispered in her ear once more. "By Krishna's order, I am your guru. Come to me, Mira. Come to me, my daughter."

# 8

# Rejection

Mira waited a week for Bhoj or Gauri to come. She embroidered veils, then picked them apart, then embroidered them again.

Why did no one come?

Perhaps they'd sent a message to her father and were waiting for his reply. Mira worried about this more than anything. She looked over the gifts he'd given her–the silk slippers, the costly garments, the gold and silver ornaments, the gems.

To match her great good fortune, he'd said, kissing her forehead.

What would he say if he heard what she'd done?

Mira sat on her balcony, trying to read the Ramayan, the scripture of Rama. It had been her mother's copy, given to Kusum by her parents on her wedding day.

Ratan had given it to Mira as part of her dowry.

"Be like Sita," he'd told her.

But Sita was a faithful wife.

Lalita rushed in. "Yuvraj is coming, Jiji!"

Oh Krishna, Mira moaned inside, pulling her veil down over her face.

He strolled in, brushing past the drapes at her doorway like a grand bull elephant striding through the forest.

She bowed and large shield-like hands gripped her shoulders, straightening her. Startled at the contact, she looked up at him.

The curling ends of his moustache touched his cheekbones as he smiled. He didn't say anything.

She fidgeted and her ankle bells chummed. "Will you sit, my lord?"

"I will," he said, seeming at ease, his smile widening.

Mira led him to a blue couch and stood before him.

"Sit with me," he said.

She sat next to him.

"You may send your dasi away. I desire no refreshments."

Mira nodded to Lalita and with an anxious look, the maid tip-toed out.

"I'm told I must punish you," he said.

Mira's stomach knotted. Well, you deserve it, she told herself. Don't complain.

"But why?"

She frowned, confused.

"You see, I've heard everything from Ma Sa, but I know her well. She tends to blow things out of proportion so I want you to tell me what happened."

Mira shook her head, blinking at him. He actually wanted to hear her side? "I don't think she blew this out of proportion."

He grinned. "At least you're being honest."

She smiled. The knot in her stomach relaxed.

He arched a brow at her. "Do you want to tell me or not?"

She sobered. What was wrong with her, smiling when this was serious? "It's about my bahu bhojan."

"Go on."

"Well, Maharani told me I had to cook meat and I said I couldn't. I've been raised in a vegetarian household."

He frowned. "It's not really meat once it's been sacrificed to Kula Devi. It's prasad and therefore pure."

"It's still the flesh of an innocent animal," Mira choked, struggling with her shock that he could say such a stupid thing.

He lifted his hands. "It's a tradition in our family."

"Does tradition make such violence right?"

"We're Kshatriyas. As warriors, we walk under the shadow of violence every day."

Mira pressed her big toe against the floor, her toe ring cutting into the rug. "We fight to protect our realm, not to slaughter innocents."

"We need meat to sustain ourselves."

"Forgive me, but we Rathores have never eaten meat and we fight just the same as you."

He looked mildly surprised. Leaning against the back of the chair, he stroked his moustache. "Hmmm," he said. "Well, you do know that the shastras permit the Kshatriya caste to eat meat, don't you?"

She looked him right in the eye. "I know that verse my self, my lord. It says that meat is only allowed to be eaten during times of war and only on the battlefield and even then, only if there is nothing else left to eat."

He blinked. "I didn't know you were educated in the dharmashastras."

"My grandfather made sure I was." Mira waited for him to say something but he remained as he was, staring at her. She dug her toe harder into the rug. Please don't make me to cook meat, she thought.

He studied her, his gaze traveling up her arms and throat to her face.

Her skin began to tingle. Was he was looking at her and thinking it was time?

"My sister Uda is very dear to me, you know."

Mira went blank. "What?"

He gave her a slow smile. "I love the way you're so forthright."

She blushed. Perhaps Gauri is right and I am ill-bred, she thought.

"What was I saying? Oh yes, Didi," he sighed and dropped his hand on his knee. "She used to be so spirited. A true Kshatraani. She would tell me and Vikram and everyone what to do and we did it. She was strong."

He looked at Mira. "People don't see that side of her now, not since her husband died."

Mira watched him, wondering what all this meant.

"Society knocked it out of her."

Mira remembered the shame she'd seen in Uda's eyes that night. It was the only thing she vividly remembered from her arrival.

After a long moment, he lifted his head. "Acha, I'll speak to my father and Raj Purohit for you."

Mira couldn't believe it! "You mean you're not angry?"

"Of course not. Your arguments are logical, after all."

"Thank you, my lord," she breathed. Now my father won't be angry with me! she thought.

"I'll take care of it. Now, I have to leave for there's much to be done in court." He touched her shoulder and strode out.

Mira leaped up and skipped around the room. Who would have thought this would happen?

Thank you, Krishna! she thought.

When she calmed down enough, she called her maids back. With Bhoj on her side, she didn't feel ashamed. She could face her people.

As the maids entered, they were grinning from ear to ear.

"Well?" Lalita asked as if she didn't already know.

"He'll speak to Maharana for me," Mira said, skipping.

The dasis, with the exception of Savitri, were laughing and clapping their hands.

"I knew he'd say that!" Janki squeaked.

"That's why you bit your nails down to the skin, is it?" Lalita giggled.

They jumped up and down together, their jewelry tinkling like mad.

"What did he say about your mandir visit?" Savitri asked.

Everyone stilled.

Mira had forgotten about that. She frowned. "He–he didn't say anything." Perhaps he doesn't know, she thought. But how could he not know? Janki said the whole palace was talking about it.

Perhaps he'd not wanted to mention it.

Why not? Even Mira admitted that her behavior had been outrageous.

He must not know. And that meant that when he found out, he'd change his mind about her.

What was it he said about Uda? That society had broken her spirit.

She's the ally I need so much, Mira thought. And if Bhoj loves her so, she must be a good person.

Then when he gets angry, she'll protect me.

*

What sort of unwomanly obstinance was this? Uda thought. And Bhoj had told the family to allow it!

He wouldn't ask such things for no reason. Then again, he was newly married and his wife was beautiful. Anything was possible.

Of course, Uda hadn't heard any of this from her family. She had to rely on Gita for her information.

There were already rumors about Bhoj's treatment of his little wife. He left her alone, they said, to grow into a woman.

As he should, Uda thought. She was proud that her brother had understood this. Her own husband had taken her on their first night together. The blood on the sheets had terrified her so much, even though her mother had told her to expect it. And it hurt, like she was crushed inside. She'd felt weak, drained.

Her husband became angry when she asked him to leave her alone for a few days. He used her several times that night.

"The family is furious," Gita told her now, "especially since your brother has asked them to excuse Mira. She will serve a vegetarian meal at her bahu bhojan tomorrow, even though all Sisodia brides have served Kula Devi's prasad for generations. They're saying Mira is bringing corruption upon the House of Merwar."

Uda was silent.

"Then, just an hour ago, Bahu Rani went into the gardens for a walk. Your Buaji was also in the garden with her own bahus. They spoke to Mira."

Uda could only imagine how the conversation had gone. Buaji, her father's sister, was known for her sharp tongue.

"Bahu Rani returned to her rooms weeping."

Poor Mira. This was just the beginning for her.

"What of my father?" Uda asked. "Surely he had something to say about this?" Maharana Sangavat wouldn't tolerate any insult to his daughter-in-law, she thought, yet nor would he allow impiety.

And what about her scandalous trip to the mandir a week ago?

The amazing thing was that now the people loved her. They were still talking about the magic that had filled the temple when she sang. Even though she'd danced before everyone, the people were so enchanted by her voice that they didn't want to admit she'd acted appallingly. They were saying that she must've had a vision to dance like that.

Uda realized that Gita was still talking.

"The word is that Bhoj went to his father directly from Mira's suite. Shortly after, a messenger was sent to all the royal households, informing them of the resolution."

"Just like that?"

"Just like that."

Yet just a few hours later, Mira left the gardens crying, Uda thought, putting down her embroidery.

She went to her balcony. The sun was making its way into the western hemisphere and she watched its descent, leaning her palms on the cool marble screen.

Her father must have a reason. He was quick to anger but quick also to be benevolent. Uda knew this, even though he hadn't spoken to her in years.

Why was Mira being so foolish? And why was Bhoj letting her?

Of course, the answer to that was as plain as the setting sun. Bhoj, adored by everyone, assumed that if he asked, the family would go along with anything.

Society wasn't like that. When Bhoj was around, they'd be polite and gracious; when he was gone, Mira would see a different side to them altogether.

Uda chewed her bottom lip. She wished she could talk to Mira but was afraid of going to her. They'd say that Uda had put the evil eye on the bahu rani and corrupted her. They probably already did since Uda had met Mira when she first arrived.

The next morning, Uda went about her routine, performing puja to her Isht Devi Durga and eating a small meal of fruit and milk.

She sat down to work on some garments for her cousins' children.

Her family may not like her but they knew she was the best at embroidery. They liked to dump garments in her arms with sheets of time-consuming patterns to sew.

She didn't mind. What else did she have to do?

By mid-morning, Uda put down a blouse to rest her eyes. She'd pricked herself too many times today.

"Raj Kumari?"

She turned to Gita.

"Bahu Rani requests an audience with you."

Uda couldn't believe it. "Bring her in!"

She heard the chum chum first. Before widowhood, she'd never have noticed it. Now, having renounced ornaments forever, she heard every kung of a bangle, and every chum of an anklet.

The girl entered.

Uda couldn't see the face for the red veil pulled over Mira's head. She extended her hands. "Welcome, sister-in-law. Come and sit with me." She nodded to Gita. "Bring refreshments."

Uda steered Mira to the couch and sat her down. "You may lift your veil in here." She smiled. "I'm your sister so surely there is no need for such modesty between us?"

The girl seemed to hesitate, then the veil slid up to reveal the gold beneath.

Even though Uda had seen Mira before, her breath still caught. Perhaps if Uda had been so beautiful, her husband would have been kinder.

Mira eyes were red-rimmed.

"They've tormented you," Uda said.

Mira was silent.

Uda looked over Mira's frame, so small and vulnerable. She felt a sickening in her stomach that such a little girl was in the power of so many cruel people. No wonder Bhoj had sided with Mira.

The girl clutched the edge of her veil against the side of her face, as if it would protect her.

"You must not have understood what you were doing. You're so young, after all," Uda said.

Mira's lip trembled. "No, I–"

Gita entered, bearing a platter of sweets and juices. She set it on the table at Uda's right hand and retreated, shutting the door behind her.

Uda poured pomegranate juice into a gold cup and handed it to Mira.

Mira took it and sipped. A drop of red lingered on her bottom lip. She didn't touch the sweets.

Uda nodded and put the dish down. "What were you saying just now?"

Mira set down her cup. "I knew I was rejecting a family tradition."

Uda wondered if Mira was just parroting what she'd heard or if she actually understood what she was saying. "So why did you do it?"

Mira's cheeks turned pink, whether from shame or anger, Uda couldn't tell.

"My Isht Dev is Krishna. I've been taught to worship him from my cradle."

Uda's lips thinned. "Just as we Sisodias are taught to worship our Kula Devi from our cradle."

"You know, you look like your brother when you do that."

Uda blinked. "Do what?"

"That thing you do with your mouth. Your brother does that too."

Uda smiled. "Really? Well, we are brother and sister–"

Wait a minute! How had the subject changed so fast? Uda narrowed her eyes. "Bhoj and I sometimes look similar but our natures aren't the same. He's too forgiving."

"He is. I was stunned myself."

"You were?"

"Yes. He actually listened to what I had to say."

Uda paused. Mira's description of Bhoj was so true.

"That's why I'm here, Didi. You're dear to him and I wanted to ask your advice."

Uda raised her eyebrows. "You may ask me anything."

Mira looked at Uda, her expression taut as a bow string. "Does your brother know what happened at the mandir? He didn't say anything about it."

Bhoj knew, all right, Uda thought. He must be saving it as an advantage over Mira.

"Perhaps he didn't see the need to say anything," she suggested.

"So he does know?"

When Uda nodded, Mira relaxed her frame into her seat. "I'm so glad."

Uda raised her eyebrows. "You're glad he knows you danced in public?"

Mira's face fell, like a pebble off a mountain. "No. I'm just glad that despite knowing, he was still kind to me." She glanced down at her hands, limp in her lap.

Uda noticed those hands were decorated with bridal henna designs, the red lines swirling and intricate. Her own hands were pale and undecorated.

There was another pause before Uda's nerves got the better of her. "Mira, you must stop this."

"Stop what?"

"This conflict. In the end, it's only you who'll get hurt. I heard what happened with Buaji."

Mira didn't move but Uda felt her withdraw.

"I don't try to create scandals," Mira whispered.

Uda covered Mira's hand with her palm. "You don't try to avert them, either."

"It's not my fault!" Mira's eyes brimmed with tears. "I didn't say anything rude to Buaji, but she was so cruel! She humiliated me!"

"Perhaps you've never known dislike and didn't know what to expect. But you can't reject family traditions and expect to be liked."

Mira snatched her hand from under Uda's and stood. "I should leave."

"Don't go."

"I feel I'm distressing you."

Uda stood. "Listen, it's best if you just do what they want. Then you won't ever have to feel lonely as you do now."

"I take my leave, Didi." Mira bowed. She pulled her veil back down over her face and left, chum chums echoing off the marble walls.

*Why is she running away?* Uda wondered in frustration.

Then she remembered that she'd touched the girl's hand. Perhaps Mira didn't want to be touched by a widow.

No, she wouldn't have come if she'd thought that way.

So why did she run? Was she so obstinate that she couldn't hear a word against herself?

Uda reached out for her juice. Her jerking hand knocked it over and the stain seeped into the faded blue of her rug. She called for Gita who rushed in with a cloth and threw it down over the puddle.

"I'll call another dasi to clean this so I can help you change clothes."

"Why would I want to change my clothes?" Uda asked.

Looking down, she saw her pure white garments stained with red.

\*

Mira retreated to her rooms, treading the blue carpet like it was a precipice, edging her way forwards, forcing herself not to run.

With Lalita and Janki behind her, she ascended the staircase, hitching her skirt up so that she wouldn't trip.

She reached her suite.

"Jiji," Lalita began.

Mira held up her hand. "Ekanth."

Janki bowed and left.

After a pause, Lalita left also.

Mira rubbed her eyes with her knuckles, feeling the kajol smudge all over her eyes.

Her rings grazed her delicate skin and she stopped rubbing to look at the jewels.

The ruby on her middle finger was the largest, the size of a knuckle itself. It burned red, rays shooting out and ricocheting off the walls.

The ruby didn't need the setting of a ring to be beautiful. If anything, it needed the sun. The sun's mighty rays would fill it and fulfill it and join it to the light of the world.

Mira caressed the stone, the red of her hennaed finger mingling with the stone's fire.

Buaji had called Mira arrogant and ugly. Her daughters-in-law had called Mira a disgusting Rathore.

Even now, Mira's body burned with humiliation. She thought of her father and how she'd brought disgrace upon him. I'm so sorry, Bapu Sa, she thought.

Uda said to do what they want. Then Mira wouldn't be insulted.

Buaji had tilted Mira's face up to the light so that everyone could see her crying.

Then they'd all walked away, laughing.

Uda thinks I've never known dislike. What was that in the garden then? And why did my own father send me away when my mother died? And why did Shakti and Kamini make me feel like–

Mira brushed her tears away. I don't care. I've lived with this pain before, I can do it again. It's not just about my honor. If I give in, I'll be impure. More impure than I am now.

What about the alliance? What about my people?

Mira moaned. Why must I make these decisions? she thought. She picked up a pillow and threw it across the room. What is it you want, Krishna?

Tomorrow is my bahu bhojan. I have to decide!

Bhoj supports me! I don't have to do what Uda said.

Then what happens when Buaji humiliates me again? What about the rest of them? Can I bear more of what I endured yesterday?

Mira looked around her darkening room. She'd sent her maids away before they'd lit the lamps. Stiffly, she went to pull the rope to summon them.

Catching her image in the mirror on the wall, she saw that the scarlet vermillion at her hair parting had streaked like a gash, specks of the powder falling to the floor with every movement. Some had fallen onto the ruby. She wiped it off and the ruby sparkled beneath her finger. Mira turned and went to her window.

The last rays of the day were falling over Chittore. The whole city was bathed golden orange.

Uda said I shouldn't reject family tradition, Mira thought, holding the ring up to a hole in the screen.

The jewel caught the sun's last rays and shone like fire, a holy fire, a yagna fire. It shone like a sacrifice.

The ruby doesn't need the gold ring, Mira thought. The ruby needs the light of the sun. She held the ring higher.

I cannot rely on others to protect me, she thought. Not Bhoj, not Uda. Not even my father. I can only rely on Krishna.

Because I too need the light.

# 9

# Sweet

Two hours before dawn, Mira bathed and dressed in her plainest garments, a light blue ensemble with an orange border around the hem of the skirt, the long sleeves, and the neckline. The veil was orange cotton, embroidered with tiny diamonds.

Having sent her other maids ahead, Mira left her suite with only little Janki yawning behind her.

The cooks, uniformed in white dhotis, were waiting.

The head cook, tall and skinny as a coconut tree, stepped forward. "Bahu Rani, everything is ready as you asked. We only await your direction."

She nodded. "Thank you Balavji. First of all, put the dhal on to cook and the milk on for the fudge."

Balav nodded to two of his assistants and they went off.

"Are the vegetables chopped and covered?"

"Yes, Bahu Rani," he said.

"Good. Start preparations for the laddoo."

Mira's mother had always advised her to begin making the sweet dishes first since they took the longest time.

So Mira set about supervising the grinding of spices and the slow condensation of milk and sugar into fudge. She took over the huge ladle to show the junior cook how to fry laddoos without burning them.

She selected how much cardamom she wanted for the sweet rice and added the right amount of gor, raw brown sugar, to the mango pickle.

She dropped bowlfuls of mustard seeds, cumin seeds, fenugreek seeds and bay leaves into hot oil and watched as they danced. When they darkened, she added twenty-five fresh chopped chilies and two nuggets of ground ginger, each as big as her fist, then poured the lot into the dhal.

Cooking was easy for Mira. She only had to know what every person in the kitchen was doing at all times and she'd been trained to do that since she was seven.

She heated masses of ghee in a pan and added a sack of semolina. She handed a wooden spoon as long as an elephant's trunk to a cook and told him to stir until she returned.

He looked stunned that a girl her size could handle such a large implement and she smiled. If there was one thing her aunt had taught her, it was to know how to do everything, even if she was never required to do it.

She left the kitchen only once, at dawn, to bathe again and perform her puja.

When she returned, she set her maids and the kitchen girls to kneading the dough, even joining in at one point. She didn't trust male hands kneading her bahu bhojan puris.

Mira looked up from inspecting the rolling of the dough to see her mother-in-law bending over the laddoo preparations.

"Bahu, I see that you have things in control here," Gauri said, dressed in magnificent violet silk that set off her fair complexion.

"I think so."

"Do you need my help?"

"I'm honored, but no. Please rest, this is a day of leisure for you," Mira smiled, hoping to seem solicitous.

"Very well. The meal must be served at noon." Gauri left through a side door.

Every person in the kitchen was staring at Mira. It was clear from their disappointed expressions that they'd expected a fight.

Because of the sheer numbers to be fed in the palace, the cooking would go on all day. Something as simple as peas and aubergine stir fry took hours because six cauldrons full had to be cooked.

On and on it went until somewhere towards noon, she took up to her suite a gold plate, a large as a wagon wheel, filled with a bit of every dish she'd cooked. She placed a Tulsi leaf in the center of the plate and offered the meal to Krishna, ringing the little bell.

She had already taken Kula Devi's offering up to the yagna hall and put aside the portion that would be given to the cows.

Newly bathed and dressed in a clean outfit of pink silk, Mira returned to the kitchens. It was noon and she directed the manservants into the dining hall bearing their huge platters.

Her father-in-law, Maharana Sangavat, was seated with Raj Purohitji at the head of the hall, on a grand couch lined with satin. Bhoj was seated at his right hand.

The men of the family were seated along the hall in lines facing eaching other.

When everything was set as she wished, Mira and her maids served Sangavat, Purohitji, Bhoj and the elders of the family, while she directed the kitchen men in serving the others. Her hands shook but she didn't spill anything.

Purohitji, as the guru of the family, said the prayer to Lord Shiv and then was observed as he took the first bite. He nodded but said nothing.

The king took a bite of the halva. "Hmmm!" he said, smiling at her. "Is that rose I taste?"

Mira smiled behind her veil and nodded.

Bhoj took a bite of his laddoo and chewed. He looked around at his family. "Ha! None of my sisters-in-law can cook like this!" As the men laughed, he turned to the curly-haired boy sitting next to him. "What do you think, Udai?"

The handsome boy took a small bite of his laddoo and munched. He swallowed. Then he stuffed the rest into his mouth.

Bhoj grinned. "Well said, Udai."

Mira couldn't hold her grin back.

The men laughed again, and began eating.

Bhoj called Mira over to him. "This is Udai, my favorite cousin. Udai, this is your sister-in-law."

"Pranam, Babhiji," Udai mumbled around the laddoo still in his mouth. He tried to swallow too fast and choked.

Bhoj thwacked him on the back.

Mira smiled at Udai. "How old are you?"

"Ten years, Babhiji."

"He has an aptitude for study," Bhoj said. "Bapu Sa has decided to send him to learn from the scholars at Benares."

"Kashi?" Mira blurted. "Then you are truly blessed, Udai. My mother once told me that Kashi was the highest of all holy cities."

Udai sipped his water. "I am very clever," he said.

Bhoj cuffed him lightly over the head. "Insolent," he said, smiling. "As Udai is so young," he told Mira, "he need not train for war yet. His mind is better spent on learning scripture." Bhoj motioned to a chubby man sitting at the other side of the hall. "That over there is Shivgan,

Udai's elder brother. He controls a fort near Kumbalgarh."

"Ji," Mira said. She wondered why he was telling her all this but then noticed how much attention Bhoj was paying to Udai. He laughed with the boy and teased him, nudging Udai with his elbows.

Bhoj loved his family. He would be a wonderful father, she realized, then almost kicked herself for having such nonsensical thoughts. She forced a smile and moved away to serve Sangavat.

When plates began to look empty, Mira sent men to fill them.

Vikram, sitting at Sangavat's left hand, dipped his middle finger into his cucumber condiment. "I don't think I've ever tasted yogurt so sweet and fresh." He looked right at her when he said it.

Mira drew back, uneasy with the way Vikram Jehtji was licking his fingers. There was something about the way he was doing it...

Don't be silly, she told herself. He's just eating.

When the men finished their meal, the room was cleared and the royal ladies entered.

Mira dismissed the kitchen men and summoned the palace maids. She served the queen and elders of the family while the maids served the other ladies. There wasn't as much laughter as when the men had eaten but Mira was still glad to escape Vikram's gaze.

Raj Purohit's wife didn't eat at the palace, just like Indumati in Merta.

Mira braced herself but the women found nothing bad to say. She'd expected at least something cruel from Buaji, but no, Buaji ate more than anyone and patted her stomach when she was finished.

Mira served a cool mint drink at the end and heard sighs around the room. Everyone would have a very good sleep now.

Everyone except Mira. She still had to feed the servants.

Leaving Savitri to direct the cleaning of the dining hall, Mira went out into the great courtyard, where everything had been set up for the people of the palace to eat.

They sat on mats in rows, leaves set in front of them as plates.

Mira went into to the kitchens where the cooking had continued as per her instructions. Everything was to her satisfaction and she ordered the buckets of frest food carried outside, marching the manservants through the palace like they were her army.

The servants of the guest quarters, the women's quarters, the west wing, the tailoring house, the laundrymen, the stables, the guard house, the dairy, the granary, they all came in by lots, with Mira smiling and urging them all to eat their fill.

Everyone ate, including the kitchen staff. The last lot stood to clean the mess.

When Mira finally dried her hands and left the kitchens, her legs were shaky and her head pounded. Entering her suite, she just wanted to collapse on her bed.

"What a feast."

Mira screamed, then saw Bhoj standing at her window.

"Don't do that!" she exclaimed. She fell on her couch, gasping.

He chuckled.

"Forgive me. I didn't mean to startle you." He sat next to her. "You didn't look as if you were nervous."

Mira rolled her eyes. "You see if you can spend all day trying to please everyone. Oh, I forgot, that's not a challenge for you, is it?"

He chuckled again. "I should spend more time here. I like your sass."

Mira vowed to shut up.

"You're tired?"

She nodded, looking at the floor.

"Have you eaten?"

Actually, no, she thought. There hadn't been time.

"I thought so. You brought a tray up for Krishna, right? It's ready for you."

Mira turned to see Lakshmi entering with the tray. She realized she was ravenous.

Lakshmi put the tray down on a low table and lay a pillow on the stool before it. "I heated everything up as Yuvraj directed, Bahu Rani."

"Thank you, Lakshmi."

When the dasi left, Mira turned to Bhoj.

"Go on then," he said.

Settling herself down, she tore off a piece of puri and dipped it into one of the sabjis. She told herself she was too tired to mind Bhoj watching her.

He sat in silence, and she wondered if he was counting her bites.

When she was finished, he arched a brow at her. "That's all?"

She nodded.

"Have some more dhal at least."

"No, I couldn't. I just want to sleep."

Bhoj gave her a long look before consenting. "Then I'll leave you."

When he was gone, Mira went into her dressing room and washed. Her face still dripping, she slumped onto her bed, pulling her veil off. As she drifted into sleep, Mira thought Bhoj was very kind to check that she ate. Very kind indeed.

*

Vikram stood in his uncle's darbar, ministers muttering around him.

Aryaji, the prime minister, leaned towards Vikram. "The court seems unsettled, does it not, Kumar?"

"Ji, Aryaji."

"It's excitement at the success of Bahu Rani's feast yesterday." Aryaji couldn't resist a satisfied smile.

"My brother's bride is perfection, Mahamantri. There was no doubt her Bhojan would be a success."

"Of course."

Vikram knew what Aryaji was thinking. The fluid flawlessness of yesterday's meal was a major disappointment to Sangavat's restless courtiers, especially since Mira's rejection of the Kula Devi had promised to be the fight of the decade.

Vikram chuckled to see Bhoj in such a diplomatic tight spot.

It was a spark waiting to flame and Vikram couldn't wait to fan it. Little Mira must burn very well.

But then Bhoj wouldn't know, Vikram thought.

He'd laughed when he heard of their arrangement. He wouldn't wait like Bhoj. He'd make his wife pregnant as soon as possible. Only then would the people know this alliance was ironclad.

Yet even as Vikram mocked his cousin, there was something good about knowing Mira was untouched.

A bugle sounded, punching everyone's eardrums in.

Maharana Sangavat, flanked by his son, Yuvraj Bhoj, graced the assembly and the crowd parted, buzzing around them like bees.

Vikram bowed with the others. A jolt of violence shot through him as Sangavat passed.

Bhoj was looking calm and composed. No pangs of unfulfilled lust then.

The king graced the throne and the usual boring business of court began. Ministers stood and gave their reports. The treasury accounts were reported, down to the very last coin, should emergency funds be needed for war. The city walls were being fortified anew, supervised now by engineers from Merta. Messages came from other kingdoms. Taxes were collected and tallied.

Vikram gave his own report on the mukhyas. There were many grievances; outbreaks of smallpox, worries about drought, requests for tax exemption.

When Vikram sat down again, he considered the men in Sangavat's government. Some ministers were prominent and had followers.

Sangavat did a great deal to dispel these factions. It was a special talent of his to sense the smallest hint of a division and then arrange a meeting to smooth things over. He never singled out favorites. There were very few who had the privilege of being called high council and these were respected fathers of the court. Aryaji, of course, held the posts of both chief advisor and prime minister.

Finally, court was dismissed for the evening meal.

Today was Somvar, the moon day, so Vikram knew Sangavat wouldn't go to the dining hall. This day was dedicated to Sangavat's Isht, Lord Shiva, the Lord of the Moon, and thus the king would fast.

The crowd milled around the main exit.

Vikram slipped away through a side door, coming out the east exit. He made his way around the civic buildings towards the Kirti Stumbh.

The guards saluted him as he entered the tower. He went up, bending his head so that he wouldn't hit the low door frames. This building was called the Tower of Victory and yet Maharana Kumbh had designed the door frames so low that people had to bend their heads. He'd said that in bending, people remained humble.

The tower had nine levels in all, each level decorated with sculptures of demi-gods and scenes from the scriptures. Writing of all languages and religions was carved into the walls. Even the name Allah was written in Urdu on a pillar to show that the Rajputs had respect for all the names of the lord.

Vikram ran up the deep cut stairs to the ninth level. This was where his uncle would come to perform his evening surya namaskar, the salute to the descending sun.

The Sisodias were Suryavanshis, descended from the sun god, and Sangavat honored his progenitor with utmost faith.

Vikram heard footsteps on the stairs and engrossed himself in the yogic movements of the namaskar, his muscular body bending and stretching in supple movement.

Sangavat came to stand next to Vikram, joining him in the exercise.

They performed it six times and then stood in silence, absorbing the last rays of the day.

"How are you, Putra?" Sangavat asked.

"I'm well, Kaka Sa. But–" Vikram pretended to hesitate, "I worry for Bhoj."

Sangavat turned to him.

Vikram cleared his throat. "Bahu Rani's arrogance has alarmed our people."

Sangavat was silent. He looked to the south of the city where the elephants were bathing in their lake, spraying each other, playing.

"The people worry that since you appeased Mira, it'll lead to further change. The people don't like change, Kaka Sa."

"I know well what my people do and do not like, Vikram."

"Yes, Maharana, of course. I only worry for my brother."

Sangavat sighed, putting his arm around Vikram's shoulders. "You've always been close to each other. Bhoj confides in you."

Always it was Bhoj. Bhoj Bhoj Bhoj.

Vikram felt the weight of Sangavat's arm get heavier. He wanted to throw it off, remembering the grim look on his uncle's face when a ten-year-old Vikram had been brought in to his court at Kumbalgarh, an innocent testimony to the devastation of war.

"Don't weep, Vikram," Sangavat had said. "Think of your parents' valorous deaths. You carry their legacy now so don't weep for martyrs."

But Vikram did weep and he hated Sangavat for giving such an impossible order. Would Bhoj have not wept? Vikram insisted to himself that Bhoj would have wept.

If Sangavat hadn't left Vikram's father Jaisingh at Chittore, perhaps both Vikram's parents would still be alive today. Perhaps his mother wouldn't have leaped into a fire to save her honor from the sultan's soldiers. Perhaps his father wouldn't have donned the saffron cloth and ridden into certain death.

But no, Sangavat had left Jaisingh with too few men to hold Chittore against the sultan of Gujarat's army. He'd wanted Jaisingh to die.

Sangavat sighed again. "I don't want Bhoj to suffer because of the attitudes of this family. He should be enjoying his time with his new bride."

Vikram's hands fisted before he relaxed, forcing his mind into the calm he felt as he performed surya namaskar. "I'll speak to Bhoj if you wish it, Maharana."

"I do." Sangavat lifted his arm from Vikram's shoulders and made to leave.

"Kaka Sa?"

Sangavat turned back.

"I've a request." Again, Vikram pretended to hesistate. "Many at court worry that we've no intelligence in the enemy camp. All we know is what we hear from our neighbors, many of whom are now bowing before the strength of Delhi."

"What is it you wish to say?"

Vikram looked into his uncle's eyes. "I'm saying that we cannot rely on others to give us the information we need."

Sangavat arched an eyebrow, just as Bhoj always did. "I have spies."

Vikram scowled. "Spies can be bought and sold for a gold coin. We need one of our own in the Shah's court."

"It's a good idea, Vikram. The problem is that I can't find anyone I trust enough to send on such a mission and still be willing to lose should he be discovered."

The sun had descended. Nightmen were walking the streets, lighting the sconces. The Kirti Stumbh was in shadow.

"Am I not a candidate, Maharana?"

Sangavat frowned. "Of course not. If you were captured, I'd have to pay a crippling ransom."

Vikram smashed his fist against a pillar. "I'd be ashamed if the Maharana of Chittore had to buy me back," he declared. "I want to go for my country and if I fail, I'll give my life before you pay a ransom."

Sangavat caught hold of Vikram's shoulders, speaking with the same passion. "Vikram, it's too dangerous! What if we should lose you? Bhoj would be heartbroken."

Vikram's pretend passion was now very real, even if his words were not. "And how can I live to see my motherland invaded? This land my parents died to defend? I'll gladly forfeit my life to protect her!"

Sangavat studied Vikram's face. "You speak as your father did."

Vikram paused. This was the first time in years Sangavat had spoken of Jaisingh.

"If he hadn't asked to defend Chittore, I wouldn't have lost him. But you're his legacy. You're my brother returned to me." He embraced Vikram. "How could I bear to lose you? To lose my brother twice?"

A cold weight settled over Vikram's chest. The hot violence that usually coursed through his veins was gone and in its place, this cold fiend sat. The heat comforted, made him strong, but this cold took that away.

Sangavat rubbed Vikram's back, as if it didn't matter if Vikram wept. "Do you truly want this mission?"

Since a knot had lodged in Vikram's throat, he just nodded.

"I would be broken if I were to lose you. You know that, don't you?"

Vikram nodded.

Sangavat moved back to look at him. "I honor your courage. If you want to go, I won't insult you by refusing."

Their embrace broke and they stood in the dark for a moment. Then they descended the stairwell and returned to the palace, parting at the central wing near the guest quarters.

Vikram made for his suite. He went into his dressing room and splashed his face, rubbing at his itchy eyes.

Now he could meet the Shah. He must send a messenger to Delhi.

So why did he feel so cold?

*

The summer was blistering. Even the dust burned.

Only a month after Mira's bahu bhojan, Bhoj came to tell Mira that her grandfather, Rao Duda, was dead.

She didn't weep until after Bhoj left. Her noble, strong, kind grandfather... He'd loved to hear her sing of Krishna. Mira wished she could have seen him one last time.

Oh, Merta! Mira thought, clutching her wet cheeks.

Maharana Sangavat sent her a message of his condolences. He said that a gallant warrior such as Rao Duda was mourned by all, friends and enemies alike.

Now Mira's uncle, Vikramdev, was Maharana of Merta.

Mira hoped her father was well, that he didn't feel the pain of losing his father too much. Mira hoped Shamal gave him comfort.

The sun burned Bhoj's skin darker every time he visited Mira until soon, he was almost black. He told her how Gauri always chided him not to get so dark yet he had to go out and train or set a bad example for his men.

He asked Mira if she disliked his darkness.

Without thinking, Mira blurted out that Krishna was dark-skinned.

Bhoj laughed. "Then I know you've no problem with it."

Mira spent most of her time in her rooms, alone. Despite the success of her feast, she was shunned by her in-laws and there was only so much she could say to her dasis without repeating herself. Even then, Lalita was the only one Mira trusted with her thoughts. The other maids were Merwari.

Two months later, when monsoon poured down on the mountain, the people danced in the streets in relief. After a day, mosquitoes were everywhere.

Mira had her maids put up extra nets over the balcony, windows, doorways, and in her sleeping chamber.

One night, a snake slipped into her bed to escape the rain.

Mira left the poor thing alone and slept on the couch outside.

Bhoj was the only one who thwarted her isolation. How annoying that the only person she didn't want to see was the only person willing to see her. Her one comfort was the drenched messenger that came bearing letters from Shamal.

When the next letter arrived on Ravivar, the day of the sun, she dismissed her maids so she could read in peace. Mira unrolled the silk, pleased to see that the messenger had protected it from getting wet.

"My dear sister Mira,

"I hope you're well and that your in-laws are kind. They must be now that your bahu bhojan was such a success."

Mira wished it were that simple.

"I'm not well. In fact, I'll likely die."

She smiled. Shamal loved to complain.

"Bapu Sa's has been acting like an ill-tempered bull and he never stops training us. It's like he expects a war or something!"

Mira couldn't help chuckling.

"He wants me to go over the ledgers again just to see if we've enough grain for next year. Seems reasonable, you say? Well, he wants to know if we've enough grain in case there's a drought.

"It's raining, my beloved sister. It's been raining for the past month. Our harvest will be the best yet. But he's making me go over the ledgers, again, just to prove it!"

Mira imagined her brother's indignant face and giggled.

"I asked him to look out the window but he wouldn't. Then he told me to stop being impertinent. When am I ever impertinent?"

Mira shook her head at him.

"Ranjeet and Raagav say I'm not dutiful enough and that Rana Ratan should make them princes instead. Naughty brats. Did you see them at your wedding?"

Mira had been too dazed at her wedding to notice what others were doing.

"They were parodying the groom's people! Ranjeet walked around rubbing his hands and grinning, pretending to be Sangavat. Raagav puffed out his chest and strutted around, pretending to be Bhoj. Then Ranjeet started clapping people on the back and laughing loudly, pretending to be Sangavat's nephew Vikram."

Mira's jaw dropped. When had this happened?

"Then Sangavat walked past and everyone almost fainted from horror. But he laughed and said they were acting just like Vikram and

Bhoj. He told the both of them to come over and entertain the Sisodias with impressions of the Rathores.

"And they call me impertinent!"

Mira giggled. Ranjeet and Raagav always got away with things. Once, they'd talked Mira into swimming in the lake, even though none of them were good swimmers. The slap Kusum gave her was unforgettable but Ranjeet and Raagav weren't punished at all. Then there was that time they talked Shamal into hiding Ratan's sword in a tree. When Ratan set the whole palace to finding it, Shamal was so scared he hid in the tree himself.

"Anyway, since the news of your bahu bhojan, Bapu Sa's been telling everyone that his daughter's the best cook in Bharat and soon Bhoj would be fat from eating her sweets."

Mira rolled her eyes. Ratan had eaten her cooking all of two times and both times he hadn't even known Mira had cooked the food.

"I wish I could be fat but the way Bapu Sa has me training, it's a miracle I manage to keep any weight on me. Last week he had me pulling a mango tree around the training field for half a day, just because he wanted to see if I could do it! Forgive me, but in war, when is one required to pull a mango tree around the battlefield?"

Mira laughed out loud.

"Do you think the enemy will be scared if I run at them and shout I'm going to smash their heads up with my tree trunk?"

She put her hand to her mouth to stop herself from laughing louder and slumped over the cushions.

Bhoj walked in.

She choked and tried to sit up.

"I heard you received a letter today."

Coughing, she rolled the letter up. "Yes, from my brother."

The image of her brother running towards the enemy, mangos flying out behind him, flashed through her mind. She bit her lip to control her giggle.

Bhoj stood over her. "His letter is amusing, I see. May I read it?"

"It wouldn't amuse you, my lord," Mira said and lifted the lid of the low desk she was sitting at. She deposited the letter inside and lowered the lid.

Bhoj arched his eyebrow. "That's what Uda always says. She never lets me read the letters she writes to her mother-in-law."

Mira bent her head back to look at him. He was far too close.

"You're wet," she said, noticing that he was dripping all over the floor.

"I went riding."

Mira went into her dressing room to get a towel. "Why were you riding in the rain?" She turned and walked right into him.

His blue eyes gazed down at her. "I like it."

She backed away and held out the towel. "I'll–er–bring refreshments."

"I'm not hungry," he said, pulling loose the strings at the shoulder of his tunic and taking the garment off. He rubbed his chest dry.

Mira stared at him. How could he take his clothes off in front of her?

He had light hairs on his chest. His whole torso was as dark as his face. He must train without his tunic on, she thought, fretting at the end of her veil. She watched the way his shoulder muscles rippled.

He said something but she didn't hear it. He was so big, she thought. Even bigger than her father.

He dropped his wet tunic on the floor.

Mira hoped he wouldn't leave it there. What would her maids think to see his clothes in her dressing room? "Er, I need something from the sitting room."

"Fine." He squelched the way back, rubbing his arms and shoulders dry.

If he didn't change his pitambar, he was going to ruin the upholstery on her seats.

Mira wondered why he'd come directly to her when he could have gone to his rooms and changed first. He turned and threw the towel at her and she caught it just before it hit her face.

"Dry my back, will you," he said, presenting his large, tanned, muscled back.

She saw droplets of water run from the nape of his neck down his smooth skin and sink into the material of his pitambar at his waist. Her mouth went dry. She took a pigeon step towards him, stretched out her arm and wiped.

His muscles flinched.

She wondered if she was doing it wrong but he didn't say anything. She stretched to reach his shoulders, stretching a bit more with every wipe. Each time, she stepped closer to him.

Her cheeks felt hot.

When he was dry, she threw the towel on the seat, not caring any more about the upholstery.

He picked up the towel again and gave his face a final wipe. As he bent, Mira saw he was grinning. He'd been laughing at her all along! He sat on what had become 'his' seat, a blue couch long enough to lie on.

Her mother's deep red couch was adjacent to his. She sat down on the far side, as far from him as possible.

He kicked off his shoes, then took off his turban and rubbed the ends of his hair dry.

"The building of our mahel will commence when the monsoon rains end," he said, rubbing his tanned feet.

She stared at his long toes, the nails white and elegant. "What?"

He looked at her. "The building of our mahel, of course."

She looked up at him. "But the plans aren't even finished yet." Mira had a difficult enough time avoiding him in his parents' house. How would she cope, living with him in a separate mahel?

"I told you just a few minutes ago in your dressing room that the plans were finished. Weren't you listening?"

Of course I wasn't listening! "I forgot," she whispered.

"Well, building will commence soon, depending on the rains."

"How long will the building take?"

"A year, perhaps fourteen months. Not long."

If Mira hadn't been sitting, she'd have collapsed. Just a year? Would he then think she was old enough?

He lounged back and she watched the play of muscles on his abdomen as he stretched.

She felt him looking at her. Feeling sweaty, she pulled at her veil.

"Can you breathe like that?"

"I'm fine," she said.

"Hmmm. Well, you just wait," he muttered to the ceiling, "I'll get that veil off you eventually."

Her jaw dropped.

"How shall we furnish the mahel?"

"The w–what?"

"The mahel. Really, my lady, are you paying any attention to me today?"

Mira was about to apologize when she saw the sly tilt to his mouth. She spoke with a bland voice. "I'm a bit distracted. I was wondering when I could watch you."

He suddenly sat upright. "Watch me?"

"Yes. I was wondering if I could come to the training field tomorrow."

"The training field?" For a moment he looked dazed, blinking at her, before his eyes focused and he scowled. "I cannot allow you on the training field! There are men and you are female and it's not allowed–"

He stopped. "Oh, I see. This is your little joke to pay me back."

"Of course not," she said. "Revenge is above me, I mean, I am above revenge."

He rolled his eyes, lounging back against the cushions.

Mira, watching his tight muscles ripple over his stomach, felt her insides flutter. She smiled at him, realized she was smiling at him, and stopped.

"So, anyway, how shall we furnish the house? Do you want to take things from here or do you want new furniture made? Either way is fine with me." He shook his hair out and put his turban back on.

Mira clenched her feet together, feeling her anklets dig into her skin. "I'd rather your mother decided."

"Oh. Well, what about the paint colors?"

Mira didn't care about the colors just as long as he left her alone. She shrugged.

"Uda is good at choosing colors. You should get her to help you."

"Perhaps you can ask her to select everything."

He gave her a long look. "What servants do you wish to take?"

She pulled at the end of her veil, trying to make it fall straight down her front. "Whoever your mother wishes to provide is fine."

After a pause, he began again. "I'd feel better if you showed an interest in planning our house." He ran his long fingers over the wet towel.

"I don't know many of the servants in this palace, so how can I choose?"

He sat up. "You cannot convince me that you've no interest in household affairs. Not after *that* bahu bhojan. I want you to make the decisions because it's your mahel and you should be happy with it."

Mira blurted an excuse. "I don't want to usurp your mother's authority."

"It's your mahel, not hers."

"But she's the queen. If I ignore her power, they'll only hate me more."

"They don't hate you."

"They do!"

He crossed his arms and glared at her. "Perhaps if you made an effort to mix with them, you wouldn't feel so neglected."

"How can I mix with them? You don't know–" she stopped. Bhoj didn't know what Buaji and the others had said.

"Know what? That you went to see Didi?"

Mira started. He knew about that?

"Didi said you seemed lonely. Why don't you visit her again?"

"I can't!" Mira stood and paced the room. "What would you have me do, my lord? Cook meat?"

He threw the towel onto his couch. "No! I don't want to drag that whole issue up again. It gives me a headache."

Mira picked up the towel to prevent the silk being spoiled. "There's no other way to resolve this problem. Even Didi said so." She paced some more.

He took the towel back as she passed. "Is that why you won't visit her?"

Mira stopped. "Yes."

He sighed. "If you won't give in then why the anxiety about usurping Ma Sa's authority?"

"There's no sense in giving them another reason to hate me."

"Don't think of them, think of me. I want you to do this."

"But they'll be angry."

"And they matter more to you than I do?"

"Well, they are many," she muttered. "You are one."

She realized too late what she'd said.

He was glaring at her, his nostrils flaring. He threw the towel to the floor and strode out, slamming the door behind him.

The servants' door on the side opened and little Janki came in, wide-eyed. "Was that Yuvraj?"

Mira nodded, her throat too tight to speak.

Janki stared at the door, still quivering in its frame. "What did you do to make him so angry, Bahu Rani? He's always so sweet natured." She noticed the puddles on the floor and looked at Mira. "Are you alright?"

Mira realized her hands were shaking.

Telling herself it was good he was upset because perhaps now he wouldn't visit her, she went into the bedroom. He has to know that he doesn't matter to me, she thought.

She fell to her knees and beat her fists against the mattress. She beat and beat but her fists were useless against its softness.

It's my fault, she thought. He's so kind and now I've made him angry. What's wrong with me?

She thought of Bhoj's gentle face, almost as dark as Krishna's. Just because he'd said some kind words, did that mean he was her husband?

No!

She straightened. He has no power over me. I have to show him that I am not his.

# 10

# Sour

Mira was embroidering vastra that would be offered to Krishna on his birthday. Thankfully, her father had sent her the quarterly income from her villages and she'd used some of it to buy the material. The rest of the income she would give to the ashrams for the poor and the cows.

She couldn't do anything else without being attacked by Bhoj's family. When her legs felt restless, she practiced her dance steps in her suite, Lalita playing the mrudunga for her.

Bhoj had gone on a border patrol for a month. Not that he'd come to see her even if he was in Chittore.

So when the patterns were so small her eyes went blurry and the material so soft it slipped from her hands, she told herself the vastra was for Krishna and had to be completed. She'd never finish twenty-one vastra if Bhoj were here to bother her.

Before their fight, he'd told her stories about his childhood and Uda. He'd made her giggle when he told her about when his parents argued.

It made Mira think of when her own parents had fought.

She remembered one time when her father came into Mira's room and put his finger to his lips, indicating that she wasn't to say anything. Then he hid under her bed.

Astonished, Mira wondered what was going on.

Then her mother entered, brandishing a ladle that dripped dhal.

"Where is he?" Kusum demanded.

"Who?" Mira asked, careful not to look towards her bed.

"Your Bapu Sa, of course! Where is he?"

"Er... I don't know..."

"Well he'd better come out. I've words to say to him!" she said, waving the ladle and splattering dhal everywhere.

"What's the matter, Ma Sa? Are you angry?"

"Of course I'm angry!" Kusum turned to leave. "If he doesn't come out soon, he'll regret teaching me how to use a mace!"

When Ratan emerged from under the bed, he had the biggest grin on his face and he picked Mira up and threw her into the air, laughing like a madman.

Mira never did find out why her mother was so angry that day.

She looked down at the green vastra in her hands and flexed her stiff fingers. It was two days before the Janamashtmi festivities. This had to be finished.

"Maharani Gauri graces the chamber," Savitri said from the doorway.

Mira leaped to her feet. Her mother-in-law was here? Now? And Bhoj was away!

Gauri entered to see Mira on the floor, trying to gather a load of green material together. "Don't you have maids to do that?"

Mira dumped the silk onto the side table. "Forgive me, Maharani, I was clumsy and dropped it." She went forward and bowed.

"I trust you're well, bahu."

"I am, Maharani. But why did you come? You should have summoned me to your quarters."

"I'd rather say what I have to in your suite than mine."

"Oh," Mira stood, unsure what to do next. "Please, sit down."

Gauri sat, her yellow outfit looking cheerful next to the red silk.

"Come sit next to me, bahu."

Mira lowered herself onto the couch.

"Lift your veil, bahu. I need to see your face."

Mira obeyed.

There were dark shadows beneath Gauri's eyes. Despite the regal beauty she possessed, her complexion seemed dull.

Perhaps she's wearing too much kajol and it's smudged about her eyes, Mira thought.

But no, the queen was wearing no kajol at all. Who went out without kajol? Mira wondered.

"I've already told your maid to bring refreshments so you needn't worry about that."

Mira nodded.

Gauri sighed.

Mira waited for a minute but the queen was silent. Mira started to worry that she was expected to speak. "Maharani, what is wrong?"

Savitri entered with a tray, preventing Gauri's answer. She placed it on the table at Mira's right hand and left, closing the door behind her.

Mira poured two cups of guava juice and placed milk sweets on a small dish. She handed it to her mother-in-law.

Gauri ate a sweet before placing the dish on the table to her left. "Bahu, I want to discuss something important with you."

Mira was glad the queen had an appetite. It meant she wasn't ill. "Ji, Maharani?"

Her mother-in-law seized another sweet and looked at Mira. "Why do you never call me Ma Sa?"

Mira felt a sinking sensation in her belly. "Perhaps I've never felt I had the right."

Gauri grabbed Mira's hand. "Of course you do. You're my son's wife."

Mira looked at her mother-in-law, whose shadowed eyes looked so tired.

Gauri ate the sweet she held and laughed a hollow laugh. "My husband is so upset at this rift. He won't speak to me until I heal it."

Mira paused. Had the king and queen been fighting over this?

Gauri gave another hollow laugh. "All my elders keep telling me I'm a fool to treat you like this. I only have one son and daughter-in-law, after all." She squeezed Mira's hand, her eyes deep and desperate. "You must become a true part of my family."

Gauri really wanted Mira to mix with the family? Mira doubted it.

"I realize you've been hurt by some of us. I ask you to forget it as we will forget our hurts."

Mira shook her head. "I never meant to insult anyone."

"I know, Bhoj told me," she smiled. "My husband told me too. So from now on, I will only concentrate on bringing you into the family as is my duty. You must know Sisodia traditions and ideals so you can teach them to your children."

Bhoj's children. Mira dug her nails into her palms and the ruby on her finger winked up at her. But she couldn't deny that she craved a friend. Her mother-in-law was right: this rift had gone on too long.

"You're the future Maharani of Merwar. We cannot have our enemies thinking our clan is divided."

Mira nodded. If the Raj Parivar wasn't strong, outsiders would take advantage and attack. The alliance was essential.

What about the meat-eating? Mira tensed. How could she associate with people who ate animals?

Endangering my people is not right either.

Mira chewed on her bottom lip. Perhaps she could do more good by mixing with them. Perhaps she could persuade them to give up their appalling eating habits. Mira didn't want to continue paining Sangavat and Gauri.

Gauri was rubbing Mira's hand, up and down, up and down. "Well, bahu? Will you help me heal this breach?"

It would make Bhoj happy.

Mira nodded.

Her mother-in-law hugged her, almost crushing Mira in her arms. "We'll start work tomorrow. I'll need your assistance with the Janamashtmi celebrations." She pulled back and gave Mira a fat smile.

Mira smiled back, though her effort was strained.

"Of course. When should I come to your suite?" Mira said.

"Directly after you finish your puja. You may breakfast with me."

"As you wish," Mira said.

"Good, then I shall leave you to your embroidery," she said, rising.

Mira stood and bowed.

Gauri swept out in triumph, her complexion renewed to its former luster.

Mira felt she'd done the right thing. With her mother-in-law's support, she could gain influence in the palace. She could make changes. That was, if her in-laws decided to like her.

The next day, mid-afternoon, Bhoj stood in Mira's doorway. "I came straight here."

Half of her wanted to apologize for the things she'd said to him. The other half wanted to make sure he never made children with her. She struggled with both emotions as he walked towards her, his eyes intent.

"I trust you are well?" Bhoj said.

How could he stand there like this was a casual meeting? He hadn't come to her for a month! Didn't he care?

She nodded and shrugged, trying to appear unaffected.

"I'm glad you are assisting my mother."

She nodded again and looked to the side now that he was so close to her.

"Are you sulking?" When she didn't respond, he leaned back. "You want to act like a child?"

She didn't reply because she hoped he'd always think her a child.

When he left soon after, she sighed but didn't know if it was in relief or something else.

A few minutes later, he returned holding a gudia, a small clothed figure dressed in a miniature skirt and blouse with a painted face. Handing it to her, he told her to play with it.

She gaped at him.

Laughing, he told Mira to dress it, bathe it, feed it, tell it a story.

She flung it in his face and ran to the balcony. Crossing her arms, Mira stuck her nose in the air and sniffed. Play with gudias! How foolish did he think she was?

He stood next to her, sobered. "You're not a small child, you know. Behaving as one doesn't become you." He looked out through the screen, the midday sun showing up in little patches on his face. One of the patches hit his eye where it made the dark blue glow with gold sparks.

Mira stood beside him, trying to cope with how fast his moods changed.

"I gave you a whole month to calm down after our disagreement. Did my strategy not work?"

To calm down or be lonely? she wondered. You knew I had no one to speak to. "Were you not upset?" she asked. He seemed so sure of himself all the time. How could anyone be that sure of themselves?

"Of course. You were very provoking. All I did was ask you to plan our house."

"I've had enough of fighting with your family. Can't you understand that?"

He looked out at the city rising from its midday nap. "Well, now that you and Ma Sa are getting on, there's no problem is there? You can ask her for help and she'll give it. Though I'm sure she'll urge you to make your own choices."

Mira doubted that, even as she moaned inwardly at the bind she was in. There was no escaping this house Bhoj was planning. The worst thing was that she couldn't help looking forward to a peaceful place where there were no taunts or insults. Her own home.

Bhoj nudged her on the elbow. "I just want my women to love each other."

She swallowed. "You think I don't? Your mother might never have wanted peace if I'd started demanding things for the mahel."

"Why didn't you tell me this before?"

"I did! You weren't listening."

He considered this. "I suppose you're right." He leaned down, a breath away from her face. "Am I arrogant?"

"Yes!" Mira snapped, before retreating into the sitting room. How did he manage to get so close?

It was only when he left soon after that she realized she'd agreed to make the plans for the mahel. She'd even agreed to do so with his mother.

He'd distracted her on purpose!

She clenched her fists, then relaxed them, sighing. At least Gauri was being nice. Just that morning they'd gone over the menus for the week and the queen had omitted all meat dishes.

Of course, it was Janamashtmi so meat wasn't allowed.

Still, it was a start.

*

Ratan sat in one of his assembly halls.

It was a grand blue marble courtyard, open to the elements, surrounded on all sides with meeting rooms. Now that monsoon was passed and the mild season begun, it was possible to sit here.

Just that morning, the last of the soldiers from Merwar had arrived. They would be sent to various forts along the borders.

Ratan wished he could rub his hands and gloat but where was the time?

His chief advisor, Bharadwaj, sat at Ratan's right hand side, steepling his long fingers.

The door opened and a guard marched in. "Mukhya Mansingh, Mukhya Jaidev, Mukhya Pratap, Mukhya Shankar, Mukhya Prasad, Mukhya Baldev, Mukhya Giridari and Mukhya Kashinath," the guard announced.

Ratan rested his hand on the arm of his throne.

Eight colorful turbans marched in. Six of these men were old and wizened, their backs bent from war.

The two burly ones at the back were much younger. One was Baldev, tall as teak. His father had passed only last year. The other was Kashinath who had deep pock marks over his face and neck. His father had died in the same smallpox epidemic three years ago.

Thankfully, the epidemic had been contained within that village. Ratan had himself gone to check the security measures.

"Rana Ratan ki jai!" the village headmen chorused.

"Welcome, Mukhyajan. Please sit."

They squatted on the floor.

"What is the news from your villages?"

The eldest mukhya stood. He wore a purple turban and was thin as a sugar cane. "Our villages live under constant fear, Ranaji."

Bharadwaj unsteepled his fingers and leaned forward. "Mukhya Mansingh, there's no reason to feel unsafe now. We have a great force patrolling our borders."

Mansingh folded his palms. "Forgive me, minister, but didn't the attack on Lingeshwar occur after the alliance was formalized?"

"There won't be another attack like Lingeshwar," Ratan said.

Mansingh's beard, red from the dust of his village, quivered. "It's not easy to convince the people of that, Ranaji."

Ratan felt the acids in his stomach churn. I give my daughter away for their protection and they still have no faith, he thought. "What would make them feel more confident, Mansinghji?"

"Well, Ranaji, if the situation weren't so threatening, it might help."

"I ask you, Mukhyaji," Bharadwaj said. "How does one make a jackal less threatening?"

"By becoming its friend, Minister."

Ratan stared at Mansingh.

Some of the mukhyas nodded.

Baldev and Kashinath did not.

"If we make a trade alliance with them, they'd leave us alone."

"No, Mukhyaji, they wouldn't." Bharadwaj's voice was calm and hard, like a sword held loosely in his hand. "They've no notion of honor in the way you or I understand it."

Ratan had a bitter taste in his mouth. "We could never trust the enemy to keep their word, Mukhyaji."

"They would honor a trade alliance."

"Only as long as it gave them what they wanted," Ratan said. "My friends, you must understand, this enemy is not of Bharat. They do not understand dharma because they are not Aryan. They've not been taught the code of ethics laid down by Manu at the beginning of time." He looked around at them. "They are not Aryans."

Mukhya Prasad stood up. Even though his supple stance gave the impression of youth, his mouth was squashed up because he had no teeth. "If they were growing rich from trade with us, what would be the need to steal our lands and cattle?" He gestured with his hands. "There'd be no need to attack us."

Ratan fought to keep control over his anger. "They don't just want our wealth. They want complete control over Bharat."

"But a trade alliance would give us time to build our defenses," Prasad said.

Bharadwaj shook his head. "It would mean they had easy access to our kingdom. They would come to know our land, our secrets. They would make allies all around us so that when it came to fighting, there'd be no hope."

The mukhyas looked at each other, shaking their turbaned heads.

Despite Ratan's anger, he understood their denial. After all, these were the people who'd be slaughtered if the Shah were to ride his men through their villages. They had a right to denial.

Everyone knew what had happened at Lingeshwar.

These men were willing to protect their womenfolk and children at all costs, even if it meant an alliance with such an enemy.

Ratan might even do the same if all he had to worry about was Mira.

"Ranaji," Mansingh spoke up. "We've heard that more kingdoms have joined the Shah's banner. He controls Bengal on the east. The whole of Punjab in the north. Gujarat in the west is his. We're surrounded."

Ratan saw that Baldev in the back was clenching his fists. Why didn't he speak if he didn't agree? "Do you forget our partnership with Merwar?"

"And what happens when that army is destroyed, Ranaji?" Prasad asked. "In the next attack, how will we replace our warriors?"

Ratan studied Prasad's face, so soft without its teeth. "There is more to this than just fighting. It is about the preservation of our culture and our ancient way of life. Would you gamble that on a trade alliance?"

"Ranaji, the people need to know they're safe. And for that, we need a new tactic." Prasad was leaning forward, pleading for sense from his ruler.

Ratan stared at the village chief, overwhelmed by a sudden need to roar in fury.

"You forget that the kingdoms the Afghans hold are not their ancestral lands." Bharadwaj stared at the mukhyas. "To trade with them would cement their place here in Bharat."

"Those lands are lost. We must look to our own," Prasad said.

Ratan remembered a time when all his advisers would come together and discuss what was for the good of Merta, for the good of the Rajputs, and for the good of Bharat. He'd never dreamed there'd come a time when Rajputs in Merta would abandon their brothers in the next state.

Mansingh looked as if he were eating bitter gourd. "Ranaji, we insist upon forming a pact with Delhi."

"Since when do you 'insist' to your Rana?" Bharadwaj.

Kashinath was looking at Baldev.

Why don't they get up and speak? Ratan wondered. They can't agree with Prasad.

"Forgive us, Ranaji, but if you don't agree, there'll be trouble," Prasad said.

"What do you mean?" Ratan asked, watching them all. To prevent them seeing his shaking hand, he placed it on his hip, staring them down.

They squirmed, the ones who sat ducked their heads, and the ones who stood shifted their feet.

Prasad almost choked on his words. "The people will revolt."

Ratan gripped the arm of his throne. He'd never imagined they would go so far.

Even the other mukhyas looked shocked.

Baldev had gone pale beneath his tan, his moustache stuck out from the tense way he was grinding his teeth. He made a move as if to rise but Prasad turned to look at him and Baldev remained seated.

The other mukhyas were silent. A sudden gust of wind ran into their backs and the older, thinner men strained against it.

Ratan fantasized it was the wind god, Vayu, punishing them. "What have I done to warrant this disloyalty? Are you taxed into starvation? Are my court judgments unjust?"

Prasad waved his hands in denial. "No, no, Ranaji. You're like our father!"

"So why this impertinence?"

"If we die to protect our country, it is a good bargain. But what if even our children do not survive to carry on our line? We cannot take that risk, Ranaji."

"This is an outrage. How dare you threaten Rana Ratan?" Bharadwaj's beady eyes burned holes into their faces.

Mansingh's purple turban was drooping to the left, his look mournful. He'd ridden into battle with Rao Duda many times and yet he was agreeing with this.

Ratan tapped his fingers on the arm of his chair. He still hoped that Baldev or Kashinath would stand and refute these threats.

Prasad cleared his throat. "That's all we wished to say, Ranaji."

Ratan waited for Baldev or Kashinath to speak. Neither did. "Then you may leave," Ratan answered Prasad.

The mukhyas filed out, grim faced.

Bharadwaj abandoned his control and paced around the courtyard.

"Was there any hint of this from our spies?" Ratan asked.

"No. They must've just thought of that threat. It didn't look as if they were planning on using it either."

"But they did." Ratan stared into space, thinking of the chaos a revolt would cause. The Shah would waste no time in attacking.

"It's a disgrace. Such disloyalty! Such *cowardice!*" Bharadwaj threw up his hands, his face red from huffing and puffing.

"Sit down, my friend. I'm tired enough as it is."

Bharadwaj sat, pulling at his own beard.

"It seems there's only one solution to this problem."

"A trade alliance?" Bharadwaj was aghast.

"Yes and no. We need allies now."

Bharadwaj nodded, catching on. "You propose another royal marriage?"

"You read my mind."

"Shamal?"

"Shamal."

*

It'd been over a month since Mira had accepted Gauri's truce. She now assisted the queen around the palace, taking care of guests and helping to direct servants.

When Gauri wasn't present, Buaji and others stopped by to inspect Mira's work.

She endured their sharp retorts that the beds weren't draped well, even though she knew that the beds were draped perfectly. She made up the beds again, under their directions, with them jeering at her efforts the entire time.

They followed her around and questioned her maids about her methods, telling them not to listen to the ugly Rathore girl. Whenever Gauri appeared, they disappeared through opposite doorways.

Mira never mentioned it to her mother-in-law. Even though she cried into her pillow every night, she never told Gauri. She wouldn't be responsible for another fight.

She missed Shamal so much. What was he doing? Was he well? He hadn't sent her a letter in weeks.

Thankfully, it was Ekadasi, a day of rest, so Mira wasn't needed by the queen.

Bhoj had told her that morning that a great sage named Sachidananda Swami had come to Chittore. He said the swami was a well known orator and had inspired thousands with his sermons.

Mira decided to go to the temple and as she left the palace, she promised Lalita that she would do nothing untoward while there, as Lalita was making a great deal of panic noises.

She hoped to learn more about finding a guru.

There was a disturbance in the crowd under the tree and people were standing up, blocking Mira's view.

She stood also, surrounded by her human shields. Straining to see above the heads, she caught sight of him when he stepped up on the raised earth at the base of the tree.

To Mira's surprise, he was young, not over forty years old.

Every renunciate Mira had ever seen had been frail and ancient, their bodies thin from fasting, their faces lined with wisdom. And yet here was a tall, robust man, who looked as if he could walk up the Himalayas and keep going.

She stared at him. How can this man have inspired thousands with bhakti? He looked as material as her father.

He faced the crowd and Mira gasped. There was a force behind his eyes that glowed and rotated.

From under bushy black brows, he studied the people. He surveyed them as a traveler might survey a road, judging the distance he needed to walk.

He sat and the crowd followed.

As he chanted mantras to his guru, Mira felt the force of his voice sweep through the crowd. It was like the monsoon rains, cool and fat, drenching everything.

The people were still, gazing up at the swami.

He opened his eyes. "I am glad to see so many young devotees here."

Mira glanced around and saw that he was right.

"It is a good sign to see such conscientious youth. It means that the evils of Kal Yuga, the age of chaos, will be fought by our next generation."

The youngsters in the crowd sat straighter, aware now of how conscientious they were.

"Youth is a great asset in bhakti since young people haven't had the time or chance to commit the sins their elders have."

The youngsters poked their sheepish elders, telling them to listen to the wise swami and scold their children less.

Mira wished her in-laws could listen to this.

"The youth don't have to spend time repenting for this or that.

They may simply devote their time to serving their Isht. That's why a righteous life must be encouraged from a young age."

That's right, Mira exclaimed in her mind. It was what she'd always thought.

"One of the best things about being young is that you're able-bodied. You can do many things that your elders cannot. Pilgrimage is one example. I myself have just been on pilgrimage to Kashi."

Mira's eyes brightened, thinking of Udai learning from the scholars. Kashi was the highest of the seven sacred cities, the chosen home of Kashi Vishwanath, one of Lord Shiv's twelve principal forms.

"They say that those who die in Kashi are liberated from the cycle of rebirth, which is why many holy people go there at the end of their lives," the swami said. "The holiest of rivers, Mother Ganga, flows down Kashi's eastern side. Just one dip in her waters washes away all the sins of your many lives. Saints and sages from all over Bharat congregate on her banks to debate the scriptures."

Perhaps my guru is there also! Mira, struck by the thought, had to restrain herself from clapping.

"There are so many different paramparas and disciplic traditions. So many different schools of philosophy. But one faith, one bhakti, one devotion. It's an ideal for all."

Everyone was nodding.

"Lord Shiv sends out a message of love in his form of Kashi Vishwanath. He teaches devotees bhakti."

Mira thought back to what Purohitji once told her.

Shiv was the third part of the trinity with Brahma and Vishnu. While Brahma was the creator and Vishnu the preserver, Shiv was the destroyer, destroying ignorance and evil. He was the benevolent master of death, easily pleased and generous with boons. He worshipped Lord Rama to show the world true bhakti. And Lord Rama worshipped Shiv to show the world that the gods were really one. Rama was Shiv and Shiv was Rama.

"There's a belief in Kashi, that when a person dies there, their ears lift up, as if they are listening to something. I myself saw it happen to a holy man who died on the banks of the Ganga. The wise say that the ears lift to hear to Lord Shiv's voice chanting the name of Rama."

Mira gasped again. She wanted to get up and run all the way to Kashi. What divine place was this that people could hear Shiv chanting? How lucky was Udai that he was there right now!

"Mother Durga, Shiv's wife, resides there in her form of Annapurna, the bestower of food. Due to her kind blessings, Kashi never goes hungry. There is always grain to be shared."

Purohitji had said that the gods would be lifeless without their female halves beside them. As Rama was lifeless without Sita. As Krishna was lifeless without Radha.

Mira shifted on the ground, the cold feeling of stiff legs sending waves of restlessness through her. Mira's reverence of Radha was as great as her envy. Krishna loved Radha above all others.

Kusum had told Mira that Krishna belonged to everyone, that he gave love and satisfaction to all. Radha was the heart that enabled him to do this. Radha was bhakti itself. Mira told herself that she shouldn't envy Radha. She shouldn't.

"Lord Hanuman resides in Kashi as Sankat Mochan, the destroyer of danger."

Hanuman was Shiv's incarnation as a monkey, descended to serve Rama. He was the emblem of humble service and a favorite of children because of his mischievous behavior towards demons, teasing and confusing them. Purohitji had always made Mira laugh when he told her stories of Hanuman, Rama's darling pet.

"Everywhere you turn there are holy people meditating and chanting. There is solemnity in the burning of the funeral pyres. The atmosphere is permeated with knowledge.

"Everyone should go to Kashi at least once in their lifetime."

Yes, yes, I have to go there! Mira thought. I have to if I'm going to find my guru. Perhaps I can visit Udai. I'll ask Bhoj.

The people were nudging each other. It looked like they were deciding to go on pilgrimage. They had family and friends they could go with.

Mira thought of her in-laws and felt her spirits depress. Even if Bhoj wants to let me go, they never will. They'll find a way to stop me.

I'll never get to Kashi.

# 11

# Betrayal

Mira set a cushion on the stool. She straightened and went to bring a water jug.

Her contingent of maids was diminished. Lalita had a cold and Janki was keeping her company. Savitri's father-in-law was ill so Mira had told her to stay at home to help care for him. That left only Lakshmi and there was only so much one dasi could do.

Mira didn't mind. It was nice to serve Bhoj in her own quarters, with no one looking over her shoulder. She skipped to the tray brought up from the kitchen.

"My lady," said a deep voice in her ear.

She jumped so high the water flew out of the clay jug in her hand and over her head. She gasped at the shock of cold wetness running down her back.

"See what you've done?" she snapped, wheeling around to face him.

He was grinning, wiping water from his hair. His turban was lying on the couch where he'd tossed it. "At least we know the water's cold."

Exclaiming, she set the jug back on the tray.

He rubbed his hand against her wet back, warming her skin under her veil.

Mira tried to hide her jerk. Moving away, she busied herself putting food on his plate. "Your meal is ready if you wish to start."

Lakshmi came in with the sweets.

Mira asked her to bring more water.

Lakshmi examined the half empty jug, gave Mira's drenched back a bland look, then left.

Bhoj grinned at Mira and she glared in response.

He sat on the stool, said his prayers to his Isht, Lord Shiv and began eating.

Mira sat at his side as he ate, waiting until an item was finished so she could fill it again.

Lakshmi brought another jug of water and Mira dismissed her.

He was almost done eating when he looked up. "I've had news from your father."

Mira perked up. She hadn't heard from her father in a long time; his only letter had been at Janamashtmi.

"What does Bapu Sa say? Is he well?"

Bhoj gazed down at his plate like it was a riddle to be solved. "He is well and sends blessings. It's the news of your brother that is of interest."

Mira stilled. "Yes?" Shamal's last letter had come two weeks ago and even though his words had been cheerful, Mira sensed he was sad. She'd dispatched her messenger immediately, asking for the cause of his melancholy.

He had to be happy, if only for her.

"He's to be married to a princess of Amber. The wedding is set for less than a month hence."

Mira felt like Bhoj had spat in her face. "Married?" Shamal was getting married? Without Mira there? And to a Raj Kumari of *Amber*? Amber was Merta's rival!

"When was this decided?"

He rinsed his hands and wiped them with the cloth she handed him. "About two months ago. Not the details of course, just the fact that Shamal would be married. Your father dispatched envoys to Amber and the alliance was fixed."

"Just like that?" But of course, Mira thought. It was how her own marriage was fixed. She went to the side table, hiding the bitter look on her face, and filled a plate for herself, heaping food on and not caring what she was doing.

Shamal would be married. Why hadn't he said anything? Was this why his letter had been sad?

"Why the hurry?" She sloshed some dhal onto her rice.

Bhoj didn't answer.

She felt his gaze and turned to face him. There was a look in his eyes she'd never seen before. It was sharp, like a broken pot's jagged edge.

"There is talk of revolt in Merta."

Her plate crashed upon the marble floor. "They wouldn't."

He got to his feet. "They haven't yet but there's talk."

"But *why?*" She clenched her hands. "My family has always served the people."

He stepped around the food on the floor and put his hands on her shoulders. "Priye, the people are afraid. They think allying with the Afghans would solve their problems."

"Bapu Sa said the enemy is treacherous," she said into his chest. "We cannot ally with them."

"He's right."

"So why don't they believe him?"

"Not everyone accepts the truth as you do, my lady."

She looked up at him, confused.

"Recently, there've been some raids. The people fear that your father and uncle cannot protect them."

"That's not true!" She shook off his touch. "My father is the best general and–" she stopped. "Raids? What raids?"

Bhoj ran his hand through his hair. "Seven months ago. A village was attacked."

"Seven months? But that was when...we married."

"Yes. The village was attacked a few days after our wedding. And just last month, a few cows were stolen and some men killed."

Her marriage had not protected her people, Mira thought. They'd told her it would but it hadn't. She felt her way around the room and sat on the couch.

Her people would revolt against her family. Against her father. Her people would ally themselves to the enemy.

The tales of valor and honor she'd been fed since birth were pulled from under her. She felt like a fallen tree.

"So my Bhaiya is to be sacrificed."

"Don't grieve, priye. I've heard his betrothed is most cultured. And Amber is a strong nation."

"Amber is an old enemy."

"Amber is a Rajput kingdom that needs other Rajput allies."

Of course, he was right. Mira thought of Shamal and his sadness. His mother was dead and his sister was far away. Perhaps a wife would be good for him. Perhaps it would be alright.

Bhoj sat next to her. Putting his arm around her shoulders, he lifted her veil up off her face. "I must go to the wedding," he whispered, drawing her towards him.

"I want to come," she said.

Bhoj shook his head. "It's not safe, priye. Everything is being kept secret until the wedding is finalized. Only our family knows where I am going."

She felt his warm hand on her throat and shivered. She looked into his blue eyes, her gaze naked without her veil.

"I must meet Shamal's wedding party in Amber. I leave tomorrow."

She felt his long fingers rubbing the nape of her neck. She shivered again, shocked by her sudden desire to move closer to him.

"I wish I could take you with me."

Mira could only nod, stunned by the feelings rising within her.

"Will you miss me, priye?"

Only now did she notice what he was calling her. Beloved.

She stared into his eyes.

He caressed her cheek with his knuckle. "I think you will. There's no need to cover your face when you're with me anymore."

She swallowed.

He pulled back. "I must make preparations but I'll return here at dawn. Be ready to see me off."

She nodded, confused by the warmth running through her body.

Bhoj smiled and touched her lips with his thumb, then left.

The next morning, she woke thinking that Bhoj was leaving today. She couldn't go with him to see her brother.

Careful to seem cheerful, she saw Bhoj off with a smile, telling him to look after Shamal.

In the emptiness of her chamber, she paced.

Her sacrifice hadn't been enough, she thought. Perhaps Shamal's wouldn't be enough either. Perhaps her people's time had come.

No! she thought. That's not possible. The scriptures say dharma is eternal. Dharma is Bharat's life force. While dharma lives, Bharat lives.

But how can there be dharma if my people are cowards?

That night, Mira went to her balcony and lay in the cold night air.

The mountain fort was close to the stars.

It seemed long ago that she'd prayed to these stars to make her constant. A stunned, rootless feeling was now a habitual gnaw in her belly. She saw herself felled in a wood full of felled trees and she was mute, her branches unable to reach the others. Soon, someone would come to cut her branches off.

She hoped this wedding would bring happiness to her brother. She longed for reassurance from him. If only he would send a letter.

She thought of visiting Kashi and finding her guru, both desires never so impossible as now.

She wondered if Bhoj thought of her. He'd told her not to cover her face around him anymore.

Winter had now set itself into the sands of the mountain. Stray cows were brought in from the cold and orphaned dogs were rounded up and herded into a dog sanctuary for the season.

Mira covered herself in soft wool shawls and stayed close to the kitchens.

The new mahel was coming along well, she was told. All the walls were now erected and the roof was being constructed.

Mira asked the queen for help with the decoration and Gauri went through everything with her, matching furniture to color schemes and paints and wall hangings.

Soon, the palace would be ready.

I feel like I'm always waiting, Mira thought, clenching her fists. For the mahel. For Shamal's letter. For Bhoj.

Sometimes, she wished it would be over, just so she wouldn't have to wait anymore. She tossed and turned in bed, waiting for him to come to her. She had dreams that there was no blood on the sheets. *No blood.* He took her again and again and always it was the same. When she woke up sweating and crying, she knew there was no escape.

Krishna, forgive me, she wept.

Two weeks after Bhoj left, he sent her a message that the marriage was finalized. Shamal was now a husband.

Mira was preparing dhal on Budhvar a week later when Bhoj's second message came: he was returning home tonight.

That evening, Buaji came with Gauri to inspect the bridal suite.

"But, Maharani," Buaji said, "your son is returning from Kumar Shamal's wedding, not his own. Have you forgotten he's already married?"

"Of course not!" Gauri exclaimed. "It's just that he's been gone over three weeks and a mother is allowed to pine for her son. Especially when he's a son such as mine," she added, rounding on Buaji with a certain look in her eye.

Mira was silent while they examined her aarti tray and sniffed at the incense she'd set to burn.

"My son likes the honeysuckle. See how well bahu knows his tastes?"

Buaji waved the sweet scent from her nose. "I would have put sandalwood," she said. "It's more auspicious."

The sandalwood is Krishna's, Mira thought to herself.

"Bahu wants the honeysuckle. I think it best not to come between the lovers," Gauri added, winking at Mira.

Mira couldn't help her blush.

"Why are you wearing green, bahu? Go put on something red," Buaji said.

Gauri looked Mira over. "She's right, bahu. The green looks beautiful but red is the sign of a married woman. It will please your husband."

Mira retreated to her dressing room to change. To her horror, they followed, walking around her as her maids changed her clothes, commenting on how she'd grown recently.

"She's much more of a woman," Buaji nodded.

"Yes, more developed. She's grown a little taller too."

Mira was dressed in an outfit of scarlet and gold before her elders left, goading each other about everything and nothing. She splashed her face to cool her humiliation, then had Lalita redo her kajol. He wasn't even here and already Mira was a wreck.

She told herself she was just nervous for her brother.

Mira stared at her newly redone kajol and nodded to Lalita that it was fine.

Trumpets sounded from outside her balcony.

She frowned.

Why was Bhoj entering the palace from this side? Shouldn't he go to his parents first?

Walking out to her front room, she ran a trembling hand over the back of her head to check that her veil was pinned to her hair correctly. She hadn't covered her face.

She looked around for her maids and they were standing behind her, grinning. Even Lalita looked happy.

He appeared in her doorway, looking too big for her quarters, and Mira felt a lurch in her stomach. She smiled.

Taking the lit aarti tray from Savitri, she went to him. Circling the lamps around his face, she noticed there were dark shadows beneath his eyes. He must be tired from the journey, she thought, dipping her finger in the little bowl of vermillion beside the lamps. I'll send him straight to bed as soon as he's eaten something, she decided. She applied the tilak to his forehead and showered petals over his head before stepping back to allow him entrance.

He limped into the room.

"My lord!" Mira dumped her tray in Lakshmi's hands.

He leaned on her and moved to the nearest couch to sit.

She knelt and removed his shoes. "Savitri, send for the vaids."

He shook his head. "Dismiss your servants."

Mira frowned but looked at her dasis and they slipped away through the servants' door. She looked back at him. "What happened?"

He looked away.

"Were you attacked?"

He looked at her and that jagged edge was back in his eyes. He touched her cheek, his knuckle gentle.

She put her hand over his, unnerved by his silence. "My lord, when did this happen? Where? Why did your messenger say nothing?"

He sighed. "I told him not to."

She waited for him to say more but he wouldn't.

"Where did the attack happen?"

"Merta." His voice was so quiet.

Mira fought the pounding of her heart. "How many men did you lose?"

"Two. Three were wounded. Your father lost more."

She gripped Bhoj's hand. "Bapu Sa?"

"It was he who was attacked."

Krishna! she thought. "Tell me everything."

He took a deep breath. "Our parties traveled together until we were in your father's territory, then we separated. They headed west, we headed south. Almost three hours later, a soldier caught up with us: There'd been an ambush. We rushed back to assist them."

Mira squeezed his hand. "And?"

"Your father's men had killed most of the attackers. Shamal took some alive for questioning. He wanted to know how the Afghans knew this route. You see, the route was kept secret."

"And my father? How was he?"

"He was well. He killed several of the ambushers himself."

She sagged in relief. "Thank Krishna!"

"Thank Krishna."

Then Mira remembered Bhoj's limp. "And your wound?"

"Shamal and I were bandaging some of the wounded and moving them to cover. Suddenly, we were showered with arrows. One entered my leg."

Mira pulled away because she was leaning on his left knee.

"No," he said, pulling her back. "It was my right leg. And it's not a bad wound. But the archers managed to kill our prisoners."

She felt him stroking her shoulder blades. "Were they found?"

"Yes, your father slit their throats. He was furious these assassins had eluded capture from his men."

Mira rose to her knees before him. "So that was the end of it?"

"No."

She stilled.

"Once your father returned from killing them, he looked to the space behind me. I looked as well.

"It was Shamal, shot through the heart."

Mira stared at Bhoj.

"He was dead."

Bhoj clasped her shoulders. "In the confusion, I didn't hear Shamal fall. Ranjeet and Raagav were the only ones who saw what was happening and they threw themselves over Shamal to protect him. They also were killed."

Mira leaned back, shaking her head. It was all a mistake. Soon Shamal would send a letter, telling Mira about his wedding and bride.

"Your father said that before he killed them, the archers told him they'd fulfilled their mission. They'd killed Ratan's son."

Shamal wasn't dead! she thought. He couldn't be dead.

Bhoj tugged her into his arms and rocked her. He rubbed her back, up and down, up and down. "Forgive me," he whispered against her temple. "I didn't hear him fall."

Shamal couldn't be dead, Mira thought. Krishna wouldn't let her brother die.

Krishna let Mira's mother die.

Bhoj kissed her forehead, holding her close.

Her insides suddenly burned red hot. Krishna let Kusum die and now he'd let Shamal die too. Even Ranjeet and Raagav.

The red hot burning made her writhe in Bhoj's arms. She tore herself away. Why didn't you protect them, Krishna?

"Priye," Bhoj tried to pull her back.

"Krishna," it was the only word she could say without screaming.

"Let me hold you, priye."

"Krishna." She turned and ran. She heard Bhoj limp after her but she didn't care. She ran until she stood before her deity.

He was playing his flute, taunting her, daring her to say a word.

Bending she picked up the hand bell she rang during his aarti. The fire at the bottom of her stomach flamed upwards and struck the scream in her throat. Flinging her arm back, she threw the bell at the wall as if it were the arrow that killed her brother.

"*Krishna!*" she screamed, and the fire roared its way up through her mouth and hit the top of her head. Then everything went black.

# 12

# Parting

Mira prayed there'd be a letter.

She ate, slept, walked, talked. She cooked, ordered, inspected, ruled.

Carrying out the tasks of her daily life, Mira found she couldn't look at him.

It was like the fire in her stomach had transformed itself into a monster that roared, always the loudest when she was before *him*. It made her head ache.

She performed puja, cooked and cleaned for him. She just couldn't look at his face.

The cold winds of winter became the soft sun of spring. Flowers bloomed and the peacocks danced and Mira's fourteenth birth anniversary came upon her.

She remembered her parents and how Shamal had clung to her when their mother died. Then their father became like the sword he wielded, cutting others away with a ruthless blow.

Mira remembered her uncle Devraj limping away from Ratan's room. There was the sound of struggling; the men were holding her father down. He was shouting that he'd never marry again, he didn't care what his family said. He'd never dishonor Kusum's memory. There were women in the next room, lamenting, weeping, telling each other that Kusum should never have had another child, that the vaids had said after Mira's difficult birth, Kusum shouldn't have more children.

Eight-year-old Mira finally understood why her mother died. Mira had hurt Kusum, weakened her, killed her. Mira had wanted to go to her father but was paralyzed. What if he hated her?

Mira remembered how, not long after, her father sent her away to the capital. He couldn't even bear to look at her when she left. Shamal wrote to her, over and over, asking why she must live so far away.

Mira never told him. How could she? He was the only one who still loved her.

Now Bhoj had lowered the flags of Merwar in honor of Shamal's death.

Mira remembered being five years old. A wedding procession was passing through the village and she dragged her mother to the window to look at it. Kusum pointed out the bridegroom on his white horse, looking resplendent with flashing dark eyes, an emerald in his turban, a red tilak on his brow. Mira asked for a groom of her own. Her mother laughed, saying that Mira was too young to get married. Stubborn Mira followed her mother all over the fort, pleading, cajoling, nagging. She cried and pulled at her mother's clothes, begging for her own beautiful groom to play with. Irritated, Kusum pulled Mira over to Krishna's altar and dumped him into her daughter's hands. 'There!' she snapped, her lotus face spitting fire. 'That's your groom. Now leave me alone!' Mira ran to Shamal and told him Krishna was his brother-in-law. He told her she was stupid but when she insisted it was true, he played along, pretending that Mira was kidnapped by demons and Krishna and Shamal would fight them to rescue her.

She remembered being a little child, alone at night, whispering to the one who was her groom, hearing the echoes of his replies.

Now the flags were raised. Merwar's roses bloomed once more. Sunny spring became scorching summer that melted into mosquito monsoon.

The roaring monster was quiet in Mira's ears, attacking only in her sleep. She woke several mornings to find her pillow in pieces, shredded by her own hands.

The wet season brought Janmashtami, Krishna's birthday and Mira distributed charity in Shamal's name.

The rains dried to cool autumn and for the first time in months, she slept without dreams.

Performing her duties, she began to think of how, even when she'd known her father didn't love her, she was certain Krishna did.

He'd taken her hand, his vastra tied to her veil, and led her around the holy fire. He'd danced with her at the mandir, holding her like she was so precious. When she'd been sent away from Chaukari and couldn't even speak her pain, Krishna had been at her side.

Even now, when she couldn't look at him, she *knew* he was waiting.

On the eve of her wedding, she'd prayed to the stars to make her constant. Yet now that she thought back to the months before Shamal's death, it was always about what Bhoj said and what Bhoj did. She'd accused Krishna of betrayal when really, she was the betrayer.

Shamal had worried for Mira so much. If only she'd been braver, stronger, perhaps his heart wouldn't have been so heavy. Perhaps he would have seen those assassins.

Merta's alliance with Amber was dust.

Merwar's rock solid partnership was what kept Merta alive. The thread holding that alliance together was Mira.

If she failed again... She couldn't fail.

She would repair what she'd broken. She would prove to Krishna she was constant.

She would save her people.

*

The bullock cart rolled into another pothole.

Vikram held onto his jaw lest the bone fall off.

He'd never noticed the bad state of the roads when on a horse. The first thing he'd do when he ruled Chittore would be to repair the roads.

Vikram adjusted his cotton tunic. Dressing as a merchant was beginning to get on his nerves. He had to pretend to sell better cloth than what he wore. The materials that he was sitting on right now were Merwari creations, fine spun cotton and gauze with bandani imprints and vivid colors. He remembered that Mira had worn a blue bandani the day of her bahu bhojan when she'd worked in the kitchens.

He knew because he'd watched from a window above.

The driver jolted the cart back into action and Vikram surveyed the land about him.

This relentless wasteland was nothing like the rocks and fields of Merwar. During the mild autumn season, this desert was sullen and watchful, like a barren wife. The monsoon rains had not fallen here. For days and days, all there was to see was sickly yellow dust wafting around Vikram's head until he swatted at it like it was flies.

In the distance he saw the approach of greener fields. He was nearing the stronghold of Delhi, the durbar of Sher Shah.

Of course, Delhi wasn't the Shah's property, just as it hadn't been Humanyun's before him or Babur's before Humanyun. They were just barbarians who rode in, chopped heads off, and lay claim to all the wonders of Bharat's culture. Why, the Shah had barely held Delhi for four years! What was four years to centuries of Rajput rule? There'd never been a time when Hindus didn't grace Delhi.

They were clever, these usurpers. Vikram had to give them that. They had to be to have gained what they had.

But Vikram was just as clever. To gain the Shah's trust, he'd given him Shamal. Sher Shah wouldn't suspect Vikram now, not when he'd sacrificed one of his own.

At first, Vikram had thought of using Shamal as an ally but the plan was unworkable. Shamal was too loyal to Ratan. Vikram had decided it was best that Shamal die.

When Bhoj had returned with his wound, his depleted force, and his sad news, Vikram had been as outraged as everyone else. He'd been the first to draw his sword and swear vengeance for Merwar's allied Rathore clan.

The court didn't know it was Vikram who'd dispatched a runner to Delhi as soon as he'd heard of the wedding. They didn't know that he'd sent a spy to Amber to find out the route and meet the Shah's men on the border.

Amber was close to Delhi. The enemy had been ready.

The cart hit a rock and Vikram's whole body shot up with the force. He landed hard on a pile of red veils that were embroidered with tiny diamonds. Grinding his teeth, he pushed his turban straight and sat back. A merchant's life was hard, he decided. Even the turbans were irritating. They were lighter, plain from lack of jewels pinned to them. He felt like there was nothing to keep him on the ground.

He also didn't like being another caste. It made him feel smaller.

There was nothing he could do about it. There'd be enemy and Rajput spies everywhere and if either party recognized him, he was a dead man. Only the Shah could know what Vikram's real business in Delhi was.

Sangavat had told courtiers that Vikram was on a border patrol with his personal guard. He'd then sworn one of his own bodyguards to secrecy and sent him with Vikram. At the same time, Koirala, disguised as old man, rode out of Kumbalgarh in a bullock cart, heading for Amber. Two days later, Koirala and Vikram had met. Vikram left Sangavat's bodyguard in charge and donned his disguise, riding away on the rickety cart. His men were told that the prince had a secret mission and if anyone spoke a word of it, their lives would be forfeit.

"Find out their secrets," Sangavat had said, "but be on guard always. They know more than we ever imagined."

Vikram wished he could shrug off that last meeting. Sangavat had embraced him, squeezing as if he wished to keep Vikram safe.

Bhoj was another thing to worry about. Even though he didn't know the truth, the way he'd watched the company ride out of the fort had made Vikram want to squirm. Memories of nightmares and crying on Bhoj's shoulder came back to him.

If Bhoj thought Vikram was only going on a routine patrol, why had he looked so serious?

If Bhoj knew... How could he know? Neither Vikram nor Sangavat had told him. It was a simple rule of politics that the more people who knew of a plan, the more likely the plan would fail.

Vikram had never liked to admit it but Bhoj could be very shrewd sometimes. He might have persuaded his father to tell him.

Still, even if Bhoj did know, he'd only know as much as Sangavat did. Right?

He wouldn't suspect, Vikram decided, chuckling. Bhoj had enough problems to worry about. His leg was healed but there was nothing he could do about his wife.

Mira was ripe, ready to take, but Bhoj stayed away because she was grieving for her brother. Bhoj had been married for one and a half years and still Mira was a virgin.

Vikram would never have believed it.

Bhoj, so charming, so handsome, such a favorite of the ladies. And he couldn't even have his own wife!

A few weeks ago, Vikram was standing on the roof of the Panna Palace when he saw her palanquin enter the Kumbh-Shyam temple complex. He watched as she emerged from the box like a beautiful bird, exotic, delicate, gracefully ascending the steps of the temple. A sudden wind had molded her red veil to her body and the sight made Vikram freeze. His hands fisted, his breath stopped.

His doubts about his plan seized him.

When she disappeared into the mandir, the bell swinging after her in the doorway, Vikram went down to the gardens and threw stones at the fish in the pond, trying to unlock the freeze in his chest.

He told himself he wouldn't watch Mira anymore.

A jolt brought his mind back into the cart. Vikram looked up to see that green fields were close.

*

Building was completed just as the winds cooled and the sun began to shrink in the sky. The masons started work on plastering, whitewashing, painting and moving furniture in.

For some reason, Bhoj had built the mahel just a garden away from the Kumbh-Shyam mandir.

The date for the vastu ceremony was fixed. The royal family and Raj Purohit arrived to witness Mira and Bhoj perform the puja to Ganesh, the Lord of Prosperity.

Mira decorated the doorstep with vermillion paste by drawing the sign of peace in the holy swastika and the eternal word AUM. She prayed to Ganesh that he fill this house with prosperity and happiness.

The lamp was lit, and the couple entered the threshold.

Bhoj named the palace Desh Bhakti Bhavan. Patriot's House.

Mira cooked feast after feast for the new home festivities and not once did anyone complain there was no meat.

Bhoj accepted it with a smile.

In truth, Mira was amazed at how easily she slipped into her role as mistress of Desh Bhakti Bhavan. It wasn't that running the palace and servants was easy. It was just that the lack of opposition was a shock. There were no in-laws here to humiliate her.

She assigned roles to the twenty servants now under her command, excluding Bhoj's guards who patrolled the walls. She kept all parts of the four-storey mahel clean, checked the food provisions regularly, and served all guests and holy people.

Bhoj left Mira to herself during this time, not just because he was busy with affairs of state but also because he was letting Mira establish the bhavan as her own.

She found his absence a relief. He called her priye so often these days.

Mira made regular trips to the main palace to sit through a gossip session with her mother-in-law. She sometimes wondered if the queen's warmth was out of relief that Shamal had died and not Bhoj. Then Mira would brush aside her tears and chastise herself for thinking such things.

"My own brothers were killed by Babur," Gauri had told her. "Not long after my marriage. Babur conquered my father's kingdoms of Agra and Jaisingpur. He slaughtered every relative I had there." She'd said it with a strange look in her eyes, as if she were seeing something not in the room.

Mira often thought of Shamal's bride, Padmavati.

The girl had been traveling on a different route and therefore had escaped the attack. After the last rites were performed in Merta, she'd returned to Amber and her parents.

Mira wrote a letter to Padmavati there. She wrote that Shamal was now with Krishna and that he'd died a martyr's death. She told Padmavati not to grieve for him for he'd simply returned to his eternal abode. She wrote that her babhi was welcome to live with Mira in Chittore.

The princess wrote back that though she'd only been with her husband for a few days, she'd come to worship him. She wrote that even if he wasn't with her, she loved his memory and that was her companionship. She wrote that she couldn't come to Chittore for she didn't want her widow's garb to depress Mira's house. She wrote that she hoped she'd be worthy of joining her husband when she left her body.

Several days afterwards, Mira received a letter from Amber's queen.

She wrote that her daughter Padmavati had asked for the right to become sati. The right had been granted and the princess had immolated herself.

Mira walked about in a daze afterwards.

The girl had surrendered her body to the fire and her husband's memory. Her husband of a just few days.

Widowhood must have been unbearable.

If only Mira had written sooner, she might have persuaded Padmavati to live.

And yet, in spite of her shock, Mira felt a deep surge of respect for the princess. Such courage. Such loyalty. She'd given up her life for Shamal.

While Mira, who'd loved Krishna for years, forgot him within months.

I shall uphold your memory, sister-in-law, Mira thought. I shall be a wife such as you.

The months crept on and the winter chill evaporated.

Mira's income from Merta arrived, escorted by a person she'd not seen since childhood. It was Raghuvir, a distant cousin, six months younger than she.

He bowed to touch her feet and Mira was struck by how handsome he'd become. He looked just like Shamal. When she told him that, he smiled and said he was honored she thought so. He presented her with a message from her father. It read that Mira was not to leave Chittore to come to Merta, not even to share her grief over Shamal. Her place was with her people.

Mira told Raghuvir she understood. Only the people mattered.

He stayed for a week and Mira spent the time feeding him, listening to all the news of her relatives in Merta, and reminiscing about their childhood in Chaukari with Shamal.

He left Chittore just as the kesari flowers bloomed, their saffron hue erupting about the city like sudden fires.

Mira wished he didn't have to go, and hugged him hard when he bid her farewell. He was a piece of Chaukari.

The people began preparing for Holi, the festival of colors. It was the one time where everyone was allowed to go mad. Boundaries of age and sex were less distinct as children and parents and men and women played together with colors.

Mira's fifteenth birthday was almost upon her and it was as if her face was molding into the hilltop fort she resided in. Her cheekbones grew higher and her jawbone grew firmer. The valleys of her cheeks deepened. Her eyes were larger, the pupils sentinel guards, watching for intruders.

Chittore received the news on her birthday: Sher Shah of Delhi was dead.

That Holi was the best Mira could remember. Singing and dancing and parading went on all day. Women decorated their courtyards with rangoli designs and cows walked around with blue hand prints all over their bodies. Boys and girls ran chasing each other through the streets, giggling and laughing as they were caught.

Mira went to the garden and joined in the fun with the other ladies, laughing as the queen threw a handful of yellow at her. She shrieked when one of the younger girls caught her skirt and doused her in pink water.

The children pummeled her with fistfuls of green and she shielded her face, screaming at them to stop. When they ran out of supplies, she seized a tub of blue water and ran after the children, flinging it at their feet so they slipped and fell over on the grass.

She was laughing so much she bent over to rub her stomach. It was a mistake.

Lalita and Janki came up behind her and grabbed her arms, pulling her backwards.

"What are you–?"

They pushed her into the pond and stood there, laughing at her.

Sitting up, she spat out purple water and green reeds, feeling the fish bumping into her body. "Thank you very much," she told her maids. Then she grabbed them, pulling them in with her.

Savitri and Durga walked up in pristine clothes.

Mira looked at Lalita and Janki.

Without another word, they reached up and pulled in the two shrieking older women.

"You shouldn't have come out if you didn't want to get dirty!" Janki squeaked.

Weak with laughter, Mira crawled out of the pond.

"Babhi!" A young cousin of Bhoj's ran up to her. "The men have attacked your husband!" She grabbed Mira's hand.

Mira, too wet and weak to resist, let herself be pulled through the garden gate and into the courtyard.

A large hand slipped around her waist.

Mira shrieked, then felt Bhoj's belly laugh against her back.

"But Maya said that you were being attacked!" she said.

"Now why would they attack me, I wonder?" He pulled blue powder from a pouch at his side and rubbed it over her face.

She wrenched away and ran back into the garden, her heart pounding.

Daylight began to fade and people were going off to bathe.

Mira went with the ladies to Lake Gow Mukh. When her elders teased her about the blue on her face, she slipped and almost drowned herself.

Now clean, the royal ladies entered the underground tunnel to go from the lake to the palace where they dressed in clean clothes.

The Holi fast was peculiar. Throughout the day people would eat dry things like nuts and chickpeas. Then at night, the Holi bonfires would be lit, where people would pray for a good harvest before sitting down to a great feast.

The family gathered in the dining hall, the men sitting down to eat as their wives served them.

Mira put a bit of everything on Bhoj's plate, making sure he got doubles of the panir sabji, a soft cheese and spiced vegetable dish that he loved. She fanned him with a peacock feather fan as he ate.

The Sisodias talked long and loud.

"Did you see the look on the king's face, Vikram," Bhoj asked his cousin, "when Aryaji ambushed him?"

"You wait, putra," Sangavat said. "I might just ambush you and throw you off the mountain!"

"You wouldn't be able to pick me up, Bapu Sa," Bhoj said, patting his rigid stomach. "My wife's cooking has made me fat!"

The Sisodias roared with laughter.

Even Mira couldn't help giggling.

After hours and many retorts, people began to get up. The men left the hall and the women settled down to eat.

For some reason, everyone was very nice to Mira. Buaji urged her to take more sabji while Bhoj's cousins asked Mira how she did her hair. The little ones wanted her to help them with their dance steps since she was so graceful.

They wouldn't let her help clean up.

"Go, bahu," Gauri said, patting Mira on the shoulder. "Go to your bed and have sweet, sweet dreams!"

Still taken aback by the warmth of their smiles, Mira got into her palanquin.

The servants at Desh Bhakti Bhavan were gathered in the front courtyard, sitting around the bonfire. They jumped to their feet as Mira arrived.

"No, no, sit," Mira told them from her box. "Enjoy the night."

Someone had remembered to light the lamps so she was able to find her suite without stumbling. Entering, she pulled her veil off her face.

Bhoj was sitting right in the middle of the room, waiting for her.

She froze on the threshold.

He smiled. "Come."

She pigeon-stepped into the room.

"I want to talk to you."

I have to tell him, she thought. It doesn't matter if he gets angry any more.

He studied her face. "You're now fifteen years of age."

She gripped the back of her couch. "Yes."

"I've fulfilled my promise to you on our wedding night. I gave you two years to adjust."

How could he speak so plainly?

His voice became smooth, like the panir cheese she'd served him. "It's time."

Mira saw the intent look on his face and swallowed the bile rising in her throat. "I can't," she whispered.

"Can't what?"

She looked at the wall, the chair, anything but meet his eyes. Her cheeks burned. "You mentioned our wedding night. Do you recall what I said to you then?"

She could see him running through his memory, trying to find something significant.

"Anything in particular I should be recalling?"

She took her sweaty hands from the couch. "I said I wanted to serve Krishna."

"Oh yes, I said that your grandfather told me about that."

So he did remember. "Well, I also said I was given to Krishna. I've always loved him as my master." She looked at the floor. "And," she whispered, "as my husband."

There was a pause. "What are you talking about?"

She tried not to twist her veil in her hands. "Krishna."

His voice changed to puzzlement. "What does he have to do with anything?"

She forced the words out. "I accepted him as my husband a long time ago."

"What?"

"My feelings have remained the same."

Bhoj cocked an eyebrow at her. "What are you saying?"

She looked up at him. "I–it's just that–"

He gave a lazy sort of chuckle. "This is a joke, isn't it? You're teasing me."

"Please don't laugh," she said.

His eyebrow dropped.

She should never have married him and put him in this hopeless position, Mira thought.

"We were married for our countries but I promised myself I'd be faithful to Krishna."

He looked incredulous. "But you're *my* wife. Have you forgotten?"

"You don't understand–"

"Then explain. This is nonsense."

How could she make him believe her?

"My lady, explain yourself."

She saw Shamal, shot in the heart. If she'd been stronger, he might have lived. "I cannot be your wife. Forgive me."

"We *are* talking about Shri Krishna, aren't we?" Bhoj burst out. "Bhagwan Shri Krishna?"

She nodded and he looked relieved before crossing his arms. "If I'm not your husband then what am I?"

"You're my..." she paused. "You're my Rana."

He clenched his jaw. "Is this not a little unfair?"

Yes, she thought, it is. I'm so sorry.

His blue eyes pierced her brown ones. "And if I don't believe this?"

Even as she wrapped her arms around herself, she knew his anger was justified. "I'm under your protection and laws. If you wish, you could force me."

He stared at her in disbelief.

Mira looked at the ground. What else could she say?

His voice was hard and grim. "You truly don't think of me as your husband? Even after all this time?"

She looked up at him.

He read it in her eyes. Turning away, he slammed the door behind him.

Mira ran after him, getting as far as the door before she stopped.

I don't deserve his forgiveness, she told herself.

# 13

# Grieving

The stars shone at Ratan as he climbed up to the parapets.

He squinted out into the night, his thick eyebrows bushing out with the effort.

By his orders, the people in the surrounding villages came into the fort at night. A thousand camp lamps were dotted around, concealed from the outside by walls of stone. His men patrolled the fort, relentless, searching the darkness for the enemy.

Sher Shah was dead, by all accounts, of natural causes. With his death, war had erupted among the Shah's sons and allies. Now was the time for the Rajputs to attack.

Every day, Ratan's men grew more focused. Their eyes seemed to sink into their heads as if they were looking in, not out. Black shadows grew beneath but the shadows were not a part of their skin. They were coming out of the eyes themselves and building forts on their faces.

To Ratan, his men now looked like Shamal.

He stared out into the darkness with a ferocious scowl.

Shamal's death was good in one way. It made Ratan glad that Kusum was dead.

Then there was Padmavati. After Shamal's last rites were performed, Ratan had asked her where she wished to live and promised that if she chose Merta, she'd be treated with all honor. When Ratan heard that she'd immolated herself, he understood why she went back to her parents' house. If she'd been in Merta, Ratan would never have allowed her sati for she was a symbol of Amber's alliance to Merta.

Sometimes, Ratan wondered if his head would cave in under the weight of his turban. Yet it still held up high.

When he'd been younger, with Kusum at his side, he'd felt like he could do anything. The threat of the Moghuls and Afghans had been a joke. The Moghuls! They who hid in their pathetic mountain villages around Kabul? No one had expected Timur's shrinking empire to challenge the might of the Rajputs. How could they? The Moghuls had no disciplined leaders, no trained army. They were just a rabble of criminals.

How different things were now.

The Moghuls and Afghans were still criminals, pillaging and torturing, but they now had the strength of disciplined soldiers and tactical skill. They knew the power of fear. They'd assassinated Shamal because he was Ratan's heir. And each day, Ratan lived with the fear that they would take his last child. His Mira.

From the reports, Mira was becoming a part of the Sisodias, establishing herself as mistress of Desh Bhakti Bhavan. She'd been the one to open the royal provisions to the people when the harvest was poor last year. She'd been the one to gather and send out medicines when there'd been an epidemic of fevers.

Mira had taken to heart her role as the protectress of her people. She was, after all, Ratan's daughter.

And yet Shamal's words haunted Ratan. *Her heart lies only with Krishna.*

She'd been married for two years. Surely she was now loyal to Bhoj.

The Sisodias wouldn't turn on her. She was their bahu rani.

Ratan looked behind him to where his people slept. Bonfires were dying down and every now and then a piece of fuel was thrown in by a soldier. Chaukari seemed like a constellation of stars floating in the night.

With Shamal's assassination, all talk of revolt had disappeared. The mukhyas would now fight for Shamal's memory for he'd not only been their prince, he'd been their son. Many demanded that Ratan attack Delhi now.

It was the time for him to swell his ranks. He would create a new regiment and call it Shamal's Guard, so that his men never forgot why they were fighting.

He looked down at the constellation before him and nodded.

\*

It was a full week after Holi that Bhoj left for Kumbalgarh. He'd be gone a month, overseeing repairs of the defenses.

Mira's maids had told her of the rumors. People were wondering why Bhoj hadn't taken Mira with him, even though it would've been a good excuse to have a holiday with his wife.

She was in the storage room, directing the shifting of grain, when Savitri came in. Mira indicated to the manservant where the bag of grain should be put, noting it down on her records. When Savitri didn't say anything, Mira looked up. "What? I need to get this finished by the end of today."

Savitri was tight lipped. "Raj Kumari Uda is here."

Mira frowned.

Didi never leaves her quarters, she thought. Something must be wrong. She looked at the manservants. "You've worked hard. Go to the dining hall for some food and rest. I will summon you back soon."

"Ji, Bahu Rani," they said, bowing.

"Come," Mira said to Savitri. Up on the ground floor, she looked around. "Where did you leave her?"

"In the receiving room."

"Bring her to the music chamber and then fetch refreshments." That room was calming with its blues and greens, Mira thought. If Uda was upset, it might help to soothe her. She took a shortcut through Bhoj's weapons room, reaching the music chamber before Uda. She sat down behind the sitar and strummed a soft morning raga that spoke of pink dawn.

There was a flash of white and Mira looked up. "Didi, you've honored me," she said, smiling. She rose and touched Uda's feet.

Uda didn't smile back.

So she *is* angry, Mira thought. What have I done now?

Savitri entered with refreshments, placing the tray on a table. She withdrew, closing the doors behind her but not before sending a glare in Uda's direction.

Mira felt a jolt of anger at her maid and clenched her fists. Savitri should know better, she thought. As Uda sat on the couch, Mira served a cup of juice and sweets on a gold dish.

"No sweets, a widow is not permitted."

"Prasad is a blessing from Bhagwan, Didi. You cannot refuse."

"Is your education so limited that you know not the rules of widowhood?"

Stung, Mira looked down at the plate in her hands. "Forgive me, I just wanted you to have some prasad."

Uda sighed. She took the plate from Mira's hand and put it on the table. "I must discuss something important with you. I'm not here to waste time."

There's always something, isn't there? Mira thought glumly, pulling the veena to her lap. "Of course. What is the matter?"

"Your husband."

Mira almost asked "which one?" but caught herself just in time. "What about him?"

A rosy blush stole over Uda's sallow cheeks. The mid-morning sunlight was streaming in through the windows and a shaft hit Uda's eyes as she turned.

Mira was struck by the purity of Uda's features. She'd never seen Didi's face in the light of the morning before. Her eyes were beautiful, wide and tilting up like an owl's, filled with light.

It was a strange beauty.

"First, I would like to say that he hasn't said anything. He's too noble to speak badly of his wife."

Mira's fingers tightened over the veena strings. "Then what's worrying you?"

"Well, whenever he's visited me this past week, he's been unusually restless."

"Could it not be the situation at court? There's talk of attacking Delhi."

"It could be, but it isn't. It's something to do with you."

Mira gritted her teeth. What business was this of Uda's?

"It's time to accept him, sister-in-law."

Mira squeezed the veena's neck and the strings squeaked in protest. "Didi, if your brother hasn't actually said anything to you then I think we should leave this conversation as it is." She strummed that soft morning raga again.

Uda reached forward and halted the strings. Her face came out of the light. "It's not in Bhoj's character to behave so...well, sullen."

Mira blinked and tried to refocus her eyes on Uda's shadowed face.

"It's my experience that men only get sullen when they're not getting what they want. So give him what he wants, Mira."

This was too much. "Didi, I respect your advice, but what happens between your brother and I is private. Otherwise, he would've discussed it with you."

"If it's so private then why are people discussing it in the streets? Everyone knows that you've yet to share a night together."

Mira gasped. They were actually saying that?

"You're young and inexperienced and don't yet know what is

important to men. You must yield."

"Didi! The situation isn't what you think."

"Then what is it?"

Mira groaned inwardly. Should she tell Uda everything? No, that would be stupid. But as Mira looked back at Uda, a shaft of sun fell over Uda's profile, lighting up a side of her face, her left eye glowing molten brown.

It was a strange sort of beauty, Mira thought. "Your brother is angry because I love another."

Uda roared to her feet. "You do not!"

"I do."

"Who?"

"Bhagwan Shri Krishna."

Silence.

"I was given to him when I was very young and I've served him since then."

"What are you talking about?"

"Bhagwan Shri Krishna."

Uda looked like she'd just been slapped. "Are you *insane?*"

Mira could see that it didn't look good. Why had she blurted it all out?

Uda loomed over Mira. "Do you mean to say that my brother has waited two years, stood by you through scandal and gossip, been faithful and loyal and gentle, and all for a mad girl?"

When Uda put it like that, it did sound bad. Mira felt her insides shrivel as she looked up at Uda.

"My brother is becoming a laughingstock and all because you're a fool!"

"I didn't know about the rumors!" Mira protested.

"So what? My brother has defended your honor more times than you know and you repay him with this foolishness!"

"I didn't mean to hurt him," Mira cried. "I never wanted to marry but I had to for Merta."

"So now you'll put Merta in danger? Didn't you consider that you must have children? Who'll be Bhoj's heir?"

Mira could only shake her head.

"You circled the sacred fire with him!"

"Didi, you don't understand!"

"Because there *is* no understanding, only madness."

"No, Didi, I cannot accept your brother or I'll betray Krishna."

Uda, still standing, looked around the room as if searching for sense. "You cannot be serious."

"Didi, you don't know. My mother is dead. My brother is now also dead. My father is far away. Since I was eight years old, I've been alone. Can you understand that?"

Uda was still.

"The only one who never left me was Krishna."

Uda clasped Mira's hand. "Bhoj will never leave you, Mira."

"Your brother is mortal. He'll have to leave one day."

Uda threw away Mira's hand. "You dare to even think of your husband's death! Have you no shame?" she shouted. "You must always pray for his long life!"

Mira felt so helpless. "*You* must have prayed for your husband. He still died."

Uda backed away. "That was my own fault, my fate."

"But you prayed for his life. So why did he die? He died, Didi, because he was mortal. Prayers strengthen us but they cannot change our destiny."

"My husband wasn't like Bhoj!" Uda screamed. "I wasn't sincere when I prayed!"

They both froze.

Uda's mouth was open, her lovely eyes filling with tears.

Mira rose and pushed her gently back down to the couch.

"I didn't mean it," Uda whispered, shaking her head.

"It's alright," Mira said, wiping Uda's tears. She saw a cloth on the tray and handed it to Uda.

Uda blew her nose with it. "I didn't mean what I just said."

Mira's voice was soft. "Didi, I can't imagine you saying anything you didn't mean." She paused. "Was he cruel?"

It was like a veil came over Uda's face and Mira couldn't see her eyes anymore. "You don't realize how lucky you are, Mira. Accept your husband and he'll make you happy."

Mira shook her head. "You feel as if you've betrayed your husband's memory by what you said. But Krishna isn't a memory for me. He is my every waking moment. So how can I even contemplate another without hating myself?"

"Have you not considered society? They will make you pay for this, sister-in-law."

"The power of society didn't prevent you from becoming a widow. I trust in Krishna to guide me, not society."

Uda wiped her nose once more. "You're a fool. What about an heir? Does Bhoj not deserve to have children?"

Mira looked away.

"You're an intelligent girl. Sooner or later, you'll realize that you must yield. I just hope it's sooner and not later." Uda stood and walked out, her back rigid.

Mira watched her, wondering how she would tell Bhoj that she could never give him children.

*

Sitting in her palanquin, Uda drew the curtains together.

She'd gone to Mira with the best intentions. She'd screwed up her courage and left her own apartments, traveling the distance to Desh Bhakti Bhavan. Uda didn't want Bhoj's marriage to be lonely and unhappy because he and Mira wouldn't understand each other. She didn't want them to be like her and her husband.

Now Uda felt as if she'd heard the worst sort of blasphemy. A woman's every breath should be for worshipping her lord. And for Mira to say that she didn't think of Bhoj as her husband? What wretchedness! What gall! Merwar would be humiliated before all of Bharat!

A woman had to bend if she was going to uphold her husband's honor. That was the way of life, of society.

Uda couldn't believe that Mira had told Bhoj this nonsense. Her poor brother! No wonder he'd been so drawn and miserable this week. How could Mira do this to him?

Every unmarried woman Uda had ever met wanted him. Yet he wanted only Mira.

And what about the way Uda had just lost control?

*My husband wasn't like Bhoj! I wasn't sincere when I prayed!*

Uda moaned and bashed her forehead against her knees. Her husband's soul would never find peace. I was sincere when I prayed! she told herself. I was!

She realized she was home. Pulling her veil over her head, she got out, heading straight for her bedroom where she lay down, trying to calm her hiccupping.

*I wasn't sincere…*

It was my anger, she told herself, chewing on her bottom lip. Mira made me so angry I couldn't think straight.

Uda blew her nose and remembered how Mira had wiped Uda's tears.

No one had ever wiped her tears before. Not her husband when he'd torn through her that first night. Not Uda's mother when Uda returned to Chittore a widow. Not even Bhoj, for Uda never allowed herself to weep before him.

Mira treated Uda like no one else did. She touched Uda's feet and smiled, as if she was glad to see the widow. Mira didn't need Bhoj around to be nice. Perhaps that was why she was so foolish. She didn't understand what the world was like, just as she hadn't understood the traditions of her bahu bhojan.

And what about Bhoj? Every day he looked more alone and unsure.

Like me, Uda thought. He looks like me. She clasped her hands together. Oh Kula Devi, please give Mira good sense.

The canopy above her moved in the breeze. There's still time, Uda thought. Mira is only young, she can be taught. I must try again and again until she listens.

When I was her age, I learned fast enough.

\*

When Bhoj returned from Kumbalgarh, his body was stained black from training in the sun. He withered Mira with a glare and went off to see his mother.

That night, Mira sat up waiting, her stomach tied in knots.

He didn't come. The next day, he came down to eat but ignored her beside him. Four weeks went by, Chittore waited for the monsoon rains, and still he didn't speak to her.

Mira felt like the tree she'd sheltered under had shed its leaves and withdrawn. He spent almost all his time at the main palace with Sumer and Vikram, who'd just returned from a lengthy border patrol. He visited Uda too. When he came home late at night, Mira heard him tread past her door, even though it wasn't on the way to his suite. Sometimes, she heard him pause outside.

The rains didn't come. Janamashtmi celebrations were thick and hot. Another month went by and still there wasn't a cloud in the sky. The heat was so relentless that pools of sweat gathered in the street if several people stood together for too long. The lake began to dry up and every day was a struggle to conserve water.

Mira made her dhal thick so that fluids wouldn't be wasted. In the sweltering heat, she dreamed of Kashi and the glorious Ganga that ran along its eastern side.

Diwali came but still there were no rains.

Maharana Sangavat sent out heralds with the decree that grain taxes would be cut down to a third of the usual.

Mira dreamed of Annapurna Mata, the giver of food, whose temple was in Kashi. Once more, Mira opened up her food stores so the people could eat.

The weather began to cool. Winds rolled over Chittore, smacking into the marble buildings like dry water.

Mira awoke one morning to chilled air. Her breath came out as fog and she shivered when she pulled back the bedcovers.

Bhoj hates me, she thought.

He'd be glad to be rid of me. Perhaps if I ask his permission to go to Kashi, he'll say yes.

For lunch she cooked his favorites. There were spiced vegetables and rice flavored with saffron. There were barfi fudges and panir sabji with puri bread. There were pakoras and sweet coconut chutney and mung dhal loaded with chilies.

He finished everything she heaped onto his plate.

As she served him more fudge, she looked up.

He was staring at her.

She could see herself reflected in his eyes, a golden spot lost in a sea of blue.

"If I asked you for something, would you give it to me?" Mira whispered.

He stared at her lips.

She looked away, conscious of her naked face.

"What would you ask for?"

It was the first sentence he'd said to her in months! She gave him a blinding smile. "I ask permission to go to Kashi."

He didn't smile back. "Why?"

The brief spurt of joy in her belly died. "I could visit Udai. And I've wanted to go on pilgrimage there for a long time."

"Since you heard the sage talk of it?"

Her lips parted. "How did you know?"

"I wondered when I would pay for my indulgence in letting you go there." He picked another fudge and bit into it. "Permission is denied."

She watched him eat the sweet, his moustache riding the motion with smooth grace. "Oh."

She poured him water.

He drank. "Why is it that I must always indulge you? Why can you not indulge me?"

Mira looked up, surprised.

"But of course, I'm not your *real* husband, am I? Why should you need or even want to indulge me?"

She placed his water at his side. "I'll always help you in whatever way I can."

He barked a laugh. "But I'm not your *real* husband so why bother?"

She felt tears sting her eyes but blinked them back.

He rinsed his hands and stood, ignoring the cloth she held out to him. "When I married you, I was so certain that you'd fill my house with love. And you have," he laughed. "You love an elusive god that'll never be within your reach. I didn't believe you at first. I thought that you were just afraid. Now I see that, strange though it is, you're telling the truth." He turned around to face her. "That's why you really want to go to Kashi, isn't it? You're following your beloved Krishna." He crossed his arms. "Well, I won't let you."

Mira knew it was a mistake, even as she went to stand in front of him. "I think it would soothe you if I were not here."

He gazed down at her. Just as he would have touched her cheek, he turned away. "My peace doesn't lie in your absence."

She searched the muscles of his back, hard as the desert floor. She remembered how once, she'd wiped the monsoon rain from his back. Then, his muscles had been supple and smooth, bunching where she touched him.

"I only upset you."

"That's not true."

"It is. Let me go, my lord."

"No!" He smashed his foot into a stool.

Saffron rice went flying everywhere.

Mira stared at the grains like a fool. Slowly, she sank to her knees and began to sweep up the rice, trying not to rub it into the rug.

After a few moments, he got down and helped her. "I shouldn't have kicked it," his voice was low.

"You were angry."

"That doesn't make it right. To insult food is to insult Bhagwan. And this is his prasad."

Mira reached into a corner to sweep up the rice that had fallen there, dropping what she found into a bowl next to her. "It's alright."

There was silence for a few minutes as they worked.

Bhoj dropped some grains onto the tray at his side.

"We've so many servants and yet here we are cleaning," he said.

A smile pulled at her lips. "It's hardly a job for a warrior."

There was a glint in his eye and he looked at her. "It's hardly a job for a warrior woman. We shouldn't be doing this."

She stopped and looked at him. "We cannot call the servants. They'll see this mess and wonder what we were fighting about."

"We'll have to pretend this never happened," he whispered.

"We'll never speak a word of it," she whispered back.

They swept up every grain, checking under seats and tables to make sure there was nothing left, then washed their hands. Just as Mira was about to summon the maids, Bhoj touched her palm.

We hadn't touched in so long, Mira thought.

"I cannot let you go to Kashi, my lady," his voice was solemn. "It's just too dangerous. We may even send for Udai though it's unlikely. Rajputs are recruiting every man they can because the Moghuls and Afghans are fighting each other. This is our chance."

She nodded, resigned.

He ran his finger down the length of her palm, his fingertip trailing to her wrist.

She watched, fascinated, as he drew circles on her skin. It tingled.

"I cannot take the chance of an ambush."

She nodded and after a moment, he drew his hand away and strode out.

# 14

# Reckoning

Vikram walked through the entrance pillars of Chittore's crowded hall.

Throughout his life, he'd envisioned this court to be the most opulent in the world. There could be nothing better than the open courtyard with its intricately carved pillars, its polished marble floor, its satin thrones and its lavish central fountain of river goddesses pouring water from their hands. He'd thought Chittore's courtiers were the most majestic, the most noble, the most Aryan.

He'd been so right.

Delhi was hell.

Oh, the city was beautiful, but then it would be. It was a Hindu king's fortress, stolen by the enemy. The palace was stunning with its lotus motifs and graceful arches.

What bothered Vikram was the crass ignorance of the enemy.

Halfway through his first meal there, an entire roasted cow was dumped on the table. The courtiers fell on it, munching off the ribs like dogs.

Vikram would have run from the city in horror if his self-preservation hadn't stopped him. He had, after all, been expecting such things. It was just that reality was far worse. Vikram had envisioned the tame image of meat chopped up and cooked in fine spices the way meat was cooked in Merwar. That, he could deal with.

But in Delhi, the more a dead animal looked like a dead animal, the better. They loved to eat off the bones.

And the smell! It passed into the pores of Vikram's skin so that he felt blasphemed, dirty, polluted. It made him remember the stench of funeral pyres; the burned flesh, the charred wood, the crackling as the body's muscles jerked about in the flames.

After the meal, a courtier called Daud had invited Vikram, alias Timur, to a game of dice.

During the game, the slant-eyed courtier had begun discussing the foulness of Bharat, and in particular, the ridiculous nature of the Rajput people. He'd thought that Timur was a Hindi-speaking Muslim from Gujarat.

Vikram memorized Daud's features so that he could kill him later on.

"The Rajputs have a warped sense of honor," Daud had said.

"Oh, really? How's that?"

"Whenever they sense they're going to be defeated, the women jump into huge bonfires, 'to escape dishonor', while the men ride out, dressed in saffron, to fight the enemy to the death. They call it johar."

Vikram knew what it was called. More than thirty-two thousand Rajput warriors and even more women had committed johar in the sultan's siege of Chittore years ago, including his own parents.

"What a waste!" Daud had said. "All those women burning to death when they could be in our harems."

Vikram had almost slit Daud's throat right then and there. Blood had filled the front of his eye sockets so that he was looking at Daud through a red haze.

Then Daud mentioned the Shah's impending marriage to a Rajput princess of Amber. Padmavati's sister Utaraa, to be exact.

That's what had stopped Vikram from drawing his blade. He'd strained against the pounding in his ears, wondering if he'd heard aright.

But yes, Daud had said, a princess of Amber was to marry the Shah.

Now, of course, the Shah was dead. Utaraa was a widow and Amber's second alliance was dust.

The blast of bugles brought Vikram's thoughts back to Chittore's court.

Sangavat and Bhoj were entering, nodding at courtiers as they advanced up to the dais.

Sangavat graced the throne and nodded to Bhoj, who sat at his right hand.

Aryaji began the monotony of the weekly report.

Vikram let his thoughts go back to Delhi.

When he'd met the Shah in that first visit, the foul snake had been reclining on a couch in one of the gardens, much the same way

Sangavat was now relaxed on his throne.

The arrogant usurper had lain back, even as Vikram approached him.

Vikram could have drawn his dagger and executed the Shah in a moment if it hadn't been in his interests to keep the Shah alive.

His death now left Vikram in an awkward position as he had no ally in the enemy camp. Daud didn't count.

It wasn't all a waste, Vikram told himself. He knew a lot about their attitudes now. He knew who was more addicted to opium than who. That was always a help.

Who should Vikram choose as his ally now? Should he side with the Afghan's or the Moghuls?

The Moghuls were headed by Humayun who was now in Kabul. The rumors were that he was waiting for his opportunity to take back Lahore and advance on to Delhi.

The Afghans, on the other hand, were headed by Sher Shah's foolish sons.

Though Humayun wasn't the best strategist or decision maker in the world, his army was boosted by the sword of his general, Bairam Khan. If anyone was going to retake Lahore, it was him.

The Moghuls who'd betrayed Humayun after his defeat to Sher Shah in Kanauj were terrified. If he returned to power, they wouldn't live.

On the flipside of that, many Afghans were flocking to Humayun's side because they knew the Afghan princes wouldn't survive.

Vikram looked up when he heard Aryaji mention Humayun's name.

The courtiers were debating retaking Delhi. No, not debating, planning.

If Vikram was to prevail, his timing had to be perfect.

The first thing he must do was send Koirala to Bairam Khan.

\*

Ravi sat outside the Kumbh-Shyam mandir for two days. When he awoke on the third morning, there was a whisper in his ear.

"Be ready."

Ravi was as ready as he could be.

The sun was pale as it climbed the sky.

He shivered in the wind and rubbed his arms. All he was wearing was his patched dhoti and tunic, both of which were almost see-through with age. He wrapped his second dhoti around his head as a turban so that it kept some warmth in.

The lunchtime hour passed and Ravi heard the priests in the temple ring the bells as they closed the curtains over the altar.

The lord was at rest.

Ravi wondered if he should go back to the dharamshalla. The manager Malyavanji was a good person to talk to. Then Ravi worried that if he went back to the hall, he might miss her and he couldn't afford that. He would rest beneath one of the sitafar trees. That way, he would see her coming.

Ravi stood and walked to the tree. He curled up on the earth beneath it and slumbered, using his turban cloth as a pillow. He kept one hand on his tambora.

The sound of bells woke him.

Some women walked past Ravi on their way into the temple.

He glanced at them but Mira was not among them. These were older ladies. One of them was short and fat but the way she walked made Ravi think of his wife.

Lona walked like a young girl.

She'd come to him when he was preparing to leave Kashi but didn't asked where he was going or when he'd be back. Looking at her nails, she just told him not to give his shoes away.

Ravi chuckled. She'd been right. That climb up the mountain would have been much worse without shoes.

A palanquin passed him, going into the mandir courtyard where it was set down.

Ravi sat up. He recognized the maids that walked alongside the box. A young female in yellow came out of the palanquin and walked towards the temple with her maids. Ravi worked hard not to jump up and down and clap his hands. He wrapped his turban around his head again and went into the courtyard, sitting on the side of the temple steps.

People walked up and down, none taking notice of the old beggar who smelled of leather.

Ravi's ears pricked. A voice from the mandir was swelling the air around him. It was his daughter singing for Krishna.

More people headed towards the temple, eager for a glimpse of the face behind the voice. Ravi saw the wonder in their expressions.

He knew Mira. He knew her past and her future and the truth in her heart. But there was nothing truer than that voice. It was her own special talent. Her strength. In slow motion so that he wouldn't miss a note of her song, Ravi stood and ascended the steps. Standing at the back of the crowd, he saw her.

She was dancing.

The devotees were around her, their arms raised and swaying.

Mira was singing of when Krishna left Vrindavan, the sacred forest of his childhood. She sang of how the Gopis went mad with the pain of his leaving. They lay in the road before Krishna's chariot and asked him to trample them so they wouldn't have to live without him.

Mira sang of how Krishna lifted each one and told her he loved her, promising them all that they were his strength and inspiration and would always be with him in his heart.

Mira sang of Radha sitting by the Yamuna river, knowing that Krishna would never more sit with her there. Mira sang of how Krishna vowed to never again play his flute because, without Radha, his flute could have nothing to say.

Mira sang like a Gopi, lying in the road, praying for death.

Ravi had seen great bhakti, deep bhakti, mad bhakti. Never had he seen such fearless bhakti.

Mira was a Raj Kumari bound by the strict rules of her status. Yet here she was, dancing for her lord, dancing before everyone.

It was like a balm for his aching legs, or a woolen shawl for his freezing body. He wanted to fall at Vishnu's feet and thank him for giving Ravi such a disciple. My lord, you've honored me, he thought.

Vishnu was watching the drama with lotus eyes.

The bhajan ended and the crowd stood around, breathless and clapping.

Ravi slipped out: now was his chance. He hurried down the steps and stood just a little behind her palanquin.

A few moments later, Mira walked towards him, her face covered by her yellow veil.

"My mind goes to sleep," she was saying to her maid. "Something inside takes control of my body and I can't stop myself."

Ravi knew what she meant. That feeling of being propelled upwards even as the mind wonders what is happening. That was Bhakti Yoga.

He stepped into her path. "Bless you, Raj Kumari."

Mira leaned back as if he were too bright for her. "Ji?"

He moved forward so he could see her better. "Your bhajan was beautiful. Your guru must be very proud."

She paused. "Ji...I don't have a guru. I've not yet found him," she sounded heartbroken and sighed.

You have now, putri, he thought. Come, Mira, recognize me. "When a disciple cannot find the guru, the guru comes looking for the disciple."

She was almost there. He could see it in the way she tilted her head, thinking hard.

"Is that true? Is a guru so compassionate?"

"A guru knows everything about his disciple, including the obstacles that bar the way."

"Bahu Rani, the bhavan awaits," a maid said.

Ravi knew it was Savitri not by her looks but by the sour look on her face.

Mira started, glancing at the disapproving maid. "Yes, just one moment." She looked back at Ravi. "I must return to the palace, Mahatma." Her frown was like the bruise on a mango.

"I know. I just wanted to give you a gift." He held out his tambora.

She gave the instrument a blank look.

"It's for you, Raj Kumari."

"For me? But it's very precious. I cannot accept such a gift from a holy man, and–"

"It's my blessing." Ravi thrust the tambora into her hands. "Use it when you sing for Krishna, putri."

Mira looked down at the instrument in her hands. "I'm not worthy–"

"That's for me to decide." He stepped back.

Her maids propelled her into the palanquin.

She dragged her feet, gripping the tambora. "Thank you for this gift. I'll play it when I sing in my prayers to Krishna."

Ravi watched her descend into the box that was lifted and borne away.

She'd be in trouble when she reached the mahel.

Her in-laws would no longer tolerate her law-breaking.

But now she was no longer alone.

*

Mira's hands were shaking; she couldn't believe she'd done it again. Around her, she could feel the devotees watching her, turning their gaze away just as she looked at them. She could feel Vishnu looking at her from his altar, a grin of mischief on his face.

The Sisodias would be furious.

She avoided her maids' eyes and exited the temple. What was she going to do now? She'd been trying so hard not to create conflict. How could she be so stupid?

From the corner of her eye, she saw people shaking their heads at each other.

Janki leaned towards her. "Bahu Rani, why did you do that?"

Mira shook her head. "I don't know."

"But now you'll be in trouble."

Mira knew it and somehow, she had to justify herself to her maid, even if she couldn't justify herself to anyone else. "My mind goes to sleep," her voice almost disappeared as she shivered from a lingering wave of…whatever it was that had happened to her. "Something inside takes control of my body and I can't stop myself."

She could feel the stares of the people in the temple complex and headed straight for her palanquin.

Then something blinded her and she blinked, leaning back.

"Bless you, Raj Kumari," said a man's voice.

The voice echoed in Mira's ears and she was mesmerized. There was so much light. She blinked and strained to see him.

The radiance diffused, the way a lamp flared when first lit and then settled into a glow. The glow hung around him, like a shawl.

He was a small man, thin as an ascetic. He had masses of curly black-brown hair that reached his shoulders and a peppery beard that flowed down his torso like a river. His eyes blazed with the light of a yagna.

Mira knew instantly that this man was older than anyone she'd ever met. It was all in his eyes.

She also knew that he was one of her own. *He belonged to her.*

How could that be? she thought. She'd never seen this man before in her life.

His clothes were tattered but he carried a polished tambora. Perhaps he was a traveling musician.

Perhaps she'd seen him in Merta. Many wandering minstrels had come to Chaukari to sing for her mother.

No, Mira would've remembered him if she'd seen him there. She'd know this sadhu anywhere.

Sadhu? How did she know he was a sadhu? By his tattered clothes, he was of low caste. He didn't wear saffron.

She realized he'd said something. "Ji?"

"Your bhajan was beautiful. Your guru must be very proud."

He was smiling as if he knew something she didn't. And why was he speaking of gurus? "Ji…I don't have a guru. I've not yet found him."

She sighed, thinking of how long she'd waited for her guru. Yet who was this man? And his voice! It was like the smoke that rose from a yagna fire, reaching the sky.

"When a disciple cannot find the guru, the guru comes looking for the disciple."

There he went again, voicing her fear that she'd never find her guru. It made her heart beat like a mrdunga drum. Mira took a half step towards him. "Is that true? Is a guru so compassionate?"

"A guru knows everything about his disciple, including the obstacles that bar the way."

Mira prayed it was the truth. She took another half step towards him and noticed that he smelled of sandalwood. But it wasn't perfume or incense. This was coming from his very pores. Who *was* he?

"Bahu Rani, the bhavan awaits," Savitri said.

Mira started to hear the disapproval in Savitri's voice. It wasn't a crime to talk to a holy man!

"Yes, just one moment." Mira wished she were not a princess. Then she could stand here all day and talk to this fascinating man. "I must return to the palace, Mahatma."

"I know. I just wanted to give you a gift." He held out his tambora.

She looked at the gleaming instrument, wondering what he was talking about.

"It's for you, Raj Kumari." He looked as if he were prompting her to take it, the glow around his form flickering as he nodded.

"For me? But it's very precious. I cannot accept such a gift from a holy man and—"

"It's my blessing." He placed the tambora into her hands. "Use it when you sing for Krishna, putri."

He'd called her daughter, not princess. How kind, Mira thought, suddenly wanting to cry. "I'm not worthy—"

"That's for me to decide." He stepped back.

Mira saw that his turban was just a rag around his head. She couldn't take such a precious gift from him when he was so poor!

Her maids were nudging her towards the palanquin and Mira resisted them, desperate to return the tambora, to spend time with him, to ask him who he was.

He smiled at her.

A koyle bird called from somewhere above and the tambora was soft in her fingers, like it was melding to her skin. Mira gasped and looked down, feeling some unnatural warmth from the wood seep into her. I'm meant to keep this! she thought.

She looked up at him. "Thank you for this gift. I'll play it when I sing in my prayers to Krishna."

He raised his right hand, as if he was blessing her.

She clutched the gleaming instrument and descended into the box. A sudden terror gripped her, as if she was being parted from her mother all over again and she looked back through the red gauze of her window at the holy man. The sight of him calmed her roiling stomach and she sighed.

He was watching after her, the wind plastering his thin garments to his emaciated frame.

Who was he?

When the palanquin turned a corner and Mira lost sight of him, she felt cold inside. She could do nothing but stare at the tambora in her hands, her eyes heavy with unshed tears.

Back at the bhavan, Mira went straight to the music room with her new tambora. It was smooth and sleek, and when she strummed it, the strings were perfectly tuned. From now on, she would always sing her bhajans with this instrument, she decided. She would take it with her to the temple. She'd play it to Krishna here at home.

She lifted the wood up to her nose and inhaled. Sandalwood…

The door crashed open.

Bhoj stalked in like a predator.

Mira almost dropped the tambora. "What has happened?" she gasped, running to him.

His hands were huge fists.

She put her own hand to her throat. "What?"

"Don't you know?"

Mira stepped back from his glare.

"What have you been doing today?"

"N–nothing. I went to the temple…"

Oh no.

"Yes, the temple. And what did you do there?"

She'd not expected him to be this angry. Even the air around him was crackling. "I–I danced."

"In public! In front of men who are not your husband!"

At that, Mira met his gaze. She'd been dancing in front of her true husband and he knew it.

"Don't start your Krishna nonsense with me today. I've had enough."

He was right, she thought. She was shameless. But it was shameful that she had to keep up this charade.

Bhoj put his hands on his hips. "How shall I punish you?"

"Punish me how you will." It mattered not. She'd been blessed by a sadhu. If she hadn't danced, would the sadhu have blessed her?

He slammed his fist onto the table and she jumped. "You know I cannot!"

Mira stared at him, bewildered.

He sat down, his shoulders sagging. "You know I cannot. That's why you do these things. You want to torment me."

"That's not true!" she gasped, moving close to his side.

He looked at her. "Don't you realize your actions reflect upon the whole family? There is enough talk about you as it is."

He was right. She tried her best to be a good bahu but nothing she did worked. And now this.

She'd thought before that she was strong enough to resist dancing. But then Krishna had called to her and she'd stood, helpless, as he took her in his arms.

She had to stop going to the temple.

"If you stayed in the mahel, there wouldn't be so much gossip."

"My lord, there'll always be talk," she said.

"Our family is being slandered!"

"I accept that I was wrong! I've told you to punish me."

"You know I won't." He glared at her again.

She threw her arms up. "How can I make you understand–?"

He caught one of her hands. "There's a way I'll understand," he said, standing close. "There is a way you can show me–"

She ripped her hand from his and backed away.

"You're my wife."

Mira looked at the ground.

He dropped his hand. "Did you know who the holy man you spoke to was?"

Grateful he'd changed the subject, Mira shook her head. She pointed to the tambora on the couch. "He gave me that."

Bhoj studied it, noting its smooth lines and delicate back. "He didn't say who he was?"

"I wish he had. There was such karuna in his eyes."

"He was Sant Ravi Das."

Mira gawked at him. "Sant Ravi Das?"

Bhoj nodded.

"Sant Ravi Das of Kashi? The one who defeated famous pandits in philosophical debates? Sant Ravi Das the cobbler? *The* Sant Ravi Das?"

Bhoj crossed his arms and nodded.

Mira had to sit down. She'd heard sages telling her mother about the Great Sant Ravi Das. "No. It cannot have been him."

"It was. He arrived in Chittore two days ago. Bapu Sa sent Arya Sumanth to welcome him and even went himself to the dharamshalla for blessings."

Mira looked at the instrument. "Sant Ravi Das gave me his tambora."

"Don't get too excited," he told her. "Many think Ravi Das is just plain mad."

"He's not mad," she said, touching the strings with her fingertips. Why did he give me this? she wondered.

He said that my guru would find me.

Mira's eyes widened and she gaped at the tambora like a halfwit. Turning, she ran for the door.

"Mira!" Bhoj caught her arm.

"I'm a fool! I didn't realize. That's why..." Mira looked through Bhoj's chest, the vision of her guru's smile before her. This is why I felt like I knew him. *Like he was mine.*

She struggled away from whatever held her and headed for the door.

"Mira. Mira!" Bhoj had to shout before she'd look at him. "Where are you going?"

"I have to find him."

"You cannot leave the bhavan today."

"What?" She really looked at Bhoj this time. "But I have to ask him something. It's important. Oh, please let me go! I'll come back straight away and I promise I won't even go near the mandir."

He took hold of her shoulders. "No."

Mira tried to shrug him off. "I have to go!"

He shook her. "Have you forgotten your duties? Have you?"

Mira blinked. "No."

He released her. "It isn't wise for you to go anywhere else today. Attend this bhavan."

She was the world's biggest fool, Mira thought. She'd wasted her chance.

But there was still tomorrow, she realized and her eyes lit with anticipation. She just had to bide her time. "As you wish."

Bhoj gave her a long grim look before setting her free and leaving the room.

She went about her duties in a fixed calm. Tomorrow, she told herself. Wait for tomorrow.

In the morning, she sent Lalita out to the dharamshalla.

Her guru had left a message with the manager, Malyavanji: Ravi would be where dying people heard Shiv chanting Rama's name.

Mira had been right all along. She had to go to Kashi.

# 15

# Foreseen

Uda didn't know what to do about her brother.

He tried to pretend everything was fine. He still called for rich food and asked the musicians to play in Uda's suite. But he didn't eat much and never even touched the meat dishes. Nor was he attentive to the musicians, even when they played his favorite midnight ragas.

His eyes were no longer deep blue. Now they gave off flecks of yellow, or gold, like the night sky filled with shooting stars. The flecks flared for a brief moment, then died.

One day, Bhoj joined Uda on her balcony as she watched the sun descend for the day. The gold sheen of the sunset flickered in his eyes and, for a moment, he looked at the marble screen as if he would tear it apart with his bare hands. Then he turned away and excused himself.

It made Uda want to shake Mira. Did the fool not understand what she was doing to him?

Uda had tried talking to Mira three times since her first attempt. Each time, Mira spouted nonsense.

Gauri had begun mentioning the birth of an heir at every opportunity. It was only a matter of time before she questioned why no grandchildren had yet been born.

The image of Mira telling Gauri that Bhoj wasn't her husband tormented Uda. She kept imagining her mother taking the great gleaming sword of the Kula Devi and cutting Mira down with one blow.

Uda knew how ruthless her mother could be. If Gauri found a way to replace Mira, it'd be a disaster in more ways than one.

For a start, the scandal could destroy the Sisodias. Merwar needed

Merta's alliance just as much as Merta needed Merwar. On top of that, Uda knew that Bhoj didn't want Mira to accept him just for the sake of an heir. He loved her.

Mira's trips to the temple were the topic of every conversation. The people were laughing at the royal family because their daughter-in-law would rather dance in public than be in bed with her husband. And on top of it, Mira was carrying around the old tambora that beggar Ravi Das had given her. Some called him a saint but most just laughed at how a mad cobbler pretended to know about philosophy.

As Uda sliced the skin off a mango for her morning meal, she knew that she had to persuade Bhoj to take control.

Just as she was sitting down to do some stitching for her cousins, Bhoj entered.

Uda looked up and smiled.

"Didi," Bhoj said, coming forward and touching her feet.

"Bless you. Sit down."

He sat. The gold flecks in his eyes were dim today.

He rested his left foot on his knee and pointed to the silk in her lap. "Is that for me?"

"No, it's for Punita's sons."

Bhoj rolled his eyes. "Why do I never get anything? Surely I deserve a bit of silk every now and then."

"This is yellow silk and it would make you look sallow. Besides, you have a wife to embroider for you now."

He winced. It vanished after a split second but she saw it.

"Yes, I have a wife." He studied his nails.

Uda made a stitch. "What are your plans for today?"

"I'm leaving for a trip to Kumbalgarh. I wanted to see you before I go." He stretched his arm over the cushion of his seat. "Vikram is coming with me."

"Really? I thought he was repairing the southeast wall."

"He was but insisted on accompanying me. He's been very protective since the ambush in Merta."

"He's right to be so." Uda set another stitch. "Promise me you'll be cautious."

He arched an eyebrow. "Suggesting I'm not usually cautious?"

"You only hear what you want to hear."

He chuckled. "Yes. That's what Mira said once."

There was a pause.

Uda set another stitch. "Sooner or later, you'll have to be firm."

Bhoj examined the speckled effect on the grey marble pillars in her room. "What are you talking about?"

Uda spoke in a slow soothing voice. "She's your wife. You have to show her who's master."

"What makes you think she doesn't know that?" he said, lowering his voice. "There are things you don't know, Didi."

"Mira told me about these 'things'. It's all nonsense, Bhoj. You have to wake her up."

Bhoj flicked a bit of dust off his shoulder. "It–is–not–that–simple."

"Bhoj, I'm saying this because I'm worried about you."

"What has she told you?" He put his foot back on the ground.

Uda set a crooked stitch. "Forget that nonsense, Bhoj. The real problem is that you indulge her too much."

"What?"

"Bhoj, a woman needs to know her husband is in charge, else she'll take advantage. And eventually, she'll take so much advantage that her husband becomes a laughingstock."

He rubbed his temples with long fingers. "What do you suggest, Didi?"

She unpicked the crooked stitch and set another. "The first thing is to do something about her mandir visits."

"I can't imprison her! She'll hate me." Bhoj paced the room.

"You have to do something."

"She's so innocent." He sounded as if he were talking to himself. "She doesn't realize what she does."

Uda shook her head. "She's innocent, yes, but not ignorant. She must be controlled before things get worse."

"I know!" He stopped pacing and stared at the floor. "I try, Didi. I try to stop her. Then she looks at me with her eyes and they tell me how cruel I am and I find myself almost begging for her forgiveness." He started pacing the floor again, following the swirling designs of the marble around and around. "If I'm strict with her, she hates me. If I let her have her way, I'm a laughingstock."

"She won't hate you. She'll respect you."

He stopped. "Do you think so?" He paced the other way, around and around the swirling pattern.

Uda had never seen him like this.

All his life, women had loved him, not just because of his looks but because he teased and played and was witty.

It was one of the reasons why Uda had ignored this problem for so long. She'd been so certain of Bhoj's infallible charm.

"Before Shamal's death, she was different towards me. I think she blames me and she's right to do so. I should've seen the danger to him."

"Bhoj, she doesn't blame you any more than she blames me." Uda watched him walk up and down the room. "Will you sit down? My head is spinning."

He leaned against the pillar at her side and gazed out of the balcony screen before him.

The trees in the garden cast slim morning shadows over the alcove.

"I must go now, Didi. My men are waiting."

"Of course. Just remember what I said, Bhoj."

He pushed away from the pillar and Uda saw golden flecks in his eyes once more.

*

The Ganga was teemed with ghats, stone steps that descended into the river. In total, there were more than two hundred, built by kings who wished to show their piety. It was on these ghats that people came to bathe, wash their clothes and dishes, and performed the last rites for their dead. It was here that the world came to cleanse itself of lifetimes of sin.

Ravi sat down in a shallow raft.

Pancha Ganga Ghat was only accessible by boat, the way on land being cut off by schools and ashrams.

The boatman, by the name of Prahalad, paddled upstream, coming closer and closer until he slowed and eased up to the steps.

Ravi alighted and gave his second from last coin to Prahalad. He made his way up the ghat to the mud hut on the bank. To Ravi, it was the most precious place in the world.

At the door, a saffron clothed Brahmin was waiting for him.

"Jai Shri Rama," the Brahmin said.

"Jai Shri Rama."

"Gurudev is waiting for you."

Ravi followed the Brahmin into the hut.

Gurudev was sitting on a straw mat on the floor. A shaft of sunlight from the window fell on his back. He tilted his head as Ravi entered.

Ravi touched his forehead to the ground at his guru's feet before sitting up. "Jai Shri Rama. I came as soon as I felt your call, Gurudev."

"Jai Shri Rama. Well done, my son." Ramanand gestured a shaking hand to the space at his side.

Ravi settled himself on the straw mat.

No one knew exactly how old Ramanand Acharya was but he had

to be over a hundred. He'd been Ravi's guru in his past life and he still occupied the same body. His skin was bleached with age and his eyes were a faded brown. He walked but complained about it and needed to rest afterwards.

Of course, Ravi knew his guru never slept. Ramanand only used it as an excuse to be alone to chant.

"You saw Mira?" Ramanand's voice sounded like the pipe of a snake charmer, shaky and hypnotic.

"Ji, Gurudev."

"And how is my granddaughter?"

"Even better than I expected."

"Did she recognize you?"

"It took her only an hour."

Ramanand chortled. "Clever girl."

Ravi laughed.

"I'm pained that I had to tear you away." Ramanand coughed and the saffron clothed Brahmin appeared with a cup of water. Ramanand took it and drank. A drop ran down his chin. "Your brother will be here soon."

"Pipa?"

"Yes. Seeking me, he'll come to you. I give you the task of testing him."

Ravi nodded.

Ramanand bowed his head and for a moment, Ravi thought his guru's mind had wandered off.

"You worry for Mira?"

Ravi started. "A little, Gurudev. She's in danger."

"I know. But you mustn't worry. You already know what's in store for her."

Ravi nodded. Now that Mira knew who her guru was, she wouldn't feel so alone. Ravi shouldn't worry.

But a father couldn't help worrying about his daughter. "I keep having this dream, Gurudev. I see spears, broken and covered in blood. I see crumbling sandstone. I see fires and smoke. And there is silence." Ravi looked down at his gnarled hands. "Then I think to myself: Mira must be strong."

"Mira? How do thoughts of Mira come into your dream?"

Ravi hesitated. "Chittore is built on foundations of sandstone. I fear there isn't enough time to protect her."

"Self doubt, Ravi?"

Ravi sighed and picked at the loose threads of his dhoti.

"You know, I remember when you took birth. Your mother and father were frantic because you wouldn't drink your mother's milk. You refused to identify yourself with such an ignorant and low caste body."

"I wanted to leave it as soon as possible."

"I went to your parents' house. They were bewildered when I took you from your mother's arms and held you. You were four days old and small as a mouse. You were crying because you hated this body and you hated this life. I chanted Rama's name and you calmed. I willed you to accept the body Rama had given you." Ramanand tilted his head, or perhaps it fell to the side. "Why did I do it? Well, Ravi, your body is that of a chamaar, a low caste, but that is not truth. Your soul is truth. And your soul was sent here to perform a job. If you'd rejected your body then, your disciples would be helpless today. Mira would be helpless." Ramanand picked up a rosary of Tulsi beads from the floor and ran his fingers over them, one by one. "Never forget that you have work to do, that Krishna himself gave you these orders. Do you doubt him?"

"No, Gurudev."

"Then worry no more." Ramanand lifted his hand and the Brahmin reappeared. "Bring fruit for my son." He turned back to Ravi. "You'll stay here tonight."

The next day, Ravi boarded another boat to take him back down the river. It depressed his heart to leave his guru. Apart from in his visions, this was the only place Ravi felt comforted. It was the only place where he wasn't hungry.

*

The day of the great trading fair came and people from all kingdoms came to the city for it. There would be processions and food and dancers and all Ravi's neighbors went to see the spectacle.

He went about his business alone in his little road, sitting inside his hut. He set a piece of stretched leather over the ground, holding it taut with rocks at the corners. Picking up a pot of red clay dye, he squatted and painted the leather with a hard twig brush. The pattern the twigs made was like the tangle of broken spears in his dream.

The ground rumbled, warning him that someone was fast approaching. He knew it was a chariot. Horses drew up outside his door and Ravi scraped twigs over leather.

A shadow fell over him.

"Mahatma?"

The dark silhouette at the door showed a tall man, wearing a large turban and a sword. The man knelt.

"Come in, Rana Pipa."

The king lifted up off his knee with the grace of a reed in the wind. He stepped into the hut. "I've come to pay my respects to Sant Ravi Das."

"I am Ravi Das."

Pipa bowed once more. "I've heard of your greatness. Sages come to my kingdom of Gondalgarh and recite your poems."

"I'm honored they find my poems fit. Is all well in Gondalgarh?"

"All is well, by your blessings."

Ravi watched as the king took a split second to survey his surroundings. If Ravi hadn't seen the glint of the king's sword hilt as Pipa turned, Ravi might never have known it had happened.

He saw doubt draw over Pipa's black silhouette as the supple reed stiffened.

Pipa stepped into the room. Thin and elegant, his chest rivaled Ravi's in slimness. He had full cheeks and a black moustache that was waxed and turned up at the ends.

"What can I do for you, Ranaji?" Ravi said.

Pipa came forward and knelt once more. "I've come to beg initiation from you."

Ravi dropped his brush back into the bowl and stirred some leather that was soaking in water. "Who am I to initiate anyone? There are many gurus and saints who are born into Brahmin families who can initiate you."

"I've heard you can guide me to salvation."

Ravi knew that Pipa had desired to see him for a long time but hadn't wanted others to know of his desire. That's why he'd come today, when all were away enjoying the great fair.

Still, Pipa was asking for initiation. He deserved something.

Ravi tipped the stone bowl so that some leather soaked water fell into his palm. "Hold out your hand, Ranaji." Don't let your pride get in the way, Ravi told Pipa with his mind.

Pipa hesitated, then cupped his hand.

Ravi poured the water into it. "Drink."

Pipa's hand jerked just a bit.

Ravi knew what the king was thinking. He was wondering how he could accept water from the hands of a chamaar, and impure leather soaked water at that!

Trust me, Pipa. "Drink. It's my blessing."

Pipa held his hand to his mouth.

In his mind's eye, Ravi saw the cool water slide down the king's hand and seep into his sleeve. "So be it," he said.

Pipa would realize his mistake soon enough.

"Thank you for blessing me, Mahatma. I'm your humble servant," Pipa said.

Ravi shook his head at Pipa. "Soon, you'll learn the ways of Rama, but first, you must learn the ways of yourself. Go now, back to Gondalgarh."

Pipa bowed and stood.

"Remember, your status as a Rana is limited to this birth. There is no knowing where you'll go next. Thus, you must consider yourself only a casteless traveling soul."

Pipa stepped forward. "Please teach me something else. Where will I go in my next life?"

Ravi stepped back. "I've already given you your first lesson. Now you must return to your city." He lifted his right hand in blessing.

The king bowed and left.

Sunlight, once more, filled the doorway.

Well, Gurudev, I tested him as you asked, Ravi thought.

He picked up his twig brush and painted the leather, scratching the brush in short sharp lines, trying not to think of spears.

A month passed. It was a better month than most. Ravi sold several pairs of shoes a week and managed to eat a meal almost every day.

Then at noon, when Ravi was trying to decide if he should cook the handful of rice he had left or save it for tomorrow, he felt the ground rumble again.

He squatted by the stove and fanned the wisps of smoke into a flame. He put a pan of water on to boil and added a long piece of leather to soften.

Outside, a chariot pulled up.

Ravi heard a pair of feet jump down and run towards the doorway.

The sunlight was blocked once more.

"Come in, Ranaji."

"Forgive me, Mahatma, forgive me!" Pipa ran in and fell at Ravi's feet, clutching them in his hands. "Please forgive me, I lied to you. I didn't drink the water you gave me. I let it fall into my sleeve." He was weeping, his nose wet and swollen.

Ravi was silent.

"I didn't want to drink impure water from a chamaar's hands. I thought my birth was higher than yours."

"And what do you think now?"

"That I was wrong!"

"Why do you think this?"

"When I returned to Gondalgarh, I gave my tunic to a washerman to clean. He gave it to his daughter and told her to chew it to remove the stains. While chewing it, she must have swallowed some of your water because now, her whole face shines with a divine light and when she speaks, it's as if Saraswati, the goddess of knowledge, is speaking. When my prime minister told me that the washerman's illiterate daughter had turned into a saintly girl, I went to see her and she told me she'd drunk the amrut in my sleeve."

Ravi pictured Namrata as she drank the drops of fortune. "She is correct, Ranaji. That water I gave you was nectar, from Sach Khand, and it contained the gift of knowledge."

Pipa placed his forehead on Ravi's foot. "Please bestow the grace of that amrut again!"

Ravi grasped Pipa's shoulders, lifting him. "Such a gift is offered only once."

Pipa looked like he'd faint.

"Do not lament, Ranaji. What happened was your destiny, as it was Namrata's destiny also. I gave it to you so that she could drink it."

Pipa's reed body wobbled. "But how will I find knowledge now?"

"You must go to your guru."

Pipa rubbed his nose. "Are you not my guru?"

Ravi shook his head. "Your guru is Ramanand Acharya."

"Ramanand Acharya? But he's your guru." His voice was full of wonder.

"Go to Panch Ganga Ghat. You shall find him there."

"How can you have such compassion for me?" Pipa covered his face with his long hands and wept. "I'm such a fool!"

"Go there, Pipa. Gurudev is waiting for you."

Pipa sobbed some more before he pulled himself together. "As you wish." He bowed again and again as he backed out of the hut.

Ravi watched him go.

Once Pipa developed love of the holy name, he would be free of his ego and his caste. He would find salvation.

Now Ravi understood why Gurudev had set Ravi this task.

In just one move, Ramanand had taught both of his students the same lesson.

Ravi couldn't change his destiny, just as Mira couldn't change hers. A guru's job was to teach his disciples to accept themselves and the truth within. The truth of Rama Naam.

*

Mira climbed the stairs, noting that tomorrow she must tell someone to dust the columns.

Savitri and Lakshmi were waiting for her.

Lalita and Janki were away, visiting Janki's family in the valley below the mountain.

Mira yawned. "You may go. I'll undress myself tonight."

Savitri came forward. "Perhaps you'd like a massage before you go to sleep."

"No, you must be tired from the feast we gave today."

Savitri took Mira by the shoulders, and steered her into the dressing room. "We'd rather serve you than sleep."

Mira smiled at her. "I don't deserve you."

Lakshmi began stirring goat's milk and honey into chickpea flour to make a paste, her efficient hands making quick work of it.

Mira gestured to the bowl. "I don't need that. Just give me some water to wash with."

"But you've been in the kitchens all day, Bahu Rani," Savitri said. "The heat will make your skin coarse if you don't care for it."

Mira thought of looking beautiful when Krishna came for her. "Alright."

The maids undid her veil and blouse. They took down her hair, removing all the jewels that kept the black mass in place then tied it back up in a simple knot. They removed her skirt.

Savitri placed a sheet on the couch and Mira lay down, closing her eyes as her maids arranged towels around her. She was so tired. There were always so many mouths to feed and so many disputes to settle. Sometimes, it felt like the servants lived to quarrel.

Lakshmi used a wet cotton cloth to wipe Mira's face and torso.

Savitri wiped Mira's legs and feet.

They smoothed the chickpea mixture over Mira's whole body, using it as a scrub.

"There, you're ready for your bath, Bahu Rani," Savitri said.

Mira rose and stepped into the warm scented water Lakshmi had prepared in the marble bathing pond. She inhaled, feeling the oils in the water sinking into her skin. Jasmine and honeysuckle filled her nostrils and she rested back against the wall of the tub, running her hands over her limbs to remove the paste. Her skin felt soft and smooth, like the belly of a cow. Through her half-closed eyelids, she saw Savitri giving Lakshmi a furious look.

Mira opened her eyes wide. "What is it?"

Savitri wiped her wrinkled face free of emotion. "Nothing, Bahu Rani."

Mira reached up and her bare breasts felt cold in the winter air. She caught Lakshmi's hand. "What is it?"

Lakshmi shrugged. "Nothing, Bahu Rani."

"Don't lie to me, Lakshmi."

Savitri pushed Mira back into the water. "I just told her there was no need to tell you any rumors today."

Lakshmi stared at the ground.

Savitri sifted through vials of different oils on the table, selecting the one she would use for Mira's massage.

Mira frowned. "That's all?"

"Yes," they said.

Mira thought of all the mortifying gossip she had to deal with every day. Bhoj was more distant than ever. "Tell me in the morning."

"Ji, Bahu Rani."

Mira splashed her face. Her body pink and gold from the scrubbing, she stepped out of the tub and lay on her front on the couch.

Whenever Bhoj did chance to be near her, she thought, he glared and snarled, like a wounded tiger limping in the grass. But it was strange. Just yesterday, she'd been walking across the courtyard and chanced to look up at the parapets. There he was, foot on wall, hand on hip, looking at her as if…as if he'd jump off the parapet if she asked him to.

Savitri pummeled her back with the towel.

Mira felt the cool sensation as Lakshmi rubbed rose oil into her back.

She never wore rose. "What's this?"

There was a pause.

"I picked it up by accident," Savitri said. "Shall we remove it?"

Mira groaned. "Half of it's already in my skin. Just carry on."

"Ji," said Savitri.

Bhoj liked rose, Mira thought.

She reared up, surprising her maids so much they jumped.

"Is there something you're not telling me?" she asked, looking from one to the other.

"Wh–what do you mean, Bahu Rani?" Savitri asked, so frazzled she'd overturned the rose vial so it spilt upon the floor.

Sweet cloying scent rampaged through the room.

Lakshmi looked at the oil seeping into the pores of her hands.

"Well?" Mira was trying not to inhale. The smell was overpowering.

"I picked it up by accident," Savitri said.

"But why was it in front of the sandalwood? You know I always use sandalwood. I never use rose. Why was the rose vial even in my suite?"

"I didn't realize what it was."

"You must have smelled it when you mixed it with the almond base."

"It's only a different oil, Bahu Rani. Please forgive me. I'm getting old and I make mistakes."

Savitri looked so forlorn that Mira paused, thinking that perhaps she'd overreacted.

However, she thought, these two were behaving odd. "What rumors did you hear today?"

The maids exchanged looks, Lakshmi looking as if she were imploring Savitri for something.

The elder maid sighed. "Very well."

Lakshmi's eyes lit with a sudden fire and she rounded on Mira. "They said Yuvraj would come."

Mira stared at her.

"It's true, Bahu Rani."

Mira jumped to her feet and shrugged on the clean blouse Lakshmi had set out for her.

"Tell me everything," she commanded.

Lakshmi trembled. "He went to Raj Kumari Uda today and we heard from a dasi who was near Uda's suite that he's determined to take his rights."

Worse and worse. "And?"

"And," Savitri said, "I heard a guard telling another guard that Bahu Rani would be a proper wife tonight."

"Tonight?" Mira whispered.

They nodded.

Mira clasped her veil to her front. "You're telling me this now, after all this time?"

"Lakshmi wanted to speak but I stopped her." Savitri bowed her head, wringing her hands so that more rose bled into the air. "I thought it'd be best if you didn't know."

"I would've found out sooner or later, Savitri! How could you?"

Savitri tightened her lips. "I thought it'd be best if you yielded to your husband."

Mira shook her head. "That's why you used the rose." She closed her eyes, her heart raging. "You've betrayed me, Savitri. How can I ever trust you again?"

Savitri lifted her hands in protest. "I'm loyal–"

"Don't say another word." He could be here any minute, Mira thought. What do I do? She ran trembling fingers over her mouth. "I have to hide."

"But where?" Savitri looked incredulous.

"This is my house isn't it?" Mira snapped. "I can sleep in any room I wish. Gather my things."

The maids rushed around the room gathering sheets and blankets and hair combs and clothes.

"I don't need the whole room!"

They nodded and were ready.

"Come." Mira said, striding through her suite to the front room. She would hide in the Blue Kamal chamber, she thought. It was unoccupied and far from here.

Her wet feet skidded to a halt.

The maids bounced off her back.

Standing in the doorway, Bhoj arched an eyebrow. "I trust you're not surprised to see me." He stepped into the room.

"Of course not, my lord." Mira hid her thudding heart by turning to her maids. "You may leave," she said in her calmest, most poised tone.

"Ji." The maids' gazes flickered from Bhoj to Mira as they edged near their door.

"Where are they taking those things?"

The maids looked at Mira in terror, the incriminating evidence plain for all to see since their arms were piled high with sheets and towels.

Mira hid her shaking hands in the folds of her skirt. "They were bringing them out here to give me a foot massage."

"Why out here?"

"I wanted some night air from the window." Mira nodded to the dasis. "Leave the things on that table and go."

There was a pause as they scurried out.

Bhoj looked at Mira standing in the doorway between her front room and inner chamber. He seemed calm.

There has to be a way I can talk him out of this, she thought.

Just remember he's not your husband.

"Will you not ask me to sit?"

"Of course, please sit." She looked around for his seat, forgetting that his seat was inside.

He chuckled. "Calm yourself, priye."

He had to stop calling her that!

He strode towards her, and she froze. Then she realized he wanted to get into her sitting room.

She felt his heat as he passed.

Mira tried to think of the usual procedure but it'd been so long since he'd been in her rooms that she just couldn't think straight. "Shall I get you refreshments?"

"No. Sit here with me."

Mira stumbled over to her mother's couch and sank onto it, digging her toes into the carpet.

He smiled again.

Was he enjoying this? How could he be smiling? He'd never been in her rooms this late, except on their wedding night and that night was now so hazy in Mira's mind that she wondered if she'd dreamed the whole thing up. She realized she was wringing her hands and sat on them.

There was no one to protect her. Would he listen if she refused him? What would happen if the servants heard the mistress screaming "no" at the master?

"I've waited long, priye. Too long. But I'm willing to admit it's my fault. I should've ended this a long time ago." He picked up her hand and squeezed it.

She could feel her palm sweating into his.

"I'll make you very happy. Don't be afraid."

She felt like a flower, rooted to the earth, unable to protest when a passerby cut her head off. She stared at their joined hands, his fingers moving in and out of hers.

Long ago dreams of bloodless sheets returned to paralyze her.

"Come with me," he stood.

Her body was so tense that when he pulled, she shot up like an arrow and landed on his chest.

"Ouff," he said and laughed. He slid his arms around her back and hugged her.

Mira was shaking so much she had to lean on him just to stop herself from collapsing. She breathed in his scent. Dust and war. Peacocks and shade.

He kissed her forehead. "You smell of rose." He kissed her temple.

She looked up at him and knew there was no escape.

He smoothed a lock of hair from her face then reached around and untied the knot in her hair so that it tumbled to her knees. "My wife," he whispered, running his hands through her long hair.

She was Krishna's wife!

"I don't want this, my lord," she whimpered.

"Shhh…" He ran his knuckles over her jaw line, touching his thumb to her mouth. "I'll make you change your mind. I promise."

"Please don't do this to me. I can't bear it."

"Neither can I, my lady. That's why I'm here."

"You misunderstand. I don't want this. I never wanted this."

His embrace tightened. "You don't know what you're saying."

The scent of dust and war and roses choked her. With a heave, Mira pulled out of Bhoj's grip. "Please stay away, my lord. This will ruin everything."

He looked taken aback at how fast she'd moved away. "I'm your husband and I have rights." He moved to take hold of her again. "If you'll just let me then I'll show you they're not so terrible."

She stepped out of his reach. "No! This isn't what I want. Forgive me, but you must leave my chambers."

"I will not." He stepped forward.

She moved back so fast she stumbled and grabbed the arm of her mother's couch. "I'm not willing!"

"Just listen to me!"

She turned and ran.

He grabbed her as she got to the doorway of her suite. Picking her up by the waist, her back against his front, he hauled her back inside. "I don't want it to be this way."

Her hair fell over her face. There was an awful ringing in her ears. Not at all like the bells at the mandir.

She pounded his forearms. "Let me go!"

"Calm down!" He twisted her about to face him. "You're making this difficult."

"Did you expect me to make it easy?" she spat out through her hair.

"I didn't expect hysterics. You're usually so composed, priye."

"Don't call me that! I'm not your *priye!*"

They stared at each other in silence.

Mira sagged against him. "I don't want to say such things. You make me," she moaned, hitting his chest with her fist.

"Do you think I want it to be like this?" He shook her. "How can Krishna be more important to you than me? I'm your husband!"

"You're not!"

"I am!"

They glared at each other.

She crumpled in his arms, weeping, and he loosened his grip on her shoulders. She smoothed her hand on his chest where she'd hit him and he pushed her hair from her eyes. She rubbed her tears away and he touched his lips to hers.

Mira slammed her palm against his face.

Bhoj rocked backwards, a vivid red palm-sized mark on his cheek. A pulse started ticking in his jaw.

He grabbed her arm and hauled her towards the bedroom. "If you wish to make us both miserable, so be it."

"No, please, forgive me! Don't punish me like this." She pulled back again and again, grabbing seats and tables to slow him down. "Please, not like this!"

"You think you're being punished? My lady, it is I who is being punished. I don't know what I did wrong in my past life. I wanted this to be otherwise but what can I do? I must have you!"

"No!" Mira grabbed a drape that hung over the arched doorway to her bedroom. He pulled and she pulled. The drape ripped in her hand.

Krishna, help me! Mira begged.

Bhoj flung her onto the bed, his chest heaving. "Don't be foolish enough to get up," he barked.

She quivered. "My lord, please don't do this!"

He pulled off his shoes and threw them into a corner of the room. He reached down and ripped her veil away. "Take your clothes off."

She stuffed her hand in her mouth and wanted to die. Please, Krishna, stop him!

Then Bhoj paused. He was looking at her.

She screamed and tried to cover the front of her blouse with her arms.

He didn't move. His eyes were glazed.

Mira shrank back against the pillows.

He stepped forward.

Mira screamed again, but he didn't even look at her face. He didn't do anything. It was then that she realized he wasn't looking *at* her but *through* her. She glanced behind but there was nothing.

He jerked back.

Taking advantage of his distance, Mira grabbed her veil and held it to her front, moving back on the bed.

He didn't notice because now he was staring at something in front of her.

Mira looked down at the bed, trying to find what he was looking at.

He jerked back again.

She gasped at the look on his face, hard and cold, his eyes jagged pieces.

He looked at her, then back at the empty space in front of her, then back at her.

She stared at him, her heart pounding.

He turned and left.

Mira heard her front door slam behind him. She waited some minutes but he didn't return. Leaning up on her knees, she looked around, trying to figure out what he'd seen. There was nothing, just that cloying choking smell of rose.

Shaking, she got off the bed and walked back into her sitting chamber. The room was a mess, tables overturned, drapes ripped, ghee lamps spilled, pillows torn open.

She sat down on the couch and waited, staring at the wall, knowing he would come back.

He didn't.

Why did he stop? she wondered, shaking. And when would he try again?

She had to get away from the bhavan.

# 16

# Haunting

Mira sat up all night, writing by the light of the stars.

She wrote to her father, asking him to call her to Merta. She wrote that she missed him and she grieved for Shamal.

She jumped when the air twitched about her, even though she knew it was just a guard patrolling below.

She wrote that she wished she'd met Padmavati. She wrote that she wished she'd seen her brother one last time. She wrote of her pain at not being with her father at this terrible time.

She'd never written such things to him before.

As the night sky lightened and the stars dimmed, she watched the bridal dawn, dressed in pink and gold, waiting to garland the sun.

Bhoj left that morning on a border patrol and Mira was relieved. The thought of being near him every day was like a mango stone in her throat. She couldn't swallow it or spit it out.

Three weeks later when Ratan's reply came, Mira was sitting and embroidering in her solar, a room that had the entire south facing wall open to the balcony. She unrolled the silk letter and read:

"Your place is with Bhoj and your people."

Mira tore the letter to shreds.

She paced and sobbed and paced some more. She crouched down and gathered the ripped pieces together. She kissed a scrap of his handwriting and whispered: "I can't bear it, Bapu Sa."

*

Ratan had been traveling for months, back and forth across his land, trying to gain support. Over and over again, he told his people he needed their sons to defeat the invaders.

These families were farmers, potters, craftsmen. They were Rajputs by ancestry but not bred to fight.

This week Ratan's men had set up camp in Rampur and the mukhya, Chandramauli, had given up the best rooms in his haveli for Ratan's use.

Rampur was close to Chaukari and the two villages celebrated many festivals together. These people had rejoiced at Shamal's birth, and danced when they heard of Mira's wedding.

Mira.

Even though he'd rejected her wish, Ratan read her letter again every night.

Was Bhoj not kind to her? Was that why she'd written such a letter?

Ratan wished he could go to see her but he couldn't leave his people for even one moment. The threat was too near. Nor could he allow Mira to come here. Shamal had been assassinated in his very presence. How could Ratan hope to protect his daughter?

Many of his people were saying they'd fight if the Rana lessened their taxes.

But how could he feed his army with less taxes?

"Rana?"

Ratan turned from the window of the haveli's best room to look at the dark figure of Chandramauli.

"You called for me, Ranaji?" His voice was like sand, dry and rough and patriotic.

"Yes, come, sit with me."

Chandramauli waited until Ratan sat down in the large rosewood throne, before sitting on a lower seat.

"I shall never forget my debt to Rampur, Mukhyaji."

"We're only doing our duty to our motherland."

Ratan nodded. He ran his hand over his moustache, twirling the waxed end around his finger.

"Why are the other villages not as willing to fight as Rampur?"

Chandramauli sighed. "You mean apart from their being cowards, not worthy of the name Rajput?"

Ratan frowned, his thick brows meeting like soldiers from opposing camps. "I will not believe that my people are cowards."

Chandramauli's yellow turban dipped as he thought. He rubbed his knee with his hand, up and down and up and down. At length, he raised his head. "It's not that they don't have faith in you. They just fear the strength of the Moghuls. In the north, Humayun holds Kabul and will surely take Punjab. In the east, the Afghans hold Bengal and Orissa but they're weak. They'll fall to Humayun. And in the west, the sultan in Gujarat is even weaker than the Afghans."

Ratan knew it well.

"The people worry about their survival. They want their next generation to live."

"What are you suggesting? That I make a truce with Humayun?" Ratan smiled a bitter smile. "I've no second daughter to give, Mukhyaji."

"I think that is part of the problem. With Raj Kumari Mira in Merwar and Shamal martyred, the people wonder what will happen if you should fall. Who'll be your successor?"

Ratan scowled. "Are you asking me, Mukhyaji?"

Chandramauli's hand stilled on his knee. "No. I'm only telling you a concern the people have. It's not good to be without an heir, Ranaji. It gives rise to internal conflict."

Ratan looked down at his hands, studying the lines on his palms. He couldn't tell the destiny lines from the battle scars.

"The people might give their sons for the sake of peace during your rule. What about after? Who would take your place? Would there be more than one candidate? Would civil war tear our land apart?"

Ratan nodded. "There is no reassurance of lasting stability."

Chandramauli was silent.

Ratan went back to the window.

Rampur was famous for its chili farms. Outside, piles and piles of red chilies dried in the sun.

Holi was approaching and the women were outside designing rangoli patterns in white and orange and green on their courtyard floors. The children were running around, skipping over the patterns and choosing which one they liked best. The cows wandered, kicking up the dust and ruining the rangoli.

Out in the fields, the men were ploughing, ready for the great spring sowing festival.

Whom could Ratan adopt to replace Shamal?

He watched as below, his men were stripped to the waist, showing the village men the basics of weapons' training. The villagers were experts in the lathi pole and wrestling. The soldiers showed them spears, swords and archery.

Ratan's purpose in Rampur was fulfilled, and he would return to Chaukari tomorrow. He had to think about an heir.

*

Uda couldn't believe the way Bhoj was behaving!

It'd been two months since he'd returned from an unnecessarily long border patrol. He now ate all meals in the main palace and as far as any one could tell, never even looked at Mira.

There were rumors he'd taken a mistress but Uda didn't see any proof of that. For one thing, if he did have a mistress, it was a sure bet that the woman would let everyone know about it. Bhoj was a prize at any time but to seduce him away from famed Mira was a rare triumph.

He spent more time on the training ground than ever before. He was losing weight. He never mentioned Mira's name and if Uda chanced to speak of her, he left the room.

His eyes now had a permanent gold sheen to them, the blue burned away. All he had to do was look at his men and they were falling over each other in fright.

There were no rumors. In fact, there was a suspiciously quiet atmosphere in the bhavan. No one seemed to know anything about anyone.

There was other news though. According to insiders, Mira had decided to re-furnish and re-drape her inner quarters. It was necessary to paint the walls and beat the drapes twice a year but to redo everything? Most of the things were new, made for the bhavan, anyway.

Also, Mira liked to sit on her balcony at night, sometimes all night long. Why? The winter months were only just passing. Was she not cold out there?

Uda had a bad feeling about it. She feared Bhoj had forced Mira.

No. He could not. He would not. Not Uda's brother.

Mira's visits to the temple were more frequent than ever and Bhoj didn't say a word against it.

Matters had gone beyond the bhavan. Gauri now wondered aloud why her grandchild had not yet been born.

Every time she did, Bhoj would turn away and growl at a passing servant.

There wasn't much time before the situation exploded.

That morning, Uda finished her puja and sat down with her prayer beads. In the quiet, she heard a scuffle outside.

She went to the window. Squinting, she made out two figures in the faint dawn light. Squinting some more, she realized the figures were

Bhoj and Vikram.

They were wearing their morning white dhotis and must have just finished performing the sun obeisance together.

Vikram had his arm around Bhoj's shoulders and was speaking into his ear. Bhoj was silent. Then he flung Vikram's arm away and stomped off. Vikram grabbed him and Bhoj shook him off.

Uda put her beads down and ran out of her chambers. Descending the stairs, she ran into an empty sitting room that had a window near where they were standing. Hoping they'd not moved, she cracked open the shutters and peered out of the screen.

"Bhoj!" whispered Vikram. "Can you not trust me? I'm your brother."

"It's not that. You just shouldn't ask such questions."

"Everyone is worried! What's happening between you and your wife? Perhaps if you tell me, I can help you."

Uda bit her knuckle to keep from agreeing aloud.

Bhoj smiled. Then he chuckled. Then he laughed. "I'd like to see you try."

"What? What's so funny?"

Vikram looked so concerned that Uda wondered why she'd not thought to enlist his help before. He was perfect for the job. She just hoped they didn't move further into the garden.

"Even if I did tell you, there's nothing you could do about it. How does one fight the immortal?" Bhoj shook his head. "Leave it be."

"What immortal? What are you talking about? Bhoj, you're not making sense."

Uda clutched the shutter hard, digging her nails into it.

"Tell me!"

Bhoj once more threw off Vikram's arm. "It's complicated."

"Try!"

Bhoj leaned the back of his head against a tree. "Mira won't accept me," he said, his voice soft and sad.

"So? Make her."

"It's not that simple."

"Why?"

Bhoj dragged his palm down the tree. Bark came away in his hand. "She loves another."

Vikram went white. "I knew that female was too good to be true!"

Bhoj let his body slide down the tree. He sat on the earth, staring at nothing.

"Who is he?" Calm once more, Vikram drew out a dagger. "I'll go right now and kill him for you."

Bhoj burst into a fevered laugh. He laughed and laughed. "If only," he choked.

Uda watched in dismay as her brother crumpled before her. Curse Mira for this!

"If you cannot kill him then drive him from her mind!" Vikram leaned over Bhoj. "You haven't taken her yet, have you? Take her!"

"I've tried!" Bhoj shouted.

Uda flinched. Her suspicions had been right after all.

"What do you mean, you've 'tried'?"

Bhoj thumped the ground beside him. "I couldn't finish it."

"*Why?*"

"Something stopped me."

"What?"

"I still can't believe it myself."

"Bhoj! Tell me what happened!" Vikram shouted. Then he glanced around the garden to see if anyone had heard him.

"I got her on the bed," Bhoj sounded like he was talking to himself. "I was determined. Nothing was going to stop me. Then, from out of nowhere, there was–"

"There was *what?*" Vikram's jaw was clenched so tight he could barely grind out the words.

"A serpent."

Vikram looked as blank as Uda felt.

That was it?

Vikram scratched his head. "You've had a snake in your bed before, my brother."

Bhoj ran his fingers through his hair. "It wasn't an ordinary snake. There were...lots of heads. And eyes, red eyes. And lots of tongues, hissing at me."

"You mean there were lots of snakes?"

"No! There was only one snake. With lots of heads."

He's insane, Uda thought.

Vikram clasped Bhoj's shoulders. "What are you saying?"

"It was there, I tell you!"

Oh Bhoj, Uda thought. What's she done to you?

Vikram sat down beside Bhoj, his movement slow and sure, as if he were worried that Bhoj might get nervous and lash out. "What did this serpent look like?" His voice was deep and soothing. "Apart from the many heads and red eyes?"

Bhoj laughed. "I knew you wouldn't believe me. Now you think

I'm mad. That's fine. I think I'm mad too. I'll go fetch Didi and we can all think I'm mad together."

"This isn't a time to joke. If you think it was there," Vikram cast his gaze around the garden, "then I believe you."

"Very well." Bhoj swallowed. "It was black. Black like midnight. It had red eyes and they were like red stars. The hissing almost deafened me."

"Did it attack you?"

"No. It just waved around in front of me. Then it started to circle Mira and I thought it'd kill her. But it just circled her. Around and around as if it were protecting her."

"*Protecting her!*" Vikram shouted, then looked around to see if anyone had heard.

The garden was empty.

"Protecting her?" he whispered.

"That's what it did! It circled around and around, never touching her or tightening around her. And it lunged at me if I moved even a step forward."

"Stop it, Bhoj!" Uda clamped her hand over her mouth.

"Didi!" Bhoj sounded like he'd just been kicked. "Is that you?"

Cursing herself, she put her face up to the screen.

They both stared at her like fools.

"Come upstairs to my room. Now." She didn't wait to hear their reply but slammed closed the shutters and ran all the way to her inner chamber.

They must have run also for they arrived just moments after she did.

She locked the door behind them.

"What were you doing there?" Vikram snapped.

"I was going to ask you the same thing!" she snapped back. "What do the two of you think you're doing, discussing private family matters in a public place? Anyone could have heard you!"

Bhoj and Vikram looked at each other as if to say, "how did she manage to turn this on us?"

"Look, we have to talk. Continue with what you were saying, Bhoj," Uda said.

He sat down and held his head in his hands. "I didn't want you to know."

"It's too late for that."

"Didi's right, Bhoj." Vikram put his arm around Bhoj's shoulders. "Just tell us what happened."

"I told you, already. The serpent went round and round and I realized it was protecting her."

"What did she do?" Uda asked. She sat on Bhoj's other side.

"Mira? She...I don't know what she did." He scratched his head.

"Did she scream?"

"No. Well, she screamed but not because she saw the serpent."

"She didn't scream at such a monster?"

He shook his head. "She just...I think she just watched me."

Vikram and Uda exchanged a look.

"Perhaps she didn't see the serpent?" Vikram said.

"It doesn't matter if she did or not because I saw it." Bhoj's voice was loud and obstinate. "It was protecting her!" He looked at the wall opposite, his eyes bright and yellow. "Do you think it was Shesh Naag?"

"What?" they gasped.

"Shesh Naag. Bhagwan Vishnu's serpent."

Vikram choked. "I think it was your imagination! What would Shesh Naag be doing protecting Mira? You were claiming your rights!"

"What if I was claiming rights from the wife of another?" Bhoj looked at Uda.

She stroked his cheek. "No, my dear Bhaiya. No."

"If this is all true, how come we don't hear about Shesh Naag rushing to protect females all the time?"

"Lakshman was Shesh Naag's incarnation and he protected Sita, Rama's wife."

"But that's in the scriptures, not reality!"

"Vikram, lower your voice," Uda said. "My rooms are remote but others might still hear us."

"I swear to you, Didi. It was there. I think it was Shesh Naag."

She took a deep breath. "Will you listen to what I think?"

When he nodded, she wiped a tear from his eyelashes.

"I think it was your guilt that made you see that serpent. You didn't want to hurt her so you made up this vision to stop yourself."

He started to shake his head and she clutched his face to stop him.

"It's alright, Bhoj. Of course you wouldn't want to hurt her. You love her."

He held his hands over hers.

"It's alright. Now you must resolve this, once and for all."

"I can't try to force her again! She hates me so much already."

"She doesn't hate you. And I'm not telling you to force her. I'm saying that we have to go and talk to her. You and me. Maybe she'll listen to the both of us. We must just remember to be calm."

Bhoj squeezed Uda's hands. "How can I face her after what I did?"

"Have faith. This can be mended."

"You need a woman, Bhoj. That's what's wrong with you. Take a mistress. Or get Maharana to find you another wife and we'll throw Mira out."

"No!" Bhoj glared at Vikram.

"Then take her! Show her who is master." Vikram slammed his fist against his knee. "Look at the state she's reduced you to! Are you a man or not?"

"Vikram!" Uda snapped.

Bhoj rose, towering over him. "You know nothing of this matter. Were you there? Did you see her terror?"

Vikram stood also.

Uda jumped between them. "This is not the time for a duel! Calm yourselves."

Bhoj slumped into his seat.

Uda pointed to Vikram's seat and gave him a warning look.

He sat.

"Bhoj, you and I will speak to Mira."

He nodded.

She put her hand around his shoulder. Her poor brother. Talking about his delusions in public! A crown prince couldn't go mad.

Despite his obnoxious opinions, Uda was glad Vikram was here. She could never have made Bhoj confide this much.

Perhaps together, she and Vikram could find a solution.

Bhoj began to shudder into his hands.

She crouched down and hugged him as he wept, looking over his shoulder at Vikram.

Vikram mouthed three words at her. *We must help.*

She nodded.

\*

Mira's seventeenth birthday came and went, marking three months since that night. Her father sent her income with Raghuvir again, and she hugged her cousin hard. She missed Shamal so much.

Raghuvir couldn't stay long and left the next day.

Unable to sleep that night, Mira sat at her altar, holding her tambora in her lap.

If only she could see Ravi Das again.

Looking up at Krishna, radiant in purple, she pleaded for her guru.

No one in the royal family would talk to her anymore. When she went to see the queen, even the maids gave Mira angry looks.

She fiddled with the strings of the tambora, tightening some, loosening others.

*Always sing for Krishna, putri,* Ravi Das had said.

She just hoped her songs were good enough for Krishna. She prayed Mother Saraswati would sit on her tongue.

"I have only one, my Krishna Gopal, there is no other for me."

She strummed the tambora and the instrument hummed, filling the space around her.

"I find mercy, love, and strength in his shelter, his door is always open."

She felt her voice strengthening, like a flower opening to release its scent.

"He is my lord, birth after birth, he commands the workings of my heart,

"I have only one, my Krishna Gopal, there is no other for me."

Now that she'd started, the words just fell out. There was no hesitation, no pause. She just knew what she wanted to say.

"Lord Krishna Gopal is my true husband, he walked with me round the fire,

"He took my hand and smiled his smile, and I knew I was his slave.

"I put my trust in everlasting Krishna, towards whose feet the whole world bows,

"The sweet, gentle, compassionate lord, he is my husband for all time.

"I have only one, my Krishna Gopal, there is no other for me."

She felt a warm breath in her ear, though the air was still outside. Warm winds wrapped around her until she felt them move through the pores of her skin. She closed her eyes.

"My dark lord is the perfection of beauty; from him all shining things rise,

"It is he who controls my flowing words and singing tongue.

"Nothing happens without Supreme Krishna's wish, we are all in his thrall,

"Act only for his pleasure and the reward shall be eternal.

"I have only one, my Krishna Gopal, there is no other for me."

Her body lifted as the wind became swift. She swayed into the currents and let them buffet her from side to side. She opened her eyes and saw blurred colors about her. Pink and blue and orange.

"Where else can I go with my lonely soul, but to my master's abode?

"His is the only path that is true for he is the path and he is the goal.

"I chant his name awake and asleep, without him life is illusion,

"My duty is his name and my action is his thought, for he is my life's breath.

"I have only one, my Krishna Gopal, there is no other for me.

"I have only one, my Krishna Gopal, there is no other for me."

She strummed the tambora, its vibrations mingling with the wind and making a painting around her. Red and green and purple swirled and whirled her back and forth. The tambora's weight lessened until it floated in her arms.

"I have only one, my Krishna Gopal, there is no other for me.

"I have only one, my Krishna Gopal, there is no other for me."

The purples churned deeper and the greens grew taller and the reds burned brighter. And through them she saw blue-skinned Krishna watching her, his pink palm held out.

"I have only one, my Krishna Gopal, there is no other for me."

He arched his eyebrow at her.

The colors stilled, like a rotating wheel had stopped spinning. The tambora dropped dead back into her hands.

"Krishna," Mira called. "Where are you?" Her knees gave way. "Where are you?"

Two hands lifted her up.

She blinked and Bhoj's face came into focus.

She shrank back.

He dropped his hold. "Was that little dancing display like what you do in public? It's very entertaining."

Something clattered to the ground.

She looked down to see her tambora lying prone on the marble. Furious with her carelessness, she bent and picked it up, smoothing her hands over it to check for damages. "How long have you been here?"

His mouth tightened, his moustache bushing out with tension. "Long enough to know I was intruding," he looked from her to Krishna and back again. "Forgive me."

It was odd but he didn't sound as if he was mocking her. She eyed him, trying to read his face but it was impossible. She would never understand him, just as he would never understand her.

"I came to tell you something but–" he looked back at Krishna, "it doesn't matter anymore."

He sounded so calm. She couldn't believe this was the same man who'd ripped her veil away. The memory made her shudder but this man before her didn't scare her at all.

His hands were linked behind his back. "You may go," he whispered.

Mira looked around to check where they were. "But, my lord, you're in my quarters."

He rolled his eyes. "I mean that you may go wherever you wish to go. If you wish to go to Merta, you may. If you wish to go to Kashi, you may."

She stared at him. "Truly?"

"Yes. Go. But seek out what you desire quickly for I will call you back if I need you."

She couldn't believe he would allow this. "I can really go?"

"Yes."

"This is so…kind of you."

"Not kind. Desperate, perhaps, but not kind." He strode out before she could reply.

It took a moment to sink in. She could go? She could go! Finally, she would see Kashi. She would see her guru.

She looked at Krishna and laughed. Thank you so much, my lord! She skipped around the room like a little girl.

Soon, she would be with her guru.

# 17

# Fathoming

Vikram strolled through the garden. He knew what Uda wanted to talk about.

Poor, mad Bhoj.

Vikram didn't remember Uda arranging any special meetings on his behalf when he'd become an orphan. No, then she was all play and mischief.

Half of him was outraged that Bhoj was so emasculated. His other half clapped in glee that Bhoj finally knew what it was to have a woman not want him.

Vikram had never realized what a coward Bhoj was. All his life, Bhoj had never flinched before a horse, a test, a battle, a woman, or anything else. And yet all it took was one Mira to make all that come crashing down.

It was a simple problem with a simple solution. All Bhoj had to do was take her and take her until she submitted. They all submitted in the end. But Bhoj couldn't do it. He'd even invented a monstrous delusion to stop himself.

Vikram laughed out loud. Mira, *still* a virgin!

He tried not to think of how his own insides shriveled like dead leaves when Mira was near.

Bairam Khan's message had arrived: he was willing to work with Vikram in exchange for information. Information that Vikram had in abundance. It was just a matter of time.

The royal family was so concerned about the yuvraj's marriage that even the king had spoken to Bhoj about it. There was talk of a second wedding. Everyone was so distracted that no one would notice when

Vikram sat on the throne.

And now Bhoj had sent Mira away. Better and better. With Mira gone, people would forget their attraction to her devotee ways. They'd forget how she served them so well.

Vikram reached the door below Uda's quarters. He went inside and ascended the stairs, preparing to put on his concerned face.

Uda was at her writing desk, a pot of ink beside her and a quill in her hand. On seeing him, she put down her quill and waved her hand over the silk so it would dry.

She must be writing to that old mother-in-law of hers, he thought.

"Come in, Vikram. I shall join you in a moment." The ink must have dried because she rolled the letter up and placed it out of view. She rose and went to him.

He bowed. "Forgive me for not coming sooner, Didi. Kaka Sa has kept me busy with diplomatic missions over the past month."

"Yes, I know." She sat down.

He sat beside her. She looked haggard with those dark shadows under her eyes and her body thin as a bamboo stick. He glanced away in disgust.

"Bhoj has sent Mira away," she said.

"Yes, I know."

"You don't know everything. We kept it quiet."

He raised his eyebrows at her. "What don't I know?"

Uda hesitated. "She went alone. Just a few days after Bhoj...told us."

"I know she went alone, Didi. I thought it odd that he sent her just as the hot season was due to start."

"No, I mean really alone. She didn't take a guard with her."

He frowned. "What do you mean?"

"I mean she didn't take a guard."

It took him moment to comprehend. His spies had told him nothing of this. "Why? How could Bhoj send her away on her own with Moghuls and Afghans roaming the land?" Daud's rat face flashed before his eyes. Vikram stood. "What was Bhoj thinking?"

"He gave her a guard but she refused it."

"So what if she refused? She has to have a guard!"

"Bhoj has indulged her in everything so far, so he indulged her in this." She grimaced.

"Does he not know the dangers around us? Anything could happen!" She could be captured, he thought, a slave to some Muslim.

Vikram wanted to vomit.

"I agree. The thought of her alone on the roads is terrifying."

"What has been done?"

"I sent four spies out to follow her. They're trained soldiers."

"So she isn't without protection?"

"No. She just doesn't know it."

He heaved a sigh of relief.

The initial shock was wearing off and he registered that this was actually good for him. Once the people found out she'd traveled alone, the scandal would be so bad that Bhoj would never hold his head high again. Merta would rise up in arms against Merwar for such an insult.

She had to return soon, however. Vikram couldn't bear the thought of her unprotected. "A few spies are nothing against a troop of enemy soldiers, should she come in their way. She must return immediately. Bhoj must act like a man and order her back."

"Don't speak like that. I'm sure that something must have happened for him to send her away with no guard. She went to Kashi, he told me."

Vikram frowned. "Kashi? I thought she'd gone to her father's house. Why Kashi?"

"I don't know but at least it's a safe place for a Hindu princess."

"Except that she has to go past Delhi, the enemy's den, to get there! Is she in a closed chariot?"

"No."

"What?" He gawked at Uda. "She's in a palanquin? *All the way there?*" Even he would never have done such a thing to a lady. And in this heat! Why would Bhoj do this?

Uda coughed. She looked at her feet. "Er…she's not in a palanquin either."

Vikram narrowed his eyes. "What do you mean?"

"She's, well, er, she's…" Uda had gone so red she looked like the pomegranate juice Bhoj loved so much.

"She's what?"

"She's on foot."

He roared to his feet. "*What!*" Bhoj had sent her away–without a guard–*on foot?*

Vikram gave a loud snigger. "Was our gracious Bhoj so kind as to give her gold for food or is she to sell her jewelry?"

"She has gold with her."

"And will no doubt be robbed and killed if she's not dead already. Why didn't you tell me this earlier? It's been weeks!"

"I did send for you but how could I write such things down or even tell them to a messenger? It was sure to get out!"

Vikram sat down, trying to think. "We must send a guard to bring her back."

He tried to think about how he could use this in his plan but all he could think was that he wanted Mira home and soon, before the unthinkable happened.

Bhoj was out of his mind! He'd handed her to every thief, brigand and Muslim between here and Kashi.

"Where is Bhoj?"

"He's with Bapu Sa in the armory."

Vikram stood. "I'll go make him send for her."

"Thank the Kula Devi you're here to do something about this, Vikram. Bhoj won't listen to me. He keeps saying this is something she needs to do."

Vikram didn't care what Bhoj was saying about it, he just wanted Mira back in Merwar. Back in the fort.

*

Ravi watched as Mira traveled all the way to Kashi.

Bhoj had known she needed no guard.

She was a devotee and a devotee was never alone.

So Ravi watched as she slept under trees in the afternoons, the shadows quivering, rotating, hissing around her. He saw how she bought fruits from old women and gave money in charity.

Whenever she came to a new temple, she would sit there and sing bhajans to Krishna, playing the tambora Ravi had given her.

People would sit and listen, wondering who this girl was who enchanted them first with her face and then her voice.

Mira just walked along, searching for her guru.

She was followed by a gang of bandits. The first week, they kept their distance, thinking she must have someone with her. But as the days passed and there was no sign of a protector, they moved in.

Four died of snake bites. One disappeared. The last escaped to spread the tale of how Mira was guarded by a monster.

She never even knew the bandits were there.

No one was foolish enough to attack her after that.

Ravi awoke one morning and knew that Mira would arrive today.

Just after the noon hour, when all others were returning to their homes for the midday meal, he brought his needle and thread outside to stitch a pair of shoes. He placed a pot of water and a mala of Tulsi beads out with him. Basking his old bones in the heat made him forget the gnawing in his stomach.

Lona arrived with food.

Her hair was grey and wiry, her face was lined, yet she stood like a youth, poised and supple.

"Why do you bring food every day when you know I won't eat it?" he asked her.

She shrugged. "Habit." She looked down at the shoe he was stitching. "Let me do that. You must rest."

"No. You need not worry about me."

"I know, I know, Rama looks after you."

"He looks after you too."

She sighed.

Ravi looked back at his stitching. "What's the matter?"

She gave him an arch look. "You mean you don't know? I thought you knew everything."

"Don't tease me, Lona."

She sobered. "I'm worried about our son."

"What's the matter with him?" Ravi was counting the stitches he'd made.

"He wants you to live with us."

"He knows that's impossible."

"Mahendra wishes it also and he's ill. He says it's only your pride that makes you live on your own at this age."

"At this age, I should have retired to the forest but here I am still living a worldly life. Tell him that."

"But if you retired to the forest, how would your disciples find you?"

Ravi looked at her. "How do you know my thoughts so well?"

She sat beside him, crossing her legs. "I'm your wife."

He couldn't deny it. "Well, I'll tell you a secret, wife." He leaned towards her. "One of my disciples is coming here today."

"Pipa?"

"No, he's not my disciple. It's Raj Kumari Mira who's coming here."

"Raj Kumari Mira," Lona repeated. "Rana Ratan's daughter? From Merta?"

He nodded. "The girl who sings in temples and plays a tambora."

Lona gasped. "*That* Mira! She's Rana Ratan's daughter? They're the same person?" She shook her head. "But she's a witch! They say she practices tantric magic and wanders around enchanting people."

Ravi laughed, his breath wheezing through his lungs like holes in leather. "Do you really believe that?"

Lona gave him a dubious look. "She's guarded by a giant snake, you know. They say it's killed five people."

"Four. And Mira is a devotee of Krishna. A vaishnav would never engage in tantric magic."

"If she's really a Raj Kumari then why doesn't she have bodyguards? Her husband wouldn't let her travel alone."

"You're right, he wouldn't. Suffice to say she has a guardian."

Lona gave Ravi a shrewd look. "A guardian of the serpent kind?"

He chuckled. "I would tell you who that serpent is if I thought you wouldn't go gabbing to your silly friends."

She threw a handful of soil at him. "Hmph! They're not silly. And I don't tell them everything."

Ravi didn't bother to remind her she'd told her friends of her pregnancy long before she'd told him. "People can be silly at whatever age."

"Well, let me tell you–"

A shadow fell over them.

They looked up to see an orange skirt, and further up, golden hands clasping a tambora. Huge eyes gazed upon Ravi as if he were not real.

He hadn't expected Mira this soon. Clever girl.

She fell and touched her forehead to the ground. "I am Mira, daughter of Ratan Rathore. I'm here to beg initiation from Sant Ravi Das. Please accept me as your disciple."

From the corner of his eye, Ravi saw Lona watching Mira in wonder.

He smiled at the girl. "Raj Kumari, you're welcome here. But are you sure you've come to the right place?"

She held out the tambora. "I know you're my spiritual master."

"But what can I teach you?"

"Whatever you teach, I'll accept. I ask only for the path to Krishna."

Ravi saw broken bloodied spears. "It's a difficult road, Raj Kumari. Full of pain."

"I'll walk it."

"Are you strong enough?"

She looked at the ground. "No."

He smiled. "Good. You must put your faith in the Holy Name."

Her eyes pleaded. "Will you teach me?"

He looked from her tambora to her golden face. "I will."

Her smile was so blinding that Ravi knew Lona was overwhelmed.

"Thank you, Gurudev." She picked up the dust at his feet and placed it on her forehead.

Ravi reached for the water pot beside him.

Mira cupped her hands, left under right, and drank what he gave her without pause.

He held out the Tulsi beads and she took them, touching them to her eyes before winding the necklace around her throat.

He looked into her eyes. "Repeat after me: Rama."

"Rama."

"Rama," he said.

"Rama." She closed her eyes.

"Rama."

"Rama." A tear slipped down her cheek.

The sun was so hot Ravi's bones were melting. "This is your mantra, the mantra of your guru and your guru's guru and his guru before him. Never forget it, Mira."

She nodded, breathless.

"I'm now your guru and a guru is like a father. His relationship with his disciple is based on trust and love. You must follow my teachings with these principles in your heart."

"Ji, Gurudev."

"It's my duty to show you the path. You must open yourself to knowledge."

"Ji, Gurudev."

Ravi gestured to his wife seated beside him. "This is your Guru Mata."

Mira touched Lona's feet.

Lona raised her hand in blessing. "May you find what you seek, putri."

Mira's eyes glowed brighter than ever before.

She's come a long way, Ravi thought. She's walked leagues of dusty plains in the hot sun, facing the dangers of bandits and thieves. She's proven herself thus far.

Now comes the test.

*

It was like a dream.

Mira didn't think about Bhoj or Chittore.

She slept in a dharamshalla not far from Ravi's hut. Every day, she went to him for instruction.

One day, she took permission from her guru and went to see Udai who, at fourteen, was now taller than her. He grinned and told her he'd heard she was in the city and had been waiting for the opportunity to visit her and Sant Ravi. He asked her to take some letters back to Chittore for him when she returned and she agreed.

After a few days, some messengers came from the King of Kashi, who'd heard that Raj Kumari Mira was in his city. The messengers conveyed the king's invitation to reside in the palace. They themselves would be her guards.

She gave them a gracious message to take back, informing His Majesty that she was at present learning from her guru, Sant Ravi Das, and thus she wished to reside near him. She also had no need for guards and did not want to burden the king's soldiers. His Majesty's hospitality was acknowledged and appreciated.

The king sent her a message back saying that should she need anything at all, she must only send word and he would provide it.

With diplomacy out of the way, Mira concentrated on her guru.

Ravi taught her that the holy name was the basis of bhakti.

"For Krishna to be supreme," he said, "every part of Krishna has to be just as supreme as every other part." Because the lord was Perfection. That was the definition of Bhagwan. That meant that all the lord's different aspects were just as potent as each other. His touch, his sight, his hearing, his taste, his beauty, his memory. His love. His name. All were as powerful as each other. His sight could also hear. His taste could also see. His touch could also smell. His name could also love.

That was what made him Bhagwan.

And yet the name was above his other aspects for the devotee could control the name. The devotee could chant and sing the name whenever the devotee wished. And in this way, the devotee could control the lord. This was the power of Rama Naam.

That day, Mira composed a song on her tambora and sang it to Ravi:

"Oh my friends, I have inherited the wealth of the Naam,

"My guru was gracious and he gave me this secret,

"Know that I'm blessed to be singing this name,

"Oh my friends, I have inherited the wealth of the Naam."

Gurudev said it'd be a famous song.

He taught her that the beauty of the holy naam was that there were so many names for a devotee to choose from. Whether the devotee chose Rama or Krishna or Gopal or Giridar, it didn't matter. Krishna said that he cared not what name he was called by, only that he was called. And if he felt that a devotee was truly calling him, he would come.

Ravi taught Mira that the Upanishad scriptures instructed a man to search for enlightenment, not riches, for enlightenment was truth. Enlightenment was Rama.

He taught her that there were three paths as defined in the Bhagavad Gita, the song of Krishna. The three paths were gyana yoga, karma yoga and bhakti yoga. Gyana, the path of knowledge, was followed through deep meditation and inner contemplation. This was the path of introverts.

Karma is the path of action. As long as one lived in this world, one must act and in actions, one created reactions. In order to reap the fruits of these actions, one must be born again, creating more action and reaction, forcing one to be born yet again. The way to break free of this cycle was to dedicate each action to the supreme with no desire for the fruit, thus nullifying any reaction.

Bhakti yoga was the path of love. Bhakti taught that in order to achieve the lord, one must have a relationship with the lord, either as a father, a son, a friend, a guru, or a lover. The relationship of a lover was the highest, for while the other four were pure and true, they were based upon the idea of superiority and inferiority. A father is superior to a son. A guru is superior to a disciple. A friend can be independent of the other.

"But a lover only loves," Ravi said. "Lovers are completely surrendered unto each other. Both believe that the other is the master. Both are humble. Both are devoted."

Mira knew that bhakti was her path. She was too foolish to follow gyana and too weak-willed to follow Karma. All she had was her love.

Ravi explained that in truth, all yogas were connected and in following one path, the devotee developed skill in the others. An extrovert could not sit and meditate but in practicing the path of action, a karma yogi would be able to calm his mind to stillness.

Ravi taught her that in all three paths, the holy name was essential. The gyana yogi meditated on the lord's name. The karma yogi acted in the lord's name. The bhakti yogi loved the lord's name.

Gurudev told Mira that in this present age of Kal Yuga, the age of chaos, it was the holy name that would save the devotees. In this age, righteousness would decline and demonic action would arise. Sages would be tortured and cast aside as mad men. War would prevail. People would believe lies rather than truth. Women would be dishonored and men would place their greed above their honor. Children would abandon their parents and parents would mistreat their children. Gambling and intoxication would bring prestige. Simplicity and peace would be disdained. Nature would be raped and Mother Earth pillaged.

Mira knew it was true. Was Bharat not now invaded by plunderers and demons? Were the Rajputs in Merta not cowards to threaten rebellion? Were there not people who dared eat animal flesh and force others to deny the scriptures?

Gurudev told her this was only the beginning. As yet, children still obeyed their parents. Honor was still precious. Nature was not yet so violated that Mother Earth refused to bear fruit. Sages were still respected.

But soon, this would be destroyed.

Mira asked Gurudev if there was no way to prevent it. There had to be a way to save the coming generations.

Gurudev told her that the holy name was the only way. The scriptures said that in this age, meditation and righteous action would be difficult. Greed, lust, envy, and anger threatened on all sides. The only shelter was the name, for the name would give rise to bhakti. It was the way out. To love the name and chant it every day was to gain peace and knowledge.

Mira remembered how long ago, Guru Mata Indumati had told her the story of Vrinda, who'd chanted Vishnu's name every day. She'd loved him and served him. She'd been a pure devotee. And her devotion had made Vishnu her husband.

"Krishna, Krishna, Krishna," Mira whispered.

"Yes, putri, you must never stop chanting his name. Never let anything distract you from this path."

"How do I stop distraction?"

He told her of the dangers and seductions of wealth. He explained how riches deluded people into thinking they were their body, not a soul, seeking the lord.

Mira abandoned her silk clothes for cotton. She slept on the floor. She gave away the gold Bhoj had given her.

She wanted to serve her guru in any way she could and asked if she could help him make his shoes.

He told her this work was not in her karma.

She asked if she may cook for him for surely that was in her karma.

He told her he never allowed anyone to do that.

She asked if she could clean his hut.

He told her it'd be a waste of time.

When one day she was frustrated that he wouldn't let her do anything, he laughed.

"Putri, you need only sing for Krishna. That is your service."

He took her to Panch Ganga Ghat.

On the way to meet her spiritual grandfather, Mira was so afraid Ramanand Acharya would deem her unworthy that she almost slipped off the raft. After all, what did she have to recommend her? She was foolish and weak and ignorant, no match for the intellectuals who came to Kashi every day to debate the scriptures.

Then she met him.

He was the sort of sage she'd once thought her own guru would be like. He was bald except for a single lock of silver hair at his crown. He dressed in saffron and sat on a straw mat in a mud hut. He looked like a flagstaff, with his back so thin and straight and his single lock of hair flopping against his scalp.

He welcomed her like the long lost daughter of his clan.

On the return back down the river, Mira wondered at how blessed she was. To belong to such a line... Surely none were as lucky as she.

"Gurudev, which of Bhagwan's names are most dear to you?"

Ravi was looking at the temples that dressed the eastern bank of Ganga. "Rama is dearest to me for he is my Isht."

"What of Krishna's names?"

"Of Krishna's names, Gopal is dear."

Mira felt the raft glide over the river. Here, the heat didn't matter. She dropped her hand into the water, feeling the purity of Ganga Mata sliding over her, cleansing her. Just one bath in Ganga's waters destroyed the sins of all one's lives. Mira was so lucky that she could bathe here every day.

Feeling the coolness of Ganga against her hand, Mira wondered why the name Gopal was so dear to him. There were so many other names.

"I am a cobbler, putri." He said, as if replying to her thoughts. "I've always felt guilty that my work is with the skin of our mother cow." Ravi was looking downstream, his face solemn.

"That is why I always buy only the leather of cows that die naturally. I hate the thought of gai mata dying so that humans can walk around in shoes. Better to go barefoot than that. And yet, even though I work with dead flesh and am so impure, Krishna blesses me with so much." Ravi looked at her, his face calm and sad. "Gopal means cowherd, and Krishna is called that because he served the cows for the first twelve years of his appearance on earth. He showed us how precious our mother cow is and that is why I love the name Gopal. The cowherd boy."

When they returned to Ravi's hut, Lona was waiting for them, holding a package.

Mira touched Guru Mata's feet and took the food.

Gurudev had told her to eat whatever Lona brought. He never ate it himself but explained that this way, his wife would feel she was doing something and Mira would be fed and Ravi wouldn't have to worry about the package sitting on the floor.

Mira had refused the food at first, seeing how little her guru ate, but he'd laughed and told her to eat, saying that it was not in her destiny to starve. He added that she was at her guru's house and by rights was allowed to eat whatever her Guru Mata served her.

A week went by, full of stories about Sita and Rama and Radha and Krishna.

Gurudev taught her how to chant correctly, inhaling deep before she exhaled: "Ra...Ma..."

Udai visited Ravi's hut twice, saying that he had permission from his masters and that he wanted to hear Ravi talk and Mira sing.

On Somvar, Mira sat on the ground before Gurudev, her tambora in her lap.

Ravi was working on a piece of leather he'd soaked, beating it with a hammer.

Mira watched the leather grow thin and supple. "Tell me more about Krishna's childhood, Gurudev."

"You know this story, Mira."

"I know but I want to hear it from you."

His rock salt curls bounced as he laughed.

Mira never saw his hair look anything but clean and soft and curly, even though she was sure that he never combed it. She didn't even think he washed it.

Ravi pulled at the piece in his hand.

Many times, she heard him muttering to the leather, whispering secrets to it. She didn't have the courage to ask him what he whispered. It seemed so private. His work was his meditation.

He set the leather near the stove to dry.

"Krishna lived for the first twelve years as a cowherd in Vrindavan."

Mira hugged her knees in anticipation. Gurudev was wonderful at telling stories. Especially about Krishna.

He picked up a shoe he was repairing and began stitching it together. "He lived in the land of Braj with his foster mother Yashoda and foster father Nanda."

Mira nodded, her chin rubbing against her knees. These were her in-laws.

"He was actually born of Mother Devki and Father Vasudev. But you know why he went to Yashoda and Nanda."

"Tell me again," she said.

He poked the drying leather with a stick to move it closer to the fire. "Putri, you know this story by heart!"

"Gurudev..." she whined.

He put down the stick. "Fine. Kansa, Devki's brother, was an evil man and a vicious king. He would capture sages and make them perform puja to him instead of the deities. If they refused, he would burn them alive or whip them to death, or force them to eat meat, or work them as animals. He was so vicious that the demi-gods prayed for the world to be free of this tyranny. Krishna, as an oracle from the sky, told them he'd incarnate himself in the house of the Yadavs to kill Kansa.

"Now, if Kansa had one good quality, it was that he loved his sister Devki. He arranged her marriage to the Yadav Prince Vasudev and even drove them back to Vasudev's house after the wedding. As they were riding in the chariot, a voice from the skies called out to Kansa that Devki's eighth son would be his death. Fear overcame his love and Kansa took out his sword to kill her. To save Devki, Vasudev swore on the honor of his Yadav ancestors that he'd give every child Devki bore to Kansa. Kansa agreed and imprisoned the couple to be sure Vasudev kept his vow."

Mira frowned into her knees. Her mother and father-in-law had suffered so much, but bore it all for they knew they would be the parents of the savior.

"In time, Devki delivered her first child. Despite her desperate pleas and his own breaking heart, Vasudev took the boy to Kansa. Kansa, however, granted it life, saying he wanted only the eighth son, not the first. Then Narad, a celestial sage, went to Kansa and called him a fool. He said that the oracle had predicted Devki's eighth son would kill him but who knew where to start counting? Perhaps this child would be known as the eighth! Kansa went to the dungeon and tore Devki's baby from her arms, throwing it against the stone wall. He killed six of her sons this way."

Mira lifted her head. "But Gurudev, I've never understood why

Narad incited Kansa. Devki's sons might have lived if not for him."

"That's why Narad did it, Mira. If Kansa had gone on sparing lives, Krishna might have reconsidered the urgency or even the need to descend to earth. Narad, however, wanted Krishna to descend as soon as possible. For that, Kansa had to be more evil than ever."

Mira had never thought of it that way before.

"Devki became pregnant with her seventh child, Shesh Naag's incarnation as Balram. Shesh Naag always incarnates with the lord. When Rama descended, Shesh appeared as his younger brother Lakshman ."

"But Balram wasn't killed by Kansa," she said.

"No. By mystical means, the fetus was transplanted into the womb of Vasudev's first wife, Rohini, who was hiding from Kansa's terror in Braj, living with her husband's friends Nanda and Yashoda. Rohini gave birth to Balram there. Kansa was so arrogant that when the signs of Devki's pregnancy disappeared, he thought the child's soul had fled in fear."

Mira laughed. Shesh Naag was fear himself, the personification of death. How could Shesh fear Kansa?

"Devki became pregnant with her eighth child. Yashoda, who was at an advanced age and had given up hope of conceiving, also became pregnant. Into her womb entered Yoga Maya, the eternal maid of the lord and the goddess of illusion.

"One night there was a terrible storm. Devki and Yashoda went into labor at the same time. In the dungeon, a miracle occurred. All the prison guards fell asleep. The chains on Devki and Vasudev's feet fell off. The locks crumbled and the doors flew open. There was a great light and Krishna was born. Vishnu appeared out of the body of the baby. He told Vasudev to take the child across the Yamuna to Nanda's house where he must switch Devki's son with Yashoda's daughter."

Mira fretted with the end of her veil, pulling it and twisting it into a hopeless crumple. She saw the light streaming through the dungeon bars, burning the locks and chains to dust. It was Krishna freeing his parents from bondage.

"Vasudev did as commanded. He carried the baby out in a basket over his head. Outside raged the terrible storm and Vasudev worried about the rain lashing his son's tender skin. Then Shesh Naag appeared to shelter Krishna with his hooded heads and Vasudev knew it was another miracle. Still, he worried how he would cross the flooded river. He waded in, praying that he would live long enough to deposit his son safely on the other side. The Yamuna rose until she covered Vasudev's head but as soon as the waters touched Krishna's feet, the river parted and a dry path was provided across the river bed."

Even the Yamuna was calmed at Krishna's touch, Mira thought.

"Vasudev reached the house of Nanda. Yashoda had delivered and fallen unconscious without even knowing the sex of her child. And no one else knew she'd given birth for a strange magic had put them into a deep sleep. Vasudev laid his son beside her and took her daughter. When he returned to the dungeon, the doors closed and the chains clasped around him and Devki. The guards awoke and saw a glorious baby in Devki's arms. They ran to inform the king. Kansa arrived and grabbed the child but Devki screamed it was a girl. She begged him to spare her daughter for the oracle had said her son would kill him, not her daughter. It made no difference to Kansa. Just as he would have flung the baby against the wall, the child flew out of his hands and eight-armed Goddess Maya appeared before him."

The hairs on Mira's arms stood up.

"'Fool Kansa!'" Ravi said, putting on a high voice for Mira's benefit.

She giggled.

"'You're a fool to think you can harm me. Your Death has already taken birth.' And saying such, she disappeared. Kansa realized the child must've been smuggled out. He sent spies to learn how many children had been born that night in his kingdom. He killed every single one and yet, try as he might, Kansa couldn't kill Krishna. For twelve years he sent demons to slay Nanda and Yashoda's son but every demon died. Kansa realized this boy must be Devki's eighth child.

"That's how Krishna lived as a cowherd in Braj until he returned to Mathura and killed Kansa."

Mira smiled. "Tell me how he was named Giridar."

Ravi rubbed his eyes. "Will you ask me everything today, putri?"

She sat up, hopeful. "If I do, will you answer?"

"I shall try," he said, laughing. He looked towards the door. "I shall tell you all there is time to know."

He turned back to the drying leather, poking it some more. "Because of all the attempts on Krishna's life, his parents, Nanda and Yashoda, were certain someone had cast their evil eye on him. They decided to do a sacrifice to Lord Indra, the king of the demi-gods, to ask him to protect their son. Indra is, of course, Krishna's servant, and he'd become arrogant of the power Krishna had bestowed upon him. Krishna discouraged his parents from performing the sacrifice, telling them to honor Mount Govardhan instead, under whose shelter they all lived. He said it was because Govardhan caught the clouds that the Brajwasis had enough rain for the forests and fields and cows. Krishna, being Krishna, talked the whole region into doing a Govardhan sacrifice. Everyone brought fruit and grains to be offered into the sacred fire. When Indra found out, he was furious. He'd thought that Krishna was Bhagwan descended to earth but the true Krishna would never stop the mortals from worshipping the demi-gods. And Indra was the demi-god king! He deserved to be worshipped."

Mira laughed. Krishna teased his devotees so much, even Indra wasn't spared! "It was Krishna's compassion, wasn't it, Gurudev? He had to break Indra's arrogance before it led to bad consequences."

"That's right, Mira. Arrogance distances a devotee from the lord. Krishna doesn't want that so he does everything he can to break the devotee's ego."

"What happened next?"

"Indra was so incensed that he summoned his servant Megh and ordered him to flood Braj. In his pride, Indra had forgotten that it was against dharma to harm the innocent. Megh filled the skies of Braj with black clouds. The people grew worried and ran to their mukhya, Nanda. They realized that the rain clouds were the result of insulting Indra. Again, Krishna talked them out of pacifying the king of the demi-gods, saying that no god was worthy of worship if worshipped out of fear. The skies opened up and destruction reigned. Houses were swept away, Yamuna flooded the fields and forests.

"The people ran to Krishna and blamed him for the calamity."

Mira moved to sit cross-legged, jiggling her knees up and down. This was her favorite bit.

"Krishna ran to the roots of Mount Govardhan, and before anyone could guess what he'd do, uprooted the mountain and lifted it above his head. The Brajwasis couldn't believe it. Yashoda and Nanda couldn't believe it. And when they looked closer, they saw he was holding the entire mountain up with only his little finger.

"He told them all to come under the mountain and to bring all the cows and other animals with them."

Mira closed her eyes and saw a Blue Boy standing with his hand stretched above his head, balancing a mountain over his devotees.

"Amazed at this miracle, the Brajwasis danced underneath Govardhan, singing 'Jai Govardhan Giridhari!'"

"Giridhari."

"Indeed. The lifter of the Govardhan mountain. That's why we call him Giridar. Because he lifts mountains. He is the shelter from storms."

"Giridar," Mira said.

"The storm raged for seven days and seven nights. At one point, the men told Krishna he should rest and they would hold the mountain up. They thought Govardhan had been pleased with their sacrifice and become light and that was why Krishna could lift him. Krishna, knowing that their love made them think he was an ordinary mortal, agreed. As soon as he removed his finger, the mountain began to sink and the men realized that Govardhan was not light. Krishna held the mountain up once more, telling them that he wasn't really that tired."

Mira's mouth was buried in her forearms, muffling her laughter.

"At the end of the seventh night, Megh went to Indra to tell him that he'd run out of rain. Indra was outraged. How could Megh run out of rain? It'd never happened before! He took out his vajra weapon and went to Braj himself. Yet when Indra tried to throw his lightning down upon the people, his arms were paralyzed. In a panic, he called out to his guru. Brahaspati, the guru of the demi-gods, appeared and explained to Indra that his pride had crippled him. Indra realized his fault and begged forgiveness. Krishna removed his paralysis."

Mira hugged herself. Giridar, Giridar, when will I see you again, Giridar?

The ground was shaking but Ravi wasn't hammering. He was sitting, cross-legged, staring into space.

He closed his eyes. "Putri, go to the door."

Mira leaped to her feet.

A chariot pulled up outside. The design of the wheels and painting was Merwari.

She felt the earth tip sideways and reached out to clutch the doorframe.

A man on a horse rode up beside the chariot. He slipped off his mount and bowed. "Bahu Rani ki jai!"

No, no, this can't be a summons, Mira moaned. Not yet!

"Bahu Rani, Yuvraj Bhoj sends this message: 'You're needed in Chittore. Pray return with all speed.'"

Mira felt misery descend over her like a sandstorm, hard and dry and suffocating. What could be so urgent that he wanted her?

"You must return to Merwar, putri," Ravi said from behind.

She turned to where he sat in the depths of the hut. "I don't want to, Gurudev."

"My karma is to be a cobbler. I don't want to do it but it is my duty. Your karma is to be a rani. You don't want to do it but it is your duty. You must remember that we perform our duty for Krishna. He is our motivation and our goal. Our every action must be for him. The day you feel your duty takes you away from him is the day you may abandon it."

"But not today?"

He smiled.

Mira swallowed. She turned back to the messenger, her head high, her manner graceful. "Have you just arrived?"

"Ji, Bahu Rani. The guard is encamped outside the city."

"Then you must rest for one day. We shall leave tomorrow at dawn."

"As you wish, Bahu Rani," he bowed.

"Come for me at the dharamshalla tomorrow." She didn't bother to tell him where the dharamshalla was. He probably knew anyway. "In the meantime, go to Kumar Udai and get the letters he wishes me to take back."

"Kumar Udai is returning also, Bahu Rani, in a few weeks when he finishes his studies. Maharana Sangavat has commanded it."

"Why does he not just come with us?"

"He will be returning to his elder brother's fort. It is a different route."

"Then go and get those letters."

As the guard rode off, the chariot remained outside.

"I've been instructed to stay with you at all times, Bahu Rani," the driver said.

Mira sighed. "Very well." She pointed to where a nearby banyan tree gave shade. "You may wait there."

Stepping back into the hut, she looked at Ravi. "You knew, didn't you? That they were coming?"

He was silent.

"I'm afraid, Gurudev. I'm afraid that I'll go back and forget everything you've taught me."

"Mira, you have faith in Krishna, but you must also have faith in yourself."

She felt fat tears gather on her lashes. "Do you have faith in me?"

"I wouldn't have initiated you unless I did."

She blinked and blinked to banish her tears. "Then I'll go. I trust you. I trust only you."

"There is much for you to learn but it will come. You must be patient."

She met his gaze and felt her tears spill onto her cheeks.

# 18

# Declaration

Her chariot rolling across the valley floor towards the mountain, Mira felt her insides tie into knots.

She didn't know what to expect when she arrived in Chittore. Would Bhoj attack her again? Would she be confined to the bhavan? Would the Sisodias shun her still?

She looked out the window.

The road circumvented the mountain, each complete circuit going higher and higher until it reached the top. It was due to this natural defense that Chittore was virtually impregnable. The enemy not only had to climb a mountain that held mountain lions and other wild beasts but also deal with the defenses at each of the seven pols. Without help from inside, the enemy couldn't win.

Mira's chariot passed through Pandal Pol, the first gate, and the guards saluted her.

She passed through Bairu Pol, where a command center stood to house the troops of the lower mountain. There was a freshwater spring here, and a storehouse of rations. There was also a stable for the cavalry horses. In times of siege, it was these troops' responsibility to get the villagers up to the fort.

Bhoj had told her all this a long time ago.

The more Mira thought about it, the more she worried about him. She didn't know what had stopped him before but she didn't think she'd be so lucky again.

She passed through Hanuman Pol, its four towers watching for intruders.

She passed through Jorla Pol and decided that, as a precaution, she'd sleep in a different room every night. But how could she sleep in a different room and not be found out?

She passed through Lakshman Pol, where another command center stood. Here, the troops were refreshed every few days, for it was monotonous work staring out at the mountainside. The lions were abundant here and troops had to be alert.

She passed through Rama Pol and the guards saluted her.

Mira couldn't understand how she'd had the patience for this before. All the endless saluting and bowing! And how would she go back to serving meal after meal when she knew she could be talking about Krishna with Gurudev?

She passed through the final gate, Surya Pol, and saw people on the road turning to look at her.

They bowed as she passed.

Sighing, she rolled towards the city and saw the white flag of the Kumbh-Shyam mandir. It was a comforting sight.

Bhoj was standing outside the bhavan with the household, his arms crossed and his feet braced apart.

Her heart thumping, Mira saw the stern set of his features.

"Bahu Rani ki jai! Bahu Rani ki jai!" The servants cheered, grinning.

They really look happy to see me, Mira thought and a spark of warmth lit in her stomach. Perhaps it wasn't so bad to be home. These were her people.

Lalita and Janki were standing near the back, Janki jumping up and down to see her.

Bhoj came around to help her alight.

She accepted his hand and stepped down. Folding her palms, she bowed. "Greetings, my lord," she said above the cheering.

"I trust your journey was safe?"

"Very safe. And you are well?" She turned and waved to the servants, who cheered louder.

"I'm fine. Come inside." He strode into the bhavan.

Mira followed him. After seeing Gurudev's simple life, the luxury of the mahel looked so...foolish. She'd returned to royal clothes and was impatient with the slickness of the silk and the weight of the gold thread. The jewels around her neck were itchy where once they'd been so natural.

They entered Mira's suite.

"I'll be brief for I know you're fatigued."

"Thank you," she said, thinking he looked strained around the lips.

"Did–" he took a deep breath. "Did you find what you were

seeking? What you went there for?"

Mira wanted to tell him about Ravi but where were the words? "Yes."

His eyes reflected her, a gold spot lost in a blue sea. "Will you return to us now?"

"Have I not just returned?"

"What I mean is, will you return to being the bahu rani?"

She looked down. "Yes."

He shifted his weight to his other foot. "I–I want to ask for forgiveness."

Her gaze slammed into his.

"What happened that night...it won't happen again. I swear it to you."

Her face burning, she remembered how he'd hauled her into the bedroom. She swallowed. "I think we understand each other better now. Please don't humble yourself."

"I want you to know you're safe." He stared at her with such blank pain that she shook.

In that moment, she forgave him. "I believe you."

The air between them thickened.

He stepped back. "I have other things to tell you but it can wait. I'll leave you to rest," he said, shutting the door softly behind him.

Lalita, Janki, Savitri and Lakshmi poured through the servants' door. Janki and Lalita babbled the moment they saw her, giving her news on everything and everyone.

Smiling, Mira took each of their hands, even Savitri's. She turned to her altar.

It was empty.

Mira looked about the room but he wasn't there. She ran through the suite, searching, before rounding on her maids. "Where's Krishna?"

Lalita smiled. "Yuvraj took him. He said it'd be a surprise for you."

"A surprise! And there he was telling me that–" Oh Giridar! She ran out of her suite and around the balcony to the opposite suite. She reached the door to Bhoj's chambers and banged on it. "My lord!"

He came to the door holding a letter in his hand. "Is there a problem, my lady?"

"Did you take Krishna?"

He stared at her a moment before rolling his eyes. He grabbed her arm.

She tried to pull away but his grip was too strong.

He yanked her down the stairs and through the courtyard into the garden, the servants jumping to get out of the way.

Mira realized they were heading for the Kumbh-Shyam temple.

The guards gawked at their struggling master and mistress but swung open the gates nonetheless.

Bhoj pulled her through them. "Here's your Krishna!"

She gaped at the little mandir before her. It was an intimate place, the roof supported by slim pillars and a small inner room for the altar. It was set behind the main mandir, built of the same grey marble, but was surrounded by enough foliage to be private.

Giridar stood on the altar, garlanded with jasmine.

"I put the flowers on him myself this morning," Bhoj said.

"You–you made this mandir?" Mira's voice was small.

"Yes! So you don't dance in front of strangers and embarrass me."

Oh.

Bhoj pointed back to the bhavan. "He's even within sight of your balcony."

She looked behind her, her balcony plainly in view.

Lalita burst through the trees. "I'll see to Rani Mira, now, Yuvraj," she panted.

He narrowed his eyes at the maid. "You don't have to protect your mistress from me, you know. She's perfectly safe!"

Lalita jumped. "Of course, Yuvraj."

Bhoj glared at them both before stomping off.

Mira looked after him, her apology silent on her lips.

*

Ratan headed towards the dining hall for the noon meal.

The thunder was rolling outside, the rains not yet begun. Ratan hoped it would be a good monsoon this year.

His brother, Vikramdev, was already seated in the dining hall. Of course, Vikramdev would never miss a meal. If he wasn't obliged to train every day, he'd lie back and grow fat with sweets. As it was, his impressive size was enough to make men bow before him.

Ratan sat down beside his brother and nodded to a dasi for the food to be brought in.

The servants trooped in bearing platters.

All the food was prasad, offered to Krishna as Kusum had liked. It made Ratan feel like she was still with him, with her devotee ways. He lit a lamp on her Krishna altar every morning and every night, offering incense and flowers to the lord.

The servants trooped out.

"How is Babhi?" Ratan asked.

"She's well," Vikramdev muttered around the food in his mouth.

"I'm glad you came. The matter is crucial and I cannot afford to leave Chaukari."

"I know. Our forces are growing. I'm pleased." Vikramdev bit into his fudge.

Ratan tore off some roti bread and dipped it into the vegetable sabji. "I just hope we'll be prepared."

"I think we will."

"Our forces are still too small. We cannot hope to fend off a direct attack of Humayun's forces, let alone attack the citadel at Delhi."

"But we won't be attacking them alone. We'll have Merwar, Jodhpur, and even possibly the sultan in Gujarat." He sounded so calm, as if he was discussing the color of a flower.

Ratan scowled at his plate. "You know how I hate that man."

"It may be the only way. It's just a matter of time before the Moghul attacks Gujarat and then our ally Merwar will have a big problem, being right on Gujarat's eastern border."

Ratan sighed.

"We have to join forces with the sultan."

In truth, the situation was better than Ratan's wildest dreams. The coalition against Humayun consisted of Merwar, Merta, Jodhpur, Gondalgarh, Amber, and now Gujarat.

It only left one question. Who would control Delhi after victory?

Amber seemed the most likely of candidates, given its close proximity to Delhi, but who knew when Amber would change sides again? That province couldn't be counted on, despite its military strength.

Gondalgarh was too small to be a candidate and Ratan had heard that Rana Pipa was too engrossed in spiritual matters to care for national security. His young son had organized Gondalgarh's involvement in the Rajput coalition, not himself.

Merta could take over at Delhi but Amber would object.

It could come down to all the kingdoms leaving representatives in Delhi to work together as joint rulers. Which, of course, would never work.

Ratan thought Bhoj was the best candidate. With Bhoj at the helm, Delhi could once more be rebuilt as a Rajput stronghold.

The problem was that Merwar and Delhi had several kingdoms between them. And should Bhoj became the ruler of Delhi, Mira would have to go with him to the Red Fort. She'd be in the heart of the conflict.

Ratan didn't want her in the heart of the conflict.

There was another roll of thunder and a flash of lightning lit the colored panes of glass in the windows.

He rubbed his temples. "I'll have to announce my heir soon."

"Tell them Jaimal is your heir."

Ratan shook his head. "Chaukari is too big a province to be ruled from the capital, Bhaiya. Jaimal's responsibilities as yuvraj are too great for him to pay enough attention."

"Nonsense, he pays attention to everything."

"It's not the same thing. Chaukari is crucial to Merta's protection. She needs her own heir and I need someone who'll lead in war."

"You speak as if you'll die tomorrow."

"I wouldn't be surprised if I did."

"There's still time—"

"There isn't. Chaukari needs an heir." Ratan poured dhal over his bhati and mashed it about. Bhati was a homely dish of wheat that was cheaper than rice and Ratan tried to live frugally when he was at home.

Vikramdev threw up his hands. "Who do you suggest?"

There was a crash as the thunder broke right above their heads. The sound of rain falling on stone and glass echoed around the hall.

The brothers smiled at each other.

Ratan swallowed the food in his mouth. "Raghuvir, Rohini Didi's son. He passed seventeen years of age a month ago at Janamashtami."

Vikramdev scowled. "You only want him because he looks like Shamal."

Ratan clenched his fist, mindless of the dhal he was rubbing into his knee.

Vikramdev continued, not noticing the look on Ratan's face. "Raghuvir isn't directly in line. He cannot be your heir."

"He's the most capable person in our family. The time for direct lines has gone, Maharana. I've been watching Raghuvir for months and he's an able warrior and a good politician."

"My son is a direct descendent of Rao Duda. Chaukari should pass to him."

"Your son will be king and he needs a loyal lieutenant in Chaukari to serve him." Ratan saw Vikramdev's brain ticking over. "He needs someone like Raghuvir."

Vikramdev picked up a pakora and dipped it into the mint chutney. "Raghuvir is too young and inexperienced. Forgive me but your plans haven't gone well over the past few years, Ratan. I think it's best if I start making the decisions."

There was a pause. The rain was now pouring down.

"What?" Ratan said.

Vikramdev looked as if the pakora had turned into a burning ember in his mouth. He gulped down some juice. "I'm saying that, er–"

"Sacrificing my children for the sake of our country was a bad idea, was it?"

"Will you sit down?"

Ratan realized he was looming over his brother like an elephant. He sat down. "I didn't plan Shamal's death."

Vikramdev gulped more juice. "Of course not. No one blames you."

Ratan noticed a sweet laddoo on his plate. Normally, he never ordered sweets with his meals but the king was dining with him and Vikramdev had to have his sweets.

Shamal had loved laddoo.

"I'll tell you what I'll do. I'll send Jaimal over here to stay with you for several months." Vikramdev returned to his food with the aplomb of a minister. "You can show him the workings of Chaukari and anything else he needs to know. Then he'll be prepared to take over when necessary."

"That's generous of you, Bhaiya, but I still think that–"

"Jaimal will be your heir, Ratan. You haven't thought this through. What if Raghuvir's promotion to Rana of Chaukari causes a split in loyalties? I won't tolerate him usurping Jaimal's rights."

"I would train Raghuvir to never let ambition come in the way of the nation's welfare."

"And what if you name Raghuvir your heir and die the next day?"

Good point.

"The matter is settled," Vikramdev said, "I'll send for Jaimal today."

*

Mira had finished her visit to the queen when she decided to visit Uda. She hadn't managed to see Uda since she'd returned, what with settling back into the bhavan, and it was time to correct her lapse.

Uda was sitting on her balcony next to the light rain, holding prayer beads. She looked up when Mira entered, watching her like she was seeing something else.

"Pranam, Didi," Mira said, touching Uda's feet. Why was Uda

looking at her like that? she wondered.

"Yes," Uda said.

*Yes?* Mira thought. What had happened to the usual blessing of good fortune? She waited to be invited to sit but Uda didn't say anything. Mira shifted her feet.

Uda blinked. "Did you find what you were looking for?"

Strange, Mira thought, Bhoj had asked the same thing. "Ji."

Still watching Mira, Uda clapped her hands and Gita came in with refreshments.

Mira accepted a piece of coconut, pure white like Uda's garments.

"The monsoon shall end soon," Mira said.

"Yes."

"Durga Mata's festival is coming up soon. I'm organizing the celebrationn."

"You must be tired with the preparations," Uda said. "I hear you're planning to have the biggest rangoli competition ever."

"I thought it'd be fun." Mira was still standing in front of Uda, feeling awkward.

"I used to be an expert rangoli artist myself."

"Really? You must show me your patterns. Perhaps you can judge the competition."

Uda didn't bother to reply.

Mira fidgeted.

"My brother pined for you, you know. He barely ate."

The coconut became dry in Mira's mouth. "You exaggerate."

"I never exaggerate."

Mira gazed at walls that needed three coats of paint. "He built a mandir for my Krishna. Have you seen it?"

"Not yet. He wanted you to see it first." Uda smiled, then frowned. She looked as if she would say more but closed her mouth.

Mira didn't know what to make of Uda's behavior. "Do you know why he did it? Surely the resources were needed elsewhere. And to complete the project so quickly, within only a few months!"

"He'd been planning it for some time. He loves you," Uda said, sounding as if it was the most obvious conclusion in the world.

Mira tried not to squirm. "Then why did he say it was just to keep me from the Kumbh-Shyam mandir?"

Uda laughed, although she didn't look as if she was sharing the joke. "It's a sound motive. You've caused a great deal of scandal."

Mira sighed.

"Now that you have your own mandir, life will be easier." Uda frowned again. She opened her mouth, then shut it.

Mira sat down, tired of waiting for Uda to permit her.

"I don't go there just to get darshan, Didi. It's the one place in Chittore where I can meet devotees, people who understand me."

Uda looked at Mira, really looked at her, this time.

"So you'll still go to the Kumbh-Shyam mandir?"

"That's not what I said."

"Good," Uda rubbed her forehead. "There's something else you should know."

"What?"

"Many in the family, they–they didn't want Bhoj to build the mandir."

Mira had a sinking feeling in her stomach.

"In fact, they were urging him to cast you aside."

Mira's sinking feeling turned into a churning maelstrom.

"In ignoring their advice, he's put his honor on the line." Uda sighed. "You're a surprising girl, Mira. You've surprised me. Now, prove them wrong."

Mira didn't know what to say. She looked at Uda, but Uda had gone back to meditating on her beads. Mira rose and crept away.

The rains stopped and a refreshing month of calm passed. The cold season arrived and the winds came upon Chittore like eagles, swooping this way and that, never settling on any roof.

It was Mangalvar when Mira heard the whisper. She was passing by Bhoj's suite and there it was, like the wind changing; a flutter and a sharp turn, and Mira's veil stuck to her body, molding her outline for the world to see.

The shutters to Bhoj's windows were open a crack.

He couldn't be whispering, she thought. Bhoj never whispered.

The courtyard below was empty. Suddenly, the house seemed unusually quiet. Where was everybody?

Her heart pounding, she edged towards the window, pressing up against the wall and peering through the shutters into his room.

Bhoj's tall, muscular silhouette was framed by the light from the balcony. He was standing by a pillar, his arms crossed, his feet braced apart. The other figure was another man, shorter, but just as muscular. His head was bent and his hands were clasped together. He stood next to Bhoj, casting lumpy shadows on the floor.

It was her brother-in-law, Vikram.

She shouldn't listen. She should walk away right now.

Mira leaned forward.

"War is here," Vikram said.

The cold whipped in and goosebumps rose over her body.

"The coalition has challenged the Afghans."

She moved closer. He must mean the Rajput coalition.

"Some thought Ratan would appoint his nephew Raghuvir as his heir. The enemy must have found out because Raghuvir's body was sent back to Chaukari last week. He'd been skinned alive."

Mira's scream sank into her knuckles. Giridar!

"He was on a northern border patrol when they ambushed his party. None of his men survived." Vikram's voice was grim.

She was still reeling from his last comment. Raghuvir, her cousin, skinned alive?

"Ratan had to act. The Rajputs cannot tolerate yet another barbaric assassination."

She was breathing rapidly, her chest rising up and down, up and down.

Bhoj's voice was hard and capable. He didn't lower his voice. "Our armies will march alongside Rana Ratan's. We'll avenge this blow."

"Yes." Vikram whispered. "I'll lead our armies. You must guard Chittore."

"What are you talking about? I'm the yuvraj, I will fight. You stay in Chittore."

Mira's bracelet scratched against the window frame and she pulled back, hoping they hadn't heard it.

Vikram lowered his voice and Mira pressed her ear against the screen.

"–put yourself in danger when–"

"I will go and that's final."

"No!" Vikram grabbed Bhoj's arm and turned him around.

She realized her whole head was visible. Easing out of sight, trying not to jangle her jewelry, she crouched below the window sill.

"I cannot let you do this," she could hear Vikram saying. "*I* must fight this war!"

"That's my responsibility."

"Bhoj, don't go! The Afghans are barbarians!"

"That's why I won't let you go."

Her eyes wide, Mira imagined Bhoj cornered by dozens of Afghans, tortured and killed like Raghuvir. Oh Krishna, no!

"What if Maharana decides otherwise?" Vikram snapped.

"He won't."

There was the sound of something wooden being knocked over.

The wind whipped about her and Mira stared straight ahead, over the balcony railing to her front door. She clamped her ankles together to stop them from chum chumming.

"We must mobilize our armies. Bapu Sa has already called to his nobles for reinforcements."

"Yes," Vikram said.

"There's not much time."

"I know."

Mira didn't want to hear anymore. She couldn't.

Sliding out from under the window sill, she moved away.

When she entered the store room, Lalita stared at her pale face.

Mira took over directing the manservants but couldn't get Raghuvir out of her mind.

Counting bed sheets, she remembered when Shamal and Raghuvir had taken her into the jungle to look for tigers. They'd not found any tigers but they'd found the end of Ratan's beating stick. Kusum had screamed that they might all have been eaten by wild animals.

Prophetic words.

Mira wiped her wet eyes with her veil.

The servants had gone quiet, seeing her tears.

Lalita touched her arm, concerned.

"It's the dust," Mira said loudly.

One of Bhoj's men came to the door. "Bahu Rani ki jai."

She stiffened. "What is it?"

"Yuvraj wishes to tell you he has urgent business at court. He won't be here for the noon meal."

Mira nodded. "You may go."

She wondered if Bhoj would tell her what was happening.

*

He did tell her, that very night as she served him the evening meal.

He said that he and the king would be leaving in two days to meet Rana Ratan. Vikram was to stay in Chittore with an eighth of the army for the fort's protection.

He didn't tell her about Raghuvir.

Mira couldn't sleep, picturing her cousin without his skin, like the goats in the kitchen. And Bhoj was going to fight the demons who'd done that to Raghuvir! What if they hurt him?

She cried and cried.

There was controlled chaos the next day as the soldiers prepared to leave. The men walked around, grimly alert. The women walked about, heaviness in their eyes.

Mira prayed. She prayed that Raghuvir's soul be protected by Krishna. She prayed that if death must come to the last men of her family, they wouldn't be skinned alive. She prayed they'd die with their Isht Dev's name on their lips.

The morning he was to leave, Mira entered Bhoj's quarters with an aarti tray in her hands. The sun tinging the eastern horizon pink and yellow, she applied the red tilak to his forehead and circled his face with the lamps.

His eyes shone gold.

She turned to his sword that rested on a cushion and applied a red tilak to the long curved blade before showering it with flowers. She lay down the aarti tray and lifted the sword, careful not to cut herself. It was heavy in her hands, rubies set into the golden hilt.

She touched the blade to her forehead and held it out to him.

"Vijay ho," she said.

Be victorious.

Bhoj took the sword from her and touched it to his forehead. He slid it into the sheath at his side and turned to meet her gaze.

"I will be."

There was a long moment when she thought he'd say more. Then he was gone.

The weeks passed and the wind grew bitter.

Mira saw the guards patrolling the walls with their eyes squeezed into narrow slits, protecting them from the swirling dust.

The pols were clamped shut and only ever opened when a soldier bearing the king's own banner rode up.

Pigeon birds flew to and from the fort, circling the parapets as they descended to sit upon Vikram's arm.

Now the armies were camped at Chaukari. Now the armies were joined by the sultan's forces. Now the armies were amassed at Amber.

Now there's a scuffle at Agra. Now there's a run-in at Kurukshetra. Now the Afghans are beaten back.

Mira spent her days in the temple with the devotees. It was the best place she could be, despite all the rumors of the past. Her people needed their faith and she must be an example.

Lamps were lit in every home that had sent a son to war.

Mira would go up to the roof of the bhavan at night and see the lamps in the windows of the city. They looked like glimmering constellations, floating in a black sky.

Two and a half weeks went by with no news, until on a Mangalvar when a messenger rode in.

The royal family rushed to the assembly hall to hear the news.

Vikram was there, standing by the throne.

Gauri walked up to him. "What is it, putra? What is the news?"

He was silent.

Mira put her hand on Gauri's shoulder. She looked at Vikram. "What is the news, Jehtji?"

He didn't look at her.

"Well, Vikram?" Uda was glaring at him for the delay.

He seemed to shake himself. "The battle is over, Kaki Sa. Our men are returning."

Cries of thanks were shouted up to the heavens.

Maharani Gauri laughed out loud. "Let there be a celebration. Send out heralds to our people: Maharana returns victorious!"

Vikram held up his hand. "He is wounded."

Gauri stiffened beneath Mira's hold, and slid to the ground.

"Maharani!" Mira caught the queen in her arms.

Uda helped lay Gauri on the floor and fanned her.

The other ladies fell to the floor also. "Maharani!" they cried.

Vikram knelt at Gauri's side.

"How badly is the king wounded, Jehtji?" Mira asked.

The others looked at him.

Vikram touched Gauri's cheek. "He took an arrow to the stomach."

The ladies gasped and started to cry.

Mira steeled herself. "Will he die?"

Vikram was pale. "I don't know."

Mira stroked Gauri's brow. "What of our men?"

"Most are returning with Maharana. Some are going to Amber for talks with the coalition."

"Did we lose many soldiers?"

"Not as many as expected."

"And what of my father?"

"He lives. It was he who stood over our king and protected him."

Gauri opened her eyes. "Where is my husband?"

"Ma Sa," Uda said, "Bapu Sa is returning and you will see him soon. You must now pray for his life, not lie in a faint."

The queen sat up. "You're right."

Mira concentrated on Vikram. "How did we win?"

"Yuvraj rode his cavalry into the thick of the battle where Rana Ratan's men were surrounded. He managed to rout the Afghans and send them retreating like the cowards they are."

"Yes, yes, that is my son! My son has won this war!" Gauri clung to Mira's hand as she rose, glaring at the women in the hall. "My son!"

"Your son," Vikram whispered.

Mira shivered. She slid her arm around her mother-in-law's shoulders and started to lead her from the hall. Mira tried not to think about what would happen should the king die.

Bhoj would be king. Mira would be queen.

No, Sangavat couldn't die.

"Kaki Sa, wait." Vikram said.

Mira turned with Gauri.

He was clutching the lion's head on the arm of the throne. He opened his mouth to speak but nothing came out.

"What is it, putra?" Gauri asked.

"Our army returns… It returns–without Yuvraj."

Mira rocked back as if he'd slapped her.

"*What?*" the ladies shrieked.

Gauri broke free of Mira and ran to Vikram. "You mean that he's staying with the coalition, correct?"

He shook his head.

"What do you mean, 'no'? It was he who won the war!"

Vikram wept over the lion. "He is dead."

Mira didn't believe it. It couldn't be true.

Gauri started beating Vikram's chest with her fists. "That's a lie!"

Uda ran to stop her mother, even as tears streamed down her face.

"Let go of me!" Gauri rounded on Uda with a ferocious look. "This is your fault. You cast your shadow over my son!"

Everything slowed down for Mira. She could see every twitch and blink. She watched as Gauri reared back and slammed her hand against Uda's cheek, the sharpness echoing in Mira's ears. She watched as Uda staggered and fell at the foot of the throne, tiny drops of blood splattering the ground. She watched as Vikram grabbed his aunt and held her, Gauri's face hidden against his chest. Mira watched as the ladies around her beat their fists against their heads, strands of hair falling from their pins. She watched as Uda held her cheek, tears making wet her white veil.

Vikram said Bhoj was dead. How could that be? Bhoj was so alive. Even when he wasn't near, she could feel him.

This couldn't be happening. Mira felt herself sway.

She fell to the ground. She thought she should help Uda but somehow, her limbs wouldn't move.

"I'm sorry," Uda moaned, clutching her face.

Mira watched as the women threw their shoes at Uda's head, some hitting Uda so hard that livid gashes appeared. Stop it! Mira tried to say but her throat felt strangled.

Uda backed out of the hall, stumbling over lamp holders and seats.

Mira turned to see Vikram rubbing Gauri's back, whispering into her ear.

He was smiling.

# 19

# Culpable

Mira sat on her couch. Her room looked so odd, smaller and yet larger, as if it were shrinking and expanding like a flower bud.

She'd told Bhoj he was her Rana.

Uda had disappeared, probably to her own chambers.

Mira knew how Uda felt, having lost a brother also. Two brothers, Mira thought, remembering Raghuvir. No, four brothers, she corrected, thinking of Ranjeet and Raagav.

Giridar, why is this happening?

Gauri was inconsolable, keening in her chambers.

Mira thought of Krishna's mother, Devki, who'd borne the pain of losing six sons.

Gauri had lost just one and was out of her mind with grief.

Lalita and Janki came in, crying into their veils.

Lalita went straight to Mira and put her hand on Mira's shoulder. "Jiji…"

Janki hiccupped and Mira laid her hand on Janki's thin back.

Lakshmi came in, her mouth open but no words coming out.

Savitri came in, silent tears running through the maze of her wrinkles. "Kumar Vikram asks that you attend the queen." She held her hands to her upper arms as if to shield herself.

Mira embraced the elderly maid. "Then let us go."

She walked out of the bhavan that Bhoj had built for her with its private little mandir right next to the Kumbh-Shyam temple. It suddenly hit Mira that Bhoj would never return to eat the meals she cooked for him. She would never again see that his clothes were washed. She would never again perform his aarti.

Walking down to her palanquin, her maids crying behind her, Mira couldn't believe this was real.

It was nearing sunset. No lights had been lit in the city.

She could hear the wailing beyond the bhavan walls, thousands mourning their prince. As her palanquin left, she looked towards the great temple.

No lamps had been lit there either. The bells were silent. Even Vishnu mourned.

Suddenly, Mira wanted to lie down and keen as loud as Gauri. She'd weakened Bhoj, just like she'd weakened Shamal.

She willed her tears back. From this moment on, she wouldn't let one drop fall from her eyes. She didn't deserve to weep for him.

Gauri lay in the dark, her hair pulled out of its pins, her body curled up as she hugged her womb. The ladies were sitting around her, rubbing her legs, fanning her.

Mira stood in the doorway. She'd never seen such a sight.

Buaji was at Gauri's head, holding a cup of water. "Babhi, you must drink. How will you care for your husband if you're so weak?"

"No, no water. My son is thirsty, how can I drink when my son is thirsty?"

Buaji's face crumpled.

Mira now realized that every word Buaji had said about her was right. Mira did deserve to be an outcast. She did deserve to be hated. She was bad luck, worse than Uda, worse than even the worst curse.

Buaji held the cup to Gauri's lips. "You must drink."

"No! My son is thirsty!"

Mira couldn't bear it. "Your son is beyond thirst and hunger, Maharani."

"Bahu? Is that you?" Gauri looked towards the doorway.

Mira met and held her gaze.

"Were you weeping all alone in your room? Yes, you were. My poor widowed Mira."

Mira forced her feet to move. She took the water from Buaji and held it to her mother-in-law's lips.

Gauri pushed it away. "My son needs water."

With a firm hand, Mira subdued Gauri's resistance. "Maharani, you must stop this."

"How can I stop, bahu?" Gauri suddenly punched her own stomach. "My womb has been robbed!"

"Maharani!" Mira grabbed Gauri's hands.

The other ladies reached in to help.

"Do you know the pain of losing a son, bahu? It's much worse than the pain of birthing him."

Mira wanted to scream her guilt. Her chest felt so tight and heavy. She wiped the queen's face.

Gauri opened her eyes. "Bahu? What are you wearing?" She turned to the women around her. "Do you see this? My Mira hasn't realized she must now wear white. Perhaps I will soon wear white also."

Buaji snapped her head up. "Babhi! No wife even imagines her husband's death."

Gauri looked at Buaji. "The mother in me is devastated today. What if my bangles break and my forehead wiped clear? What then, sister-in-law? Then I will be a widow, just like my wretched daughter."

"Maharani," Mira said, "whatever happens, you're still our queen and the people look to you for strength." She wiped the drops that rolled down the queen's cheeks, feeling the weight of the other women watching her. "You're a Kshatraani," she told the queen. "You know that the ultimate meaning of a Kshatriya's life is death in battle. Your son has died saving his people. Be proud of him. Be proud."

Gauri gazed at Mira. "I would rather hold him in my arms than celebrate his death."

"You must celebrate it. He is a martyr."

"But this pain, bahu! I held him in my arms and taught him to walk. And he called me Ma Sa and kissed me and hugged me."

"I will call you Ma Sa. I will hug you."

Gauri touched Mira's cheek, her tears falling silently. "How kind you are, bahu. Keep praising your husband's memory. It makes me feel he is close."

"He wasn't my husband, he was your son. He was what he was because of you."

Every lady was watching Mira, respect in their eyes.

Gauri lifted her hand to wipe away Mira's vermillion.

Mira pulled back. "You must save your strength, Ma Sa."

Gauri lowered her hand. "My poor Mira, so kind, so strong."

*

Maharana Sangavat was carried on a litter into the palace, maids showering him with pink and red petals. His skin was grey as he clutched his sword to his side.

As Sangavat passed the ladies, Mira held Gauri's hand.

Yuvraj's pyre was lit on Merta's soil, the generals were saying.

As the king lay on his bed, the Raj Vaids cut off his bandages.

Mira stared from his feet. His stomach looked like the poor slaughtered sheep she'd once seen, hacked to pieces by the cook. She gagged and clapped her hand over her mouth.

"Maharani…" he whispered and the queen knelt at his head.

The vaids were measuring medicines, mixing them with boiled water. They began cleaning the wound.

Mira prayed to Krishna. Perhaps the wound wouldn't look so hopeless once cleaned.

One of the vaids explained that the arrow had been removed and the wound sewed but the stitches came apart when Sangavat heard of Bhoj's death. The king hadn't allowed anyone to touch him after that.

Bloody cloth after bloody cloth was heaped in a pile on the floor, making the marble slippery. The more blood they wiped from the king, the more spilled out onto the bed, like a dam had broken.

The vaid continued, saying that he'd given the king herbs for the pain but the wound was deep. There was no telling how much he'd bled internally.

The head vaid was boiling a needle and thread.

The steam was such a relief. Mira felt drops of clean water on her face.

Another vaid held a cup to Sangavat's mouth. "Drink this, Maharana."

He turned his face to the side. "Let me die."

"No!" Gauri cried. She wiped the sweat from his brow. "You mustn't speak like that, my lord."

Sangavat's body heaved as he coughed. Blood rolled into his beard. Gauri wiped it as best she could.

"Our son was like a lion, my lady," he told her. "The whole battlefield heard his roar." He coughed again, and his wife wiped up the blood.

Mira saw how they held each other's hands. She turned to Vikram and the generals. "This room is too crowded, my lords. We must leave the vaids to their work."

Vikram studied her with Bhoj's blue eyes.

She was stunned by the pang in her heart.

"Is that Mira?" Sangavat asked. He lifted a red hand towards her.

Vikram motioned to the generals to leave the room.

Mira turned away from Vikram and knelt at the king's feet.

"Come closer," he coughed.

She sank down at Gauri's side. "Maharana, you must rest."

"I have a message for you, bahu."

A message?

The red and pink rose petals had mixed with the blood to make thick, clotted syrup. As Sangavat writhed, clumps of syrup fell to the floor with soft plops.

How could one man hold so much blood? Mira wondered.

The head vaid shook his head at the others and turned to a servant. "Call Raj Purohit."

The end was near, Mira realized. "Maharana, shall I call Uda?"

"No!" Gauri snapped. "That girl shall not enter this room."

"Call her." Beads of sweat sank into the pillow.

Mira nodded at a servant who ran from the room.

"Where is Vikram?"

"Here, Kaka Sa."

Mira almost jumped out of her skin to hear Vikram behind her. She'd thought he left with the generals.

The head vaid was trying to sew up the king's stomach but Sangavat was heaving about and the vaid couldn't get his stitches accurate. The other vaids tried holding Sangavat down, pressing cloths hard on the wound to stem the blood loss.

Sangavat went from grey to white.

Mira watched Vikram go to the other side of the bed and take his uncle's hand.

Sangavat squeezed as a spasm overtook him.

"If only you'd let me come with you," Vikram whispered.

Sangavat sagged. "I'm glad you didn't come," he panted. "I'm glad Bhoj is dead and not you."

What? Mira thought. *What did he just say?*

Gauri nodded, even as she cried into the bed sheets.

Mira realized how little she knew of this family. She looked around at their faces, so fair and tense and private. She didn't belong here.

"I couldn't have faced my ancestors or my brother had I lost you, Vikram."

His brother, Vikram's father.

Mira saw Vikram searching Sangavat's face, his own pensive.

"Kaka Sa, how can you say this?"

"I swore I'd hold your life dearer than my own son's. It was my promise to my brother."

Vikram stared.

"Now you must rule Merwar." Sangavat's face contorted.

Then he went still.

"My lord!" Gauri screamed.

"*Kaka!*" Vikram shouted.

Sangavat's mouth opened and his words were so faint, all three leaned down to hear it.

Uda ran in. She swayed at the sight of her father.

"Uda?" Sangavat whispered.

Mira leaned in. "Yes, Maharana, she is here."

Uda knelt behind Vikram.

"Putri?"

Uda's tears fell hot and wild and free, like the monsoon rains.

Sangavat seemed numb, not even noticing the pressure the vaids were putting on his stomach. "I'm sorry I didn't console you, putri."

Uda rocked back and forth. "No, Bapu Sa."

Gauri wiped her husband's forehead. "But it's her fault!"

Uda's owl eyes were wet and blurred.

Don't listen to her, Didi! Mira thought.

"We were wrong to blame her," Sangavat said.

"Bapu Sa, just rest," Uda pleaded.

Mira gazed at Sangavat. She wished she'd known this man who'd fathered Bhoj and Uda. Bhoj used to tell her wonderful stories about him.

"Putri, I think he knew he was going to die." Sangavat said to Uda. "The morning before the last battle, he told me things he'd hidden for years. Things about you."

Uda was immobile, her eyes fixed on her father's face.

Mira was frozen, wondering how Bhoj had known he would die.

"He told me how your husband abused you. How you always denied it but he knew it was true."

Gauri stared at Uda.

Mira wasn't surprised at Sangavat's words.

"Uda, I failed to protect you."

"Bapu Sa, it wasn't your fault. I failed, not you."

He went into another spasm, and blood made pink his clenched teeth. He sagged once more. "That's not what Bhoj said, putri. Forgive me."

Uda shook her head, her mouth screwed up like her mother.

"Mira?" he rasped.

"Ji?"

"Bhoj said that–" He spasmed, heaving under the pressure, twisting Vikram's hand up and down.

Everyone reached in to hold him down lest the wound open more.

"My lord!" Gauri screamed.

Sangavat was suddenly calm. He looked about. "Mira?"

"Ji?"

"Bhoj said he was sorry. He prayed that you and Shri Krishna would forgive him."

She clutched her throat.

"Is he forgiven, bahu?"

"There was nothing to forgive, Maharana," she choked. "Nothing at all." Mira saw the light in his eyes grow dim, just like Kusum, and she swallowed. "Turn your mind to your Isht, Maharana. Remember your Isht!"

The vaids lifted their hands from the king's body.

Raj Purohit had arrived, a beacon with his silver hair and pure white garments.

Mira sank back in relief.

"Sangavat?"

Sangavat turned his head to the priest.

"It's time to let go of this world, putra. Turn your mind to your Isht Shiv."

Sangavat closed his eyes. "Aum namah shivaya, aum namah shivaya, aum namah shivaya," he chanted.

His ears lifted, as if they were trying to hear something.

Then silence.

*

Mira watched as Gauri bathed, pouring water over her black head. Her forehead cleared of vermillion.

Maids cut off her hair, lock by lock, until there were only tufts of black poking out of Gauri's scalp.

She wrapped white garments around herself and removed her mangalsutra, the necklace given to her by her husband on their wedding day. She smashed her glass bangles against a pillar so that shards fell to the ground, some embedded in her wrists.

She didn't tell Mira to change into widow's garb.

The ladies returned to the king's chamber to ready him for his final journey. They washed his body of the red and pink and brown and dressed him in clean clothes of white silk.

The maids brought in a garland of flowers, jasmine and rose.

Mira laid it around his neck with Gauri looking on.

The men entered. They placed the king's body onto a litter and hoisted it to their shoulders, carrying him to the great hall where the court would pay their respects.

The ladies followed as did Uda, who was somewhere at the rear.

Raj Purohit, accompanied by Brahmins, chanted mantras. "Oh Lord Narayana, grant salvation unto the departed soul."

Lord Narayana, Vishnu's other name, Mira thought.

"Protect him from the coil of rebirth and accept him into your abode."

Mira prayed with the priests that Sangavat's soul find liberation. Let him never have to come back into this world, Narayana.

Vikram performed the son's duty of offering oblations to the deceased.

The family stepped in line of rank to offer their respects.

Gauri laid her flowers at his feet. With a face of stone, she touched her forehead to his toes. She circumambulated her husband clockwise, once, twice, three times. She bowed and backed away.

Mira offered her flowers, circumambulated, and backed away.

Uda offered her flowers. She circumambulated her father with hollow eyes.

The men of the household came next, uncles, cousins, brothers-in-law, nephews, friends, generals. Udai, Bhoj's favorite cousin, offered white rose petals.

The ladies came forward, sisters, aunts, cousins, sisters-in-law, nieces, daughters-in-law of the clan.

Raj Purohit found an auspicious time for the cremation at the height of the noon hour.

The men, led by Vikram, hoisted the king's litter onto their shoulders and carried him away from the women.

Mira knew that Sangavat would ride through the fort in state on an open chariot so his people could take their last darshan of him. Once his party reached the cremation ground outside the city, Vikram would say the last prayers and set the king's body aflame.

*

Thick night fell before Mira crept out of Gauri's bedchamber.

She still couldn't believe this was happening. She kept thinking that Bhoj would soon return to Chittore, triumphant.

How could he not when she loved him so much?

Oh yes, she loved him.

He'd sent that message with Sangavat and now something inside her was shattered.

He wanted forgiveness when, in truth, she should have begged forgiveness of him.

If Mira now wore white and proclaimed to be his widow, he'd never forgive her. He'd think she was mocking him, when he had sacrificed everything for her.

She prayed that he knew she loved him. Her Rana. Her Bhoj.

She prayed that he forgive her.

\*

As the new sun rose over the city fort, Vikram watched the priests sweep up the last dusts of his uncle's body and place them into a great casket, ready for their immersion into the holy Ganga.

The other men had gone to the gates where servants waited to douse them in water before they entered the city.

Vikram stayed on the cremation ground.

Sangavat had cared more for Vikram's life than Bhoj's.

Yet it had been Vikram who'd sent messengers to the Afghans and Moghuls, telling them everything about Sangavat and Ratan's strategies.

Vikram had betrayed his own blood.

Mira knew Bhoj was dead but she didn't know his hands and arms had been cut off, bit by bit, before he'd fallen under the killing blow. Now she was mad with grief, they said. She wouldn't change into widow's garb.

Vikram had never felt so cold. He was sitting in the Himalaya ice like Bhagirath, except that Bhagirath had borne the ice for his clan's salvation, to appease Lord Shiv and bring the holy river Ganga to earth. Vikram sat in ice for his clan's death.

Now he had what he wanted: the throne of Merwar.

He'd never felt so cold. Like Lord Vayu, the wind god himself, had poured into Vikram's nostrils and descended into the pit of his stomach.

Sangavat had loved him. He'd valued Vikram's life higher than his own son's.

Why had Sangavat never told him this? Always, it was Bhoj this and Bhoj that. What does Bhoj think? How does Bhoj feel? Mustn't upset Bhoj!

Vikram tried not the think of that long ago evening in the Kirti Stumbh, when his uncle had worried for Vikram's safety.

Sangavat had never shown Vikram any love. He'd never soothed

Vikram's nightmares. Instead, he'd told a young boy not to weep. Not to weep!

Vikram watched the priests pour the ashes into clay pots. He sat on the ground, wrapping his arms around his knees, curling into a ball the way he had when he'd been a young boy. He rocked himself back and forth, the stony ground bruising his skin. How could he not weep?

Bhoj hadn't wept.

All the generals swore the same thing: Bhoj had not wept, even when his arms lay in pieces about him.

Vikram had killed his own cousin and uncle, and for what? The land his father had died defending? The fort his mother had burned herself alive in? Were his parents smiling down at him, proud of his victory?

Now there was no Sangavat to tell him not to cry. There was no Bhoj to hold him when he woke in the night, crying for his burning mother.

Vikram rocked himself back and forth.

If only his uncle had held him, and just once said he was sorry Jaisingh was dead. Instead, he left an orphaned boy alone to face the world. That wasn't love!

*Love.* It was all lies.

Vikram stared at the fire-blackened earth before him. Dust. Sangavat's words were just dust. Just lies.

He didn't stop to wonder if a dying man would lie.

If years ago Sangavat had thought his own brother so precious, why didn't he send more troops to defend Chittore against the sultan? He'd known that Chittore hadn't had enough! Why weren't the women taken far from danger? Why?

Why had Vikram lived the cursed life of an orphan?

Sangavat could have prevented it. Now he was dust and Vikram held everything in the palm of his hand. Chittore, Merwar, Mira.

Mira? She was Bhoj's widow.

It mattered not. Vikram was now the king and his word was law.

*

Two weeks later, the courtiers came to the assembly hall. Many of the nobles were here to see to the succession before they took their forces and returned to their own forts.

Vikram entered with his head bent so all would see his humility and his respect for his uncle.

He'd just returned from his mission, days of hard riding with his closest bodyguards. He'd taken Sangavat and Bhoj's ashes to the Ganga.

There could be no mistakes, Aryaji had told him. The king and yuvraj's ashes had to reach the holy river without disturbance. The scriptures instructed that this be done without delay.

Vikram watched his peers from the corners of his eyes. They looked restless. He took his seat among them and waited.

Aryaji stepped onto the dias. "Merwar is faced with a grave problem, my lords. This is a dangerous time for a kingdom to be without a king. Therefore, I nominate Vikram, son of Jaisingh and Rati, nephew of Maharana Sangavat, to be crowned immediately."

There was a roar of approval.

Among the clapping cheering nobleman, a slim young man wearing a red turban stood. Vikram saw that it was one of Bhoj's friends, by the name of Bhimasen. "My lords, if I may be allowed to speak."

The cheering died.

Vikram gritted his teeth and waited. He'd never been one of Bhimasen's favorite people. They'd been rivals for Bhoj's counsel.

"I believe that Kumar Vikram is the best candidate for the job." Bhimasen said. "He's as cunning as his father, as just as Sangavat, as noble as Bhoj."

The courtiers gave each other dubious looks.

Vikram's nostrils flared. How dare the underling mock him!

"He's perfect except for one thing."

Vikram clenched his hands. Did Bhimasen know something?

"His claim is not direct. He is the son of Sangavat's younger brother, not the son of Sangavat himself. Therefore, the court must consider all claimants to the throne before appointing anyone."

"Who are you thinking of, Bhimasen?" Aryaji asked.

The rubies on Bhimasen's red turban glittered as he bowed. "I believe Kumar Shivgan is also a claimant."

Everyone turned to look at fat Shivgan sitting next to Bhimasen.

"He too is descended from the great Maharana Udaikaran, Sangavat's grandfather. Shivgan's father Sagar died in the last battle against Babur just as Vikram's father Jaisingh died against the sultan of Gujarat. Shivgan is a good politician, firm in his convictions, and courageous. I nominate Shivgan."

Everyone jumped to their feet and started shouting, some telling Bhimasen to be quiet and some telling him he was right. They were waving their fists at each other; Vikram was elbowed in the face by an impassioned courtier.

He longed to send his fist into Bhimasen's mouth. How dare the fool bring up Shivgan's ancient, meaningless claim?

Handsome Udai was sitting behind his elder brother Shivgan, looking unconvinced and Vikram wondered at it. Didn't Udai want his brother to be king?

Bhimasen and Shivgan were childhood friends. If Shivgan was on the throne Bhimasen would have the same influence he'd had when Bhoj was around.

Fine, Vikram thought. He didn't mind having to dance around the issue. It was what he wanted anyway. Arranging his face into dignified, humility, he stood.

The courtiers turned to him.

"My dear friend Bhimasen is trying to spare me the burden of ruling. He knows I've no desire for it."

The courtiers looked at Bhimasen who was frowning.

"My claim to rule is not important. This throne belonged to my uncle and my brother Bhoj. My father Jaisingh died defending it so that my uncle could remain king. Truly, I don't want the throne for I do not feel worthy of it. My brother Shivgan should be crowned."

The courtiers roared even louder this time and the crowd began jostling about, elders trying to calm the youngsters and being pushed out of the way.

Aryaji called for order from the prime minister's dais.

"My lords, I believe we should hear what Shivgan has to say."

That's a brilliant idea, thought Vikram. Let the idiot speak and ruin his chances all by himself.

The noblemen turned towards where Shivgan was standing, his round belly sticking out over his dhoti and his too loose turban sliding backwards off his head. He caught it just in time and set it back on. He cleared his throat. "My friends, I believe that what Bhimasen has told you is true. Maharana Sangavat himself said that if he died without an heir, my claim would be foremost in the court."

The courtiers looked at each other, frowning.

Vikram raised his eyebrows. It looked like Shivgan had prepared himself. Better say something to neutralize the attack. "Indeed, brother, you're the right person to follow Sangavat. If my brother Bhoj were here, he would say the same thing."

"But Kumar Vikram, Bhoj often told me that you were the cleverest man ever born into his family." General Ashtabuj was frowning. "He said there was no one who'd be able to outsmart the Moghuls but you."

Nice, Vikram thought. And I'm not even paying Ashtabuj.

"Kumar Shivgan only has a claim if Sangavat left no heir," said Minister Danvantari, a small yet formidable man. "And the vaids tell me that before he departed, Maharana named Vikram his successor."

Better and better, thought Vikram. He looked at Shivgan who was looking at Bhimasen who was looking at Danvantari with tight lips.

Starting to worry now, aren't you, Bhimasen? Vikram's lips twitched but he turned it in to a mournful expression just in time. He stepped forward. "My lords, I appreciate your support, but I'm not worthy of the throne. What have I done for Merwar? Nothing. I'm not the person to head our army, nor am I good with the treasury or with foreign diplomacy."

"Then why did he leave you in charge of defending Chittore?" General Shantanu boomed.

"And why did Maharana always trust you to inspect the taxes every year?" Minister Kuber said. "I want you to succeed Sangavat, Kumar."

Vikram held up his hand. He kept his voice smooth and soft. "But I'm not good with foreign diplomacy."

"Then why did Maharana Sangavat trust you to visit the sultan in Gujarat last year to begin negotiations for the coalition?" Minister Devgan said.

"If Maharana trusted your judgment in all of these things, he must have thought you worthy." General Ashtabuj looked about the hall, his gaze intense. "We must trust Maharana Sangavat's judgment and make you our king."

"We want you to be our Maharana!" someone from the back called.

"We want Vikram as our Maharana!"

"Maharana Vikram ki jai! Maharana Vikram ki jai!" The chant swept through the hall, the courtiers stamping their feet.

Vikram folded his palms and bowed to the nobleman. "If this is the will of the court then I will obey. But I tell you now, I will rule only in trust for my brother Bhoj."

"Maharana Vikram ki jai! Maharana Vikram ki jai!" The courtiers stamped their feet.

Aryaji shouted from the dais. "It is settled! Raj Purohit has found an auspicious time for the coronation at dusk. Till then, we make the preparations."

The courtiers grabbed Vikram and shoved him up onto the dais. He stood there, looking down on them all, his hands folded in humility.

Shivgan had been pushed to the side where he and Bhimasen were watching the hysteria, their lips curled.

Pushing his elation to the back of his throat, Vikram embraced Aryaji, the eldest man in the court, and stepped down to embrace his noblemen.

He would be crowned at sunset! Everything he wanted was within his grasp.

And Bhimasen? Vikram smiled. He'd deal with Bhimasen later.

*

Mira heard the bugles sound as Vikram's procession set off. Enclosed within the palace walls, she could hear singing and dancing as the people celebrated.

How fast the world moved from grief to joy.

She was taking the route through the gardens lest Gauri ask her where she'd gone. Then Mira could say that she'd been for a walk.

There was no one at Uda's door so Mira entered without being announced. "Didi?"

No reply.

She walked through the suite. "Didi?"

There was a rustle and Mira turned to the side.

Uda was sitting on her balcony floor, weeping into her prayer beads.

Mira ran forward and crouched down, clasping Uda's bony shoulders. "Didi," she whispered.

Uda shrank away.

"Didi, look at me."

"Go, before I cast my shadow over you again."

"You've never cast your shadow over me."

"I must have."

Mira knew only too well that Uda wasn't to blame. She sat. "His death was not your fault."

Uda scrunched her beads in her hand.

Mira took them and dried them in her skirts. She laid them around Uda's neck. "These are for prayers and hope, not pain."

Uda caught Mira's hands. "Even widowed, you're so strong. How do you do it?"

"I'm not strong, Didi."

"You're not a widow either, are you?" Uda let go. Her tilted eyes glistened gold in the light. "That's why you still wear red, isn't it?"

Mira was silent.

"Did you know this would happen? That Bhoj would die?"

Mira looked at her hands. "There's only one certain thing in life, Didi: we all die."

"Except your Krishna?"

"Except Krishna."

The sounds of the celebration floated over the trees in the garden.

Mira imagined Vikram proceeding towards the coronation tree on foot, the royal chariot trailing behind him. His body would be shielded by the great blue and yellow umbrella of the Sisodias.

The coronation tree was outside the city, near to the Bhima Kund. It was where Vikram would have his purification bath with jal from the holy rivers. There, Raj Purohit would annoint his brow with the Raj Tilak.

From the sounds Mira could hear, hundreds of dancing girls were preceding him, showering his path with spring flowers. The Brahmins must be walking alongside him, chanting ancient Vedic mantras of kingship.

"I know now," Uda said. "I know why you wouldn't allow yourself to love Bhoj."

Mira wanted to say she'd loved Bhoj very much. But she was silent.

"I never imagined there'd be a day when I wouldn't have Bhoj near me." Uda's voice was soft. "I remember telling you to accept him and that he'd make you happy forever." She looked up at the dying rays that filtered through the screen in a dotted pattern before her. "If you'd listened to me then, your pain now would be unbearable."

Mira touched Uda's shoulder, her throat clenchng. "You've lost a father and a brother." She touched her own chest where it ached. "I know that pain." There was a long, strangled moment before she could speak again. "You mustn't blame yourself for their deaths."

"How can I not when even my own mother hates me?"

Gurudev had told Mira that the laws of karma dictated an individual's destiny. Everything that happened was only a reaction of past deeds. Uda was not to blame for Bhoj or Sangavat's destiny.

"You cannot hope to be understood or loved by society," Mira said. "Even if you were to achieve it, such love never lasts. There is only one love that'll never fail you and that is Bhagwan's. Put your faith in him, Didi, and he will give you strength."

"Will he? Will he care about a wretched widow who wasn't sincere when she prayed for her husband?" She looked at Mira. "It's true. I didn't want him to live. Then he died and it was my fault."

"He abused you! Perhaps Krishna was punishing him for his

crimes. Perhaps he was saving you. Perhaps so many things! The law of karma states that we are all responsible for our own actions. Your husband's karma led him to an early death."

"Then my karma must have been to suffer his abuse."

Mira sighed and looked at the grey pillars of Uda's rooms. "Who knows what acts we've committed in our past lives? Perhaps we must just accept it and try to be better."

"Just as you accepted your marriage to Bhoj, even though you never loved him?"

Mira was silent. She'd loved him but she'd never accepted him. Was it her destiny or her mistake?

"What did Bhoj do that he had to die this way?" Uda whispered.

Mira's eyes were hot and dry and open. "Death isn't always a punishment, Didi. It can be a reward."

For a moment, Uda said nothing. "How can you be so wise?"

Mira choked. "I'm not wise, Didi, only blessed with a guru."

Uda looked up at the orange sky. "Who?"

"Sant Ravi Das." As soon as Mira said his name, she felt a calm touch her, like the warmth of the descending sun.

Outside, the people were cheering as they followed the great procession, singing the glory of their new king.

A conch shell was blown, like the mountain's deep call to the sky. The hairs on the back of Mira's neck stood up.

Vikram was now king.

"I don't think you should wear red anymore, Mira."

"Is my fear of society deeper than my loyalty to my husband?"

"Mira–"

"Didi, I've made my decision."

Uda chewed on her bottom lip.

Mira sighed again. Gurudev had said her duty was to be a queen. She would never be queen now that Bhoj was no more but she was still a symbol of the alliance between Merta and Merwar.

"Ma Sa wants you to live with her now," Uda said.

"Yes. I'll return to Desh Bhakti Bhavan only when she wishes it. But I must return. I cannot worship properly in her quarters."

Uda smiled. "Too many schemers?"

The corners of Mira's mouth tilted up. "Something like that."

Uda's smile died. "She won't let you leave. When she decides on something, she's like a rock that won't move."

Mira held Uda's hand. "It's only her grief that makes her hurt you."

Uda was silent, threading her fingers through Mira's.

Drums beat to a ferocious pace somewhere far away, causing Mira's heart to thump madly. The new king, seated in his golden chariot, was greeting his subjects.

Mira didn't know how much longer she could stand the gloom in Gauri's quarters. It wasn't the way to remember a man like Bhoj.

# 20

# Enduring

Ratan and Vikramdev sat together in the king's private chamber.

Neither brother knew what to say.

In the small hours of the night, Merta's capital was at uneasy sleep, jerking at the slightest sounds in the darkness.

The Afghans had fled, some going to Humayun, some retreating to Bengal.

Ratan and his brother had left their most trusted generals in Delhi to take part in the coalition sovereignty of the Rajputs. Merwar, Jodhpur, Amber and Gujarat had done the same. Pipa's son, Yuvraj of Gondalgarh, was there himself.

Jaimal had been wounded in his left arm but was training as hard as ever.

Ratan was barely scratched.

Vikram, son of Jaisingh, was now Maharana of Merwar.

Ratan would never forget the sight of Bhoj's last assault on the battlefield, his cavalry charging into the fray like madmen. Bhoj, further ahead than his men, had smashed all in his path, letting out such a roar that the ground trembled. Then arrows came from behind and the yuvraj fell from his horse. His men were too far away to help him.

The Afghan thugs had descended, hacking away at his limbs, taunting him, delaying his death, while the Afghan cavalry rallied against Bhoj's regiment, keeping them from reaching the crown prince.

Bhoj had stood firm. Even with an arrow in his back and his arms in pieces.

Now Mira was alone.

Ratan had gone to war with the intention of wiping out the blot on humanity that was the Afghans. His victory was at a terrible price. And there was still Humayun of the Moghuls to contend with.

Ratan wished he could go to Mira and tell her of Bhoj's glorious triumph but he didn't think he'd be able to bear seeing her in widow's garb, never destined to have children. And another dilemma weighing on Ratan's mind—Chaukari still had no successor.

There was only one option, though it chilled Ratan to the bone.

Jaimal would be his heir.

It was clear that the enemy liked to kill Ratan's heirs.

"We must step up the security around Jaimal."

"I was thinking the same," Vikramdev said. "I'll double his guard."

"It can't be just anyone. Only our best may be his bodyguards."

Vikramdev nodded.

"But they must be secret. No one must know we've increased the security around Jaimal. If spies are observing us, which they are, they must not know how Jaimal is protected."

Vikramdev nodded.

"We'll station guards around him as ordinary servants, friends, maids. We'll do everything we can to keep his security secret." Ratan looked at Vikramdev. "Even Jaimal must not know how many are guarding him."

"Yes," Vikramdev said.

Ratan fell into silence once more, contemplating the random speckled pattern of the polished marble floor.

He wished he could see Mira.

*

In the light of the hot summer sun, Uda sat with her prayer beads, chanting the twelve-syllable mantra. She remembered Raj Purohitji teaching it to her when she'd been a child and he'd told her it was one of the mantras that brought salvation.

"Aum namo bhagavate vasudevaya," she chanted, twirling a bead on her finger. She thought of how Krishna had so many names. Madhav, Giridar, Gopal. Vasudev, as she was chanting. He was everywhere. That was what Vasudev meant.

"He who is all-pervading," Raj Purohitji had explained.

She'd known this mantra for years. Why had she never used it?

With every bead Uda chanted upon, every whisper of Vasudev, she felt the darkness lessen. She thought of Bhoj and didn't feel crushing grief. She thought of her father, who'd not spoken to her in years and she didn't feel regret. He'd loved her in the end and she was blessed.

No longer did her father and brother have to suffer. They had gone on to salvation. To moksha.

Mira was right. Death wasn't always a punishment. Not everyone's end was as pure as Bhoj or Bapu Sa's.

"Aum namo bhagavate vasudevaya," she whispered and felt light stir in her breast.

Let me have such a death, Vasudev. Let me come to you on a chariot of glory.

"Aum namo bhagavate vasudevaya," she whispered.

Uda craved the honor with which Bhoj had died. She wanted to be venerated as a true Kshatraani.

Let me have such a death, Vasudev. Let me come to you in glory.

"Uda."

She opened her eyes.

Gauri stood before her.

It couldn't be, Uda thought.

"Uda?"

It *was* her mother. She stood, stumbling over her skirt hem. "Ma Sa?"

Gauri looked tired in her white garments. She'd lost her plump beauty.

Just like Uda.

"Forgive me, putri."

The room tipped sideways. Her mother was calling her daughter?

Gauri looked at her feet. "I should have listened to your father but I was too angry. I had to blame someone."

"It matters not."

"Yes, it does. I'm your mother but I didn't think of how you felt. I didn't understand. Now I'm living the same widow's existence and I see what you've endured all these years."

"Ma Sa–"

"Let me speak, putri." Gauri took a step forward, lifting shaking hands to touch Uda's face. Then she stopped. "I've lost the right to touch you, haven't I?"

Uda didn't know what to say.

Gauri lowered her hands. "I gave all my love to my son and left my daughter to rot in her fate. Your father realized the truth because Bhoj told him what it was. Bhoj never neglected you." Gauri lifted glass eyes to Uda. "Did your husband truly abuse you?"

There was a terrible pause as Uda struggled with the truth. But she'd hidden the ugliness for so long and she was tired of it. She nodded.

"What did he do to you?"

Uda was silent. How could she possibly say out loud the things he'd done?

"Did he beat you?"

Uda drew a shaky breath and nodded.

"Did he–?" Gauri blanched, tight lipped. "Did he–against your will–?"

Uda's lips trembled. She nodded.

"And you never told your mother?" Gauri's glassy gaze melted and she collapsed. "You never told me?"

Uda crouched before her. "How could I tell you?"

"You should've said something!"

"It would've made it worse."

Gauri looked up at Uda. "How often did he do this to you?"

Uda bit her bottom lip.

"Every month?"

Uda swallowed.

"Every week?"

Uda closed her eyes.

"Every day?"

Uda saw visions of scratches and fists. "Whenever he felt like it."

There was a strangled pause.

"Kula Devi, forgive me," Gauri said. She wrapped her arms around herself. "I failed my children, Durga Mata. How can I repent?"

Uda opened her eyes, beating the memories back. She pulled her mother into her arms.

"You didn't fail me, Ma Sa. It was my fate and one cannot change one's fate."

"But how could he do that to you? And you bore it without even a whisper. You never said anything! Then you came back as a widow and had to bear even more."

"It doesn't matter now, Ma Sa."

"Kula Devi, Durga Mata, protect your children. Protect this house."

"Ma Sa…" Uda prayed to Vasudev to help her mother.

"I abused you for your widowhood, Uda. I thought there must be something lacking in you that your husband died so young. But now I'm glad he died or he would've been hurting you all these years. And you would never have said a word to anyone. Beaten and raped, and so often too! And Bhoj told your father everything."

"Bhoj only knew of the beatings."

"How did he find out?"

Uda paused as the memory came back to her. "Bapu Sa sent him training on the western border. He was still just a boy at the time. He was passing our fort and stayed with us for a day." She looked down. "I was serving his meal and when I turned, he saw the bruises on my back. He was ready to kill my husband."

"Why didn't he bring you home?"

"I ordered him not to. I told him we'd an argument the night before and that I'd provoked my husband. I told him all was resolved."

"And he believed you?"

"I made him believe me. He was just a boy, Ma Sa! Too young to sort out my troubles. And my marriage alliance was good for Merwar."

Gauri stopped rocking and looked up at Uda. "Putri," she whispered. She caught Uda in a fierce embrace. "My putri."

Uda held Gauri just as close. It'd been so long since her mother had held her. The last time had been on Uda's wedding day.

*

Uda moved in with Gauri and together they embroidered silks for the family. They talked about the happy times of Uda and Bhoj's childhood, when Gauri had scolded them for their mischief. They laughed about how Sangavat had tickled Uda with his beard and let her sit on the front of his saddle when he went riding.

No more did Uda dread Gauri's words. No more did she creep out of rooms to escape her mother's accusations.

Months later, Mira still wore red and the gossip was turning vicious. She danced in the temple, they said, and behaved as a loose woman.

Gauri allowed Mira to return to Desh Bhakti Bhavan.

Alone, she told Uda she didn't know what to do. She'd sent Mira to the bhavan to protect her but it wasn't working.

Uda told Gauri they were wrong about Mira just as they'd been wrong about Uda. Mira was good and pure and only danced because she found comfort in Krishna.

"What else does she have?" Uda asked her mother.

Gauri agreed, saying that she feared hurting anyone the way she'd hurt her own daughter. Who knew what pangs Mira suffered?

Then Uda heard some women muttering that Mira should be stoned for her audacity. Uda's embroidery became more and more crooked as she agonized over what to do.

\*

Mira walked through the master's quarters. Somehow, looking at Bhoj's things here was less painful than looking at his one blue chair in her room. Yet try as she might, she couldn't remove his blue seat from her room.

She went into his majestic sleeping chamber, where the bed was covered with a white sheet. It was funny how she'd never dared come here when he'd been alive.

Now that Mira was all alone to sing for Krishna, she discovered she couldn't find the words. Her chest hurt too much. It was only when she came to Bhoj's rooms and sat here for a time that she was able to play her tambora.

Sometimes, the pain was so bad she had to go to the Kumbh-Shyam mandir, all by herself, just to stop thinking. In the temple, the need to dance overcame her and words spilled out, words that Gurudev had taught her.

Nothing was said about it. The devotees were so kind.

Yet Mira knew the royal family despised her. She was glad that now, with her widowed status, she'd never again have to attend a family event.

That left her all alone in the bhavan, with Bhoj's rooms, her tambora, and her need to sing.

"Jiji?"

Mira turned to Lalita in the doorway.

"Raj Kumari Uda is here."

Mira looked at the bed and wondered what color the covers were underneath the white sheet. She'd look later, if she had the strength.

"I'm coming," she told Lalita.

Mira touched a silver bowl that was at her side. It must have contained perfumed herbs to sweeten the air. Raising it to her nose, she tasted the lingering scent of roses. And dust.

In the music room, Uda was standing near the tablas, examining the different sized manjiras that were hung on the wall.

"Didi," Mira said.

Uda turned and smiled, coming forward to take her hand.

Mira attempted a smile but found the pulling at her face too much of a strain.

Uda led her to a seat and sat with her. "How've you been?"

Mira shrugged. "It'll be Diwali soon."

Uda's smile died. "You don't seem too excited."

"I'm just tired."

Sitting back, Uda looked at the manjiras. "The servants you sent back to the main palace miss you."

"There was nothing for them to do here." No soldiers or guests to feed, Mira thought. No yuvraj to please.

"I know."

There was a pause.

"Shall I send for refreshments?" Mira asked.

"Yes. I'm hungry."

Mira clapped her hands and Janki came in with a tray of fruit.

"That maid of yours has grown so much." Uda said, looking at Janki's retreating back. "She was ten when Ma Sa sent her to you, wasn't she?"

Mira nodded.

"Will you be getting her married soon? I know you got Lalita married a few years ago."

Mira shrugged. "If Janki wishes it."

"You must hurry before she gets too old. I'll ask Ma Sa to recommend someone. There's bound to be a suitable boy in our household."

"Only if Janki wishes it. I'll let you know."

Uda opened her mouth to say more but didn't.

There was another pause.

"You know you must stop going to the mandir."

Mira stared at the floor.

"They're tearing your reputation to shreds."

"Why? They think I'm a widow and a widow's supposed to spend her time in prayer."

"It's not that simple!" Uda sighed and massaged her temples with her fingers. "A widow is an outcast. She is not supposed to dance in public, nor is she supposed to sing, or talk, or do anything else that brings attention to her."

"Is that what you think? That I want attention?" Mira looked at the painting on the wall before her. It was Krishna playing his flute, standing in a circle of adoring Gopis. Perhaps she did want attention but it wasn't the sort that Uda thought.

"A widow is an outcast and outcasts are never welcome."

"In Krishna's house, everyone is welcome."

"Don't you understand, Mira? Before, you were protected by Bhoj, but now you rely on Vikram. You must be careful."

Mira remembered the day the wind had changed, a snap and then a flutter. "I rely on Krishna to protect me."

Uda seized Mira's shoulders. "They're calling you a *whore*."

Mira recoiled.

Uda looked as if she had a bitter taste in her mouth and she dropped her hands. "They say you never honored Bhoj in his life and still won't now he is dead."

Mira stared at Uda.

"They say you must be pleasuring all the men of the family."

Mira covered her hot cheeks with her hands, her eyes wide.

Uda looked so helpless. "You see? I told you to behave as a proper widow and you didn't listen."

"They think all that just because I go to the mandir?"

"Don't forget the rumors of the past."

"But they were the opposite. They said I denied Bhoj."

"That only adds fuel to the fire! They say that you humiliated Bhoj by giving yourself to all but him and that's why he let himself get killed in the war. Mira, they've come to know that you went to Kashi and not Merta. They know you stayed with a man."

"That was my guru!" Mira leaped to her feet, sparks flying from her eyes. "They dare slander my guru? They *dare?*"

Uda gestured weakly. "What else are they supposed to think? You give them nothing but arrows to fire at you."

"But they're lies!" Mira's hands were fists at her sides.

"Unless you show them you can behave as a widow, they'll continue to believe these lies."

"How can they think such things?"

"It's human nature."

"It's not!" Mira screamed. "Gossip and lies! Is this the society your brother died to protect?"

Uda stood. "He died for higher things."

Mira stared down at the marble beneath her, the swirling lines of randomness sprinkled across the jade green. "Didi, I'm not a–a–"

Uda crouched before Mira and pulled her into an embrace. "I know."

Mira thought how Uda's arms were so different from Bhoj's, so slim and fragile. She pressed her forehead down onto Uda's sharp collarbone and prayed for an end.

She'd lived with the rumors before because they'd been true.

But these were lies. How could she go to the mandir and face

Vishnu and know that people were saying such things about her? They thought she was a–a–

"Vikram has forbidden the family from commenting on the rumors. The servants have been warned, on pain of death, against gossiping about you. He told me he wanted you to stay in the bhavan."

"Jehtji said this? When?"

"Just this morning. Stay out of sight, Mira. It's dangerous outside."

They might stone me, Mira thought in horror.

"I won't go to the mandir, Didi."

Uda's chin bumped Mira's head as she nodded. "It's for the best, my sister."

\*

That night, Mira tossed and turned in a fitful dream.

There were greens and blues and reds and oranges and she stood in the middle as the colors whirled around her. The greens became a forest. The reds became the flowers and the blues, a peacock. The oranges became a lion, circling her, graceful, lazy.

A circle of rocks around her kept the lion at bay.

There was a banyan tree, its branches plunging into the ground, its roots embedding in the sky. A parrot sat on a branch.

Mira knew it was a parrot though she couldn't see its body. She could see only its left eye, watching her.

If she moved from the circle of rocks, the lion would get her.

The parrot watched.

She shifted her feet and found the earth moist and warm. Her ruby toe ring glinted up at her and she dug it into the loose soil.

She looked to her right and saw a stream, the water clear as glass, flowing over a golden streambed. Her throat was parched and she longed to drink from that spring.

The lion passed by.

Her lord stood before her, dressed in a yellow pitambar, his blue torso bare. He reached down and scooped up some water, cupping it in his pink palms. Droplets fell to his bare chest and slid down his taut abdomen, leaving glistening trails on his skin.

He held his hand out to her, his pink palm filled with sweet water.

Mira reached out but she was too far away and the lion was close.

The animal passed by.

She had to go now, before it came again. Mira took a step forward and stumbled over the rocks.

She jerked awake.

The canopy of her bed looked down at her.

Sitting up, she ran a trembling hand over her sweating forehead.

He'd been so patient, waiting for her and she'd stumbled over those rocks. Those stupid rocks!

Mira beat her fists against the bed. How could she stumble over the rocks?

Crying out, she thrashed the insect nets aside and stood, her limbs shaking. She paced the floor, trying to bring strength back into them, trying to remove the feel of the rocks.

And then she knew.

She'd thought they were protecting her. She'd been wrong.

# 21

# Remedy

Vikram signed letter after letter.

His hand was cramping but he kept signing. In the year and a half since he'd become king, he'd become used to this tedious task.

His scribe, a man he'd appointed last year, stood next to him with another load of letters in his arms. The scrolls of silk were all pledges of support, sent to him from the mukhyas of all his vast territories.

Vikram signed the letters, showing his acceptance of their pledges and acknowledgement of their loyalty.

It wasn't enough. He would have to tour his kingdom. Letters couldn't show him what was in the hearts and minds of these men. Who knew what plots were being concocted?

He had to find a way to show them all he was in charge. It had to be a domestic matter since he couldn't afford to lose any men in battle.

Luckily, he already had a plan.

Before he'd left to complete his uncle and Bhoj's final rites on the banks of Ganga Mata, he'd sent out Koirala to spread the rumors of Mira's visit to Kashi.

On returning, he'd learned the people were so outraged that Mira was in danger of being attacked. They were mourning their hero and here was the hero's widow behaving shamelessly.

That was when Vikram forbade the family and servants to speak of the rumors.

He signed another letter.

The matter of her garb did confuse Vikram though. With all that he knew of Mira, he hadn't expected this of her. His aunt Gauri had told him Mira was confused with grief and thus it wasn't her fault.

Had she loved Bhoj so much? Then why reject him as she had? There must be another reason. Was this all deliberate trouble-making or was she really mad? If it was deliberate, why was she doing it? Was her vanity so great that she wouldn't lessen her beauty by cutting her hair and removing her jewelry?

That didn't sound like Mira.

He signed another letter.

One thing was for certain: she was unaware of her effect on men. She'd reduced Bhoj to incoherent ramblings and hallucinations yet she'd not used her power to extract riches or silks or influence out of him.

Instead, she'd made Bhoj send her, unescorted, to Kashi. What sort of woman went anywhere without her entourage? It was a miracle nothing had happened to her. Uda had told Vikram that the four men she'd sent after Mira had never been obliged to lift a finger.

He signed another letter but the end of his quill snapped and his scribe took out a knife to sharpen it.

Somehow, nothing made sense when it came to Mira.

Vikram wanted her powerless, friendless, on her knees before society. Because he was society's head. He had the power to strike or show mercy.

The scribe handed the quill back to him and he signed another letter.

Uda had come to see him this morning as he was dressing. She'd said that even though she'd told Mira not to go to the temple, Mira still went and the people were very angry. She told Vikram to send Mira to Merta.

Vikram had to stop himself from chuckling in front of his scribe. Uda thought Merta was safe!

He had, of course, agreed. Then he'd sent out a man to spread the word that Mira was being kicked out of Merwar.

She was in more disgrace than she imagined. Even now, she was probably in that mandir Bhoj had built for her, strumming that nasty old tambora, when outside a storm was brewing to destroy her.

Vikram would be seen as the righteous king, expelling the wicked harlot. He would be hailed as the preserver of values, the protector of dharma. Even family members wouldn't be spared from justice.

And Mira would be within his grasp.

*

Mira had returned to her uncle's house in Merta to find that her younger cousins, once so sweet and loving, now shunned her. Her cousin Jaimal ignored her.

Her aunts and uncles, the maids and manservants, even the guards, all avoided Mira like she was an attack of smallpox.

One day, she'd come in from the garden to find all her red cotton garments lying on the floor, torn to bits. She was glad her father kept sending her income or she wouldn't have been able to replace them.

Mira retired to her rooms, avoiding her relatives like they were dangerous animals.

No food was sent to her suite; she had to buy her fruit from vendors outside the palace grounds.

Savitri and Lakshmi had remained in Merwar, for they'd never seen Merta and Mira knew they wouldn't like it. Janki had also never seen Merta but she and Lalita were so close it would've been cruel to leave her behind. Both came with their husbands.

When Mira had left Merwar, the people had gathered to watch her leave, their stony-faced silence testament to their hate.

Vikram had ordered a guard to go with her, headed by Commander Sumer, one of Bhoj's best friends.

Mira had fed Sumer on many occasions and was glad he was with her on this journey. He reminded her of those days with Bhoj.

Then she'd arrived in Merta and wondered at how small the fort looked. The walls were so short and the gate was so small. Was this really home?

Her people had stood alongside the road to greet her and Mira felt their eyes harden when they saw her red attire, confirming the rumors that she was sent home in disgrace. These were the same people who'd cheered at her wedding.

At the palace, she met Shakti, older and grumpier than ever.

Shakti had said Mira was to go to her suite and not come out until she was summoned.

No one summoned her, not for one whole year.

Sumer and his armed escort remained with Mira, even though she told them to return to Chittore.

"Maharana Vikram told us to protect you, Babhiji," Sumer told her. Since he and Bhoj had been very close, Bhoj had told him to address Mira as sister-in-law.

Ratan didn't come to see her.

She couldn't go far from the palace because she knew her family would get angry. She didn't go to any of the temples outside, and she missed the Kumbh-Shyam mandir a great deal.

Mira wasn't surprised by her family's rejection. Just hurt. Every night she prayed to Krishna that her uncle might not be angry, that her father might come to see her.

There was only one good thing about being home: Girija Shankar Purohit.

One day, Mira had gone into the gardens before sunrise and Purohitji was crouching on the grass, gathering flowers from a jasmine bush. She'd bowed and turned to leave, thinking he wouldn't want to speak to her.

Then he said: "I heard you found your guru."

It was such a shock to hear a gentle voice that Mira didn't know how to reply. Thankfully, he spoke instead, giving a long list of Ravi Das' accomplishments and prowess in poetry.

Mira, in a rush of gratitude, told him all the things she'd seen in Kashi and how Gurudev had given her a tambora and how he'd helped her understand the holy name. Then the sun rose and gardeners came in, and both Mira and Purohitji realized it was late.

From that day on, she spoke to her old tutor often in the gardens. Sometimes, he brought Indumati along and the three of them discussed songs that Ravi Das had composed.

On Shukravar, a messenger came to Mira's suite. "Rana Ratan is waiting to see you in his room."

Mira dismissed the messenger before she even realized what he'd said. Her father? Her father was in the capital?

She summoned Lalita and Janki and tiptoed out of the suite, hoping not to run into any of her cousins.

Then they were at Ratan's door and she told her maids to remain outside.

He was standing by the window, resting his hand against the wall, his shoulders hunched inwards as if he were bearing a great weight. He wasn't wearing his turban and his once black hair was peppered with grey locks.

Mira thought she should be afraid but the truth was that she'd felt so much anger directed towards her, she no longer feared it.

"Bapu Sa?"

He turned. His eyes were darker than ever. "Putri," he said, stepping towards her.

It'd been eight years since he'd given her away to Bhoj. Eight years since they'd seen each other.

She ran into his embrace.

He held her as if she'd disappear.

Mira thought of all those they'd lost. Bhoj, Shamal, Ranjeet, Raagav, Raghuvir, even Sangavat. She knew that her father was thinking of them too.

After some time, they pulled apart.

Ratan shook his head at her. "You look so grown up."

"I'm now almost twenty-one years old." She took his hand and kissed it. "I've missed you so much."

He pressed her head against his chest and held her as if she were a little girl again, crying because Shamal had broken her gudia.

After another moment, Mira lifted her head. "I thought you didn't want to see me."

"There were a lot of things that stopped me. Now I'm here."

There was another pause.

She pulled away. "I'm back from Chittore, Bapu Sa."

He led her to the couch. "Putri, I think you should return there."

She looked at him in dismay. "They've kicked me out."

"Vikram sent word that we're still allies. He only wanted to keep you safe from civil unrest. His messengers now say the atmosphere in Chittore has calmed down."

"If we're still allies it's because you protected Maharana Sangavat when he was wounded on the battlefield."

"No, Mira. We're still allies because of you. You're the symbol."

She lowered her gaze. "I no longer have any dignity in their eyes, Bapu Sa."

"Because you're a widow?"

"Because I refused widowhood."

For the first time, Ratan looked down at what she was wearing. There was no reaction on his face but Mira saw a flicker in his eyes.

She fretted at the end of her veil.

"Mira?"

"I don't consider myself a widow, Bapu Sa."

"I saw Bhoj fall. It was a hero's death but it was still death. He's gone, Mira."

She shook her head. "My husband isn't dead."

"Mira…"

"Bapu Sa!"

He jumped.

She glared at him. "You never listen to me. Even when I told you I didn't want to marry, you still made me do it. I obeyed because I was your putri and would do anything for you." Her face crumpled, her features tumbling in an avalanche. "But don't ask me to do this. I cannot."

He studied the way she kept her shoulders straight, even as she held her tears back by sheer force of will. "You're strong, Mira. You're stronger than Shamal ever was."

She looked up at him.

"He couldn't ever be happy when you were not. Your Ma Sa and I both knew it."

Mira took Ratan's huge hands in her smaller ones. Gold on gold, like when she'd been little.

"After your wedding, he told me he'd never forgive himself for failing you."

She squeezed his hands.

"He told me you wouldn't let go of Krishna. Even if the whole of Merwar turned on you, he said. You wouldn't let go."

Mira swallowed.

"Did Bhoj know?"

She nodded.

"Did it make him angry?"

"At first. Then he said he'd always protect me. Now he's dead."

"He was a good man, putri."

"I know."

There was a pause.

"You must return to Merwar. Go now when the weather is cool."

She closed her eyes.

"If you stay here, it'll remind our people of our losses. Morale will lessen."

"Is there still talk of rebellion?"

Ratan started. "How did you know of that?"

"Yuvraj told me."

Ratan sighed. "There's been no more talk since Shamal's murder."

Of course, Mira thought.

There was another pause.

She knew her father was right. If she stayed here, the people would be reminded of how great heroes like Bhoj and Sangavat had fallen. Fear would grow.

"I'll go, Bapu Sa, but not to Merwar."

He frowned. "Then where?"

"I'd like to go to Kashi. Gurudev is there."

"You have a Gurudev?"

"Ji, Sant Ravi Das. I met him when he was visiting Chittore. Do you remember how Ma Sa always wished she could meet him?"

He looked at her in wonder. "*The* Sant Ravi Das accepted you as his disciple?"

Mira nodded.

Ratan smiled. "Well then, you must go to him."

*

Gurudev was chanting and it was one of Ravi's favorite pastimes to watch his Gurudev chant.

Ramanand inhaled, his frail chest swelling with air. "Ra...ma..." he blew out, his chest relaxing as he exhaled. There was such perfect symmetry in the timing; swell, "Ra...ma..." relax; swell, "Ra...ma..." relax. His breath came out as fog in the cold air.

Ramanand opened bleary eyes. "Is that you, Ravi?"

Ravi bowed.

"For a moment there, I thought you were Rama," he chortled.

Ravi grinned. "Rama's hair isn't as curly as mine."

Ramanand touched his beads to his eyes before laying them aside. "I need to talk to you."

"That's why I came."

Ramanand nodded. "Things aren't looking good for Bharat."

Ravi waited.

"I feel it's time you went on another yatra. You've been getting restless."

It was true. The vision of broken spears was clearer every day.

"You're not sleeping well either. It's not good to be anxious when practicing bhakti."

"As you said, Gurudev, this is a dangerous time for Bharat."

"When will Mira arrive?"

"I expect her within two days," Ravi said.

"And your plan?"

Ravi didn't answer.

"You feel guilty already."

"She's vulnerable, Gurudev."

"Sometimes lessons are hard. Your duty, Ravi, is to spread knowledge. Remember what the Gita says: *Concern yourself not with the result of your action but only with the action itself.* You cannot control the result, putra."

Ravi nodded. "I only wish there were another way."

"Isn't that the test? If there's another way, she'll find it. We've already agreed she's a clever girl."

Ravi smiled.

"Do only your duty, Ravi. To do more or less than your duty is to not do your duty at all."

\*

Sitting outside his hut, he brushed the dust off a new pair of shoes. They were small, wide at the toes. The blazing sun warmed his bones and he felt fit enough to walk up Chittore mountain.

Lona had come and gone, leaving her food package on the floor.

Ravi's son Vijay had visited with his son, Shravan. The child was growing bigger every day because he was fed and he was healthy.

Just as Ravi set aside the new pair of shoes, Mira walked up.

She knelt and bowed at his feet. "Pranam Gurudev. Jai Shri Rama."

He lifted his hand, glad she'd arrived. "Saubhagyavati bhavah, putri."

When she didn't straighten, Ravi looked around. "Where's your chariot?"

"I left it outside the city." Her voice was muffled with her head so close to the ground.

"And your guards?"

"They're waiting just a little way from here."

"Why do you not rise?"

Mira raised her face. She looked like she'd been rained on, feverish and cold at the same time. "I just wanted to rest at your feet."

Ravi knew her guilt hadn't allowed her the privilege, the release, of tears. "Rise, Mira. Sit with me."

She pulled herself into a sitting position, crossing her legs. "Yuvraj is dead."

"You're not responsible for his destiny."

She searched the ground. "So this was fated?"

"Fate is a strange thing, Mira. We make our own yet we don't even recognize it when it hits us."

"So it was my fault?"

"You know better than that. Think back on what you said to Uda."

She didn't look as if she wanted to. She covered her face with her hands.

"We answer for our own actions. No one else can be responsible."

She lowered her hands. "I hurt him, Gurudev. I hurt him so much."

"Any man's pride would've been hurt."

"Uda said he loved me. I denied it. Then Maharana Sangavat said that Yuvraj knew he'd die that day. *He wanted to die.*" Her lower lip trembled. "Because of me."

Ravi rested his forearms on his raised knees and his bony elbows stuck out. "Many terrible things happen in this world, putri. We call it Kal Yuga, the age of chaos."

"That doesn't make it acceptable."

"You were honest: you always told him how you felt. You couldn't have done any more than that."

"I drove him to his end."

Ravi shook his head. "He did what he did for his people, and more importantly, for Krishna."

She frowned. "What do you mean?"

He looked up at the sky above them, a shining blue summer sky. "In the end, he understood who and what you were. That's why he asked you for forgiveness. Really, he was asking forgiveness of Krishna."

"Why?"

"Perhaps Bhoj realized what was most important."

"He said I'd never have to fear him again," she whispered.

"That was part of his realization."

Mira scooped up a handful of loose earth and looked at it in her palm. "What was the other part?"

"That his love for you wasn't selfish. It didn't have to be returned for it to live."

Mira closed her fingers around the earth.

"He did love you, Mira. That was his salvation."

"What do you mean?"

"To love a devotee is to love Bhagwan, putri."

Her tears fell onto the dirt in her hand, causing muddy trails to run through her fingers. "Thank you, Gurudev."

"Thank Giridar, Mira."

*

Over the next months, as the days heated, Ravi talked to Mira about the scriptures and listened, as slowly, she composed new songs. Still, her voice lacked lustre.

Together, they went to the mandirs around Kashi. At sunset, they watched the aarti to Ganga Mata, performed on the banks of the river by strong young priests.

The priests had to be strong because the aarti was almost an hour long and consisted of first an incense aarti, then a duph or smoke aarti, then the lamp aarti, which was a tall pyramid as large as a man's arm. Then came an aarti with water-filled conch shells, then a flower aarti, and then a great fire aarti which was a single flame held in a brass bowl that the priests wielded from a chain. Then there was a camphor aarti, lit so that it burned and smoked at the same time, releasing its refreshing aroma. This was followed by another conch shell aarti with water, a perfume aarti, and a flower petal aarti, after which the petals were thrown into the Ganga. Then the priests performed a peacock feather aarti, fanning Mother Ganga before blowing the conch shells. Last was the chamadh aarti, where the priests used a yak tail to ward insects away so that Ganga Mata could rest undisturbed.

Ravi knew Mira found some peace in watching the ancient rite, even though she didn't speak of it. She lit a lamp and set it on the water, watching it long after it had joined the other lights in the midst of the river.

Ravi then bent all his thought towards Lona: he needed reinforcements. The next day, he glanced up from his altar to see her in the doorway.

"What at you grinning at?" she asked.

"Nothing. Come inside."

She peered into the hut as if there were a demon lurking about. "I woke up this morning with your voice in my head. Is this a trick?"

"Why would I play a trick on you?"

"How would I know? You just seem a bit too pleased, that's all."

"That makes you wary?"

"Hmm." Lona came into the room. She peered around once more. "Where's Mira?"

"I sent her for flowers."

"Hmm."

"I promise there's no conspiracy planned. Actually, I need your help."

She raised her eyebrows. "How?"

Ravi sighed. "Mira has fallen into melancholia and I need you to snap her out of it."

Lona sat next to him. "What do you want me to do?"

"Just follow my lead."

"I've been doing that all my life."

He snorted.

"Hmph! Don't get derisive. Your Sita and Rama know the truth."

Ravi looked at his little mud deities. "Indeed."

Mira appeared in the doorway, clutching the end of her veil to her stomach. It was bulging with flowers that she dropped in the bowl next to Ravi. "I think the rains might start soon," she said, a sheen of sweat on her forehead. "The air feels wet."

"Don't be too hopeful," Lona said, wiping her own sweating forehead. "It often gets like this in Kashi. The Ganga, you know."

Mira had lost weight in the month she'd been in Kashi, despite the daily meals from Lona. Her collar bone rose out of her shoulders like the axle on a chariot wheel.

Ravi worried about it. He didn't want her to waste away.

"Putri, sit here before me and make a garland for Rama," he said.

Mira sat down, picking up the needle he kept by the altar. She threaded it.

Ravi nodded at Lona who then sat beside him. "Lona, why don't we tell Mira about Sita?"

Lona's white hair crinkled as she tilted her head in question.

"We can tell her about when Ravan kidnapped her."

She smiled. "You mean the way we used to tell Vijay when he was a boy?"

He nodded.

"Who gets to tell it this time?"

"You," he told her.

Lona turned to Mira. "Well, putri, as you know, King Dashrath had four sons, Rama, Bharat, Lakshman, and Shatrugna. Rama, the eldest, was the epitome of goodness, a perfect son, an ideal brother, a loving husband, a clever statesman, and a skilled warrior. He was loved even by his enemies."

Mira began stringing flowers together but her attention was on Lona.

"When the time came, Dashrath decided to put Rama on the throne of Ayodhya and the kingdom was overjoyed at the news. However, Kaikaiya, Dashrath's second wife, was not amused. She wanted her son, Bharat, to succeed, though Bharat wanted only to serve Rama. She reminded the king of two boons he'd promised her long ago when she'd saved his life in a battle. For her first boon, she asked that Bharat be made king. For her second, she asked that Rama be exiled for fourteen years."

"Tell Mira about the kidnapping," Ravi said. "She already knows how Rama was exiled."

"*I'm* telling the story," Lona said, frowning at Ravi. "It is necessary to first set the base." She turned back to Mira. "So, Dashrath was heartbroken that his beloved queen would do such a thing and pleaded with her to retract her demands. When Rama heard of the situation, he immediately prepared to go to the forest, telling his mother Kaushalya that it was his duty as a son to honor his father's promises. The rest of Ayodhya was devastated, including Sita, Rama's wife. She insisted on accompanying him, despite his warnings that life in the forest would be too much for her. He told her that the rules of exile were that one had to dress in the clothing of poverty, walk barefoot, eat only fruits and leaves, and never enter any city. He told her she wouldn't be able to bear these austerities. She told him that the pain of walking barefoot through the forest would be less than the pain of separation from him."

Lona turned to Ravi. "See what I'm doing?"

"Alright, alright."

Mira hid her smile behind her hand.

Lona continued: "Lakshman also decided to go with Rama for he'd never been separated from his older brother for even a day. Together, the trio left for the forest and, as the years passed, made their way south, seeking the darshan of the holy people. Actually, Rama was traveling over the land to meet his devotees, something that, had he been crowned king, he wouldn't have been able to do. So his exile was all part of his plan."

Mira pulled a flower apart and used the petals as pattern breakers.

"For the last year of their exile, they settled in Panchvati Forest. It was when they built their ashram there that Ravan, the demon king of Lanka, heard of Sita's beauty. One day, when Rama and Lakshman were away from the hut, he kidnapped her."

"You didn't tell her about Shurpankha!" Ravi said.

"Do you want me to get to the point or what?" Lona asked. "We'll be here all day if I stop to talk about how Shurpankha wanted to marry Rama and Rama said that he was already married to Sita and had vowed to have only one wife and then Shurpankha tried to kill Sita and Lakshman cut off Shurpankha's nose and sent her to her brother Ravan where she told him all about Sita's beauty."

Ravi winked at Mira who hid her laugh behind a cough. Lona was brilliant at this, Ravi thought.

"Actually, now that you mention it, I forgot to talk about Rama's glorious looks, since that was why Shurpankha wanted to marry him." Lona leaned towards Mira. "He was very handsome. His skin was dark as a forest at night and his eyes were tender as lotuses and vast as two oceans. His hair was soft and black and curly like the clouds and his arms were long and powerful, trained to wield a bow with effortless skill."

Ravi rolled his eyes. Lona always waxed lyrical on Rama's looks because she thought it got on Ravi's nerves, only it didn't. He knew from experience that Rama was even more beautiful than Lona described.

Mira's eyes were dreamy, clearly thinking of Giridar.

Both ladies sighed.

Well alright, perhaps it was getting on Ravi's nerves. He cleared his throat, loudly. In the back of his mind, he could hear Rama laughing at him.

Lona shook herself. "So, anyway, Sita was stolen away by Ravan. Rama and Lakshman looked everywhere for her, finally coming to Kishkinda, the monkey kingdom, where King Sugriv ruled with his loyal servant Hanuman. Hanuman, as you know, was a great devotee of Rama and had waited years to meet with him. With his help, Sugriv and Rama became friends and Sugriv sent out search parties to look for Sita."

"You missed the part where Rama and Hanuman first met and how Rama killed Bali because Bali was holding Sugriv's wife captive. Oh, and you missed the part about Mother Shabri."

"Will you stop interrupting?" Lona huffed. "You can tell her about Shabri another time. Right now we're focusing on Sita.

"So, anyway, Hanuman took his party south and they came to the southernmost tip of Bharat. Lanka lay across the ocean and they knew Sita must be there. Hanuman, who was the son of the wind god Vayu, was able to leap over the ocean and reach Lanka. He snuck into the city, searching for Sita and he discovered her in one of the gardens where she sat under a tree, weeping for Rama."

Lona beamed at Mira. "You see, putri, even though Ravan had kidnapped Sita, she had forbidden him to touch her else the force of her curse would destroy him. In a rage, Ravan sent hoards of demonesses into the garden to terrorize her. Despite all their efforts, Sita remained steadfast.

"At night, when the demonesses had tired of tormenting her and left her alone, Hanuman came down from the tree and gave her the message that Rama would soon arrive with a great army. Sita, overjoyed, blessed Hanuman as her son and told him to tell Rama to hurry for she was dying without him."

Ravi saw Mira's face fall. She understood Sita's pain.

"Hanuman returned to Kishkinda where he told Rama that Sita

was alive in Lanka. Rama was overjoyed and told Hanuman he'd never be able to repay him. Sugriv immediately prepared his army of mighty apes for war. They marched to Lanka and camped right outside the gates of the city. Ravan was astounded that Rama wasn't just the wondering beggar he'd previously thought. However, Ravan readied his forces, confident that he'd defeat Rama. Rama, being Rama, sent a peace envoy to Ravan to say that all Rama wanted was Sita. If the demon king complied, Rama would leave in peace. Ravan, being Ravan, refused. War began. One by one, Ravan's powerful generals fell under the attacks of Sugriv's army. Hanuman and Lakshman destroyed each and every one of Ravan's mighty sons. Soon, Ravan himself came out to fight and after an epic battle in which Ravan used all sorts of dark magic, Rama slew the demon king.

"Sita was rescued but when she was taken to Rama, he told her to stop where she was for she still had to prove she was chaste."

Mira frowned.

"The truth was, putri," Lona said, "that Rama had no doubt of Sita's chastity. He knew she loved only him and that she was faithful. But, in the eyes of society, she had to prove herself. It was time for her agni pariksha."

Ravi saw Mira's eyes harden at the word society. Her hands clenched.

"Sita ordered Lakshman to light a fire before her. She declared that if she was pure, she'd be able to walk through it and reach the other side, unharmed. If she was impure, she'd be destroyed. Lakshman was outraged that Rama would test the very wife who'd left the wealth of the palace to live with him in exile. However, Sita made Lakshman comply because there was a great secret behind this test. A secret that only the divine couple knew."

Mira leaned forward, transfixed. "What secret?"

Ravi leaned forward too. This was the whole point of today's lesson.

Lona leaned in to cement the circle. "Rama is Bhagwan and Sita is his other half, the mother of the universe. The whole plot of her kidnapping was a charade from the beginning to the end, executed by Rama and Sita themselves. They knew Ravan would kidnap her and thus she hid, leaving behind only a shadow of herself for Ravan to steal. Sita called upon the god of fire, Agni Dev, and asked him to shelter her and that was where the real Sita had been all this time. So after the war, Rama wanted the agni pariksha so that he could get his Sita back, and at the same time, make the world believe that Sita had passed the test of purity. Even though, in fact, there was no test."

Mira looked at the deities of Sita and Rama, so serene as they smiled at her. "It was all a charade?"

"Yes and no," said Ravi. "Carry on, wife."

"Well, putri, Sita walked into the fire and disappeared, astounding the warriors of Sugriv's army and causing great fear in Hanuman and Lakshman. Suddenly, she reappeared with Agni Dev. The fire deity announced that Sita was as pure as Ganga and that her love for her husband was true. Husband and wife were reunited."

Lona turned to Ravi.

Now is the time for explanations, he thought. But let's see how much Mira has understood. "What did you think it meant when I said 'yes and no', putri?"

Mira chewed on her lip before answering. "The agni pariksha was a charade because Bhagwan already knew the truth. He is the truth. And yet the pariksha was necessary for Sita's fame. Without it, the world would have forever wondered if she'd been unchaste."

Ravi nodded. "Anything else?"

"The agni pariksha is the test we must all face. The ultimate test of our love. We cannot reach Bhagwan without passing through fire."

Ravi and Lona exchanged looks, both of them impressed.

"And how will we pass it?" Lona asked.

"With unswerving courage."

"Just courage?" Ravi asked.

"And faith. And devotion."

"And how do we create these qualities within ourselves?" Ravi asked.

"By being in the company of the devotees."

"And?"

"By chanting the holy name."

Lona smiled.

Ravi smiled back. Mira didn't need him at all.

Now he must only set her free.

# 22

# Inevitable

Uda's head felt like it was hot iron being pounded by a blacksmith. Her limbs were broken spears, splintered and shattered.

She hadn't called a vaid. It would only irritate the rest of the family. Besides, she wasn't really ill.

She clutched the bed sheet to her chest.

Now that Mira was gone, the people needed someone else to blame. Once more, Uda was the black-hearted witch. She'd killed her husband and now she'd killed her father and brother.

Uda tried to remember that everyone had to suffer their own karma. She tried not to hate her family for their words. If only Mira were here to reassure her.

If Mira were here, Uda thought, she would be the target of those words. Uda hoped Mira never came back.

She wondered if it was possible to die from words. She remembered how, when she'd been young, Purohitji had told her about how the scriptures mentioned the power of words. They stated that there were sages so truthful and pure that a single word from them could protect a village, or destroy a demon, or even bring the rains.

Now, in Kal Yuga, the power of lies reigned.

Uda had lain with other men and that was why her husband had died, they said. She'd crept away at night and been a whore, they said. Even if she'd prayed for him, her prayers would never have reached the Kula Devi because she was so unclean, they said.

Uda tried to shut out the voices. She screamed in her mind that they weren't true. She'd crept away only to escape his beatings.

He'd not been faithful. He'd let his courtesans into Uda's house and her bed. They'd worn her clothes and jewels, and she'd looked on, too weak from his beatings to fight them.

She'd been faithful! She'd prayed for his life! Black and swollen from his punches, she'd prayed. Was it her fault if she couldn't mean those prayers?

She wondered if her husband hated her for it. Was he in Narak? Did he curse her that she join him there?

She clutched the sheet to her chest. Please, Vasudev, I don't want to join him in hell or anywhere. I'm sorry I didn't mean my prayers.

She stared at the white canopy above her bed.

In this year and a half of Mira's absence, Uda had realized how much she'd lessened the pain. Even with the tension of Bhoj between them, Uda had always felt Mira was a sister. A friend.

Her throat ached.

She thought of how Bhoj had told her and Vikram about the magical serpent. She'd not believed him then.

Now she knew it was true. Those men she'd sent to follow Mira had returned with fantastic tales. Uda was so overcome that she hadn't known what to say to Mira. She'd only known she couldn't interfere with Mira's bhakti. Just as Bhoj had known it.

Uda clutched the sheet, longing for night to come.

Before Mira went to Merta, she'd asked Uda to care for Giridar. So at night, when all others slept, Uda covered herself in a shawl and hurried through the darkened halls and lanes of Chittore to Mira's mandir. She brought Krishna food and asked forgiveness that it'd been cooked with her own unclean hands. She dressed him in the beautiful clothes Mira had made, and applied the tilak to his forehead.

It was a secret. Not even Uda's maid Gita knew.

Uda sang to him. She sang songs she'd learned in her childhood. She sang Gopi Geet, songs of loneliness and separation. She looked into Krishna's lotus eyes and felt a stirring in her heart. Uda then knew why Mira couldn't give him up.

She turned on her side and stared at the white nets that hung around her bed. It was winter but she kept the nets up. She never took them down.

Vasudev, Vasudev, Vasudev, she thought.

Did my shadow kill my father and brother, Vasudev? Because I was a bad wife?

No! I never meant it. I did pray for him. I did.

Vasudev, my throat aches. Make it better, my lord, I can't bear it.

Is Mira safe? Does her family treat her well? Vasudev, my Giridar, let her never be this lonely.

The whiteness stared back at her.

"Uda?"

Blinking, she looked towards the door.

Gauri came forward, "I heard you were ill." She put her hand on Uda's forehead and gasped. "Putri, you're so cold!"

"Don't touch me, Ma Sa. My shadow will cover you."

Gauri sat on the bed, rubbing Uda's arms. "You must stop this. We both know it's not your fault."

"Our people think it is."

"They're wrong, Uda!" She paused. "This is why you left my quarters when I was ill, isn't it? You didn't want me to be maligned for being near you."

"I'm not a good person, Ma Sa. I shouldn't be near good people."

"No! You've done so much for us. You protected Mira when no one else could. I know it was you who sent her to Merta. In her stead, you took the brunt of society's anger."

"I deserve it."

Gauri stroked Uda's forehead. "Why must they blame you for everything? I'm a widow yet they say almost nothing to me."

"You gave your son and husband in battle. My husband died of illness."

"It wasn't your fault!"

Uda rolled on her side, turning from her mother. "Ma Sa, go, before they say I've poisoned you."

Gauri pulled Uda back around.

She moaned, her limbs hurt so much.

"Uda, something is truly wrong with you!"

Laughter bubbled up within Uda's aching throat. "That's what they've been saying all these years."

"No, I mean you're really ill. I'll call the vaid." Gauri moved to rise.

Uda grabbed her hand. "No."

"At least let them check–"

"No, Ma Sa!" A sudden weakness overtook Uda and she dropped her mother's hand.

Gauri stroked her hand over Uda's temple. "Why, putri?"

"It's my own karma, Ma Sa. My own deeds."

Gauri sighed.

"You must trust Giridar, Ma Sa. Trust him for he's all that's certain in this world."

Gauri leaned down, her face close to Uda's. "Putri, do you know who you sound like?"

"Who?"

"Mira."

Uda closed her eyes. "Then perhaps all is not so bad."

Perhaps the voices would be silent. Perhaps her throat would stop aching.

*

Ratan sat thinking about Jaimal's obsessive training. Something had to be done to slow him down but who could reason with Jaimal?

Only Shamal had been capable of that.

"Rana Ratan ki jai ho," said a man from the doorway.

Ratan looked up to see a black shrouded figure. "Come in," he said, watching the bent old beggar limp through the doorway.

The beggar closed the doors and looked about the room.

"We're alone," Ratan told him.

The bent man straightened and was tall and strong. He pulled the shawl off his head and looked at Ratan with youthful eyes.

Ratan smiled at him. "Come closer, putra. Sit with me."

"Ji, Ranaji," the young man sat next to Ratan.

Ratan studied Ranjeet's lean face, made leaner by the years he'd spent in disguise.

When Ratan had laid out Shamal, Ranjeet and Raagav's bodies, he'd discovered that Ranjeet was still alive. Right then, he'd seen his chance.

Whispering to Ranjeet to remain quiet, Ratan told everyone that he was dead. That night, he cared for Ranjeet's wounds, stemming the blood loss and sewing the torn flesh. He gave Ranjeet herbs for the pain and told him again to not let anyone see he was alive.

When Ratan performed the last rites for the three, he kept Ranjeet's face covered, for the body they were cremating wasn't Ranjeet's but one of the Afghan assassins. It had galled Ratan to treat an assassin with such respect, but it was for Ranjeet's protection and Ratan had done what needed to be done. He secreted Ranjeet back to Chaukari as one of the wounded soldiers, and once there, he hid Ranjeet away in Shamal's rooms.

Slowly, the boy recovered and Ratan explained why he must remain dead to the world.

Ranjeet created a new personality for himself and limped off towards Kabul, that place of ever eager thieves.

"It's a good thing all here think I'm dead. It's difficult to remain concealed in Delhi." Ranjeet said.

"Why?"

"I think the enemy has a Rajput informant."

Ratan recoiled. "What!"

"I couldn't believe it myself."

"Did you learn his name?"

"No. The Afghans gave vague descriptions. I don't think any of them know his true identity. But I realized at once that he was a Rajput."

"How?"

"Things they said about him. He rarely ate with them. He never went to the mosque. He spoke only Hindi."

Ranjeet had spent six months learning Persian so that he could blend in.

"When did you learn there was an informant?"

"Only recently. It took a while for the Afghans to start talking. From the way they joked, it was as if the informant had been around a long time. Perhaps since Mira Ben's marriage."

"Since Mira's marriage?" But that was almost ten years ago! Ratan ran his hand over his beard. How had they learned nothing of this for *ten years?* So much had happened in that time. And an informant had been telling the enemy about everything. Everything, of course, except Ranjeet.

"What about the Moghuls?" Ratan asked.

"You mean whether or not this traitor is informing them too? I can't say."

"It makes sense if he is. Humayun is making rapid progress into Bharat from the north. It's only a matter of time before he strikes Delhi."

"If the informant is selling secrets to the Moghul, no one mentioned it in Kabul. But Humayun is strong, my lord. He's not a great strategist but his general, Bairam Khan, is clever and ruthless. And our coalition is weak. The representatives in Delhi bicker and squabble over the spoils when they should be rebuilding defenses."

"I know! But if I go there to inspect progress, our allies will think I'm taking control."

"The representatives from Amber have tried to take command several times but Chittore's representatives and our own generals won't let them. Gondalgarh's yuvraj is also resistant. And as you know, the sultan has taken his share of the spoils and pulled out."

Ratan scratched his beard. "The only way to end the squabbling is to give Amber control. But to do that would make them stronger than Merta. And we cannot trust them not to take advantage of that and attack us."

"Amber has always coveted our land."

"There has to be a way of making the coalition work. There has to be!" Ratan looked at Ranjeet, thinking of the impossibility of a Rajput traitor.

"Who could it be?" Ratan asked, thinking aloud. He stood and paced the room, not minding Ranjeet seeing his nerves. A small part of him even liked it. It was like having his son back.

Ranjeet's voice broke through Ratan's thoughts. "You always said the enemy knew too much. How did they know of Shamal's route? How did they even know of his wedding? How did they always know how to counter our strategy in battle?" He shook his head. "Admit it, my lord, you suspected an informant long ago and that's why you sent me over there."

Ratan rubbed his eyes. "But why would one of our own betray us?"

"Someone who stood to gain." Ranjeet said.

Their heads rose at the same time and they stared at each other.

"It couldn't be." Ratan said. "Sangavat always spoke so highly of him. Bhoj told me himself that Vikram was loyal."

Ranjeet threw up his hands. "Perhaps too loyal! Think about it, Ranaji. Bhoj and Sangavat are dead and Vikram has taken the throne."

"Vikram wasn't even at the battles! He didn't know where we'd be." Ratan paused, staring at his hands. "But he was in a position to find out. Any of Merwar's men could've helped him." He paced the other way. "They could have alerted the enemy." He turned to Ranjeet, his voice gruff. "But why help assassinate Shamal?"

Ranjeet's eyes darkened. "To weaken you. Everyone knows you are the real ruler of Merta and Merta is essential if the enemy wants Merwar too."

"Then why has Vikram not handed Merta over to the Afghans already?"

"The Shah died just a year after Shamal's death, remember? Vikram, if he is the traitor, must have been in a dilemma over what to do next."

Ratan nodded slowly. "Then came the battle. There must have been some agreement that Vikram would take Merwar while the Afghans take Merta and the other countries in our coalition. It makes sense."

"Yes." Ranjeet rubbed his left knee at the place where the arrow had entered. He'd never walk straight again. "Things didn't go to plan."

He pulled off his ragged turban and ran his hands through his hair. Clouds of dust fell off him. "Something went wrong."

"Of course..." The realization hit Ratan like a rock. "The truth is that the Afghans had won. They were decimating us and there was no way for us to counter-attack because they'd cut off our reinforcements. If Bhoj hadn't suddenly plunged into the fray with the last of his cavalry, I'd be dead along with Sangavat. He surprised the enemy enough to make them retreat. Then our reinforcements broke through the barricade and drove the Afghans back. The enemy never counted on Bhoj being that reckless.

"His suicide attack saved us." Ratan concluded.

Ranjeet slammed his fist down against a table, thunderstruck. "Thank Krishna for Bhoj!"

They fell into silence, considering the possibilities.

Ratan lifted his head. "We're jumping to conclusions. The informant might not be Vikram."

"Even if it isn't, the logic still fits. It must be someone who stood to gain. And Vikram gained more than anyone. He was the *only* person that gained."

Ratan frowned. "If that's so, why did he refuse the throne?"

Ranjeet paused.

"It's true. He protested his coronation before the whole court, saying that he wasn't worthy and that his cousin should be king."

"Which cousin?"

"Shivgan, a distant cousin. He has a claim three generations old. Perhaps he's our traitor. My spies tell me Shivgan was stating his case before the whole court before they overruled him in favor of Vikram. Shivgan obviously wanted power."

"I still don't like Vikram, my lord. I don't trust him."

"Why? He carried on our alliance despite the fact that Bhoj was dead."

"Shamal never trusted him."

Ratan gaped. "What do you mean?"

"When he first saw Vikram at Mira's wedding, Shamal didn't like him at all. He said Vikram looked hungry."

"Hungry?" Ratan exclaimed.

"That's what he said. Hungry."

Why did Shamal never tell me this? Ratan thought. He looked up at Ranjeet, who was now standing near, watching over Ratan with anxious eyes.

"Are you alright, my lord?"

Ratan clasped Ranjeet's arm. "Go rest, putra. We shall speak more of this later."

"Yes, but are you alright?" Ranjeet was wringing his hands.

In spite of himself, Ratan smiled. Ranjeet had always had that habit of wringing his hands, even as a young child. Shamal and Raagav had teased him about his anxiety but Ranjeet had never grown out of it. Now, in his disguise, it served well as an aging effect.

Krishna planned things meticulously.

Ranjeet blinked down at his palms. "How is my father?"

Ratan felt his head beginning to ache. "He's well." Every time Ratan looked at his friend Lakshman Singh, he was weighed down with the knowledge that Lakshman's only son was alive but Lakshman could never know it. And that was Ratan's fault.

"And my mother?"

"I haven't seen her but I hear she is also well," Ratan said.

There was a pause. "Go, putra. I'll come to discuss more with you late in the evening. For now, I believe there is fruit in Shamal's room for you. I shall bring more food."

"Ji," Ranjeet stood and bowed. He limped towards the wall on the left.

"Wait," Ratan went to him, thinking of how lonely Ranjeet must be without his parents or his friends. Without a wife. "Ranjeet, your motherland is forever indebted to you. Your sacrifice is great."

Ranjeet shook his head. "I can never be greater than my motherland. And a mother is never indebted to her children. I live for her and I die for her."

Ratan gazed at him. "Why does that sound so familiar?"

Ranjeet smiled. "Because you said it."

Then Ratan remembered: an afternoon by the elephant pond, Shamal and his friends sitting on the ground as Ratan tested them on their slokhas, Mira playing on an elephant's back.

"You still remember that, Ranjeet?"

"Those were the happiest moments of my life, Rana."

Ratan put his arm around Ranjeet's shoulders. "I need you. You're my secret weapon."

Ranjeet nodded and pressed his hand against a small catch in the wall. A door swung open and squeezed shut behind him so that, once again, the wall looked just like any other wall.

Ratan stood there, praying that the traitor would be discovered soon. He would show the villain no mercy.

*

Kashi's roads were exactly like Chittore's—noisy, loud, constant movement.

Mira couldn't help wondering how her own people were. She hoped there'd been sufficient rains and that the harvest was good. She hoped there was peace. Most of all, she hoped Uda was well.

Her guard was still with her, even after the year she'd been here. They camped outside the city and took turns to come in and guard her. Mostly she was with her guru and thus they weren't needed, yet they still insisted on patrolling around Ravi's hut.

She'd told them to return to Chittore so many times but they refused, saying their duty was to protect her.

Mira suspected they liked it here. Many times she spied them when not on duty, taking darshan at the mandirs and bathing in the Ganga.

Her father had been sending her income to Kashi all these months so she'd been able to pay for their upkeep.

The time here had been so good. Gurudev and Guru Mata had told her wonderful stories to make her laugh and cry, and all the while Mira felt herself grow strong.

She felt the naam running through her veins as she'd not felt it since Bhoj's death. She felt it like it was Vayu's son Hanuman carrying her over the ocean, or Agni burning away false Mira.

Yet it was now different from before. The naam felt harder, swifter, as if the secret currents of the Ganga consumed her. Mira's stride was sure, her motions swift. She worshipped the ground with her feet, running along the banks of the Ganga, feeling the mud slide between her toes.

For the first time in years, she felt truly clean.

Down the lane, she spied Gurudev's hut, so innocent among the trees and the grass. Kashi was so green, so lush, the juice of sweet grass bursting outwards as Mira walked over the blades.

Inside, Gurudev was pounding on leather with a hammer. Khud khud went the ground. He looked up and smiled at her.

She felt her heart leap into her throat. She'd never get over his smile.

"Did you enjoy your walk?"

"Ji, Gurudev," Mira said. She sat before him on the ground. "The fog on the river looks like the clouds have descended to worship Ganga. It's beautiful."

Khud khud. "If only Uda could see our Mother Ganga. It is a shame that she's not well enough to come here."

Mira frowned. "Didi is unwell?"

"She's being tested."

Mira's lips parted. "Will she pass?" Even as she asked, her heart sank for she knew what he'd say.

Khud khud. "Your time in Chittore isn't over, putri."

It wasn't fair, she despaired. She'd thought she was free.

"But you're not free, Mira. Your thoughts still take you to Chittore. You go there every day, even though you don't realize it."

She started.

"You're still attached to your role as their queen. Until your attachment fades, your duty to them cannot fade."

"But they don't want me. I'm not attached to them, I only worry..." Of course, she thought. I worry. "How will I know when my time there is over?"

"You will know, putri."

She folded her palms. She thought of not seeing his smile and her voice grew shaky. "When will we meet again?"

"Don't come to Kashi. I won't be here."

She gave him an alarmed look.

"Worry not. I'll be on pilgrimage."

"Where will you go?"

"Everywhere I can," he said, smiling.

"Then how will I find you?"

"I will find you."

Why wasn't he giving her a straight answer? "What is the purpose of your pilgrimage, Gurudev?"

"Suspicious?"

She raised her eyebrows at him.

He laughed. "I should have known. Daughters are like that."

"Well?"

He looked away. "I go to the north, Vrindavan, Mathura, Delhi."

Oh no. "It's dangerous to go there, Gurudev. Please don't."

"I must."

She was appalled. "But the Moghuls can attack at any time!"

"I must trust in Bhagwan to protect me." He gave her a look. "Just as you must trust in him."

"May I come with you?" Perhaps she could find a way to make his route safe.

"No. I go because it is my guru's order."

She slumped. How could she could argue with that? Still, she wondered why her grandfather was sending Gurudev into such dangerous territory.

"Jai Shri Rama, Mira."

She understood: it was time to leave. She touched her forehead to the ground at his feet, then rose and gazed at his face. "Jai Shri Rama," she whispered, before rising and walking out of the hut, her first steps back to Chittore. Just when she'd thought her ties to the world were cut, they were tied again.

Yet these were her guru's orders and she would obey.

# 23

# Protest

Lona put her food package on the floor.

Ravi was placing flowers at Sita and Rama's feet.

"Why did you send her back?" she said, coming further into the hut.

"It's what was best."

"But she was just beginning to live again."

"It had to be done, I'd put it off for far too long."

Lona saw the white bundle on the floor. She stilled. "You're leaving too?"

Ravi nodded. It was something else he'd put off.

The silence between them lengthened until it became a piece of string, pulling them back and forth.

He looked at her wizened white hair and her young eyes.

She blinked back tears. "When will you return?"

He couldn't lie. "I may not."

She understood. She'd always understood. "Will you see your son before you go?"

He looked away. "Perhaps it's best if I don't."

"Please see Vijay. Otherwise, he'll think you've just abandoned him."

Ravi turned to Sita and Rama and sighed. "Send him to me."

She turned to leave.

"Lona."

She looked back to him.

"You know I must do this."

"I know."

For a moment, she looked just as she had when they'd first married. Like a bird that flew off at the slightest sound.

If not for her, Ravi would never have trodden this path. "Forgive me if I've hurt you."

"You've never hurt me, my husband." She left, her graceful feet taking her away.

A few minutes later, Ravi slung his bundle over his back. He knew that Lona would come to serve the deities every day so he needn't worry about them.

He went outside and sat on the ground, bracing himself.

Vijay walked up to him.

His son had always reminded Ravi of Lona. Straight-limbed and smooth skinned. Supple, dark. But then, Ravi was also dark.

"Ma said you were leaving," Vijay said, his voice slow and quiet.

Ravi nodded.

"May I come with you?"

First Mira and now Vijay. "You have a wife and son to look after."

"You also have a wife and son."

"My son is grown. He can look after himself."

"But who will look after you, Bapu? Let me come with you."

Ravi shook his head. "Rama looks after me."

Vijay shifted his weight onto his other foot. "It's always been Rama, hasn't it?"

Ravi was stunned at the bitterness in Vijay's voice. "Vijay…"

"I just wish you'd share something with me."

Ravi rose to his feet. "I've nothing to share except Rama. You know that."

Vijay turned to leave. "I understand."

Ravi grabbed his son's shoulder. "You think I've neglected you, don't you?"

Vijay was frowning.

"But how can I treat you as my son when I've never been able to look after you? I have no rights as your father."

Vijay opened his mouth to speak.

"It's true," Ravi said. "A real father is one who supports his family and I could never support you."

"But Bapu–"

"Hear me. My commitment to my guru means I must distance myself from that which is worldly. When bhakti awakens, attachment to the material world lessens. But that doesn't mean I don't love you. In fact, I love you more because I see Rama in you."

Vijay clutched Ravi's hand.

"I no longer see a boy I conceived with his mother. I see a divine flame that's part of my lord. That's why I'll never worry for you or fear for you. I know that Rama is within my son and knowing that gives me peace." Ravi leaned his forehead against Vijay's. "Never think that I don't love you."

Vijay moved back. "Then let me come with you."

"It's not your path, putra."

"What is my path?"

Ravi closed his eyes. "I cannot see that. But I know I cannot take you with me."

Vijay straightened his shoulders, just as Lona did when she was upset. "Forgive me. It wasn't right for me to be an obstacle but I wanted to try. I thought I should at least try."

Ravi touched Vijay's shoulder.

"I never thought you neglected me," Vijay muttered. "It just feels lonely sometimes. I wish you'd let me look after you."

"You've fulfilled your duties to me beyond anything I ever imagined. I'm proud of you."

Vijay took a deep breath before looking up at the sky. "It's getting late. You should leave soon."

Ravi pulled Vijay close and embraced him. "My blessings are always with you, putra. Never forget that." Releasing his son, Ravi pulled his bundle over his shoulder and walked away, the lush grass beneath his shoes softening the pain in his knees.

Never had he spoken so frankly to his son before. Vijay truly made Ravi proud.

Lona had been right. But then, she was always right.

\*

Mira lay on the carpeted floor, the roof of her tent suffocating her.

This was nothing like the first time she'd come to Kashi. Then, she slept outside, under the trees, the calls of the forest around her. The open air had felt like she was next to Giridar.

Now, with guards around her, she couldn't feel that way. Once more, she felt like she was on her balcony, trying to glimpse the stars through the holes.

She turned on her side and tried to sleep, ignoring the cot her guards had set up for her. Pilgrims didn't sleep on beds.

There was a shuffling noise.

She sat up. The guards were well trained and they knew to be quiet. Who was making that noise?

There it was again. Shuffle scuffle, like something had fallen down.

She crawled to the opening of her tent and peered out. Through the crack, she saw struggling shadows. Oh Krishna, was the camp being attacked?

She wasn't about to let her men fight and die without her.

Perhaps this was Krishna's test. Perhaps this was how it was meant to end. And she had no weapon!

Then she remembered the katar Sumer had given her.

She went to the table by her bed where the dagger lay. She clasped the handle as she'd been trained, her hands encircling the central metal holder as the protruding metal bars fitted along the sides of her hand. The blade was long and slim and triangular, perfect for stabbing. She pulled the sheath off and a slice of moonlight from the tent opening flashed over the steel.

The scuffling sounded again. There was a shout.

She pushed the tent flap away and ran out, katar at the ready. The scene in front of her, however, made her stop.

Her men were standing in a circle around her tent, fending off veiled women. No, not just veiled women but old men as well, many of them clutching packages, and making pleading gestures to the guards. One old man lay on the ground, rubbing his shoulder.

The people were pushing against Mira's guards and when they caught sight of her, their voices rose. The guards closed ranks to form a tight band.

"Return to your tent, Rani!" Sumer called to her.

"What is this, Sumer?" Mira demanded. "Who are these people?"

A soldier named Marut pushed a woman who leaned too far inwards.

"Marut!" Mira ran forward to stop him.

The crowd silenced.

"Raniji, they are troublemakers." Sumer came up to her. "Please, Babhi, return to the tent so that we may dispose of them."

"What do you mean, 'dispose of them'? Sumer Bhai, these are women and elders." She looked up at him. "Well?"

"Forgive me, Babhi, but we have to be alert. What if they're enemies in the guise of women?"

Mira looked at the woman who'd been pushed down. She was an older lady, with a thin face, lined like a coconut. "What is your name?"

"Satya. I only wished to get your darshan."

That was the most surprising thing so far. "*My* darshan? But why?"

"You're Sant Ravi Das' disciple." She stood and took a step forward but Marut pushed her back again.

Mira grabbed his shoulder. "I think this one's female, Marut. Let her through."

"But, Babhi—" Sumer began.

"Let her through."

As Marut stepped aside to let the woman in, the others spoke up, pleading to be let through also.

Mira couldn't believe so many wished to see her. She held up her hand to quiet them. "Who are you all and why are you here?"

An older man with the shaved head of a vaishnav leaned over his staff. "We've come from Naagpur. You passed our village earlier."

A woman leaned in, catching her gold bracelet on a guard's armor. "We wish to have darshan of you," she said, yanking her bracelet out of the kink in his shoulder.

Mira shook her head at them. "You're mistaken. I'm no longer a princess of any importance and therefore my darshan is useless."

"We haven't come to see a Raj Kumari. We've come to see a devotee. We've come to see Sant Ravi Das's disciple."

Mira tried to see the face of the elder who'd spoken but he was in shadow. "My guru is great but I am not."

"Sant Ravi Das takes only worthy disciples, Mirabai," another shadowed woman said.

Mira froze. "Why do you call me that?" she whispered.

"You are a great lady, Mirabai," said another elder.

Mira shook her head. "I'm not worthy of this honor. I'm only Mira, simple Mira. Please return to your homes."

The people raised their voices in protest.

"We came to hear your bhajans!" Mira heard in-between the shouting.

She raised her hands to quiet them once more. "If you wish to hear a bhajan that is one thing, but please do not call me Mirabai. I'm only Mira."

"Yes, you're Mirabai, Rana Ratan's daughter, we know," a woman said.

She was so short that Mira couldn't see her head until a guard shifted position and Mira spied her through the soldier's armpit.

"We've heard that your voice charms even the birds and that when you dance, it is like the Gopis dancing raas with Krishna."

Mira's heart skipped a beat to hear the little woman's words. News of her dancing had reached so far outside of Merwar? She danced like a Gopi?

Mira held her hands before her like a shield. "No, please, I'm not what you say."

"My name is Vamini, Mirabai, and I'm your follower. I've walked a long way to hear your bhajans."

Mira was trembling like a flower blossom in the rain. When she'd suspected an attack, she'd not trembled at all. She'd grasped her katar and determined to meet death head on. Now these people said they were her followers and she wanted to run screaming from them all.

She wasn't *Mirabai!*

The crowd raised their voices again, pleading for a bhajan. The guards pushed them back.

"Sumer Bhai, stop your soldiers!"

The guards ceased.

"These are women and elders and they will not be abused. Let them through."

Sumer opened his mouth to reply but nothing came out.

The look on his face made Mira understand. 'This has happened before, hasn't it?'

He bowed his head. "Yes, Rani. I thought it best to send them away."

"You could've at least told me!"

"You seemed so lost in your thoughts, I didn't want to disturb you."

He was right, Mira realized. She'd not paid her men the attention they deserved. She'd been neglectful. "Let them through and rebuild the fire," she said, her voice more sedate.

"As you wish."

The people, free of the barricade, approached her with folded palms.

She greeted them and asked them to sit while she fetched her tambora.

It's just as Gurudev said, Mira thought. I must keep singing for Giridar, that is my service to him and his devotees.

As her chariot rolled over the plains, closer and closer to the mountains of Merwar, Mira found that whenever she went near a village, a crowd would come and ask for her songs and stay with her all night long.

Mira shared her joy in the holy naam with all of them, even though it delayed her arrival in Chittore for weeks. Her twenty-third birthday came and went with song and dance.

No one listened when she asked them not to call her Mirabai.

*

"Maharana is here. He requests an audience with you," Gita said.

Uda hadn't seen him in months. No, years. Not since Mira had left.

She pushed the sheet off and stood. Her bones felt frail, weak, as if they'd shatter if she took a wrong step. She pulled her wrinkled veil over her head.

For a moment, she thought it was Bhoj sitting in her front chamber. He sat so straight, so regal, a sapphire pinned to the front of his turban. He looked taller. Even his moustache looked thicker. It was all she could do to choke out her greeting.

"Maharana ki jai ho."

"I hear you're not well, Didi."

He was a bit late in hearing it.

She couldn't bear to look at him, this pretend Bhoj. "I just feel a bit weak," she said, fixing her gaze on the floor.

"I trust you're recovering," he said.

Why do you care? she thought.

"I need you to be well, Didi. I've work for you to do."

That made her look up.

He sighed, looking as if all the world's burdens were on his head. Bhoj had never looked like that. This was Vikram after all.

She took a step towards him, careful not to jar her bones. "What can I do for you?"

He rubbed his temples. "Mira is returning to Chittore."

Mira! "How do you know?"

"My spies. She's raised quite a tempest, you know."

Uda frowned. "What do you mean?"

"Wherever she camps, a huge crowd of devotees join her and she spends the entire night in satsang with them."

The corners of Uda's mouth curved upwards. She smiled. She giggled. She shrieked with mirth.

Vikram glared. "I expected sensible behavior from you, Didi."

She held her hands against her stomach. "Doesn't it seem funny to you?" she gasped. "All but her own people have recognized who she is."

He made an impatient sound. "I've no time for riddles, Didi! This is a dangerous situation."

She stopped laughing.

"I cannot allow any civil unrest. We need internal peace if I'm to defeat our enemies."

Uda gestured around the room. "What can I do from in here?"

"She may listen to you."

"Mira only does what she thinks is right. Don't try to change her, Vikram." Uda fingered the table at her side. "I've tried it before and it doesn't work."

"I'm worried, Didi. I cannot refuse her entry because it would jeopardize our alliance with Merta and on top of things, Mira is dear to Raj Mata. But if she is to remain here, she must conform. I leave this responsibility to you, Didi."

Uda frowned at him. "What do you mean?"

"Make her don widow's garb and stay out of sight."

"You'd have her be like me?"

"I need the women of this family to be quiet."

She gaped at him. "Then you're a fool!"

His lips parted in shock.

"Do you still not realize who Mira is? What she is?"

His mouth worked but nothing came out.

"Mira is a *devotee*. If it were not for her, this land would have been destroyed long ago."

Vikram clenched his fists.

"It's true. Do you not think the alliance with Merta saved us? And it was Ratan, Mira's father, who stood guard over Bapu Sa's wounded body and protected him from the Afghans. You know very well, Vikram, that if the Afghan's had captured our king–"

"Any girl would have done in the alliance!"

"Mira was the center of our defense! Bhoj knew it and so did my father. And it's not just that. This land is protected because there are pure souls like Mira who walk upon it. For whom else would Krishna protect us if she were gone?"

Vikram waved a fist before her face. "This land is protected by the strength of men, not by the mystical nonsense of a foolish female. This land is protected by me!"

"You think it is. You who sit on the throne and pretend you're Bhoj. But it was Mira who gave Bhoj his strength. She made a true Kshatriya out of him."

"You've lost your mind! Is the whole of Bharat going insane?"

Uda prayed for strength. "Vikram, listen to me. Don't try to torment Mira or make her change. You must dispel the rumors about her. Therein lies your dharma as a king and a brother-in-law."

He kicked the table next to him and fruit went flying about the room.

She jumped.

"I'm trying to run a kingdom. I don't have time to debate stupidity. I've told you to do a job and as my subject, you're bound to obey me."

She crossed her arms.

"That's all I have to say." He stomped out, not looking at all regal as he picked his way through the guavas and grapes.

How dare he! Uda thought. She was his older sister and he had no right to order her.

She wanted to tell Mira not to return but she didn't know what route Mira had taken or how far away she was. And Uda couldn't deny how much she longed to see her friend. Just the knowledge that Mira was returning made Uda's bones feel stronger.

She had to do what Vikram wouldn't. She had to tell the people the truth. Even if they stoned this widow for daring to speak, she must do this, for Mira.

*

Mira couldn't believe it.

The people of Chittore were standing at the roadside with their palms folded, watching her ride past.

But they hate me, she thought.

There was a scuffle as someone pushed his way to the front.

Mira looked at the man.

He was tall but his body was bent with age. As he pushed people from his path, she saw he walked with a limp. He seemed anxious to reach her before she passed.

Her heart skipped a bit. No, it couldn't be–it wasn't–

Mira told herself it was nerves. Her mind was playing tricks on her.

Except that when that old man looked at her and she met his eyes, she felt like she was looking at a friend. A dear friend.

A dead friend.

Her chariot passed on.

She couldn't help looking back into the crowd, trying to catch a glimpse of the old man, but he was gone. Perhaps he'd never even been there.

When the chariot drew up to the palace, Mira was shaking so badly, she didn't know what to do with her hands. Her unexpected vision bothered her but the silence of the fort was much worse. Even the royal banners had ceased flapping.

Mira descended and told Sumer to take the men to the barracks. Then they were free to go home to their families. She went up the steps and headed for the ladies quarters. All along the way, servants bowed and were silent. What was going on?

She arrived at teak double doors. "Tell Raj Mata that Mira wishes to pay her respects," she told the dasi.

The dasi bowed. "Please enter. Raj Mata is waiting for you."

Mira walked through the doors and saw that no one was in the front room. She went into the solar.

Gauri was sitting in the speckled sunlight that filtered through the marble screen. She looked up from her embroidery, smiling. "Bahu!"

Mira went forward and touched her mother-in-law's feet. Crouching on the floor, she saw that lines had burned their way into Gauri's fair face. Her forehead was weathered with grey hairs, as if the ashes of Sangavat's funeral pyre had settled on her head.

Gauri lifted Mira and embraced her. "Live long, my dear. How was your journey?"

Mira shook her head. "Fine, but why has everything changed? The whole fort is different, and the people, they–"

"They are respectful? Yes, I know. Uda told me."

"Didi! She has recovered from her illness then?"

Gauri gave Mira an odd look. "How did you know she was ill?"

"I–I heard about it," Mira stuttered.

"Well, she was ill. Then she heard you were returning and I never saw such a fast recovery."

"She's well then?"

Gauri sighed. "Not quite. Still, it is Uda you have to thank for the change in our people. She's taught them much in your absence."

"What? But she never leaves her rooms. She–"

"She's become like you."

"Me?" Mira sat on the couch with a thud. "Ma Sa, what are you talking about?"

"When she heard you were returning, she went out and told the people all about the things you endured, the torments, the humiliations, all so that your people would be safe under the alliance. She told them what you sacrificed for them, and of your bhakti for Krishna." Gauri reached out and touched Mira's cheek. "She told them of your kindness to everyone, even a mother-in-law who was so cruel to you."

Mira stared at Gauri.

Gauri smiled. "Why don't you go into my bedchamber? Uda's resting there."

Mira rose and ran for the room.

Uda was asleep in bed. She looked pale, hollowed out somehow.

Mira stopped at the bedside, dismayed. "She looks lifeless," she whispered to herself.

"I'm not so lifeless, Mirabai."

Mira started. "You too, Didi?"

"The name suits you."

Sighing, Mira knelt beside the bed. "Didi, what's the matter? What is this illness?"

"It's nothing, really. I just feel a bit sleepy."

Mira put her hand on Uda's brow. "You feel weak? Have you been eating?"

"It's not that. It's nothing, Mirabai, really."

Mira cast a despairing glance at Gauri in the doorway.

Gauri was smiling. "She's been calling you that ever since she heard it. She was even angry that she hadn't thought of it herself."

I can't believe these people, Mira thought. "Didi, how long have you been feeling weak?" She took hold of Uda's cold hand.

Uda yawned. "Not that it matters, but I think it started a little while after you left."

"It started when the whole city turned on her." Gauri's voice was loud.

"What do you mean?" Mira looked from mother to daughter.

"Ma Sa..." Uda whined.

"It's true, Uda," Gauri said, coming around to the other side of the bed and sitting on the mattress. She glanced at Mira. "When you left, the people turned the brunt of their anger towards Uda and she's suffered ever since."

A heaviness sat on Mira's chest. Once again, she'd hurt someone she loved.

"They've cast their evil eye on her," Gauri said, stroking Uda's brow.

Mira squeezed Uda's hand. "Sit up."

"I can't."

"Sit up. For me."

With Gauri supporting her back and Mira pulling at her shoulders, Uda heaved her bony frame upwards.

Mira sat on the bed, facing her. "Didi, why do you listen to them?"

Uda looked at Mira with bleary eyes, an owl discomfited by

daylight.

Mira kissed Uda's hand. "Vasudev knows who you are and nothing they say can change that."

Uda shook her head. "I tried to tell myself, Mirabai, I did." Her lips trembled. "But I fear what they say is true and that Vasudev must hate me as much as they do."

"Vasudev would never hate you."

Uda's face looked hollower than ever, as if she were the inside of a coconut. "They say I killed my husband and Bapu Sa and Bhoj."

"No!" Mira clasped Uda's face, trying to force life into it. "You mustn't listen to them!"

"How can you be so sure, Mirabai?" Uda rambled. "It makes sense really. Everything I touch is destroyed."

Mira almost choked. "To die, to end, to change, that is the nature of this world, Didi! Don't take it all upon yourself." She prayed that Giridar would help Uda. "The only thing you did wrong was to put your faith in society and not in Krishna."

Uda raised her black gaze. "I know." She held Mira's hand against her cheek. "I've felt him. But I'm not strong like you, I'm not good enough to keep him with me."

Mira wiped Uda's tears. "He's always with you. He's everywhere, in everything, in every moment. Once you understand that, you'll feel him always."

Uda moved into Mira's embrace, resting her head on Mira's small shoulder. "I felt so alone when you were gone. It felt worse than when he was beating me."

Mira closed her eyes and held her sister. She should never have left Uda in Chittore.

"I should've taken you to Gurudev, Didi."

"Sant Ravi Das?" Uda whispered as Mira rocked her back and forth. "You saw him?"

"When your brother died, I felt so lost. Gurudev helped me see Krishna again."

"I wish I could meet Sant Ravi Das. Then I might not be so wicked."

"Shhh…" Mira rocked Uda, cursing her own selfishness. Poor Didi had braved her worst fears for Mira and all the while, Mira had been singing and dancing.

Gauri's eyes were far away. "When Sant Ravi Das came to Chittore just a few years ago, your father showed him all honors. He even went to Ravi Das for blessings." Gauri sighed. "Such a happy time."

"What did Bapu Sa say about him?" Uda's voice was so young. So innocent.

"He said that when Ravi Das lifted his hand to bless him, there was a white spot of light in the center of his palm."

"Really?" Uda was wide-eyed.

Mira held Uda as Gauri recounted all the things Sangavat had said about Ravi Das. None of them surprised her. She herself had seen the jyoti in his hands.

There was no leaving Chittore now that Gurudev had ordered Mira to stay. Indeed, he'd sent her to care for Uda. Mira would make sure that Uda recovered. Together, they'd never again feel the pain of loneliness.

# 24

# Grapple

It was hot and wet the next morning. The coming of monsoon hung in the air like an insect waiting to bite.

Mira bathed and dressed in a red cotton sari. She rolled her hair into a bun at her nape and applied vermillion to her parting. She picked up one of the trays Janki had readied and went down to Krishna's mandir.

The garden was empty.

She went up the steps and opened the door to the inner sanctum.

Dressed in his light sleeping clothes, he looked so charming.

Mira rang the bell to wake him. She bathed and dressed him in a saffron silk dhoti, seeing that he was shiny from the massages Uda had given him.

Mira painted sandalwood designs on his feet, adorning his toes with Tulsi leaves.

Janki and Lakshmi entered with more trays. They set them down and left.

Mira sat and threaded a needle before stringing flowers into a garland. When she could no longer hear her dasis' footfall, she smiled up at Krishna. "Now I have you all to myself," she told him. Looping jasmine flowers together, she sang of how the grass sprang up to pad Krishna's feet and the cows followed his flute through the forest. The peacocks danced when they spied him and the birds sang for his pleasure. The deer walked up to him to be petted and the monkeys brought him fruits. The land of Vrindavan bloomed as a bride, all for the pleasure of beloved Krishna.

She placed her garland around his neck, white flowers lush against his dark shining chest.

"Will you make a garland for me?" said a voice behind her.

Her heart stopped at the sensation of whispers. She swallowed, then turned.

He was standing at the entrance to the mandir, leaning against a pillar.

He looked so much like Bhoj, she almost fainted. Surely Vikram had never looked so much like Bhoj before. Her legs shaking, she walked towards him, folding her palms. "Maharana ki jai ho."

"Greetings, Mirabai."

"Please don't call me that, Maharana. I'm not worthy of the name."

He arched a brow. "Indeed. How was your journey?"

She suppressed a shiver, even as the hot wetness of monsoon lay on her skin. "It was safe. Who could ask for more?" She noticed a white petal, moist with morning dew, clinging to the back of her hand. She lifted her other hand to brush it off.

Vikram lifted his hand and it collided with hers.

"Oh, forgive me," she said.

He plucked the petal from her skin. "No need."

This is all wrong, Mira thought. Even Bhoj never looked at me like that.

She shook off the feeling, telling herself she was just nervous because no one else was around. "How are you settling into your responsibilities as head of the family, Jehtji?" For some reason, she needed to remind him he was her brother-in-law.

He was rolling the petal between his fingers, caressing it until it bruised. "I see you still wear your jewels."

She squelched her urge to step back.

He touched her cheek with a fingertip.

She pushed his hand away. "Jehtji! What are you doing?"

"I can give you jewels, Mira." He slipped his arm around her waist and bent to kiss her neck.

"Let go!" She slammed her fist into his ear.

He reared backwards.

She ran a few steps into the mandir. "How *dare* you touch me!"

He must have recovered from her blow because he bounded up the last few steps towards her. "Come now, Mira. I think we should stop pretending."

She glared at him, backing away. "What are you talking about?" She came up against the altar. Giridar, she thought. Do something!

"I think we both know. Don't fear me, Mira, I'll give you jewels.

How about emeralds? Or rubies? Rubies look good on your skin." He reached out.

She slipped behind Krishna.

"I can't marry you, of course," he said. "But I'll look after you. You'll never fear society's tongue again."

Mira realized this was actually happening. He was really saying these things to her. "How can you even think like that?" she cried. "You're Maharana!"

He laughed. "Precisely. Whether you agree or not, you will accept me." He groped at the end of her veil.

She grabbed Krishna's flute and hit Vikram's hand with it.

There was a blinding light.

Mira screamed and covered her eyes. She heard a hissing sound. Giridar, what was happening?

Vikram howled.

She peered through her fingers.

A huge serpent was at Vikram's feet. No, not a serpent. It had more heads than a serp–*more heads!* Mira lowered her hands and looked again. It *did* have more than one head. And it *was* a serpent! It slithered towards her and Krishna, its scaly black body encircling her.

She'd have screamed if she'd not been frozen, inside and out.

Giridar, she thought. Giridar, Giridar, Giridar.

Vikram gave her a dazed look, then howled again.

She realized the serpent had bitten him on the hand. She thought it was the same hand that had touched her but she couldn't tell for sure. There were just too many heads. At the same time, the serpent was circling her. How could the serpent lie at Vikram's feet and be circling her at the same time? How could it have so many heads? It had to be lots of different snakes. But Mira *knew* that it was just one.

Where had it come from?

She clutched Krishna's flute and watched in mute horror as it wound around her, sure to tighten at any moment.

Vikram howled again. He grabbed his left calf and staggered back, moaning.

Mira thought the bites couldn't be poisonous because Vikram hadn't collapsed. There was no white froth at his mouth.

The serpent wasn't killing him, only driving him back.

Around and around her went the great serpent.

It lunged to bite Vikram again but he lurched away, stumbling down the steps with his lame leg. He disappeared into the garden.

Mira looked down at the serpent.

It was gone.

She stared at the space where it had been circling her but there was nothing there.

Had it ever been there?

She peered into the moist air outside.

Vikram was gone.

She couldn't believe he'd tried to attack her. Had the world gone mad? Had Mira gone mad? If it hadn't been for the serpent–the serpent! She looked from the empty floor to Krishna standing before her. "The serpent..." she breathed, stepping around to face him.

Now she remembered the look Vikram had on his face, the same look Bhoj had worn that night. Was that serpent what Bhoj had seen?

"My lord, my lord," she said over and over. "How can I thank you enough?"

She fell and touched her forehead to Krishna's feet, kissing his sandalwood painted toes. The coolness of the stone soothed her sweating brow. Nothing could harm her now.

Vikram thought he was powerful? Mira laughed to herself. She would never fear him again.

*

He didn't stop until he was in his dressing room.

Vikram grabbed a cloth and wet it in the basin, then threw the cloth away and stuck his hand in the water, it was itching so much. He looked down at his calf. It was red but not swollen. It looked more burned than bitten. He couldn't understand why he'd not collapsed yet. Perhaps it was a slow moving poison. He had to call the vaids.

What was he talking about? Poison? There'd been no poison! He must have burned himself on a lamp and not realized it.

Bhoj's tormented words came back to him. *It wasn't an ordinary snake. There were...lots of heads. And eyes, red eyes.*

Vikram was losing his mind and it was all Mira's fault! She had to be a witch.

How dare she reject him! He raked his nails over his itching calf. The skin came away in his hands.

Her face blazed in his mind, just as she'd looked when he'd tried to kiss her. Her skin had looked so soft, beads of moisture clinging to her neck and her cotton veil molded to her body. He could see through it to her lushness underneath, her curves reaching out to him.

How dare she reject him! She should be up here with him right now, seeing to his demands. The only reason she lived was so that she could warm Vikram's bed. Didn't she realize this?

He moaned, the burning sensation spreading up to his elbow and he picked the wet cloth up off the floor to wrap his arm with it.

He would have made life so easy for her but she thought she was above him. Above the king! He'd show her.

He'd not forced her because he was noble. He didn't like to hurt women. That was why she was still down there in her little mandir. If Vikram had wanted, he could have dragged her up here and done whatever. She could do nothing about it.

In fact, he thought, that's what he'd do. He would drag her all the way here and make sure she screamed like she'd never screamed before. Hit him with Krishna's flute, would she? He flung the cloth to the floor and stamped towards the door.

His leg gave way beneath him. The pain was like a thousand tiny insects running around inside his leg. He squeezed his eyes shut and moaned. That snake had made him a cripple!

What snake? He'd burned himself on a lamp!

It was she who'd caused this. She'd confused him with her whorish ways and he'd burned himself. Somehow.

"Dasi!" he shouted.

A slim young woman in red came running into the room.

He liked all his dasis to wear red.

She gasped to see him on the floor.

"Call Raj Vaid," he said through gritted teeth.

She ran out.

His hand itched and he scratched it, the skin raking away with his nails.

The witch. She practiced black magic and that was the cause of his injuries.

He would see her punished. No one practiced black magic in his kingdom. Reject him, would she?

He turned onto his back to take the pressure off his throbbing leg. The thousand little insects crawled their way towards his groin, running around under his skin. He cried out.

Was Bhoj right? Was Mira protected?

He realized that he couldn't move his hand. His fingers were stuck in a crooked position like an old beggar.

He would kill all snakes in his province!

Mira would pay for this. It might take time but he'd make her pay.

So what if everyone loved her now? He could change that. He

could make them hate her anew.

Because everyone hated a witch.

*

Uda moved into Desh Bhakti Bhavan with Mira.

Neither she nor Mira were responsible for the royal households because Vikram had appointed his other female cousins to the job. It was fine by them. Now they had all the time in the world to devote to Krishna.

After three months of rain, news came that Delhi had fallen to Humayun, or rather, to Bairam Khan. The coalition was in pieces, the Rajput forces scattered. With Delhi taken, it was only a matter of time before the Moghuls came for Merwar.

Mira and Uda worried about the state of fear that pervaded, hoping that Vikram would do something to calm the people.

Vikram married a princess of the Jodhpur Rathores, one of Mira's distant cousins.

Mira caught a glimpse of Maharani Renu once in the gardens, looking so young and tender. There was a bruise on her left cheek. When Mira tried to talk to her, the girl ran away, retreating into the palace.

Mira thought that if she tried to help Renu, it would only backfire. Vikram didn't need excuses as it was.

Nine months after the wedding, Renu gave birth to a stillborn boy.

Some whispered that the child had died from the beatings.

In Uda, Mira saw renewed memories of brutality. Horror glazed her eyes until Mira had to shake her from it.

Mira's face grew more sculpted as one, two, three years passed and she approached twenty-seven as if an artist was chipping away at her. The valleys of her cheeks grew into ravines and her chin that had once been so delicate was now a cliff, terrifying in its severity.

Seeing the way Renu had to live, Mira understood, now more than ever, how blessed she'd been with Bhoj.

Then the news came that Humayun had died, dispatched to the afterlife by a fall from the steps of his astronomy tower. Bairam Khan was now officially in charge because Humayun's son and heir, Akbar, was only a boy of thirteen.

Bairam Khan consolidated Akbar's forces over the next two years, rounding up Afghan rebels and executing them. Sikander Shah Sur, an Afghan chief in Punjab, surrendered to Akbar.

Yet there was little talk of challenging the Moghul. The years went by in peace.

Uda accompanied Mira on trips to the Kumbh-Shyam mandir. The devotees swarmed around them like waves against a boat, pushing and pulling and steering them towards the height of the song.

And after every few months, when Mira's income arrived from Merta, she and Uda went on pilgrimages near and far. They cooked feasts for the sick and homeless, feeding the cripples with their own hands. And to all who thanked them, Mira and Uda said that it was by Krishna's grace that they were doing this. Krishna and Sant Ravi Das.

Bairam Khan was assassinated while on pilgrimage to Mecca. His influence over Akbar had been too strong for the other Moghuls to bear.

For the people of Chittore, it was a show of even greater monstrosity. The Rajputs had been as eager to kill Bairam Khan as anybody but they'd never have attacked him when he was on a holy journey. Such a thing was against dharma.

Akbar was now nineteen years old and, it was said, his blood burned to subjugate the Rajputs.

Maharani Renu gave birth to two more stillborn sons.

Vikram married again, this time to a princess of Gondalgarh and it was whispered that he didn't go to Renu anymore. His new bride was beautiful and spoilt and Vikram was enamored of her.

Mira noticed that where Uda's paleness had once matched her garments, now her skin shone with a brighter hue. Pink had entered her cheeks and there was a sparkle in her eyes. Her bony frame was overtaken by health and flesh. Now past the age of forty, Uda looked like a rose that had bloomed in winter.

For Mira's thirty-third birthday, Mira and Uda decided to visit the holy city of Pushkar, the only place on earth that housed a temple to the creator Brahma. Mira wanted to bathe in the famous lake, the Bindu Sarovar.

They set out in the middle of winter, planning to return home in the middle of spring, thereby avoiding the worst of the cold and the worst of the heat.

As always, a crowd of holy men and devotees accompanied them. Many widows also joined them. Commander Sumer and his guard protected them on Vikram's order, though Mira tried to tell Sumer he wasn't needed.

It was now tradition for Mira's camp to host a satsang in the evenings. Devotees would come from nearby villages and Mira would play on her tambora and sing.

Sumer never liked the arrangement. He said it was dangerous.

They reached Pushkar and stayed in a dharamshalla there. They bathed in the Bindu Sarovar and went for darshan in the Brahma temple. They sat before the priest and heard the history of Pushkar.

It was said, the priest told them, that at the beginning of time, Vishnu was sleeping on Shesh Naag in the midst of the cosmic ocean. As he slept, a lotus grew from his navel and when the lotus opened, Brahma was sitting in the middle of the blossom. Brahma then asked Vishnu what his purpose was. Vishnu told Brahma to meditate to find the answers. They both meditated and a pillar of fire appeared before them. The fire was Shiv and as an oracle, he told them to search for the end of the pillar. Brahma flew upwards and Vishnu descended. They looked and looked for eons but couldn't find the end. They returned to the original spot to discuss their findings. Vishnu, being truth personified, admitted that he'd not found the end of the pillar of fire. Brahma, however, wanted to outdo Vishnu and said he'd found the end. Shiv, knowing that Brahma had lied, cursed Brahma that he'd create the entire world but never be worshipped for he'd also created falsehood. Vishnu, who spoke only the truth, would be loved by all and worshipped forever. Brahma recognized his fault and begged forgiveness. In his mercy, Shiv told him there would be one place on earth where Brahma would be worshipped. Brahma meditated upon Shiv's name by the Bindu Sarovar, and gained the boon of his temple.

It was said, the priest told Mira and Uda, that if a son were to bathe in the Sarovar and pray for his deceased father, the deceased would gain immense spiritual benefit.

Mira bathed in the Sarovar and gave money to the poor. She paid for a feast to be served to the poor Brahmins of the city. She did it in Bhoj's name.

She and Uda remained in Pushkar for over a month, visiting the temples of Saraswati and Gayatri, Brahma's wives, the mothers of the vedas. Mira's fame drew the holy men and they spent hours in satsang, talking of the great stories. Mira sang her songs for them, composing new ones also.

Still, it was the songs she'd written with Gurudev that were her favorite.

Spring approached and Mira and Uda decided it was time to return to Chittore. Rama Navami was almost upon them and they wished to be home to celebrate it with Gauri.

Three nights after they left Pushkar, Mira sat in the usual satsang.

Uda was asleep in the tent, tired from their long day.

Mira sang about Mother Yashoda's pain when Krishna left Vrindavan. She sang that Yashoda's tears made a second Yamuna river, even holier than the real Yamuna for Yashoda was Krishna's mother. She'd suckled him and loved him and taught him to walk on his tender feet.

She finished the song and the crowd pleaded for another.

Then a man stood up. He was younger than most of the men there, with a thick moustache that ran down to his jaw and up to his ears. He wore a turban, though it looked a bit loose for him and slipped down his head.

Mira saw he had red hair beneath it. She wondered why her guards had let him into the camp since it was Sumer's established rule that young males were not allowed in.

An older man stood with the red haired younger one. He had a lock of hair that was longer than the rest, and he wore a vaishnav tilak on his forehead.

He must have been why the younger one was let through, Mira thought.

They came forward and knelt before her.

"Pranam," they said.

"Ji, pranam," she nodded.

The turbaned man put his hand on his heart. "I've never heard such a voice before." His voice was soft and oddly accented.

He must be from a distant land, Mira thought.

"I'd like to offer a gift in exchange for your beautiful bhajan." He took out a golden necklace embedded with emeralds.

Mira drew back. "I'm obliged to you but I don't sing for gifts."

"I know. You're free from the vice of greed. Still, I beg you to take it."

She clutched her tambora. "I thank you but no."

"Take it for your Krishna deity. I'm told you have one."

"Of course I have one." She'd brought Giridar with her to Pushkar.

"Then give it to him and that will satisfy me. Please, I must give you something for your song and this is the greatest jewel I possess."

Mira was about to say no again when a grandmother nudged her.

"Take it, Mirabai. The poor boy offers it with such humility."

Mira felt hot with frustration, the deep valleys of her cheeks growing red as she flushed. "What will I do with such a gift? My bhajans are not to be bought."

The older man spoke for the first time. By his voice, Mira knew he could sing very well.

"Ji, Mirabai, it wasn't the lad's intention to buy your bhajan. He only wished to express the joy he felt at finally hearing your voice. Please take it for Krishna and we'll be satisfied."

The crowd called out to her to take it.

He does offer it with faith, Mira thought. She could see the sincerity in his eyes.

He held the necklace out, the gold glittering in the campfire.

She wouldn't take it. It wasn't right. She didn't want other devotees to hear she was accepting gifts and descend on her with offerings.

Mira looked at the man. He wanted her to give it to Krishna.

She shouldn't accept it. Giridar didn't need jewels.

"Take it, Mirabai," the crowd called. "Honor the boy's faith!"

"Please take it," the red haired man said, looking like Raagav had looked when she'd refused to laugh at his foolish pranks.

Mira sighed. She gestured to the ground before her. "Place it there. I'll give it to Krishna as you wish."

He glowed, wrapping the necklace up in a silk cloth and laying it before her. "I thank you."

Mira forced a smile for him and shifted backwards to avoid touching the gift.

# 25

# Secret

Ratan wondered if Mira would visit Merta on her way home to Chittore. Pushkar wasn't far from Merta.

She might come to see her old father.

It'd be wonderful to see her, not to mention a great morale boost for his subjects now that Mira was revered throughout Bharat. Ranjeet had been there to witness her return to Chittore years ago. He'd seen how the people bowed to her and flocked to the temple to hear her sing. They called her Mirabai.

Of course, that hadn't been Ranjeet's mission. He'd been there to find the traitor, if indeed the traitor was from Merwar. He'd found a soldier who talked of a certain malnourished man named Koirala.

Well, Koirala wasn't a Rajput name, was it?

Ranjeet found out that Koirala worked for the state in some sort of administrative position, although no one was really sure what he did. Koirala frequently took trips away from Chittore, saying he was going to Kumbalgarh on business. Ranjeet went to Kumbalgarh to investigate, but found that no one there knew a man named Koirala.

How could a non-Rajput be allowed to work in the palace and then take trips away for no reason? Where was he going? Who was he?

When Ranjeet sent word that Koirala worked in the army barracks, dealing with soldier records and such, Ratan felt unwell. A great deal of information went through such places.

Then, quite suddenly, Koirala was dead, found in the barracks with a dagger in his throat.

The murderer hadn't been found.

Ratan's chest began to burn after every meal. His vaids prescribed cooling drinks and ordered that all hot spices be cut from his diet.

If Koirala had been involved with spying then by whose connections had he gained a position working for the state? Who was his true employer? The Afghans? The Moghuls? Someone else?

Ranjeet's one clue was gone.

And now Jaimal was ill with fever. The vaids said it was exhaustion.

Vikramdev was frantic.

Jaimal kept insisting on seeing to his duties and it took three men to restrain him. Even now, he was performing documentation in bed, reading messages and letters.

Two years ago, Amber had proved true to its reputation and allied with Akbar, giving the Moghul one of their daughters in marriage. The princess was now known as Empress Maryam Zamani, given a Muslim name to please Akbar's Muslim court.

The emperor had abolished the practice of making Muslims privileged citizens by doing away with burdensome taxes on non-Muslims. He'd even taken on some Hindu royal customs such as appearing at his window on certain days for his subjects to see him. He was even inviting famous Hindu artists and musicians to his court to integrate Hindu and Moghul culture.

Hindu kings were talking about allying with him and even entering into his service. They said that he was not so bad a tyrant as Babur.

The world was going mad.

Akbar was just as bad as his father and grandfather, Ratan thought, except that he was taking control of Bharat with cleverness rather than brute strength. He knew that the Hindus wouldn't submit to him unless he showed tolerance towards their beliefs.

It was said that Maryam Zamani—Ratan choked on the name—was allowed to practice her bhakti in a tiny temple within her apartments.

Vikram of Chittore was sending messages that they couldn't attack Akbar now: he was too strong. They had to wait for the strategic moment.

Ratan agreed that they couldn't attack, but he didn't agree that waiting was a good idea. How long would it be before more Hindu rajas married their daughters to the emperor?

If only Ratan knew who the traitor was, he could devise a strategy to weaken Akbar.

The only one Ratan trusted was Ranjeet, whose last message had been four months ago, saying that he was heading for Fatehpur Sikri, Akbar's capital. Since then, there'd been nothing.

Every night, as Ratan drank his cooling drinks to douse the burning in his chest, he wondered where Ranjeet was. Perhaps Ranjeet was on his way to Merta right now. Perhaps he'd found the traitor and was trying to kill him. Perhaps he was deep in Moghul territory and there was no way of sending a message.

Perhaps he'd been discovered and was dead.

*

When Mira and Uda arrived in Chittore, the first thing they did was visit Gauri.

They told her all about the holy men they'd met and how she should've come with them even though she told them she was too old to travel anymore.

The next morning, Mira made her way down to Krishna's mandir. The spring air was ripe with scents of the sweet champaa and kesari flowers.

Today, she would begin arranging the celebration for Rama's birthday. She wanted dancers to perform at the Kumbh-Shyam mandir with a play and a great feast to be served afterwards. She also wanted satsang to go on all day in Krishna's mandir, and she was planning to ask some of the holy men to give sermons on the Ramayan.

Vikram was planning a procession and had invited her to it.

She hoped he'd mended his ways. She'd never understood the madness that had possessed him. Since the serpent, however, he must have come to his senses and she hadn't seen him.

Mira had wanted to be in Chittore for Rama Navami so she'd not taken the time to visit Merta. She regretted not seeing her father, but he was always so busy that she doubted he would've had the time to spare for her anyway. She'd write him a letter tonight.

As she bathed Krishna, Mira sang of when Krishna saved Queen Draupadi from her evil brother-in-law Dushashan who'd tried to disrobe her before the royal court of Hastinapur. Mira sang of how Draupadi had called out to Giridar Gopal and he'd blessed her, making her veil never-ending so that Dushashan pulled and pulled and never found the end.

Mira dressed Krishna in a light blue cotton dhoti since it was so hot. She wrapped a turban around his head, inserting the tip of a peacock feather into the folds. Lastly, she untied the knot she'd made at the corner of her veil. A necklace slipped out, gold and studded with emeralds. An emerald the size of Bhoj's thumb dangled from its apex.

Mira fastened the necklace around Krishna's neck and stepped back. The green-blue fire shone against Krishna's blue chest, nestled amongst the white and orange flowers.

Mira sighed. "Krishna, there's no one more beautiful than you."

She'd felt uneasy taking the necklace but now seeing it on Krishna, she knew it'd been made for him. She prayed to Giridar to bless the young man who'd given her the necklace.

Janki and Lalita entered the temple with the bhoga trays. They gaped at the jewels around Krishna's neck, in particular the huge emerald on his chest.

Since they, along with Lakshmi, had stayed in Chittore to look after Raj Mata, none of them knew what had happened on the journey from Pushkar. Mira had retired Savitri a year ago.

"Where did you get that, Rani?" Janki asked, her eyes wide. Even though Janki was a grown married woman, she still had the air of a young girl.

Mira shrugged. "A traveler. He asked me to give it to Krishna."

The maids exchanged looks.

Mira arched a brow at them. "What are you looking like that for?"

Lalita hesitated. "Jiji, that's the biggest emerald I've ever seen. I don't think even Maharana has a jewel that big."

"Of course he wouldn't. It's only fitting that Bhagwan's jewels be greater than anyone else's. That's probably why that man gave it to me for Krishna."

"Did that man say who he was?" Janki said.

"No. But he seemed generous."

Janki's round eyes latched on to the emerald. "Very generous."

Mira busied herself inspecting the bhoga trays. There were fruits, sweets, saffron milk, flowers, rose water. Mira had decided that she didn't hate rose so much after all. In fact, she'd grown to love the husky romantic yearning of the scent, sweet and unfulfilled. She'd even begun to offer it to Krishna every day as part of his breakfast. She did it in Bhoj's name.

The maids left, looking over their shoulders at the necklace.

Mira shook her head at their silliness and offered Krishna his food.

She stepped out of the inner sanctum of the temple, the garbagraha, and shut the doors so that Krishna could eat in peace. There was a string on the side wall that was attached to a fan above Krishna's head and she pulled at it to fan him.

Opening the doors once more, she heard a shuffle behind her.

"Pranam, Mirabai."

She paused. This was the first time is years he'd had the courage to face her, she thought.

"Pranam, Maharana," she said, smiling as she turned.

Her smile disappeared fast enough.

He looked so *old*, standing there at the foot of the steps. His face was ravaged, his blue eyes red and bleary. She wondered if he was ill. Perhaps the snake bites had caused him more injury than she'd thought.

Mira felt a pang as she remembered how he'd howled.

His gaze was fixed on the floor. "I trust your yatra was successful."

She walked to the top of the steps, keeping her gaze on his face. "Ji, it was."

"And did you manage to do all that you desired?"

Why the sudden interest? "We did, Maharana."

"And you were safe at all times?"

Mira almost smiled again. "We were."

Then Vikram looked up at her—no, not at her but at Krishna. "I see you've acquired a new treasure."

She was perplexed. "No, Maharana, Giridar has always been with me. Don't you remember?"

"I'm speaking of the necklace around his neck."

Mira followed his gaze to the emerald. "A devotee donated it for Krishna."

Vikram stroked his moustache, now straggly and thin. "Indeed."

Mira wondered why such a simple gift should cause so much talk. Perhaps Vikram was jealous at not possessing such an emerald himself, as Janki had said. If he was, Mira thought, he should rid himself of such thoughts. Greed was not a virtue, especially in a king.

But there was a calculating look in his eyes as well.

The air vibrated when Vikram spoke again. "Who gave it to you?"

Was it the look in his eyes that made her suspect? Or was it the way his hand curled at his side, as if he were resisting something? She stepped back.

Why did she feel so nervous? He couldn't hurt her! "It was a man sitting in the satsang one night."

He leaned forward. "Achaa? A man?"

"Yes," she said, forcing her voice to stay even. "A merchant." Perhaps it'd been a mistake to take the gift after all, Mira thought. She'd get silly questions like these now.

"What did this devotee look like? Surely as the head of the family, I should find him and express my thanks."

"That's not necessary. He gave the gift with the intention tnat it be given to Krishna. He didn't want more than that."

"He must have been a rich man."

"Yes, as I said, he was a merchant." Mira wished this conversation was over.

"A merchant, you say?" Vikram stroked his moustache.

"Yes, a merchant." Mira spoke quickly because she just wanted him to leave now. He was using up the morning and she still had things to do before the lunch hour. "He looked a bit unusual, actually, fairer than most and he had red hair."

"Red hair?" Vikram looked more interested now than ever.

Mira swallowed her nerves. "Yes, red hair. In every other aspect, he seemed an ordinary person."

"Indeed?"

"Yes, indeed."

Vikram looked from the jewel to Mira. "This is all fascinating and I wish I could discuss it more. However, I have duties so if you'll excuse me, Mirabai, I'll take my leave."

"Pranam, Maharana," she said in relief.

He turned and left, his fingers still running through his straggly moustache.

When she returned to the bhavan, she busied herself with festival preparations and tried to forget her strange encounter. The only problem was a nagging little voice in the back of her mind. By the end of the day, she almost wished she'd go down to the mandir and find the necklace gone, stolen away by a thief.

Of course, the jewel was still there when she went down that evening. No one in their right mind was going to steal from Krishna.

Mira sighed and offered him his meal, lighting the lamps and fanning him. She sat thrumming her tambora when Uda came up the steps, chewing on her bottom lip.

"Who's that for?" Mira asked, nodding at the yellow silk Uda held.

Uda glanced down. "It's a gift for one of the pujari's children." Her voice sounded tense and short. "We'll have to give them gifts at Rama Navami."

What's so upsetting about that? Mira wondered. "I've finished a few sets of clothing myself." She thrummed some more on the tambora before setting it down. "What's wrong, Didi?"

Uda glared. "I heard *he* visited you this morning."

Mira paused. "It was fine, Didi, I promise. He only asked about our yatra to Pushkar."

Uda looked over at Krishna, blowing so serenely into his flute.

"Did he mention the mala?"

Mira sat up. "Why is everyone so obsessed with it? It's just jewelry!"

"Yet even you are agitated about it."

Mira tried calming herself with a deep breath. It was that stupid nagging voice in her head again. "Forgive me, everyone is just so enamored of that jewel. It's vexed my nerves."

Uda just looked over at Krishna. "Vasudev," she whispered.

The next day wasn't so eventful. Or the day after. People gawked at the necklace when they came to Giridar's mandir but no one said anything.

Mira thought less about Vikram and more about the upcoming festival. She still had to prepare a new song for the lord's birthday.

The week passed and everything was set for the great day. The menu was fixed and the ingredients all accounted for. The dancers were happily practicing their play and the holy men were thinking up their sermons. Mira considered putting in an appearance at the procession but she knew that cooking and the kirtan would require most of her attention. It was best if she stayed near the bhavan.

She was in bed resting after the noon meal, listening to the chum of her anklets as she tapped her heel on the mattress, when Uda burst in on her.

"Mira!"

"What's wrong, Didi?" Mira sat up.

Uda wrung her hands. "You have to leave. Now!"

Mira rose. "What are you talking about?"

"Please, Mira!" Uda grabbed Mira's arm and pulled her towards the dressing room. "There's no time. They might come at any minute!"

"Who?" Mira dug her heels in. "Calm yourself and tell me."

Uda yanked at her arm.

"Aiee!" Mira squeaked. "What's wrong with you?"

Uda dropped Mira's useless arm and began grabbing clothes from the chests, flinging them into a pile on the floor. She took a sheet and bundled the garments together, tying them up with a big knot.

"You must go!" Her hands were trembling. "Oh Vasudev, what will happen now?"

"Didi! What is it?"

Uda turned to the doorway. "Where are your maids?"

"I sent them to rest."

"Even Lalita?"

"Yes, why?"

"The less they know, the better." Uda shoved the bundle into Mira's arms. "Time to leave."

Mira dropped the bundle to the floor. "First tell me what's happening."

Uda looked at the doorway again, her eyes wide. "There are terrible rumors about you."

Mira rolled her eyes. "It wouldn't be the first time, Didi. Although I do admit, I've no idea what they're upset about now. But you know I don't care."

Uda shook her head. "The law will care. You must leave *now!*"

"What?"

"The law, Mira! They'll put you on trial."

*Trial.* "For what?" Mira laughed. "Madness? I'm afraid I'll have to plead guilty."

Uda clasped Mira's hand. "This isn't the time for jokes! I'm serious."

"But trial for what?"

"Treason."

Mira blinked. *"Treason?"*

Uda pounded her forehead with the butt of her hand. "We can't waste time! You know what the sentence for treason is." She picked up the bundle.

Mira took it and threw it on the floor. "I want to know!"

Uda groaned. "It's the necklace."

"What are you talking about?"

"It was Akbar who gave it to you, Mira."

Who? Mira wondered.

"Akbar! The Moghul Akbar! Badshah Akbar!"

As soon as she understood what Uda was talking about, Mira decided that it was the most stupid thing she'd ever heard. It wasn't even funny. "Akbar? And just how is that possible?"

"Vikram's spies say that Akbar hasn't been at court in Fatehpur Sikri for the past two months. He was seen in the area of our camp just three weeks ago. The man who gave you the necklace–he had red hair correct?"

"Well, yes, but–"

"Akbar is known for his red hair! Red like dirty copper, they say. And he's also known for his love of music. There was a man with him, yes?"

"Yes, *a Hindu man!* Why would Akbar be with a Hindu man?"

"Because that *Hindu* was Tansen, Akbar's famous court musician!"

Mira shook her head in disbelief. "Tansen? And Akbar? Really, Didi, you should know better. Why would they come to see me of all people?"

"Because you're famous too! Tansen must have told Akbar about you and Akbar wished to hear you sing."

"So they disguised themselves and snuck into our camp?" Mira rolled her eyes. "And why give me a gift?"

Uda threw up her hands. "Does it matter? Perhaps Akbar was truly moved by your bhajan. The fact remains that his emerald is in your possession and the whole city believes it payment for your treachery."

Mira couldn't credit this nonsense. "But how—?"

Uda shook her. "That jewel is so huge it could only belong to a king!"

Mira shrugged her off. "Even if it was Akbar, I didn't take it as payment for anything. I gave it directly to Krishna as requested."

Uda slumped. "That's not how they'll see it, Mira," she moaned.

Mira stepped out of Uda's reach as she tried to digest what had been said.

Akbar. And Tansen. And the necklace.

Her people thought she was a traitor.

Traitors were put to death.

Mira closed her eyes and pictured Krishna as he'd looked that morning, the emerald shining from his blue chest. She saw his pink palm, cupping the pure water of the golden stream. She saw Giridar, a mountain resting on his fingertip.

Was this his final test? she wondered, opening her eyes.

"Please, Mira, you must leave. I'll stay behind to ward them off." Uda took a bag of gold from her waist and slipped it into the bundle. "Take this and go."

Mira grabbed Uda's shaking hand. "I'm not leaving, Didi."

Uda gaped at her.

"I cannot leave. Gurudev ordered me to stay. Perhaps this is why he sent me back."

"To face this? Trial and death? No, Mira, you must go." She squeezed hard on Mira's hand. "I cannot bear it if they harm you!"

Mira smoothed Uda's hair down. She remembered the serpent in the temple as it had circled her. When death itself was Krishna's servant, what could Vikram do to her? "Nothing will happen to me," she whispered. "Have faith, Didi."

Uda wept into Mira's hand. "How can I?"

Behind them, Mira's suite door crashed open. "Rani Mira!"

Uda stared at the walls in horror. "Quick, the servant's door."

The servant's door crashed open. Guards flooded the room. The dressing room doorway darkened as more guards flooded in from there.

In the middle, Uda clasped Mira like a little child.

So many men to catch just one woman, Mira thought. Vikram was still thinking of the serpent, after all. She almost giggled at the thought.

The leader of the fray came forward. It was Sumer.

In the split second that he met her eyes, Mira saw his shame.

"Rani–" All the times he'd protected Mira were in his voice. "I'm under orders from Maharana to escort you to prison."

Uda's eyes blazed gold. "How dare you, Sumer!" she shrieked. "Of all people, I never expected you to do this. Have you no obligation to my brother? To your *dead friend Bhoj?*"

From the way he flinched, Mira thought he had a very strong sense of obligation. "Didi, this isn't Sumer Bhai's fault," Mira said. "He's under orders from the king."

"But he knows these charges are baseless. He was there! He should protect you!"

"He should do his job, which is to obey Maharana," Mira said.

Both Sumer and Uda looked at her.

Mira smiled at him. "I don't blame you, Sumer Bhai. May I take my tambora with me?"

His moustache was scrunched up from the way he was grinding his jaw. He'd heard her sing many a song on that tambora. He'd even requested a few songs himself. "Of course you may take it, Babhi." He motioned to one of the men to fetch it.

"I'll get it," Mira said, lifting her chin. She didn't like anyone else touching Gurudev's blessing.

The soldiers, all members of the guard Bhoj had created for Mira, bowed as she passed them, shuffling their feet.

She took the smooth wooden tambora from where it lay on its cushion on the table. "I am ready."

Keeping Mira in the middle, they trooped out. It wasn't much different to when she'd walked to her wedding, except that this was easier, and she was not being clutched by bodiless hands. Also, there was no one to embarrass her with crude jokes.

Just as she passed through the doors, she turned back to Uda who stood with her hands in her mouth. "Look after Giridar, Didi."

Uda nodded, mute.

Mira smiled. Now we'll see what Vikram has in store, she thought.

\*

Walking through Madhuvan, Ravi breathed the sweet air. He watched a herd of elephants pass up ahead, their graceful swaying bending the trees backwards. He watched as the cows wandered, munching on juicy grass.

Lushness bloomed, roses sprouting in clusters, champas falling off bushes, lotuses growing in ponds.

Ravi had come to Braj after wandering all over Bharat. He'd gone to Ayodhya and Rishikesh up north. He'd bathed in the Sariyu and the Ganga and even gone so far northeast as the Brahmaputra River. He'd gone down south to Ujjain and bathed in the Shipra and Narmada, and taken darshan at the Omkareshwar and Mahakaleshwar Jyotirlingas, two of Lord Shiv's twelve high temples. He'd traveled east once more, this time going to Bhubaneshwar and to the great Kali Mata temple in Kolkata.

And everywhere he stopped he met people and told them to chant the holy naam. He told them it was Bharat's salvation.

Now in Braj, where Krishna had played and frolicked with the Gopis, Ravi was overwhelmed with sadness. This land would soon be laid waste by Akbar.

Braj, or Vraj, as some called it, was less than a day's ride from Delhi. The Moghuls had already been here. Luckily, they hadn't realized the importance of this land, thinking they were only destroying another region. The Brahmins had taken the deities from the temples and hidden them so that no Muslim barbarian would lay his hand on their delicate lord. Some deities were buried, some lowered down wells. Some were even hidden in the trunks of trees.

Now, with Akbar's power growing, it was only a matter of time before Moghuls came again so the devotees didn't want to restore Krishna to the altar. Their love for him was so deep that instead of seeking his protection, they sought to protect him.

Ravi laid his hand upon a dark tamal tree. Rama hadn't visited him for months now. Neither had Gopal. Not for months and months.

Ravi found himself weeping at nothing. Water tasted sour. Day seemed like night and night seemed like the blackest day. Where was Rama?

Ravi sighed. He'd seen Vikram's power rising like a palm tree. Too thin to be noticed, too high to give shade. Ravi had sent her to it. Had he done right? Would she be safe?

Of course she would. She was ready. Wasn't she?

Death was always the final test.

He looked up at the tree branches that hung around him. Gopal, give her strength.

Ravi slid to the ground, his back against the dark tamal trunk. "Gopal, Gopal," he whispered.

"Yes, Ravi?"

His head shot up.

A Blue Boy, holding a flute loosely at his side, smiled at Ravi.

The scent of flowers was sweeter and the leaves of the trees greener. The earth at Gopal's feet sprouted soft grass even as Ravi watched. The birds let out purer notes than he'd ever heard. And golden light was everywhere.

A calf appeared at the Blue Boy's feet, grazing on the soft fresh grass.

The Blue Boy patted its head.

Ravi prostrated himself on the ground. Sandalwood filled his senses.

Krishna's lotus feet were painted with swirling sandalwood patterns, Tulsi leaves clinging to his toes like lovers.

"What did you want, Ravi?"

"Want, Gopal?"

"You called me."

"I called you?" Ravi asked.

"Yes."

"I only wanted your darshan, my lord."

"Well, here I am." The Blue Boy sat down beside Ravi.

The earth burst forth with new grass to cushion him.

Ravi couldn't breathe and at the same time, he didn't need to. Gopal had never sat next to Ravi before.

"Do you know how dear this land is to me, Ravi?"

"No, Gopal. How dear is it?"

Gopal plucked a blade of grass from the ground and another four burst forth in its place. "This land is like my mother. It does nothing but love me."

Ravi stared at the blade in Gopal's hand. It grew longer and greener, even though it'd been plucked. It curled around Krishna's hand.

Gopal laughed. His ocean eyes curled upwards, his lashes so long that they touched the arch of his eyebrows. "See how it tickles me?" He stroked the bit of green with his finger. "But I've no time to play, Little

Blade. I must think of my Mira."

Ravi found his lungs and inhaled. "Mira, my lord?"

"Yes, Ravi."

"Was I wrong to send her back?" He couldn't help blurting it out.

Gopal studied the blade in his hand. "You cannot do wrong, Ravi. Your place in her life is higher than anyone's. Even mine."

"Even yours?"

Krishna smiled. "Of course! I'm only her husband whereas you're her guru. A husband must always honor his wife's relations. That makes you my guru."

Ravi gaped at him.

"Why do you think I appeared the moment you called? One must always obey one's guru."

It was too much for Ravi. "How long will you tease me, Gopal? Be merciful!"

Krishna shook his head, laughing. "Arre, I'm trying to make you happy and you're protesting!"

"Please don't raise me so high," Ravi begged. "Let me stay here at your feet."

Krishna grinned. "As you wish."

Ravi was so relieved he almost melted into the tamal tree. Then he felt the ground rumble as Gopal stood.

"Is this Mira's final test, Giridar?"

"Tell me, my dear, is there ever a final test?"

Ravi thought of the constant gnawing, the pain of leaving Lona, the guilt of leaving his son. "No," he said. "Will this test mean her death?"

"The soul never dies, Ravi. You know that."

"Then she'll come to you soon?"

"What is soon? A day in Brahmaloka is as long as the life age of this earth. Is a day in Brahmaloka soon?"

Ravi smiled. "The Gopis were right when they named you Nuthkhut, my lord. You're so naughty."

Krishna laughed. "That's why they love me, you know."

Then he was gone.

The calf grazed where the fresh grass had grown.

Ravi leaned forward and touched the cow's feet, beloved as they were to Gopal.

# 26

# Confession

Mira sat on the dirt floor, straw littered about her as a bed.

Above, the world was playing in the spring sun, whilst here her breath came out as white mist. She wrapped the end of her veil around her shoulders but it didn't warm her. This dungeon had no windows, just three little slits in the roof.

She'd not known it would be so dark.

She missed the soft cushions of the palace and the clean marble floors. She missed the light.

I'm too attached to luxury, she thought. Gurudev isn't attached to anything except Rama. He lives with dirt floors and fog. I should follow his example.

She closed her eyes. "Giridar, it's just you and I."

Sandalwood and jasmine filled her nostrils. A peacock feather brushed her cheek and Mira lay on her back. Warm air caressed her. Her skin tingled where the feather trailed down her throat.

"Giridar," she whispered.

The feather lifted away.

She opened her eyes. "Giridar?"

The sandalwood and jasmine melted away.

"Giridar?" Her breath came out white once more. She sat up.

"Come back!" she screamed, pounding her fist on the dirt floor.

Silence.

She rose, wandering about her cell, trying to catch his scent. "Please come back," she whispered.

The decaying smell of cold closed in around her.

Mira threw her veil off her shoulders. She undid the knot in her hair and let it tumble down her back. She picked up her tambora and strummed it, thinking of what she should sing.

"Soon," she told herself. "It will be soon."

What could Vikram do to her? What could this dirt floor do to her? Even here, Krishna would come. He was with her always.

She feared nothing.

*

Mira wasn't sure but she thought it was two days later that a pale bull of a guard opened her cell door. Despite the darkness, she could tell that the guards were pale. They didn't get much sunlight.

Vikram stepped into her vision, his hands clasped behind his back. Mira stood.

"You've been called to court."

She shrugged. "Tikh hai."

He looked pleased at her acquiescence. "Follow me."

She smiled at him. "I'll never follow you."

He glared. "You just agreed to come to court!"

"Yes, so that justice may be done. But to walk behind you? Never."

Vikram's gaze shifted to the guard standing behind. "It is just this sort of disloyalty that brought you here, Mirabai."

He stomped out and she listened to the stones resonate from Vikram's offensive footsteps.

The bull came forward a step. "Mirabai."

She nodded. Holding on to her tambora, she walked into the thick of the guards waiting outside her cell and marched with them down the passage, coming to a set of ascending stairs.

She lifted her skirt a little off the floor. I've come too far to break my neck now, she thought, chum chumming up the steps.

Reaching the top, they passed through a single door, wide enough for three people to walk side by side. They entered a cavern filled with chains and locks, obviously a communal prison hall built for short term guests. Sconces lined the walls and a single window was high up in the corner. No light shone through it: it must be night.

It hadn't escaped Mira that today might be Rama Navami. She regretted not singing for Rama at noon, the hour of his birth. She hoped that Uda had gone through with the plans for the feast. Mira had worked hard on them.

They turned left and went up another set of stairs.

There was a door at the top that led to the outside. It swung open as they approached.

A guard appeared in the doorway, a black spot framed by the orange light of sconces. "We'll show you the way from here, Raniji," he said.

Mira stepped into the new hub of soldiers. She could feel the tension in the way they were holding themselves, as if they would pull out their swords at any moment. Mira wondered why they were so tense about escorting just one woman.

In the distance, the street torches lit up a crowd being restrained by rows of guards. When they caught sight of Mira, they began shouting and pushing against the guards.

"Mirabai ki jai! Mirabai ki jai!" she heard people on one side shouting.

"Traitor! Traitor! Widow!" people on the other side called out.

The sounds of struggling increased and Mira saw that the crowd had turned on itself. She wanted to tell them to stop fighting but her guards ushered her out of sight.

They reached a set of high double doors that opened as they approached. This was the royal court. Here, Raj Purohit himself presided as judge. His decision was final, his authority absolute. Even the king sat below him.

Gold light emanated from the ghee lamps. Mira's sensitized eyes blinked and she looked up at the open night sky to soothe her vision.

"We'll take Rani Mira from here," a tall, slim guard said. He was dressed in blue livery, his sword sheath decorated with pearls.

Mira assumed her position amongst this new set of guards and advanced into the building. She could hear the sounds of chatter and anticipation as she neared the open courtyard.

The chatter stopped the moment she entered.

Her blue guards melted away.

In that hall filled with ghee lamps, where the roof was open to the sky and the stars glittered down, Mira could smell only dust. She could feel it filling her nostrils and getting under her nails. It stiffened her hair and stained her clothes. It wasn't like the dirt of her dungeon cell. That had been fine and dark and humble. This dust was coarse and fair, the dust of battlefields.

She fought the urge to cough and her skin felt tight.

The royal family sat in the balconies. The generals and prominent merchants sat on ground level at the sides, facing inwards. Brahmins sat on the dais, surrounding Raj Purohit on his throne at the top of a grand marble stair. Pillars stood at his left and right hand.

Mira walked to the middle of the hall.

She looked up at Raj Purohit. She'd met him many times—at her entrance to Chittore, at her wedding feast, at her bahu bhojan. The last time she'd seen him had been at Sangavat's last rites.

His silver hair was even longer than she remembered. He carried sacred rudraksh beads in his right hand and wore a necklace of them around his neck. He opened his mouth and his voice boomed. "Let the hearing commence. State the crimes of the accused."

An elderly Brahmin came forward with a scroll. He unrolled and began reeling off the charges, his nasal voice carrying far.

"Raj Purohitji, Rani Mira is accused of violating marriage law. She has stayed alone with men other than her husband, Yuvraj Bhoj, even whilst he was alive. Now that he is martyred, she refuses to accept widowhood and insults his memory by continuing to wear her vermillion and jewelry."

Mira almost rolled her eyes. This was old news, she thought. She noted there was no wind tonight which was lucky as none of the lamps were flickering and she could see Raj Purohit's face clear in their light.

"She is accused of treason against her country for providing information to the enemy and by accepting a gift from Akbar of the Moghuls."

The court burst into agitated whispers.

When could I have given the enemy information? Mira wondered. Out of the corner of her eye, Mira spied Uda sitting in a pew above and Mira shifted her feet, trying to catch Didi's eye so that she could smile at her.

"Silence!" Raj Purohit boomed.

The whispers ceased.

He looked at the Brahmin. "Is she accused of any other crime?"

"Ji. She is accused of inciting the subjects against Maharana Vikram, their lawfully consecrated king."

That's new, Mira thought as whispers broke out again.

Raj Purohit looked at her. "Do you plead guilty to any of these charges?"

Mira saw herself as if from the sky, small and insignificant. "I have only one, my Giridar Gopal, there is no other for me." She stopped, surprised. She'd not planned on saying that, but now her throat felt as if it were lined with silk. The dust had cleared.

Purohitji frowned. "What do you mean by that?"

The words just fell out of her mouth. "Lord Giridar Gopal is my true husband, he walked with me round the fire."

"Giridar? Who is this Giridar? Let him be brought forth."

Everyone looked around, shifting with unease.

Vikram's balcony level was just below Raj Purohit's. He narrowed his eyes at her.

Mira met Vikram's gaze. "He is the lord of all three worlds, against him, your power is nothing."

The court looked to her.

She strummed her tambora and smiled. "The sweet, gentle, compassionate lord, he is my husband, birth after birth."

Purohitji leaned forward. "Do you mean to tell this court that Shri Krishna is your husband?"

She inclined her head.

"What of Yuvraj Bhoj? He was your husband by law and dharma."

"No. My marriage to him was a farce to protect our people. My true husband was always Krishna."

The court erupted in outrage.

"Silence!" Raj Purohit thundered. He looked back at her. "Do you realize what you are saying, Rani Mira? Your words may earn a harsh punishment."

"It is he who controls my flowing words and singing tongue. His will is my only law."

"Rani! Are you saying you don't accept the authority of this court?"

"Nothing happens without Krishna's wish. We are all in his thrall."

Raj Purohit clenched his hand around the arm post of his throne. "What say you to the accusations of treason?"

"I act only for Giridar's pleasure."

"Is it Giridar's pleasure that you be a traitor? What of Akbar's gift?"

She picked at the tambora strings, loosening some, tightening others. "A devotee gave a gift to the lord."

"He gave the gift to you, not the lord."

"A wife is entitled to hold her husband's possessions."

Purohitji gaped at her.

He thinks I'm mad, Mira thought, and her smile widened.

"Did you give the Moghuls or the Afghans information?"

"The only information I have is the holy naam and I will give it to any who ask."

"You have traveled over long distances for many years. Even whilst Yuvraj Bhoj was alive. You may have passed our secrets out at any of those opportunities. What of the third accusation? Have you been inciting the subjects against their Maharana?"

"What has Maharana done wrong that he's worried about rebellion? Only tyrants suffer revolt."

Vikram growled. "Liar! Admit that you've been poisoning the minds of the people against me!"

Mira raised her eyebrows. "How have I done that?"

"With your songs!"

Her eyes widened. He even accused her songs!

"I sing Krishna's names and his pastimes. I sing of my devotion to him."

"And my slander! Don't think I don't know!"

"Enough!" Raj Purohit said.

Vikram bowed his head. "Forgive me, Purohitji. I'm made angry by her betrayal of my brother."

Mira laughed aloud and the crowd gasped.

Purohitji, however, was looking at Vikram. "Control your anger, Maharana. A good king knows when to be angry and when to be calm." Raj Purohit turned back to Mira. "Do you plead innocent or guilty?"

"Who among us are innocent?" Mira replied.

"So you plead guilty?"

"I have only one, my Giridar Gopal…"

Purohitji looked strained. "Your crimes have been heard and you've been given the opportunity to respond. Your trial begins tomorrow at dusk. This court is now adjourned."

Blue guards materialized out of thin air to escort her.

Mira gripped Gurudev's blessing and prepared herself for the darkness of the dungeon. It mattered not. It would end soon enough.

\*

At dusk the next day, she returned to stand in the center of the court, waiting in the silence for what would come.

Raj Purohit tapped his fingers on the arm of his chair. "Rani Mira, you know what crimes you're charged with. What is your defense?"

She shrugged. "I've stated my reasons."

"You've nothing else to say?"

"No."

Purohitji stroked his silver beard. "You say Yuvraj Bhoj wasn't your husband but Krishna is. Tell me, has Krishna given you children?"

Mira met his gaze. "My relationship with Giridar is not of the body but of the soul. It's not a question of blood ties." She thought of Gurudev's instructions on the nature of bhakti and strummed her tambora. "Still, if you insist then I can tell you he has given me children."

There was a collective gasp.

"I know what is mortal and immortal, powerless and the most powerful. I do not fear you or this court and my courage was born of my trust in Krishna. I care not for the opinion of the world because I need nothing but him. My trust in Krishna gave birth to my knowledge and renunciation. These are my children and I will sacrifice much to protect them."

The court burst into loud voices.

Raj Purohit nodded. "I admire such bhakti, Mira. I truly do. It's amazing that you're so fearless." He looked grieved. "Yet I cannot permit you to renounce your lawful husband. It is a bad example to all the women of this land."

"I have an eternal relationship with Krishna. I will defend my love in this court and the next because that is my duty as a wife. Is that a bad example?"

"But you're a royal lady and Yuvraj Bhoj was your husband."

"In this life I was born a royal lady. You were born a Brahmin. But were you a Brahmin in every birth? Will you be one in the next? What is the value of your caste if it is not eternal?"

Vikram roared to his feet. "Mira! How dare you speak to your guru this way?"

"My guru is Sant Ravi Das of Kashi. I will call no other my guru."

"She's a scourge upon our pure land!" Vikram raged to the court.

Purohitji kept his gaze on Mira. "Calm yourself, Maharana."

"Forgive me, Raj Guru."

Purohitji took a deep breath. "Is that who you stayed with in Kashi? Your guru?"

"I stayed in a dharamshalla near my guru's hut and I went to him every day for instruction."

"But you were alone with him?"

"My guru is never alone. Rama is with him." She directed a fixed glare at Purohitji.

He had the grace to look ashamed. "What of Akbar's gift? Do you not realize he's our mortal enemy? By taking his jewels, you've betrayed us. Did you give him information?"

"As I said, I gave him only the holy naam. I'm Krishna's wife. A devotee gave me a gift for my husband and I passed the gift to him with all speed. Krishna doesn't look at people and see their bloodline or caste. He sees only what is in their hearts. Perhaps he saw this devotee's love and inspired me to take the gift."

Purohitji leaned forward. "So now this is all Krishna's fault?"

She shook her head. "Everything happens according to his will. If Giridar had not wanted the gift, he never would have allowed me to put it on him."

"She's mad!" the people shouted. "Lock her away!"

Mira looked at Vikram. He knew as well as she did that Krishna had ways of expressing displeasure.

Purohitji glanced in the direction that Mira was looking to see Vikram. He frowned. "Silence!" he roared at the court, before turning back to Mira. "Did you incite the subjects against their king?"

She raised her eyebrows. "What king? I see no man worthy of the throne here."

Amidst the shouting of the crowd, she pointed to where Vikram sat. "That throne is the seat of righteousness. Until my brother-in-law rules with truth and justice as his aides, he'll never be worthy of it."

The jeers of the crowd drowned out her last words.

"I will have silence!" Purohitji roared and the court finally stilled. Purohiji closed his eyes for a long moment before looking at her.

"You've given me no choice, Rani. This court finds you guilty of all three crimes and the punishment would normally be death. However, seeing your sincere bhakti, I will be lenient. If you accept your faults and ask forgiveness, I will change your sentencing from death to lifelong imprisonment within your bhavan grounds. What say you?"

Mira looked down at the marble floor and noticed it was peach colored, speckled with orange. No, not orange. Saffron. "I cannot ask forgiveness when I'm not sorry."

"Mira," Raj Purohit urged, "you are too innocent to comprehend what you are saying. Think again."

"I comprehend more than you know, Purohitji. Death is not the end of my journey or anyone else's."

He studied her calm features. "I'll give you time to think over my offer. We'll meet again at dusk in five days on Shunivar. If you don't ask for forgiveness then, you'll be sentenced to death by poison. Do you understand?"

Hanuman Jayanti, the birthday of Rama's darling pet, was on Shunivar. It was, indeed, an auspicious day to die.

*

Mira came to the door of her cell, squinting to make out her visitor.

"They won't let me inside." Uda's voice sounded like a mouse scratching in the corner. "Can you believe their insolence?"

Mira felt Uda's tears on her fingers. "Be careful else the bars will rust."

Uda choked. "How can you joke at such a time?"

"If only you'd met my guru, Didi, he'd have taught you how to laugh." She wiped Uda's cheeks. "Don't weep," she whispered.

Uda clasped the bars. "If only you'd run when I told you to!"

"I carry in my veins the blood of Rathores. I cannot run."

"Mirabai, I could never be as brave as you."

"What is there to fear when Giridar is with you?"

Uda pounded on the iron bars. "Vasudev, why? Why do this to your own Mira?" Shuddering, she fell to the ground.

Mira knelt. "Didi, would your brother have expected you to weep like this?"

Uda moaned. "He'd be weeping even more than I."

Mira shook her head, refusing to believe it. Bhoj would never have wept.

Uda felt her way through the dark, grabbing Mira's hands. "Ask Raj Purohit to forgive you, Mira."

"I cannot do that."

"He wants to save you! All you have to do is ask."

Mira forced her voice into the stoniest of sounds. "Didi, I have chosen Giridar."

Uda was silent.

They sat, holding hands.

The pale bull appeared. "Raj Kumari, you must leave now." His voice was quiet.

"I won't!" Uda snapped.

"You must," Mira said. "And listen," she said, feeling like there was a rock in her throat, "my deity is yours now. Care for him with all your bhakti."

After a moment of silence, there were white dashes of Uda's veil as she nodded. Her skirts rustled as she stood.

"And Didi?" Mira said. "You understand that I must prepare. Don't...come back."

There was another long moment of silence. Then Uda whispered, "as you wish, Mirabai. Jai Shri Krishna."

"Jai Shri Krishna."

Mira waited until she heard the last of Uda's footfall before slumping against the bars. "Help my Didi, Giridar. She has no one."

\*

Gauri came and ordered Mira to plead mercy.

"I'm sorry I wasn't a good bahu, Ma Sa," Mira replied. "I tried."

Sumer came and begged forgiveness. He told her it was his fault for allowing Akbar through and that even though he'd told Vikram this, the king had ignored him. Sumer told Mira to place the blame on his head and he'd gladly accept death for her.

She told him he wasn't guilty. She told him that Merwar needed honorable soldiers like him. She told him to trust Krishna.

Her maids, including decrepit Savitri, came to see her, begging her to give in to Raj Purohitji.

Mira told Lalita to take her husband and children to Chaukari. "Tell Bapu Sa I love him. And tell him not to break the alliance."

She bequeathed her four maids with her wedding jewelry except for her mangalsutra. She was to be cremated wearing it.

When she was alone, she thought of her guru, wishing she could have seen him one last time. She prayed she'd meet him in the next life.

Her last day came upon her and Mira sang all the songs she'd ever written. She sang the songs her mother had sung. She sang Gurudev's poems.

The pale bull appeared and his voice broke when he told her that it was time.

She walked over to him.

"Promise me that tomorrow, you'll watch the sun rise."

When he touched her feet, she placed her right hand on his head.

The crowds outside the jail were struggling against the guards, shouting words that Mira blocked out.

Entering the court, she blinked her eyes against the glare of lamps.

Sisodias, Brahmins, Raj Purohit: all awaited her decision.

"I will not ask forgiveness."

"Rani Mira, are you certain?" Purohitji asked. "I'll give you another chance: do you repent?"

She lifted her eyes to the stars above her. "I repent all moments of my life not spent worshipping Krishna. I repent all moments when I allowed my selfishness to fight his will. I repent all moments when I didn't trust him." She fell to her knees. "Forgive me, Giridar. I was weak. But I promise you now, I am weak no more."

Raj Purohit's silver beard was wispy and forlorn. "I sentence you to death by poison. You will drink it now, before the court." He nodded to his assistants and there was a collective intake of breath in the court.

There were footsteps at Mira's left.

She glanced around and saw a thin little man coming towards her, a copper bowl in his hands. She remained on her knees, waiting.

I come to you now, Giridar, she thought. Please accept me.

The man held out the bowl, his gaze sliding to the side.

Mira took the bowl from him, her hands firmer than the mountain Chittore was built upon. She turned to face Raj Purohit.

The court was transfixed, horror mixed with gruesome fascination.

She brought the bowl to her lips. Giridar, take me away, she thought.

Bitter liquid slid down her throat, bitter like the water Gurudev had given her on her initiation. She swallowed every drop.

Giridar, Giridar, Giridar, she chanted in her mind.

The bowl clattered to the saffron speckled marble.

Mira felt her body lower. Giridar, Giridar, Giridar...

"The poison should take effect within half an hour."

She heard Raj Purohit's words and thought his voice strange, distant.

"Rani Mira will be taken to her bhavan. Call her dasis."

Mira knew her union was near. She could feel it. "Giridar..."

Familiar hands placed her in a litter.

Giridar, Giridar, Mira chanted as she was lifted and taken outside.

The air was soft, the fighting crowds now gazing in silence at her still form.

Her litter was placed on the grass at the steps of her temple, near the banyan and sitafar trees. The Kumbh-Shyam mandir was just a few paces away.

This was where she'd first met her guru. Where she'd learned so much. Where she'd danced. Giridar...

There was no pain. Her limbs were so light it felt like they were floating. As if she were pulled upright by a golden breeze. Giridar, I want to dance with you.

She raised her arms, knowing his embrace. She felt a peacock feather touch her cheek. He whirled her around and around and she laughed. She was warm. She was free. Giridar...

A hand touched her shoulder. The golden breeze faded.

Mira opened her eyes to see Uda staring at her with a face whiter that ever. She looked like a dungeon guard.

"Didi, why are you here? I must die alone."

"You're not alone, Mira. Look around you."

Mira looked and saw hundreds of people holding torches.

Uda shook her head. "It's been two hours, Mirabai. We've all waited but you're not dead." She felt the warmth of Mira's body. "You should be dead."

Mira blinked. "But how–?" She looked up at the twinkling stars.

"The poison's never failed before," Uda whispered.

It couldn't be. Mira looked from the people around her to Giridar's temple. She ran for the steps.

"Giridar!" She swayed and had to grab the doorpost to keep from falling. She staggered up to Krishna who was dressed in saffron and gold. He looked more stone now than ever.

"Why, Giridar?"

Uda came running but stopped in the doorway.

"Giridar, I can't bear it," Mira wept, falling to his feet. "Take me with you! Take me with you."

# 27

# Regret

The vaids came but she didn't let them near her.

What had she done wrong? Mira wondered, sitting in the temple, staring into Krishna's face.

Six hours had passed and she wasn't dead. It was midnight.

The people were still outside, muttering that Mirabai had been saved.

This isn't salvation! Mira wanted to rage at them. And the cruelest, most painful, most pressing question of all: why didn't he want her?

"Vasudev has saved your life, Mira," Uda said from behind, her voice glowing. "Your every action is now vindicated to the world."

"Who *cares*, Didi?"

"I do! The whole world must now beg your forgiveness."

"But I don't want that! I want Krishna. Why can't I have Krishna?"

Uda sounded astonished. "Do you think he saves everyone the way he just saved you?"

Mira shook her head. She must have committed some unforgivable crime.

She had to get out of Chittore. She knew now, beyond any doubt, that her life here was ended.

It was years since she'd seen Gurudev. He'd told her that he'd find her but he hadn't come. Where was he now?

She couldn't go to Merta. It'd be the same there as it was here. There would be her father and aunt and Jaimal and everyone, and all that she knew they'd say to her. She couldn't go back there.

Where could she go then?

Vrindavan.

Of course, she thought. Gurudev said he was going that way. Perhaps he was still there! Mira realized there might be another reason why her life was prolonged. Perhaps there were other things Giridar wanted her to do. Perhaps this was what Gurudev had meant when he sent her back to Chittore.

Mira would leave tonight.

*

She sneezed for the hundredth time. Her head felt fluffy, as if it'd been stuffed full of cotton. The point between her eyebrows was aching.

Her limbs felt like she was wearing the millions of jewels she'd worn on her wedding day, except that she wasn't wearing millions of jewels. She was wearing her mangalsutra, her earrings and two glass bracelets, one on each wrist. It was the least amount of jewelry she'd ever worn.

Her little bundle contained a pair of spare garments, her anklets, her tambora. She didn't have any gold to spend but then, she didn't really need it.

The sun was beating down on her and there was very little shade to hide in. The trees were sparse here on the road near to Ramthambhor.

She hoped to find some water soon; perhaps there was a village nearby. Her throat was itching.

The heat had been so unbearable the last few days that Mira had walked only in the early morning and through the night. She found berries here and there in the wild.

She hadn't found any water, however, for two days now, and she wondered if she'd collapse.

She wondered if her father knew what had happened. He must know by now, even if Vikram hadn't told him. In any case, she was glad her father hadn't come to stop the trial.

Mira didn't need him to rescue her anymore.

She stumbled over a twig in the road and rubbed her aching toes. She noticed the hem of her skirt was ripped and for the first time in days, she smiled.

Wouldn't Gurudev be proud to see me now? she thought.

Mira wiped her sweating brow with her forearm and tried to breathe through her nose, but it was too stuffy. Her throat itched with thirst.

Up ahead, a cobra slithered across her path, heading eastwards.

She wondered if it was heading towards water. Ignoring her

throbbing feet, she walked after it.

It slithered and slithered and at times, Mira had to run to keep up. After an hour, she noticed the ground was softer. There was a cow grazing in the distance and that meant people were nearby.

That meant water.

She had a dull taste in her mouth. Her legs were so heavy she just wanted to drop and sleep. She sneezed again.

The sun was right above her, burning into her skin.

She squinted to see where the cobra was.

It was gone.

Oh no, it must have gone too fast, she thought. She tried to run after it, but her offended legs rebelled. She collapsed, gasping for air, sweat beads sliding down the small of her back.

I must have water, she thought, laying her head on the parched earth. Water…

"Arre, who is this? There's a woman on the ground!" A voice, coarse and old, came from a distance away.

Mira heard the voice but didn't have the strength to raise her head.

"Are you listening? Come here and see! She looks ill." The man came closer.

Another voice, female, called out. "What woman? Have you gone mad?"

"No, there's really a woman. Looks like a traveler but what woman would travel alone? She must have people with her but I can't see them."

The woman's voice was closer now, almost right next to Mira.

"Arre, you're right! Where's her family?"

"I don't know but look, she's married. See, she's wearing vermillion. Where's her husband? Where do you think she's from?"

"Hai Bhagwan! First give the poor woman some water and then ask questions."

Mira felt drops of blessed jal fall onto her cracked lips and she licked them, turning her face up to drink more.

"Here you go, sister, drink this," the woman said. "You must have gone without water for a long time. Didn't you bring a water pot with you? It's always good to travel with a little water, sister."

Mira wanted to say she'd lost her pot. Actually, she'd given it to a holy man in a mandir. He'd been so poor, and his eyes were so deep that she couldn't help but think of her Gurudev. She'd given the man her water pot and store of fruit and left before he'd had the chance to give them back to her.

Mira didn't open her eyes as the woman poured water down her throat. She just concentrated on the sensation sliding down her itching throat, cooling her body as it went deep into her belly. Thank Giridar, she thought.

Feeling life swish around her stomach, she blinked up at the pair.

They were elders, man and wife, their bodies thin and dark from a life of labor in the sun.

The old woman, her face pointed and shiny, patted Mira on the shoulders. "Poor thing, just rest a bit and then you can tell us who you are."

The cloudless sky was whizzing around Mira's head. She grabbed the ground to steady herself.

"Ouff, she looks very ill, this one. Poor thing," the woman said to her husband.

"She looks young. Where's her family?"

"Shhh...are you going to talk nonsense before the girl has even spoken? Let her rest."

"I'm alone, Ma. I've no family with me." Mira said. And I'm not young anymore, she added in her mind. I'm a woman grown.

"No family? No children? But you're married, sister!" the old woman exclaimed. "Surely you have family somewhere. Where are you from?"

"Chittore."

"Chittore? That's so far! It's all the way in the mountains, not that I know, mind you, but I've heard it's far away and up a high hill and it's very difficult to get to. You came from there?"

Mira put her hand to her temple and sat up. The world swayed. "I have to go to Vrindavan."

"Vrindavan? All by yourself?" The man shook his head. "I don't like it."

Mira squinted against the sun's glare. Her bundle was at her side on the floor. She picked it up to check that her tambora was alright but her feeble fingers couldn't undo the knot.

"Let me do it for you," the old woman said, pulling the knot apart.

Mira picked up her tambora, her hands shaking from the effort. It was fine, no harm done at all. Sometimes it amazed her how invincible this instrument was. She'd carried it around all these years and there wasn't even one scratch to show for it.

The woman and man looked at each other.

"Are you a traveling singer then?"

Mira smiled though her brain was spinning. "Something like that.

Can you tell me where the next village is?"

"Virpur is one hour that way," the woman said, pointing towards the east.

One hour! moaned Mira inwardly.

"What's your name, sister?" the woman asked.

"Mira," she whispered.

"Mira?" they said in unison.

She could feel them looking at each other, then at the tambora in her hands and the vermillion on her head.

"Hai Rama," the woman whispered, "you're Mirabai."

Mira blinked to make her eyes stop blurring.

"Mirabai..." they whispered together.

"Swami, can you believe it? Mirabai! On our land! The others will never believe it."

"Quick, give her more water," he said. "She looks like she's going to faint."

"Mirabai can't faint. She's protected by Shesh Naag himself." Still, she tipped the pot over Mira's mouth.

Shesh Naag! Mira thought, gulping. How do they know about that?

"We'll take you back to our house. It's closer than Virpur. This is our land you know."

Mira, her head cleared a bit by the water, looked about. She was in a chili field, piles of red all around her. How had she missed all this when she'd been running after the snake?

She was lucky there wasn't any wind to blow the chilies over her or she'd have been in trouble. She looked back at the elders. "I'm most obliged to you. I wish I could give you something but–" Mira stopped. She pulled out her pyal from her bundle, the bells chum chumming. "Please, take these as my thanks."

The woman shrank back. "We couldn't take anything from a holy person."

Mira shook her head. "I'm not a holy person. Please take them, I don't want to be indebted to anyone."

The man and woman shook their heads.

"We couldn't take anything from you. It'd dishonor our ancestors. But–" the woman beamed at her husband, "if you do wish to repay us then you must come to our hut and let us serve you."

Mira squinted at them. "I'll be a burden. No, no, I must go to Vrindavan. Please take my pyal."

"How will you go anywhere in your state?" the man said. "You need food and rest. Please, stay with us and bless our family."

Mira shook her head. "Bless you? I'm only Mira, not a sant. I must be on my way."

"Mirabai, it is too hot to travel. Your skin is already burned. Stay with us and you can teach our daughters your songs."

"Your daughters, Ma?"

"They're disciples of yours. It'd be such a blessing if you were to stay and teach us."

Mira's sensible half was telling her she was too ill to go anywhere, while the other half was horrified at being called anyone's teacher. However, if they wanted to do kirtan then she couldn't refuse them. Her guru had ordered her to sing.

Still, it was a delay she couldn't afford. Something inside her told her to reach Vrindavan as soon as possible. She would go to their house, sing a bhajan or two, then leave.

She retied her bundle, gritted her teeth, and rose, trying to ignore her aching feet. Just when she thought she'd try taking a step, her legs gave way.

"Hai Rama!" the woman cried, reaching out to catch Mira as she fell. "Mirabai, you can't leave like this. Let us look after you."

Mira knew when she was beaten. "Tikh hai," she croaked, her voice sounding foreign and ugly.

The old woman crowed and the old man chewed his toothless gums in excitement.

Mira tried to smile but felt a sinking sensation in her stomach. Gurudev was waiting in Vrindavan.

*

A week passed before the old couple allowed Mira to leave. She spent the week resting and listening to her own songs sung by their three daughters. It was with a tender heart that Mira said goodbye to them all and set off eastward.

She didn't know whether it was Akbar who'd given her that emerald necklace but it was his men who greeted her as she passed into his territory.

They were Hindu, she was surprised to see, both of them sporting tilaks on their foreheads.

Jay and Vijay, as they introduced themselves, came with a palanquin and asked for the honor of escorting her to Fatehpur Sikri where Akbar was eager to greet her.

She refused, telling them she was on her way to meet her guru and didn't need their assistance. They asked that she at least come to Fatehpur Sikri to meet the badshah but she refused, saying she was on pilgrimage, not a diplomatic mission.

They asked that she at least make use of the palanquin they'd brought her.

She refused, saying that the land of Bharat was sacred and she'd vowed to travel it on foot.

Before returning to their master, the soldiers told her she would be free to travel in Akbar's domain.

Mira didn't bother telling them she already knew that.

She traveled onwards, through the ravaged territory of the Delhi plains, land that once belonged to Rajput kings. There were temples that had been blasted into oblivion, while others had been defaced and turned into Muslim places of worship. She saw one Shiv temple where the deity of Nandi, Shiv's bull, had been beheaded. In the next, she saw sculptures of Vishnu and Lakshmi that had their faces chiseled off. In another, she saw the walls were covered in blood and when she asked whose blood it was, the children told her it was the blood of the head priest, killed because he'd refused to convert to Islam.

Everywhere, she saw that trees had been cut down and to her horror she saw dead cow carcasses littering the ground, even in the temples.

They were killed, the people told her, to degrade the purity of the land.

Mira was overcome, feeling the loss of pride and freedom that characterized Rajput ideals. And in spite of everything the Moghuls had done, Hindus like Jay and Vijay bowed before them. They'd accepted Akbar's sovereignty and because of that, Mira knew Akbar would never leave Bharat. This savagery would prevail and Kal Yuga would take root.

She wondered if she should warn Vikram but knew that, with his spies, he must know all of this already. He was a wily man, after all.

Two weeks passed by as Mira wandered from mandir to mandir, her hemline ripping more with every desecration she came upon.

In the villages, the women came to her. They said they'd heard of Mirabai's miracle escape from the poison and they wanted her to be their guru. They cried, holding out their veils in the gesture of begging and pleaded with her to show them the path.

Mira told them to have faith, for no one could escape the laws of karma. The Moghuls would ultimately be destroyed. She urged the women to never forget they were Hindus, the children of Bharat, and that dharma was in their soul. She told them to never give up hope.

She always ended by telling them she was no guru, only their sister who had suffered as they. She told them her only good deed was that she followed Guru Ravi Das and that he'd opened her eyes. She told them to take shelter of the naam, for that would always be with them, even if the mandirs were gone.

Passing by Agra, she was approached by more Hindu soldiers who asked Mirabai to come to the Moghul's capital.

She told them to thank Akbar but she wasn't here to entertain the emperor. She was on pilgrimage.

Mira reached the banks of Yamuna and bathed in the holy river.

Gurudev had said that Yamuna's waters had once been fair but that she'd meditated on Krishna's name and form with such fervor that her color had darkened to match his. People then called her Kalindi, Dark One.

Dipping her head into the water, Mira felt a strange sort of peace. A peace born of defeat, she thought.

The temples were destroyed, the earth polluted, the cows slaughtered. Nothing sacred was safe. Even this Yamuna could soon run red with blood, should the Moghuls choose to make it so.

The only refuge was the name. They couldn't desecrate that. It was the only thing Hindus could keep within themselves, a secret weapon; the most powerful weapon of all.

Gurudev had been right.

Mira lay in the water, yearning for the time of raas, the dance of love, when Krishna and the Gopis united under the full moon on the banks of Yamuna.

She washed her hair in the river, her dark tresses camouflaged in the dark waters until she couldn't tell water from hair.

Gurudev had said the Yamuna was bhakti and bhakti was Radha and that made Yamuna another form of Radha. He'd said the holy ones wrote verses to Yamuna's beauty, her purity. They said the ripples on her surface were the lines on Radha's neck, and the waves, Radha's breath. They said her two banks were knowledge and sacrifice, and her reflection at night, the stars in Radha's eyes.

Mira bathed in Yamuna, water sliding off her skin like dew off a lotus. She prayed the river's bhakti would purify her. Mira wanted to be beautiful for Krishna, even though she could never be beautiful enough.

She could never be Radha.

# 28

# Revelation

Vikram couldn't understand how she'd managed to escape his clutches.

What tantra was she practicing that she'd rendered the poison useless? He'd personally supervised its concoction!

Now Raj Purohit had forbidden anyone to chase her or harm her in any way. He'd told Vikram that she'd drunk the poison with the entire court as her witness and still she'd survived. It had been an act of Bhagwan.

Raj Purohit's eyes had narrowed as he'd looked at Vikram, studying the way Vikram responded.

His own guru was suspicious of him!

It was a simple enough conclusion for these simple people, Vikram thought. If Mira had been saved by Bhagwan then she must be innocent which made Vikram, who'd put her on trial, wrong. And if Vikram was wrong about this, how many other things was he wrong about?

She'd disappeared into the night and none had known where to. None except Uda, of course, but who could get a word out of her?

Fortunately, Vikram had sent out spies and knew she was on her way to Vrindavan. Right into the heart of Akbar's lair.

Wasn't that proof she was Akbar's whore? She'd been sentenced in Chittore, used black magic to free herself, and had now gone running to the Moghul.

But the people of Merwar wouldn't listen to a word of it. Vikram had sent out his best men to spread the tales but every single one of them had returned black and blue from the beatings the people had given them.

If she was going to Vrindavan then she was on pilgrimage, was the people's angry retort. She was innocent and a sant and her name would be honored by all who didn't want to die.

Vikram was at a loss.

Mira had been gone for three months. She'd reach Vrindavan in time for the monsoon, his spies told him.

He hoped it was a good monsoon this year. Decent rains would be a sign to the people that he was a good king and his reign was righteous. Their faith in him would be restored and all would think the trial had been an honest mistake.

The much-disputed jewel remained in its pride of place on Krishna's neck. Uda was now the guardian of the small mandir, a place that had become a main attraction for pilgrims as Sant Mirabai's temple.

Uda led the satsang and all pilgrims came out of the temple glowing at the thought that they'd had darshan of Mira's deity.

Vikram had half a mind to destroy the building but even he thought that'd be wrong. It wasn't Krishna's fault Mira was a traitor.

Ratan wasn't helping the situation. He'd sent messages that were nothing more than threats and had even gone so far as to send Jaimal to Chittore. Ratan *suggested* that Jaimal assist Vikram in the defense of Chittore. This would show the people that despite Mira's absence, the two countries were still allied.

Jaimal was, of course, a spy.

Vikram couldn't refuse Ratan. His own popularity among his people was so low that if he resisted Ratan's wish and Merta attacked, his people might just side with Mira's father over their own king.

So Vikram welcomed Jaimal with open arms and appointed him general-in-command of Chittore's defenses.

It didn't take long to see that the reports about Jaimal were true. Wily and shrewd, the man was fanatical about training and expected complete obedience from everyone, whether it was his maid, his wife, his men, or his horse. He installed a new rigorous training program for the soldiers, telling Vikram the men had slackened since losing Bhoj's direction.

"Their quickness, their strategy, their strength: it's all gone. They're a pathetic excuse for an army," Jaimal said.

Vikram wanted to rip out Jaimal's tongue but, of course, he smiled and apologized and told Jaimal to do what he could with the louts.

It was odd how Jaimal watched Vikram in court, as if something was fizzing away in his brain, waiting to go off like the cannons Vikram was so desperate to acquire.

Akbar had many cannons.

The people of Chittore waited for the monsoon rains, eager for the swell of clouds that would bring relief from the heat.

A month went by and the rains didn't come. Another month passed and still the rains didn't come. Janamashtmi was celebrated and still the rains shunned Merwar.

Uda breezed into the court one day, a sea of male faces looking at her. She *suggested* to Vikram, in a tone of supreme irreverence, "that it might be advisable for Maharana to open his granary to the people.

"Since there won't be much crop this year, we wouldn't want our people to starve," she said before breezing out.

Despite the white locks that now streaked Uda's hair, she carried herself with a grace Vikram had thought only Mira capable of. Even Uda's skin was firm and glowing. Vikram wondered where her bony ugliness had gone.

Vikram saw Jaimal watching Uda, a gleam of admiration in his eyes.

Jaimal's wife was not in Chittore at present. She'd gone back to Merta to tend to Jaimal's sick mother.

Vikram decided that, diplomacy or not, he'd tell Jaimal straight that if he touched Uda, he'd die. The last thing Vikram needed was another scandal involving his family.

Jaimal smirked when Vikram came out with it. "Uda is Mira's sister and that makes her my sister. *I don't touch my sisters.*"

Vikram went pale, wondering if Jaimal knew. But no. Jaimal would've killed him already if that were the case.

The weather cooled and Merwar settled into the depression of drought. The toil of the entire year went without fruit.

The next year was even more difficult. Vikram's third wife gave birth to a stillborn son. Again.

He'd blamed his first two wives for the deaths of the boys but now here was proof that it hadn't been their fault at all.

There was something wrong with him.

The vaids were giving him medicines, herbs to improve his seed quality and instructions for diet so that his children would be healthy. He'd even stopped going to his concubines. The next year, all three of his wives miscarried.

Vikram considered marrying again but didn't think he had the energy for it.

Akbar was sending messages proposing friendship but how could Vikram accept? His people hated him enough as it was. If only Bairam Khan hadn't been killed! He and Vikram had had an understanding.

A corner of the eastern province revolted. And who was leading the revolt? Shivgan, of course.

Vikram, not wanting to seem unmerciful towards his cousin, negotiated and agreed that Shivgan have complete sovereignty over that area so long as Shivgan handed over such-and-such an amount as taxes. He also sent over two of his own men to assist Shivgan in the ruling of that territory and insisted that Udai, Shivgan's brother, reside in Chittore as one of Vikram's lieutenants. This way Vikram had a hostage should Shivgan try anything else.

"It wouldn't happen in Merta," Jaimal said, snorting. "Rathores are loyal to the bone. We'd never go against our own flesh."

Vikram's retort was silenced by the memory of a long-ago lesson in scripture: "*Corruption breeds corruption.*"

Secretly, he sent a man to a Jyotish. The learned scholar consulted the skies, calculated the stars, and concluded that Merwar was being punished for torturing a sant.

Vikram broke a lot of furniture and roared at his wives before he was able to sit down and think.

She had to come back. It was the only way. Mira would be the resident holy person and everyone would bow before her. Even Vikram would bow, if it'd make it all better.

Yes, he thought. He'd call Mira back to Merwar.

*

She'd been in Braj for two years, staying in an ashram for lady pilgrims.

Gurudev, she learned, had come and gone and Mira agonized over her slowness, for she was told that he'd left only weeks before her arrival.

Her father had found out where she was and sent her income every few months.

She'd been to Gokul village, where Krishna spent the first three years of his appearance on earth. She visited Nandagaon, where Nanda and Yashoda moved to escape the demons that mysteriously kept attacking baby Krishna. Mira wandered around the hills of Barsana, Radha's sweet little village.

Mira went to Govardhan, the mountain that Krishna held for seven days on his little finger and thus became Giridar, the mountain-lifter.

Every dawn, she bathed in the Yamuna and spent the dawn hours walking up and down the lush green banks, hoping to catch a glimpse of Radha in the waves.

She met with holy men and asked them to tell her stories about Krishna.

The people of Vrindavan were so matter-of-fact about the land's holiness, it sometimes surprised Mira to hear them speaking so casually about places like Govardhan or Gokul.

To her, it was *Gokul* and *Govardhan* not just Gokul and Govardhan. These were the most sacred places on earth, not just where to go to get the cheapest fruits.

But that was the charm of Braj. Even in the scriptures it was stated that the Brajwasis never knew Krishna was Bhagwan. He was their darling, their prince, their mischief-maker. He was everything to them and yet they never knew he was Bhagwan.

To the Brajwasis, Krishna had never left them. He was always there, playing with the Gopis and trysting with Radha.

Mira believed they were right. After all, how could Krishna have left Braj, where love flowed in the dark Yamuna? How could he leave Radha and Mother Yashoda and the Gopis? How could he leave his beloved cows?

Some sages even said that only Krishna's shadow had gone to Mathura to free Devki and Vasudev and kill wicked Kansa.

But then Mira thought of the stories Gurudev had told her. Stories of how Devki and Vasudev sent Krishna to school once he'd killed Kansa. At the ashram of Sage Sandipani, Krishna's classmate Sudama asked Krishna if he missed Braj. Krishna told Sudama that he missed Braj so much he wished he could fly there at night, just to watch Radha sleeping.

Sudama asked why Krishna didn't write letters. Krishna explained that he tried. He picked up pens to write to Mata Yashoda but the next time he looked down, all he'd written was Mata, Mata, Mata, Mata. He could never write anything past her name because he couldn't put his pain into words.

Did he leave Braj? Did he not? Mira didn't know. Radha had never left and Radha was bhakti personified. The Brajwasis wrote her name on the trunk of every tree, and the brick of every wall. Radha's name was everywhere, even more than Krishna's.

Early one misty morning, Mira made her way to Mount Govardhan to circumambulate it. Strumming her tambora, singing Krishna's name, she circled the hill, breathing sweet air deep into her lungs. The cows were chewing on the grass around her and she stopped under a tamal tree to drink some water.

"Mira."

Her eyes growing wide, she watched him approach through the mist.

"Aren't you pleased to see me?" He walked up, grinning.

"Pleased? I–you–"

"I thought I might surprise you."

He was here. He was really here! She dropped and touched her forehead to the ground. "Gurudev!" she cried, looking up at him.

"Jai Shri Rama," he said.

"Jai Shri Rama. I've waited so long to see you!"

"I know. I couldn't come earlier."

She laughed out loud. She couldn't believe she was finally with Gurudev!

He sat down in front of her. "I see you're well."

She moved to sit cross-legged. "Yes. But Gurudev, where've you been all these years? Did you go back to Kashi?"

"I've been wandering, much the same as you. Do you like Vrindavan?"

His hair was as curly and long as ever. He didn't look a day older, she thought, shaking her head at him.

"Of course I love Vrindavan."

"I thought so." He looked at the earth beneath them. "You did well in Chittore."

Her mouth parted. "I did?"

"Yes. I was never as proud of you as I was at that moment."

She blinked at him, pleasure flushing her cheeks pink.

"It just proves what I suspected some time ago. You don't need me anymore."

That shook off her giddiness. "What do you mean?"

He smiled. "You've gone beyond what I can teach you."

"But–but–"

"You're pure enough to know what truth is now. You passed one of the most difficult tests a devotee can face."

"How can you say I don't need you anymore?" she gasped. "I'm your disciple!"

"You'll always be my disciple, Mira. That doesn't mean you'll always need my answers. You've proven yourself."

"Why are you doing this?" she cried.

"Mira," his tone was reassuring, "this is the natural progression of study. A student comes to a teacher and a teacher gives him lessons. But when the student learns all the lessons and passes all the tests, what more can the teacher do? It's time then for the student to leave school and engage in work for the good of society."

"This isn't school!" Mira dashed at the tears running down her cheeks. "I'm not just a student, I'm your daughter! How can you say I'm just your student?"

Ravi shook his head. "You are willfully misunderstanding me. Mira, you're grown up now. You know that I'll always be your guru and you'll always be my disciple. What I'm saying is that you've ascended to a higher level. You no longer need my direct instruction."

"But what do I do now?" she wailed.

"You do what needs to be done."

She stilled, thinking of all the women who came to her and begged her to teach them.

"Yes, Mira. You have followers and you are capable of instructing them."

"I cannot be a guru!"

"Whether they're your initiated disciples or not, you must still instruct them. If someone comes to you for help, you must do what you can for them. Of course, you didn't need me to tell you that, did you?"

Mira refused to answer. "Can I at least spend some days with you here?"

He looked grim. "I'm sorry, putri, I must leave Vrindavan."

He'd only just arrived!

"Fear not, Mira. We'll meet again."

She cried into her hands. Everyone she loved always left her.

"Will we meet again *in this life?*"

He looked rueful. "You've become wilier than ever, haven't you?"

"You taught me," she muttered, wiping her cheeks.

He chuckled.

"But really, Gurudev, will we meet again in this life?"

"I promise you we will. Now I must leave." He rose, his curls bouncing upwards with his body. "Jai Shri Rama, Mira."

"Jai Shri Rama, Gurudev." She bowed at his feet and watched him walk away, the dust and mist mingling around him until she could only see a cloud.

*

Uda returned to the bhavan after a day at the mandir.

Preparations were underway for Janamashtami and she'd been overseeing the rehearsals of the plays and dances, as well as the acrobats. All that meant a lot of music, and more importantly, drums.

Uda's brain was banging in her head.

Udai and his wife Kaveri were helping her organize the performances. Udai often said that he missed hearing Mira sing the way she used to in Kashi. Kaveri often expressed grief at never having heard Mirabai sing.

Uda wished Mira were here but wouldn't dream of letting her know that. She'd rather die than be an obstacle to Mira now.

Janki came to the door of the dining room. "Maharana is here, Raj Kumariji."

Uda raised her eyebrows. After all this time, Vikram had something to say to her? "Send him in."

"Ji," Janki disappeared and returned with the king.

Disgusting pretender, Uda thought, with his stupid straggly moustache. She'd never forgive him for what he'd done.

His head was bowed, apparently deep in thought.

Uda wondered what malice he was planning.

He walked up and without even looking at her face, bowed and touched her feet.

She was so surprised that she blessed him. "Sukhi ho."

He didn't reply and she drew back. "Sit down," she said, gesturing to the couch behind him.

He sat. "Forgive me for disturbing your meal but I needed your advice."

She resumed her seat on the dining stool. "In what, exactly?" She picked up her cup of milk.

"I wish to call Mira back."

Uda stared at him, forgetting her milk halfway to her mouth. "When will you grow up?"

He looked at her.

She tore her gaze away, unable to bear his stupid expression. "You've opposed her, hurled accusations against her, tried to kill her, and now you want her to come back? Are you mad?"

He looked bewildered. "I admit I was wrong. I want to restore her to her rightful place."

Uda set her milk down with a splash. "Why didn't you come to these great conclusions *before* you tried to kill her? Believe me, she doesn't need you to give back her 'rightful place'."

He scowled. "Things were different then, Didi. I did what I thought right."

"Oh, things were very different. You weren't so old and wise. Nor were you so generous in your character assessments. What was it you said to Bhoj? To just 'lock her up until she submits'?"

He looked at the floor. "As I said, things were different then."

"Well, thank Krishna Bhoj didn't listen to you."

"I did what I thought was right!" he snarled. "Will you stop bringing Bhoj up over and over again?"

Uda blinked: she'd only brought Bhoj up once. "Vikram, calm yourself. You're spitting all over me."

He drew a shaky breath.

"Whatever you think, you cannot call her back now."

"If I call her back then perhaps the weather will improve and our lands be safe." His veins were bulging out of his temples.

She smiled. "So you finally admit that Mira's presence protected us."

"Yes, yes." He was impatient. "That's why I have to call her back!"

"Don't you understand, Vikram? You've lost the right to ask anything of her."

He looked so miserable that Uda couldn't help herself. She patted his arm. "What you must do, Vikram, is look for peace."

"With the Moghuls?"

"Of course not!" she gasped. "You must find peace within yourself. Once you do that, things will get better. Believe me, Vikram, I know a lot about bad luck."

He frowned. "How can I do what you say?"

"First, you must send a messenger to Mira, not to call her back, but to ask forgiveness. Second, you must pray to your Isht, be it Krishna or Shiv or Durga. Find your faith, Vikram."

He rubbed his temples with his knuckles, just like he used to when they'd been children.

She was startled to see it. It'd been so long since Uda had thought of him as her cousin, a brother she'd grown up with. Her voice gentled. "It's the only way, Vikram."

She could hear him breathing in and out, in and out.

"What if that doesn't work, Didi?" he whispered.

"It will work."

There was a long pause as Uda waited for him to agree.

"I don't think that's good enough, Didi. I think she has to come back for things to get better." His eyes were red and sore.

Uda leaned back. "Don't do this to her. Your problems stem from your conscience, not from her. If you ask forgiveness and try to better yourself, things will improve."

He shook his head, staring at the wall before him with bloodshot eyes. "You don't know what's happening, Uda. Some of my courtiers have joined Akbar against me."

"*What?*"

"She must come back." The chair toppled behind him as he stood and strode out.

Uda looked after him, reeling from the news. He'd endangered Merwar with his games and now he wanted to destroy Mira's happiness too? Well, Uda wouldn't let him.

\*

Mira was glad to see the gateway up ahead. She'd been searching all over the forest for the hermitage.

Sanatan Goswami lived there, a great disciple of the mysterious Chaitanya Mahaprabhu.

Mira stood outside the gateway, waiting for a disciple to see her.

Sure enough, a saffron-robed man spotted her and came to the gate. He was young with smooth skin and keen eyes. "May I help you, Devi?"

"I desire an audience with Goswamiji. Will you tell him that Mira, disciple of Ravi Das, is here?"

The student started. "Mirabai? Of course, I'll immediately inform my master."

Her heart swelling in anticipation, she watched the young student run towards a straw hut. There were some who said that Chaitanya Mahaprabhu was Krishna's incarnation. She couldn't wait to meet his disciple.

The young devotee appeared. Keeping his gaze on the ground, he shuffled back to her.

"My master conveys his deepest respects to you, but he is a sanyaasi and has taken vows against meeting women. He asks that you forgive him."

Mira blinked. "Oh." She stepped back. "Oh."

She turned away. "Forgive me, I thought there was only one man in Vrindavan. Clearly I was wrong." She walked away down the lane, wondering at the sage's thinking.

"Mirabai!"

She turned around.

The disciple was running to her, panting. "My master wishes to see you. He asks that you come back to the ashram."

Mira looked behind him at a saffron-clad figure walking down the lane, leaning on his staff for support.

"Goswamiji?" she said as he reached them.

His head was shaven but for a lock of grey hair at his crown and his back was thin and fragile like Ramanand Acharya. He folded his palms. "Forgive my ignorance, Mirabai. Please grace my ashram."

"But I'm a woman," she said.

"So am I, Mirabai. You opened my eyes. The only man in Vrindavan is Krishna, and we are all his Gopis."

Mira looked from Goswamiji to his disciple, both of them humble and hopeful. She folded her hands before the great sage. "I've desired your darshan for a long time, Goswamiji, but I only learned the secret of your ashram's location recently."

"I've heard many of your songs, Mirabai, and many tales of your life. Come, let us do satsang."

The three of them returned to the ashram, the disciple one step behind Mira and his master.

Goswamiji invited her to sit on the porch of his hut and told his disciple to wash her feet. This done, he offered her prasadam.

She took a grape.

"I'm glad I could meet you," she told him. "I'll soon be leaving Vrindavan."

His eyes widened. "You're leaving? Why?"

The heaviness that haunted her came into her eyes. "I can't bear the viyog anymore, Goswamiji. Sometimes I think I'll go mad."

"You feel the separation so deeply?"

Mira closed her eyes. "I can no longer sleep. All I think about is the agony Radha and the Gopis must have gone through when he left them."

Sanatan Goswami's single lock of hair flapped in the breeze. "The pain can be terrible."

She let silence speak for her.

He frowned. "Where will you go? Vrindavan is closest to Krishna."

"Yet I find no peace here. Everywhere I go, I'm reminded that he left the Gopis, his dearest devotees. He left Vrindavan for Mathura and then he left Mathura for Dwarka. So now I go to Dwarka to find him."

Goswamiji smiled. "That's what the Gopis did, you know. They went to Dwarka looking for Krishna and in the end, gave up their lives there. The place is called Gopi Talau and it is said that the earth there smells of sandalwood."

"I've heard the story."

His saffron garments rustled as he moved. "Will you sing me one of your bhajans before you go?"

Mira looked at the tambora in her lap. She touched the strings, so delicate and fragile. "I'll try to sing, but I warn you that my skills have lessened of late. The viyog has lodged in my chest and I can't get my words past it." She strummed the instrument, feeling the tension in the strings. "I have a question, Goswamiji. May I ask it?"

"Of course."

"It's said that your guru is an incarnation of Krishna. Is that true?"

Goswamiji looked her straight in the eyes. "Yes."

"Then why did you leave him to come here?"

His eyes filled with tears. "Because he ordered me to. And whatever my master orders, I will obey, no matter the pain of viyog."

Mira's tears flowed down the deep valleys of her cheeks. "You're braver than I."

# 29

# Abandoned

Mira found her way west through the Aravali mountain range and stumbled into Gujarat.

The Bhils, tribal people who lived in the wild lands of Merwar's territory, helped her through the rocky passes where avalanches were common. They sang her songs and brought her berries and nuts to eat. They protected her through mountain lion haunts and showed her where to find water.

When she expressed her gratitude, they bowed, saying only that it was their duty to serve their queen.

Mira's destination lay on the westernmost tip of Bharat, the island of Dwarka.

The further she got from the mountains, the more lush the lands around her became. There were vast golden fields of wheat and the villages thrived with cotton industries.

Mira had heard that Akbar was eager to seize this fertile land from the sultan of Gujarat. She must to get to Dwarka before Akbar did.

Mira traveled down the dusty roads, rutted and dry from the carts that rattled over them. The roads in Merwar were much better than these, she thought. Vikram had seen to it.

She came to the temple of Shamalaji, the name meaning dark-skinned Krishna. She passed numerous villages, learning the language of Gujarat on her way. The people didn't speak Rajasthani or even much Hindi here. Their language was soft, dominated by shu and che sounds. Mira liked it.

She soon learned that even here, they'd heard of Mirabai.

Whole villages gathered before her and pleaded for bhajans. She didn't know how they knew that this lone woman in tattered red garments was Mirabai but they did.

Women came to her, holding the front of their veils out. They asked her to give them bhakti.

She told them stories from the scriptures, of Vrindavan and Kashi. She explained that no one could give them bhakti for that was within them. They had only to draw it out with the holy name.

Due to the extra days she spent in the villages, it took her weeks to reach the holy village of Dakor, where the famous Ranchodrai temple was. Ranchodrai, another one of Krishna's names, meant "he who runs from battle". Mira was surprised by this name and asked a holy man at the temple what it meant.

The holy man, fat from feasting on Ranchodrai's prasad, explained that Krishna was known by this name because of his pastimes. He left Mathura for Dwarka because the demon king Jarasantha was attacking his people. Of course, Krishna could have killed Jarasantha but he had other plans for the demon and thus he ordered a strategic retreat in order to protect his subjects. When his court told him that the world would call him Ranchod, Krishna said that he didn't care, that he would rather be known as a coward than a king who allowed his people to be harmed. He also said that it didn't matter what name people called him by because if he felt they were truly calling *him*, he would answer.

And thus in Dakor, Krishna's devotees loved him as Lord Ranchod, their protector. He was so adored that some, out of respect, wouldn't even say his name. They would only call him Thakorji. Master.

The holy man, his belly as round as a laddoo, told Mira that this temple housed the original Dwarkadish deity, brought here on the order of Krishna, the Lord of Dwarka. There was a four hundred year old story of a devotee who spent his whole life walking from Dakor to Dwarka and back again for darshan of Dwarkadish. One day, Dwarkadish told the devotee to take him back to Dakor, for the devotee was old and feeble and would no longer be able to walk the distance. So the devotee went into the temple that night and took Dwarkadish. He put the deity in the back of a cart and started driving home but due to his age, he couldn't stay awake. Dwarkadish told the devotee to sleep while he himself drove them to Dakor. Such was Krishna's will that the cart reached Dakor the next morning, an impossible feat for mortals.

And thus the people of that place built the Rachodrai mandir for their sweet Krishna who'd forsaken the grandeur of Dwarka for their humble village.

Mira was stunned by the tale. "So Dwarkadish no longer resides in

Dwarka?"

"Oh no, he's still there. There are two halves of Dwarka, you see, Gomti and Bhet. Our Ranchodrai comes from Gomti, the main part of Dwarka where Krishna ruled as king and protector. Bhet Dwarka is where Krishna kept residence with his family. The original deity in Bhet Dwarka is still there.

"In Gomti Dwarka, the people were heartbroken to find that he'd left them. Krishna then appeared in a dream to the King of Dwarka and told him to shut the mandir for six months, after which he was to find the new Dwarkadish inside. The king shut the temple and during the months of waiting, the priests could hear banging and scraping inside. After four months, the king could bear the wait no longer and opened the doors. There was Krishna, the Lord of Dwarka, his form dark and beautiful. But because the king had been impatient, the deity was incomplete. The eyes were only half-open and remain that way to this day."

Mira was fascinated. At least the original Krishna was still in Bhet Dwarka, she thought. She would stay there in her husband's house.

The noon rest was over and the mandir doors opened for Darshan.

Mira's heart sped at the thought of seeing Dwarkadish.

The crowd was just as enthusiastic as her and they pushed and pulled to get inside. Mira had to hold her tambora above her head to avoid squashing it. She was propelled up the stairs by the mass of devotees and through the archway into the brilliantly painted temple. Everywhere, sweating bodies bumped into each other in their eagerness to see Ranchodrai. Mira hopped on her feet but she couldn't see him above the heads of all the men.

"Ranchodrai ki jai!" the crowd shouted out.

A graceful young lady with astonishing green eyes grabbed Mira's arm. "This way, Mirabai!"

Mira was pulled towards the right side of the temple and, thinking that the woman was taking her out, she tried to wrench away. "I haven't seen him yet!" she cried.

The lady pulled Mira harder. "There's a separate space at the front for women!"

This space was no less sweaty but it was nearer to the inner sanctum and Mira had hopes that she might spy him over the women's heads. She and the green-eyed lady pushed themselves through the mass of women, and Mira learned that it didn't matter if a woman was old, her elbows were just as strong as any youngster's.

"Ouff," Mira groaned as another one bashed into her belly.

Then she spied him and forgot her discomfort.

His eyes were the biggest she'd ever seen. They were huge, like two moons side by side in the night sky.

Mira felt a tug at the back of her head but she ignored it, concentrating on the eyes of Ranchodrai. She leaned over the head of a tiny woman and gazed at him.

He was like nothing she'd ever seen. Ranchodrai...

Something was pushing on her back but she resisted it, digging her heels in.

She caught a glimpse of his feet, covered with shoes made of yellow silk and adorned with jewels. His body was so graceful, she expected him to lift his feet and walk towards her. Her heart thumped.

Something hit her back with such force that she went flying into the space in front. Looking behind, Mira saw a hoard of angry women who'd been waiting for darshan. Backing away from them, she could no longer see Krishna, so she looked around for the lady with green eyes, wanting to thank her.

The lady wasn't there.

She must have gone out, Mira thought and headed for the side doors. She descended the steps and tried to remember what the lady had been wearing but couldn't. All she remembered was those amazing eyes. The complex circled the temple and Mira wandered around and around, trying to find her in the crowd.

Finally, she resigned herself to the fact that it was impossible to find the lady here. Perhaps she went home, Mira thought.

Inside the temple, the crowd was chanting "Ranchodrai ki jai!"

Mira joined in the chant, lifting her arms and dancing to the beat. She smiled, thinking of his eyes, twin moons in the sky.

Giridar, Ranchodrai, Dwarkadish, she thought.

There were Tulsi plants in the garden by the temple and Mira walked around them, admiring the graceful green leaves.

When she returned to the dharamshalla in which she was staying, she noticed two young men standing on the street outside. They were wearing Merwar's blue livery and were holding the reins of two royal looking horses.

Her heart, a moment before so full, deflated.

They knelt before her. "Rani Mira ki jai!"

"What is the message?"

They looked at each other.

"We bring a message and a request from Maharana." The one on the right said, tilting his chin up.

Looking into his face, Mira saw his deep pride in being sent on this mission, despite his callow age. What was Vikram doing, sending these youths across Bharat? Mira wondered. She prayed that Uda and Raj Mata were well.

"Maharana Vikram wishes to ask forgiveness for the accusations held against you. He realizes now they were wrong. In your absence, our country has fallen on difficult times. There's been a drought for the past two years and now, just before we left, Merwar suffered a most ferocious storm. There were devastating landslides where much of Chittore mountain slid down into the valley."

Mira stared at the man.

He returned her gaze, his eyes beseeching. "Hundreds are dead, thousands are trapped and many homes are destroyed. Maharana asks that you return to Chittore to aid him and his subjects in the recovery."

Mira couldn't understand why there'd been storms at this time of year. The crop fields would be devastated, not to mention buried under the landslides. Her brain raced through all the things that could be done to help her people—supplying clean water, clothes, dry land. Medicines would be needed in case of outbreaks of diseases. Children and the aged would be most vulnerable. She thought of how she might organize the provisions kept in storage and–*wait!*

Mira shook her head. She was no longer a queen. This wasn't her duty. Vikram and Uda would know what to do.

The man's underdeveloped moustache trembled. "Please, Mirabai, come home. Merwar needs you."

"I cannot come, Senikh. Chittore isn't my home any more." She was going to Dwarka to live in her husband's house, she thought, seeing visions of children lost without their mothers.

I'm no longer a queen, she told herself.

The men looked at each other, their thin shoulders slumping.

She turned away, unable to face their disappointment.

"Tell Jehtji that I thank him for his apology and that he has my forgiveness. However, I cannot return to Chittore."

The one who had been silent buried his face in his hands.

"I will pray for Merwar," she whispered. "You two should pray also."

Feeling them staring after her, she entered the dharamshalla, strumming her tambora and thinking of Merwar.

*

Ravi took the boat to Bhet Dwarka, his stiff legs jolting in the rickety craft.

Summer had settled in but here on the coast, the wind was cooler. The salt of the ocean was in the air and he tasted it on his skin.

Ravi knew that Vikram's men were not far behind.

Though Mira didn't need him, he'd promised her one last visit. He would use it to warn her.

When the boat docked, he wrinkled his nose against the appalling smell of fish that hung in the air. Since the sultan's capture of Gujarat, the fish industry had grown. Now, even Dwarka was polluted with the stench of it.

Ravi knew that Mira hadn't taken it well, her heart rebelling against the torture of innocent sea creatures. But what could she do? The sultan was in power and he merely tolerated Hindus in his land. To him, the sacredness of Dwarka was as ridiculous as the life of Krishna.

Foolish, foolish ruler, Ravi thought. He would fall soon enough.

Ravi would take darshan and see Mira. Then he must be off back to the mainland, where Akbar was mobilizing his forces. It wouldn't be long now.

Ravi made his way up the steep slopes to the top of the island, where Krishna's palace lay. There, Dwarkadish was worshipped.

Panting from the climb, he bought some flowers to offer Krishna. He took darshan and went out into the temple grounds which were really lanes between the rooms of Krishna's palace. He wandered around, following his instincts, until he spied a slim red figure in the distance. Squinting against the sun, he saw that the woman carried a tambora.

He walked up behind her. "Mira."

She turned. "Gurudev!"

She looked just as she always did, like a beautiful young girl despite the toil of her years. He lifted his right hand. "Saubhagyavati bhavah."

She rose from bowing at his feet, laughing. "I knew you were coming! Somehow, I knew it. I've missed you."

He smiled. "No, you haven't. You've been far too busy with your husband."

She blushed. "Gurudev, he's so beautiful and kind, I can't explain to you—"

"You don't have to," Ravi chuckled. "Let's go to the courtyard, putri. We shall speak there."

Mira one step behind him, they walked back down the lane.

348   J.A.Joshi

He sat on the raised earth under a tree. Mira sat on the ground before him.

"Can I get you anything, Gurudev? Some fruit? The coconut water here is very sweet. Shall I get you some?"

"No, putri. I'm fine."

She studied him. "You are, aren't you? You've even put on weight."

He grinned. "I've been eating a bit more than usual."

"That's a relief!" she said, grinning back, "you never did eat enough."

"I'm sustained by my Isht Rama, you know that."

She sobered. "Yes, I do."

"Good." He paused. "You seem very happy here, Mira."

"I am," she breathed.

"You've done well. There are many who are stronger now because of what you've taught them."

She looked at the ground. "It wasn't me, Gurudev."

"I just want you to know I'm proud of you. Now look at me."

She lifted her gaze.

"Never leave your husband, Mira. He is your fate."

She paled at the seriousness of his tone.

"You're close, putri. So close. Don't leave now."

Mira gazed deeply into his eyes and straightened her shoulders.

"I swear to you, Gurudev, I won't leave Dwarka for all the rest of my days."

Ravi sat back, satisfied.

*

In the month since Gurudev's visit, there'd been two more messages from Vikram, both asking her to return.

Mira had refused them, her promise to Ravi fresh in her mind. She wasn't stupid. Gurudev had told her to remain here for a reason.

Sitting in the courtyard where she'd sat with her guru a month ago, she strung flowers into a garland for Dwarkadish. She hummed a song to herself, a song about Krishna's parents Devki and Vasudev, and their joy of when Krishna found them.

A shadow fell over her, blocking the hot rays of the sun.

Two blue liveried men knelt before her.

"Pranam Raniji," said a man with an impressive waxed moustache. It was almost as regal as Bhoj's had been, except Bhoj's curled more and he'd never waxed it.

"Our king begs you to return to Merwar," the second one said. He was older, his face broader and more lined. He was so familiar to her, but she couldn't think where she'd seen him.

"He begs?" Mira couldn't imagine Vikram begging for anything. She looked from the elder, with his strong cheekbones, to the younger with his proud whiskers. Both were so strong and sincere as they knelt before her. "You two were in the guard Yuvraj created for me, weren't you?"

They nodded, grim faced.

"You are Marut," she said to the older one. "And you are Sameer," she said to the other.

They nodded once more.

"We also bring a message from our commander, Sumer," Marut said. "He asks that his Rani returns to care for her subjects. They need her blessings, as does he."

Mira bit her lower lip. It had to be bad for Sumer to call her back into Vikram's lair.

"Please, Rani, return with us. Bless us with the chance to guard you once more."

Mira closed her eyes. "I cannot, Sameer."

The men looked desperate.

"But why, Rani?" Sameer asked.

"I have vowed to remain here for the rest of my life."

"Chittore is your home!"

"This is my home now." Mira looked around her, from the cows wandering, to the flower girls sitting at the temple doors, to the holy men sitting and chanting. "I belong here."

The soldiers just looked at her, mute.

"We know we're not worthy to be your guards, Raniji," Marut said. "We're the ones who took you to the dungeon. But please don't punish Merwar for our crime."

Mira shook her head at him. "Neither of you committed a crime. You were following the orders of your king and I don't blame you. I only tell you the truth when I say I cannot leave here." She put her garland down. "Come to the dharamshalla and I will write a letter for Maharana." She had to send some sort of comfort to Vikram.

She wrote the letter within half an hour, chewing over her words. She wrote that she held no grudges and that he wasn't to feel guilty. She told him she prayed for Chittore and hoped Merwar prospered. She told him to look towards his Isht for strength.

She handed the letter to the messengers and bid them farewell, watching as they trudged back down the slopes to the dock and the boatmen.

Mira then turned and walked the distance back to the courtyard, her steps small and slow.

Poor Vikram. What could be so bad that he begged her to return?

She hoped things improved. She hoped Uda was well.

Uda! Oh no, Mira should have sent a letter for her too. She ran all the way to the docks but the men were gone, their boat halfway to the mainland. There was no use sending someone to catch them because they'd be gone by then on swift horses. She'd have to send her own messenger.

Mira could tell Uda to help Vikram. Then Merwar would be strong again. Why hadn't she thought of this before?

The next day Mira sent her letter.

A month went by, another month, a third, and four months later, as the rains fell, Mira still hadn't received a response.

Perhaps Uda wasn't able to send a messenger because the monsoon rains were on time this year. It wouldn't matter because the young crops would've been destroyed in the storm and resulting landslides but still, if it rained, that would explain why Uda hadn't sent a message.

Mira dressed in her best pink cotton garments and made her way to Gopi Talau, an area outside the city. This was the famous pond where the Gopis gave up their lives.

Tonight was Sharad Poornima. On this full moon night, Krishna danced the raas with the Gopis, fulfilling their desire to be his.

Tonight all the people of Dwarka came together to celebrate this love between the lord and his devotees. The people had asked Mira to sing but she'd told them she would only dance tonight. She would be a Gopi.

The enclosure was lit by torches around the perimeter and by the lamps set around Krishna's feet. The drums were beaten and the conch was blown; the garba dance began. Krishna stood in the middle as the devotees danced around him.

Mira clapped and swayed. The stars twinkled down and she thanked them for helping her bend.

The devotees danced with dandyaa sticks, knocking them together in rhythm, following a pattern around the circle. One of the musicians played a melody on the flute, the strains sounding like the swaying leaves in Vrindavan.

Mira played with the dandyaa, laughing with the other devotees as they accidentally hit her fingers. She felt the golden light of the torches mingling with the white light of the moon. She felt the clean clay earth beneath her feet and the gentle wind swirling around her.

The drums beat for hours until all were tired and thirsty. Mira knew the raas would end soon but she didn't want to leave Gopi Talau this night. She decided to sleep here under the moon and stars so that she could feel Giridar right next to her.

The devotees packed up the prasad that was on the altar for distribution, wrapped Krishna in soft shawls and placed him on a cart, then made their way back to the city.

Mira remained where she was, bidding goodnight to them all. When they were gone and the night was quiet, she lay upon the ground and felt the air stir.

The torches still burned but she didn't mind.

She named the stars she knew and guessed at the ones she didn't. Her eyelids felt heavy and she let them slide downwards. "Giridar," she whispered as she fell asleep.

She could hear sweet singing as the Gopis danced with Krishna. It can't be, she thought, the devotees have gone home. I'm alone here. All alone…

A fingertip touched her palm where it rested next to her head. The heat of the finger made her skin tingle. It traced its way down into the crevice of her elbow and up to her shoulder.

Mira quivered.

The fingertip trailed up her neck and touched her lips, caressing them, parting them.

Sandalwood filled her senses until she could taste it and she stretched. "Giridar," she whispered.

"I'm here." The words grazed her, running over her lips as she opened her eyes. Twin moons gazed down at her, so close.

She felt his breath coming into her. She felt his fingertip wonder along her collar bone like it was the bank of the Yamuna.

He kissed her, putting his arms around her and rolling over the sweet scented earth, over and over until they were laughing.

Mira melded herself to him, her hand to his hand, her chest to his, and danced the raas with her husband.

*

She opened her eyes to a pink gold sky.

A green parrot sat in the tree above, looking down at her with round eyes.

Her skin was goose-pimpled in the chill dawn air. She turned to her left side but he wasn't there. She looked to her right but he wasn't there either.

Radha suffered constant pain when Krishna wasn't with her. Mira knew her own fate was to be the same.

She sat up. The top hooks of her blouse were undone and she reached to fasten them when she felt something.

Resting inside her blouse, on her left breast, was a peacock feather.

# 30

# Message

Mira looked up from the Mahabharat scripture she was reading. A priest from the mandir had lent it to her.

The manageress of the dharamshalla was at her door.

"What is it, Ma?" Mira asked.

"There's a messenger for you, Mirabai." The round lady with a head of wiry grey hair gave her a knowing look. "I think he's from your terrible relatives in Merwar."

Mira shook her head. "They're not terrible, Ma."

They had this conversation every time messengers came from Merwar.

Mira followed the manageress down the steps to the courtyard of the dharamshalla. A Brahmin stood there, a holy man with wild dreadlock hair that she recognized from the Kumbh-Shyam mandir. She bowed to him.

He handed her a letter in silence.

It bore Uda's Aum mantra seal, thank Krishna. She looked back at him. "Babaji, will you sit and take some refreshment while I read this?"

He nodded.

She went into the kitchen to fetch him a plate of fruit and a cup of coconut water. She laid a mat on the ground for him and placed his meal before it. "Please accept this and take some rest. I will read this and then write a response for you."

He sat down, folded his hands in silent prayer and ate.

Mira took her letter into the corner to read.

"Jai Shri Krishna, my dear Mirabai. I hope you're well and healthy.

"I received your letter some months ago but was unable to reply because of unforeseen circumstances. Then Babaji was kind enough to volunteer delivering my letter. By the way, he has taken a vow of silence so don't think he's being rude if he doesn't talk to you.

"I wish to allay your concerns about Vikram. He's in good health and is as stout-hearted as ever. You mustn't worry about his ruling abilities. They are as they ever were."

Mira frowned.

"You must stay where you are, where it's safe and you're at peace."

Where it's safe? Is Merwar not safe anymore? Mira wondered.

"Vikram is only calling you back because his conscience is attacking him and he believes the only remedy is to make you return. I'm trying to convince him, daily, that he must only find peace within himself. You need not return."

The rest of the letter was filled with banalities about life in Chittore and little bits of news about devotees here and there. So-and-so has married. So-and-so has had a baby. So-and-so has joined Sumer's regiment. Mira must not return to Chittore.

Uda was definitely hiding something.

What did she mean when she wrote that Vikram's ruling abilities were "as they ever were"? And why should Dwarka be safer than Merwar? Both were threatened by Akbar.

And why had Uda repeated over and over again that Mira was not to return to Chittore? Of course Mira wouldn't leave Dwarka, but why Uda was so insistent about it?

Mira wrote a quick and blunt response. She had to make Uda tell her the truth.

Three months later it was the heart of winter and Dwarka, being on the coast, was treated to freezing winds and bitter mornings.

Mira woke extra early on the morning of Gita Jayanti.

This was the day when Krishna spoke the Bhagavad Gita to his friend Arjuna on the battlefield of Kurukshetra, revealing the secrets of the universe.

The priests performed a special yagna for Krishna today and thus Mira rose when it was still dark. She bathed, not bothering to heat the water, simply dousing herself with a frigid bucketful. Her skin bumped up in reaction and she rubbed it hard to warm herself. She dressed in a yellow blouse and skirt with a red border at the hem and neckline. She pulled her black hair into a knot and covered it with her veil. As a special treat, she put her ankle bells on and chum chummed down the lane towards the temple courtyard.

The yagna would begin soon. The Brahmins were already here,

some had been here all night, preparing for the event. As the secondary priests placed offerings of grain and ghee into the fire, the head priest would chant the entire Gita without pause.

Mira was eager for it to begin. She loved the magic of yagnas and the heat of the sacrificial fire.

When the invocations were spoken and the holy fire lit, the priests began their offerings. The flames rose high, licking the ghee that was poured into it. The priests threw grains in, chants of "Swaha!" "Swaha!" reverberating around the courtyard. The head priest chanted the Gita to the rhythm of the ocean waves, up and down and up and down.

Mira watched, transfixed by the potency of the fire, consuming offerings like the earth swallowing the sea. The wind whipped about her, molding her veil to her body and she shivered.

She heard the chanting of the Gita, up and down, and saw that the flames were dancing to the rhythm, flickering and fluttering. She stared deep into the heat and saw the plains of Kurushetra, the dust rising in the wind. It was a vast yellow land, an ancient battlefield that had seen more blood than anywhere else on earth. Then she saw spears, shattered spears, lying in a heap on the yellow dust. Then the plains were gone and suddenly it was sandstone, like the foundations of Chittore, and it was red and black with blood. The spears, shattered before, were bloody and tangled, mutilated and scattered. And all around was fire, a grand fire, a devastating fire. Mira could smell charred flesh, like the meat once cooked in the royal kitchen.

She cried out.

"Mirabai!"

She pushed her way through the flames, trying to find the burning flesh.

"Mirabai!"

She stumbled over spears and felt her feet cut but she couldn't find the bodies. Where were the bodies?

"Mira!"

She gasped and looked up.

The priests of the temple were standing over her, worried looks on their faces.

She swallowed the bile in her throat. "What?"

"You had a seizure," one of the younger priests said, his round eyes concerned as he offered her a cup of water.

She took it and looked around. The yagna was still going but even the head priest was staring at her as he reeled off slokas of the Gita. She gulped some water. "Forgive me, I'm not feeling well." She stood, her limbs weak and shaking. "I'll go walk and compose myself."

They nodded, and Mira saw one of the priests gesture at his small son to follow her.

She walked out of the temple complex, shivering, trying to understand what had just happened.

Was it a vision? She'd never had a vision before. What did it mean?

She looked down and saw that her feet weren't bleeding.

She took another gulp of water but her hand was trembing and she sloshed it all over her neck. Had she really seen Chittore in her vision? She'd not recognized the streets or the buildings. What about the burning meat? Her stomach churned and she swallowed bile once more.

"Please, Giridar, don't let there be a war," she whispered.

*

She fired off another message to Uda, asking questions that she'd not thought to write in her last. She asked whether there was any news of Akbar or the Afghans and if the alliances were upheld. She asked if Ratan was well and the roads safe. She asked if the people were afraid and if the army ready.

She calculated that it would be at least a month before she received a reply.

After two weeks, her vision hadn't reoccurred. Perhaps it'd just been a dream after all.

Her mind eased and she was able to think of other things, specifically, the night of Sharad Poornima.

He hadn't returned yet. Perhaps that had all been a dream too.

But no, she still had the peacock feather. She kept it next to her heart when she slept.

Again, Mira wondered how Radha and the Gopi's had been able to bear such pain. There was nothing like this pain in all the world. Not the death of one's mother, or one's brother. Not losing her reputation, not losing her status, not even missing her guru could compare to this. All she wanted to know was why she wasn't good enough.

Radha was his beloved, his strength, his other half. Mira could never be as perfect as she. But even then he left Radha in Vrindavan.

Radha and Krishna spent their lives apart, visiting each other in dreams, crying when they felt the other was crying but never meeting face to face. It was only when they both left Earth and returned to their divine abode of Golok that they reunited.

If Krishna was the spark of life within all beings, Radha was the spark of love. She was what inspired the lord to unite with his devotees. She was the mother who showed the children their father.

Mira knew that Radha was within her and because Radha was within her, this pain of viyog would never leave. It was what made Mira rise in the morning, what made her sing, what made her dance to the rhythm of the mantras.

She began to understand what she hadn't in Vrindavan: she needed this pain.

Without it, there was no reason to carry on.

*

Ratan opened his eyes to see a carved marble ceiling above him. His legs were cramped. He looked down to see that he was lying with his head touching one wall and his feet touching the other. There was a deity of Krishna next to Ratan on the floor. Krishna's legs had been smashed off.

Ratan looked into the deity's eyes.

"Where am I?" he asked.

"You're in a mandir, my lord," said Ranjeet's voice. "They already stole what they could so they won't be back here. I thought it the safest place." He was sitting behind the altar, stirring a pot. He held it up. "It's kitchi for you."

"Good, I'm starving," Ratan said, ignoring his confusion to focus on the problem at hand. He moved to rise and gritted his teeth against the shock. His shoulder was on fire! Then he remembered that bastard Moghul had run a sword through it.

"Don't move, Ranaji, You'll tear the stitches." Ranjeet put his hands beneath Ratan's back and helped him sit up. He ran his hands over Ratan's bandage to check the bleeding had not begun again.

"Is the food offered?"

Ranjeet picked a leaf from a plant behind the altar and put it into the bowl. He held the bowl to the fallen, legless Krishna and spoke soft prayers under his breath. He lifted the food. "It's offered." He began spooning soft kitchi into Ratan's mouth until he saw the rana's glare and handed the bowl over. "I thought you might be too weak."

"Never that." Determined to ignore the pain, Ratan lifted the spoon to his mouth. He almost gagged on it. "What happened?" he mumbled to cover his discomfort.

Ranjeet's face looked as if it'd been carved from the same marble as the ceiling. It even had the same funny lines all over it, running over his nose and forehead. "There was nothing left when I dragged you from the battlefield. Everyone was dead which was why, I suppose, no one bothered to take you to safety."

"When did you arrive?"

"A day ago."

"I've been unconscious for a day?"

"You were bashed on the head several times. I thought you might not wake up."

Ratan was suddenly assaulted by the worst headache he'd ever had. How could he not have noticed that headache before? It throbbed from his crown, the pain bubbling like a freshwater spring all the way to his eyebrows.

He groaned.

"Drink this." Ranjeet held a cup to Ratan's mouth and this time Ratan took his help, gulping down the liquid. Ranjeet waited a few moments before he spoke again. "There's nothing left, Rana. Chaukari, Merta, it's all gone. Many of our people are dead and the ones who still live will only scream in grief."

Ratan felt a miraculous lightheaded sensation, then a heavy one, as if someone had just thumped a hand over the top of his head. But the pain was gone. "What did you give me?" His voice was slurred, as if he was drunk except that he'd never been drunk in his life.

"A mixture of poppy seeds."

Ratan stared at him.

"It's not enough to kill you, only enough to dull the pain. I learned it while in Kabul. The Moghuls are addicted to the vile plant but I thought I should give you some, regardless."

"Poppy seeds?" Ratan said, despising his drunkard voice.

"Yes. I know we shouldn't use such strong plants but I've nothing else to give you for the pain. I'm sorry, my lord."

Ratan held up his hand. The pain in his shoulder was gone. "I can't believe you gave me poppy seeds." He shook his head and it didn't hurt. "Tell me what happened."

"You were injured and fell from your horse. I brought you here." Ranjeet's face hardened. "The siege must be over in Chittore by now."

"My brother is dead?"

Ranjeet's eyes were hard. "I kept him close by so you could perform his last rites."

The poppy seeds made Ratan feel nothing. "What about the rest of the family? My nieces and nephews and cousins?"

"They're dead, my lord."

"Has there been word from Merwar?"

"I've waited on the road for the past day. There's been no word."

The next day, weak and trembling, Ratan lit his brother's pyre.

\*

For two weeks, he regained his strength. He rid himself of the disgusting poppy relief and breathed to control the throbbing the way his father had taught him. His shoulder healed, and once the pain was gone, it was amazing how young Ratan felt. The burning in his chest that had plagued him for years was gone, and the stiffness of his joints seemed to melt into the ground he slept upon.

Ranjeet told him of how the prominent Brahmins had been forced to convert. Those who didn't had their wife, mother and daughters raped. If they still refused, their sons or grandsons were killed. If they still refused, they were tortured, some skinned alive, some impaled, some mutilated beyond recognition. Then they were killed.

Ranjeet had found some of Ratan's soldiers, dragged to safety by their comrades. They were hiding the way Ratan was, in little destroyed temples and ashrams, finding food in ghost villages.

Ratan told Ranjeet to gather them for a meeting in Dhairya Babbaji's ashram, the hermitage of the now dead holy man.

When Ratan reached the place, he saw a force of at least four hundred soldiers, battered and bruised, but Rajput soldiers nonetheless. Many of them were the village lads he'd recruited some years ago.

"We're alive and that means we're still fighting," he told them, looking around at their grave faces. "They cannot beat us because we'll not surrender."

It was just like that night, so many years ago, when Ratan had imagined that his men were no longer looking out. They were looking in, seeking the light in the darkness.

And they fought. Wherever they discovered a Moghul camp, Ratan sent his men to cut off food supplies and steal horses and cut the throats of the perimeter guards.

He wreaked havoc among the unsuspecting Moghuls, setting off explosions of gunpowder in weapons tents, and burning the food when the soldiers scurried to find their invisible foe.

Ratan cut free the young girls who were tied up, their clothes ripped, their legs splattered with blood both dried and oozing. Some of the girls were already dead when he cut them free.

"What about Mira?" Ranjeet asked one night.

"Mira?" Ratan said, staring up at the constellations.

"Yes. Who shall we send to protect her?"

For a long moment, Ratan could only look up at the night sky, feeling the air quiet and cool about him. He thought of his sweet, innocent daughter, and wished he could've seen her one last time. Then he looked at Ranjeet. "Don't you know? Mirabai needs no protection from us."

Ranjeet was quiet for a moment before he nodded and stole away to another Moghul camp.

Whenever Ratan spied a commander, he went in to kill the man himself. No one else was allowed to kill commanders, only Ratan.

His company made their way south down to the Vindya mountains and Chittore. Sweeping over the valleys under cover of dark, Ratan heard the whispers of cannon fire, and knew that Chittore's walls were being assaulted.

She'll hold, he told himself. Jaimal is in there and he will make her hold.

And when Ratan's men crept up the mountainside, skirting Moghuls and mountain lions, Ratan held his weapons close. Months ago, Jaimal had sent word of hidden caves the Sisodias used in times of need and Ratan found them, deep in the mountainside. He secreted his force inside and sent off scouts, men who were small and light-footed, to gather information.

Two returned to tell him Chittore still held, if barely. Six of her seven gates had been breached and the Moghuls had set up their camp within them. Akbar himself was in there, a drunk singing in that guttural language, Persian. The few Merwari people still alive had retreated into the inner fort.

Ratan set men all over the mountain to kill the Moghul runners, thus cutting off Akbar's communications. He sent more men to kill any horses the Moghuls had, asking forgiveness of the horses for the slaughter. His only defense was that their deaths were necessary.

Then his third scout came with a message: Jaimal was dead.

Ratan couldn't understand what he felt. It was like something broke inside him. All these weeks he'd hoped that Chittore still held because Jaimal was there to hold her. Now Merta had no heir, no king, no protector. The Rathore line was dead.

What should he feel? His Merta, his people, defeated by barbarians, and all those he loved were gone. All but Mira.

Ratan didn't know what he felt, but as he unsheathed his sword and cut his own palm, he swore that he would die defending his people. He swore it and his men swore it and as the drops of their blood fell to the cave floor, Ratan felt free.

*

Uda stood next to her mother.

The women were gathered opposite the Brahma Vishnu Shiv temple. Here, the holy trinity was worshipped in a three-headed shivling stone as the united creator, preserver, and destroyer.

Gauri had decided this would be the right place.

Huge pyres were before them, fueled with all the wood in the temple's supplies. It cast Uda's face a saffron hue.

They'd all known this would happen, Uda thought. So many women had taken their children in their arms and accepted fate.

Behind them, before them, around them, cannon fire raged. Little bits of stone were flying around, ricocheting off the ground and hitting the women. The walls were falling.

"Soon," Gauri said.

The younger women were whimpering, their faces hidden in their veils. Only when the elders reprimanded them for cowardice did the girls emerge from their veils, their tears still falling but their heads high.

For the first time in their lives, these Rajput women were not surrounded by guards or even maids.

"Never forget you are Kshatraanis," Gauri told them. "Now is the time to prove it."

The ground shook with a deadly explosion.

Uda grabbed her mother and in the process, dropped her copper vial.

Gauri picked it up. "Don't lose this, putri."

Uda turned to see that across the gardens the gate to the inner fort was breached, the wall broken. Moghuls were streaming in, brandishing swords. Rajput soldiers were rushing to face them. Both Moghul and Rajput archers shot arrows from their vantage points on the parapets.

"Now," Gauri said.

Some hands shook, some did not, but the women pulled the tops off their vials. They lifted them to their mouths and swallowed.

No one saw that the top was still on Uda's vial.

One girl, a pregnant cousin of Uda's, gagged on the liquid. Her mother-in-law patted her back.

"Remember your husband and your Isht," Gauri told them.

There was a moment as every woman closed her eyes in prayer. Then:

"Durga Mata ki jai!" Gauri cried, walking into the pyre.

"Durga Mata ki jai!" the women cried after her.

Uda watched them join Raj Mata Gauri, their garments curling in the flames. The grey tendrils of her mother's hair glowed and it looked as if fire was emerging from her head. The ladies dropped silently onto the pyre, their bodies overcome by the lethal dose of poison.

Vasudev...Uda thought, her breathing harsh as she watched her mother engulfed by fire. I need you now, my lord. It is just you and I.

She held her vial and backed away from the flames.

Gauri had ordered Uda not to do this.

The saffron-robed Rajputs were clashing with the Moghuls, their swords fierce, flashing in the sunlight.

Uda turned and ran through the gardens to the Kirti Stumbh. She hurried all the way up the stairs to the ninth level. Panting, she rubbed the stitch in her side, then picked up the bow and quiver she'd left there earlier. Now was her chance.

Vasudev, give me strength, she prayed.

She set an arrow on her bow and took aim, pulling the string right back to her ear the way Bhoj had taught her. She let go. The arrow whizzed down and pierced a Moghul in the shoulder, just as he would have stabbed a Rajput in the back.

Uda set another arrow and took aim. The string twanged and the arrow raced off, finding its place in the thigh of another enemy very close to his groin. He screamed and she smiled: at last, some fun.

She sent more arrows flying through the air and brought seven more enemies down.

One of them, his rat face thin and ugly, spied her. He shouted something to his comrades and they began running Uda's way.

I am not afraid, she thought, bringing two of them down as more soldiers joined the race to the tower.

They leaped over limbs and dead bodies and parts of walls, closing in on the Stumbh. When they approached the Shiv temples, one of them deliberately stepped into a yagna kund.

Uda shot him in the leg for it.

She wished Mira's serpent was here now, confounding them with its many heads.

But there were too many Moghuls. Uda kept shooting, holding her position even as she heard them shouting on the stairs. She shot an enemy as he tried to grab a woman's limb in the pyre. She shot a man as he threw a pail of water over the flames. She shot a Moghul as he urinated against Shiv's temple.

There was another explosion and the Kirti Stumbh vibrated. In the distance, the inner fort wall collapsed. There were few saffron robes still standing. She saw a sea of Moghuls streaming in through the rubble, waving swords and slashing all in their path.

She picked up the vial she'd placed on the floor, pulling the top off. Below, she heard the frustrated voices of barbarians as they climbed the stairs to reach her. They must have been cursing but she didn't know their coarse language.

Uda thought of that last letter from Mira that she'd been unable to answer. Akbar's army had reached the foot of the mountain by then, using elephants to haul massive cannons, so there was no question of allowing another messenger out. The birds were being used to contact Vikram's forces over the land, calling them to Chittore's aid.

Thank Vasudev Mira wasn't here.

Behind, Uda heard the swarthy voice of a soldier as he reached the ninth level. She swallowed the poison. It was sweet, like honey. She wondered if her mother had put honey in it to cover the bitterness.

Uda crouched on the window sill, looking down at the yellow sandstone of Chittore. This was her motherland. She would die for her mother.

Uda felt the man reach for her, his hands reeking of blood and sweat. She could feel his glee at finding the only royal woman alive.

I go now to my Vasudev, she thought. "Aum namo bhagavate vasudevaya..." she whispered.

Up ahead, Uda saw something that made her blink. A golden chariot, pulled by four white horses, was streaking through the blue sky. As she watched, it turned and flew towards her, the horses swift and sure.

The man behind her was joined by several others. She felt the air swish as they raised their swords and Uda was struck by the thrill of death. She smiled.

"Aum namo bhagavate vasudevaya." She gazed at the chariot that was almost upon her and pushed away from the sill, away from the heat of the hands that reached for her.

She didn't feel the ground. She felt only, "Aum..."

*

"Didi!"

Mira sat up on the floor.

Outside, the sun was cooling and people were rising from their naps to return to work.

Mira's heart thumped like a mrdunga drum. Why had she just said Uda's name? She'd not even been thinking about Uda. Remembering the vision of shattered spears, Mira shivered. She could still smell the burning flesh.

If only she'd returned to Merwar.

But she couldn't! She'd promised she wouldn't.

The messenger. The messenger hadn't come. That's why she was so anxious.

Mira took deep breaths and told herself she was worrying over nothing. She just had to wait for the messenger.

# 31

## Ties

Vikram was hiding in a cave on the eastern side of the mountain.

Most of his men were dead.

Akbar was living in Vikram's palace.

Vikram's forces in his other forts were under attack. They couldn't come to aid the capital.

The last months had been endless. Akbar's cannons had assaulted the walls over and over again.

Jaimal saw to it that each night all damage was repaired.

There was no way for the Moghuls to break through and for a few days or so, Vikram had thought that Akbar would retreat.

Then Akbar tried to plant mines beneath the walls by digging tunnels but this backfired when one of the mines blew up too early, killing hundreds of his men and alerting Jaimal to his plan.

It took him months but Akbar finally realized that he was never going to penetrate the fort. Ruthlessly, he made his men pile sand and dirt into a little mount that he called coin hill, for he offered his men a gold coin per basket of dirt they contributed. He lost many soldiers in the venture, for the laborers were easy pickings for Vikram's archers, but Akbar had his hill built. With it, there was a highter vantage point from which to fire his cannons into the fort, and with the amount of Rajputs concentrated inside, the casualties were enormous.

Jaimal was one such casualty.

With fewer people to repair the walls, it was only a matter of time.

When Chittore's food supplies, already exhausted in the long drought and devastating landslides, ran out, Vikram realized that once again, johar was the only way, just as it had been for his parents.

Silently, he removed his armor and donned the saffron robes.

His men followed.

Together, they rode into battle, intent on laying down their lives.

Vikram was shot in the thigh with an arrow and fell off his horse. When Akbar came along to kill him, the fool hadn't spied Vikram trapped and unconscious beneath the animal.

The Moghuls went back to their camp to feast on the cows they'd killed and Sumer pulled Vikram from beneath the horse's rump and brought him to the cave.

Vikram's leg was broken in three places, but it didn't matter. He was supposed to be dead, killed like his father in johar.

"Ratan arrived with a small brigade," Sumer was saying. "It was enough to fend off the rascals trying to rob the bodies of our dead."

"Where is Ratan now?" Vikram asked through clenched teeth.

"He was martyred."

If only Mira had come to Merwar when I asked, Vikram thought, Akbar might never have attacked. Ratan might still be alive.

Stop it! Vikram screamed in his mind, pounding his head with his fists. Just stop it!

This wasn't Mira's fault. It had never been her fault.

Vikram finally recognized the cold within him as the shame it was. *He* had done this to Merwar, to his family. Who would mourn him now? He wasn't even dead! He lay crippled in a cave while Akbar slept in his bed.

If only Ratan hadn't lost Shamal. Now Jaimal had fallen too.

If only Bairam Khan were still alive. Bairam Khan would not have attacked Vikram. They'd understood each other. Right?

All Vikram's wives must be dead by now. Vikram had no sons to succeed him.

If Bhoj had been alive, this wouldn't have happened. The outer provinces would never have revolted. The nobles there would never have joined Akbar.

At least I sent Udai away, Vikram thought. Udai, Bhoj's favorite, Shivgan's younger brother, would live to fight on.

But not Vikram. He'd failed many times but not again.

Dry-eyed, he told Sumer what to do.

Sumer went out, captured two horses and brought them in.

Vikram chose one and gripped its mane. He hauled himself onto its back, pushing his broken leg into place. The agony of moving it was nothing to him.

Sumer climbed onto his own mount's back.

His other men were on foot, their swords held tight, their faces shadowed. The last of Ratan's men stood with them.

"Now we follow in the footsteps of our fathers," Vikram told them. "Remember always that we are Rajputs."

He unsheathed his sword and kissed the blade. "Hail Merwar, my Mother, my Goddess. Forgive me for my sins."

He rode out of the cave and up the steep slopes to the enemy.

The Moghuls guarding the gate saw them and raised their bows, arrows cocked and ready.

Vikram held up his sword.

*

Mira stood in the middle of the courtyard, looking at the messenger before her.

He was tall and dusty, his eyes black and his hair wild. He knelt before her. "Rani Mirabai ki jai ho."

Mira gazed at Sumer's lieutenant. "What has happened, Lakshmikant?"

"The worst, Rani."

Mira felt a strange sense of dizziness.

"Our people are dead."

Mira stared at him. What did he mean? All of them? Every last one?

"Akbar waged a siege against Chittore. The royal family is destroyed. The only survivor is Udai, your late husband's cousin. On Maharana Vikram's order, he went over the mountains with his wife, Rani Kaveri, to the southwestern corner of Merwar."

"Vikram's order, of course," Mira nodded again, her head light with a feeling she couldn't grasp. "Did you say the royal family is dead?"

He nodded.

"Everyone?"

He nodded again.

That meant Uda too. And Raj Mata Gauri. "What about Maharana Vikram's wives?"

"They committed johar with Raj Mata, Raniji."

There was a pause.

"Johar," Mira said, looking at the way his unwaxed moustache stuck out at odd angles, stiffened by dust and sweat. She felt her legs give way and she sat down on the stone floor.

She saw women jumping into flames and men riding out in saffron.

Mira could ask how and why but somehow, all that seemed irrelevant. She looked up at the soldier and he was haggard, like a demon had whipped him all the way to Dwarka. "What is Udai going to do, Lakshmikant?"

"He will build a new city in the mountain valley."

"That's good," she said, nodding like a fool. "And Merta?"

"Destroyed, Raniji. Your cousin Jaimal and father Ratan were martyred in Chittore."

Krishna...Jaimal was dead? Mira clutched her tambora. Her father and uncle and all her cousins too. Her father was dead!

"Raj Kumar Udai begs that you join him in his Aravali camp. He desperately seeks your assistance."

"Me?" What can I do? Mira thought.

I knew this was going to happen, she realized. I didn't want to believe it but I knew.

She shook her head to clear the horrifying thoughts. "Return to Udai with my blessings and tell him I'm sworn to remain in Dwarka."

"Raniji, we beg you to reconsider. We need your help!"

"How can I help anyone, Lakshmikant?" Her voice was dazed. "I cannot even help myself."

"We need your faith and your Giridar. We need him so much."

Mira swallowed. "Giridar is with you always. You have only to call out to him."

The soldier closed his eyes. "Do you have any advice for Kumar Udai?"

"Tell him not to commit johar." Mira hugged her tambora. "And tell him not to return to Chittore. The Bhils of the Aravali mountains are loyal to the Sisodias. Tell Udai to recruit them."

"As you command, Raniji." He rose.

Mira took a deep breath and forced her legs to stand. "May Krishna bless you, Lakshmikant."

She watched him walk away and wanted to do something, anything, to straighten his tired back. Yet there was nothing she could do. Just as she'd done nothing for her father.

She should've warned them. She'd known this would happen.

No. She'd known nothing. Nothing.

*

Mira sat on the temple floor, looking up at Krishna.

The priests, as always, gave her space.

What can I do, Giridar? she wondered.

Krishna said in the Gita that this world was temporary, that the real war was within the human heart. The way to win this war was to surrender heart, mind and soul to him. Then there would be peace.

Mira prayed that Ratan and Uda and Gauri and even Vikram were now with Krishna.

Poor Vikram. Mira should have returned to Chittore when he'd asked. She'd denied him his last wish.

But Gurudev had told her to stay here.

Mira was to blame for all those deaths. Hundreds of thousands of her people. Merwar, Merta, both of them her countries. She'd worked all her life to protect them; she'd even married a man who wasn't Krishna. Now her people had been slaughtered.

She couldn't bear to look at Krishna. In her selfishness, she'd failed her people. She'd failed *him*.

"Mira."

A tall man was looking down at her. He looked like a reed, his body so slender and flexible that it waved when he shifted his feet.

She'd never seen him before but she knew who he was. "Rana Pipa?"

"I am Pipa."

"Ramanand Acharya's disciple?"

He nodded, and the single lock at the top of his head floated about. "I am your guru's brother. And that makes me your uncle."

She stared at him.

He smiled. There was a glow around him, as if the sun were shining from behind, except that the sun was not behind him. Pipa gestured to his left side.

A beautiful lady stood there, her cotton garments wrapped around her like silk around a doll. "Mira, we've come to see you," the lady said, her voice soft.

"This is your aunt," Pipa said.

"Jai Shri Krishna, putri. I am Sitasarchari," the lady said.

Mira gaped at her. "Jai Shri Krishna," she whispered.

The golden glow was around Sitasarchari's head also. Where had these two come from? Mira wondered. She realized her uncle and aunt were standing before her and she'd shown them no respect. She touched her forehead to the ground at their feet.

Sitasarchari lifted Mira up and kissed her brow.

They sat before her.

"We bring a message from my brother," Pipa said.

"Gurudev sent me a message?"

"He wants you to be strong, Mira. You must be strong."

Mira's eyes were glazed. "They're all dead, you know. Everyone."

Pipa and Sitasarchari looked at each other.

"Nothing happens that is not destined to happen, putri," Pipa said.

"But how could this be destined? Why?"

"Our destiny is determined by our actions."

Mira looked from one to the other, the glow around their heads arresting her. "It's my fault, I should've done something."

"There was nothing you could have done," Pipa said. "Remember Kurukshetra? Even Krishna tried to avert that war but he couldn't."

Mira thought of the ancient war in which the whole world had fought—the horrific war of the Pandavas and Kauravas fought at Kurukshetra, where Krishna spoke the Gita to Arjuna.

"Akbar has won."

"Only the battle, Mira, not the war. The war is within ourselves and we will win it. You will win it also, if only you are strong." He smiled at her. "Come, Mira, you were only saying this to yourself a moment ago."

She saw the glow shift and rotate at the back of his head. "Kaka Sa, why is there this tej on your faces?"

The couple smiled.

"We've just received darshan of Dwarkadish and Goddess Rukmini," Sitasarchari said, her voice tender.

Mira's eyes were whirlpools. "Where?"

Pipa lowered his head. "We'd been performing penance for years, trying to achieve Krishna's darshan. Finally, we despaired and jumped into the ocean to end our struggle. Then they appeared."

Mira gasped. "And then?"

"They saved us. They loved us. They sent us back," Sitasachari said.

Mira looked from her aunt to her uncle and back to her aunt. "Sent you back? But why?"

Sitasarchari shrugged. "They always have their reasons. And here is one right before us: you."

Mira hugged herself. "I thought I didn't have anyone left."

Pipa laughed. "A devotee is never alone. You must trust Krishna even in the darkest moments. Trust him as he trusts you."

Her uncle was right, she realized. Krishna was always with her.

Just as she'd trusted him the night of Sharad Poornima, she had to trust him now. She had to believe he would show her the way.

# 32

# Warrior Woman

Mira sat with her Tulsi beads, meditating under the banyan tree outside the temple. Her hips felt stiff and she ignored the discomfort, accepting it as the aging of her physical self.

"Rama," she whispered, chanting the mantra her guru had taught her. She cleared her mind of all other thoughts, concentrating only on the vibrations of the holy name. "Rama..."

The sounds of cows clomping or devotees talking faded away. She heard only the sound of Rama.

A light appeared in her mind. It was violet then deep purple then violet once more, the light spinning like a wheel on an axis. She concentrated on that light, spinning to the chant of Rama. The violet deepened to pure white and Mira felt it rush over her. Her skin goosepimpled and she bathed in the light.

"Rama Rama Rama," she chanted, listening to the syllables roll off her tongue.

Coolness washed over her, even though the spring sun was heating up the marble paving of the ground. Her heart slowed, pumping in time to the chant.

She looked at the spinning chakra and listened to the rhythm of Rama's name. After some hours, she felt the sun's rays fading and knew it was time for Krishna's aarti in the temple. She let the chakra go back to violet, and then to deep purple.

"Raghu Pati, Raagav, Raja Rama, Patita Pavana, Sita Rama," she said. It was a verse she'd learned in childhood and she said it whenever she ended her meditation. Glorious Rama, she thought.

Since her talk with her aunt and uncle a week ago, she'd stilled her mind to the news of Merwar's fate. Because that was what it was. Fate.

That didn't mean, however, that she could sleep. Every time she half-dozed, she saw Uda standing at the top of the Kirti Stumbh, a great fire burning beneath her. Then there was Ratan standing in a cave, his palm bleeding.

Mira blinked, opening her eyes to see devotees streaming into the temple complex.

From her vantage point of the raised earth under the banyan, Mira spied an old Brahmin, his white clothes tattered and dirty, his right hand clutching a staff. His face was streaked: he'd been weeping.

It was the Sisodia Raj Purohit.

He'd seen her. He brushed through the gate, not even paying attention that he was entering the great temple of Dwarkadish. He walked right up to her in the middle of the courtyard.

"I've come to take you home." He held his staff as if it were a weapon. His beard, once silver and glorious, hung in clumps from his shrunken cheekbones.

Her heart ached to see it. "I can't come with you. Forgive me."

The clumps of hair scrunched as he clenched his jaw. "I've sworn to Rana Udai that I'll only return to Merwar with you."

"And I've sworn to my guru that I'll remain in Dwarka with my husband."

"How shall this be resolved?"

Mira folded her palms. "Purohitji, I know and understand what you're feeling but I cannot come with you. For me to return to Merwar would only be a burden to Udai."

"No, Rani. Merwar needs you."

It was like being on a raft, jostling from one bank of the river to the other. "I've sent my blessings to Udai, Purohitji."

"That's not enough. I declare that if you do not come back to Merwar with me, I'll remain here, in this very spot, day and night. I'll not eat or drink and I'll not move until you agree to return."

She stiffened. "You can't do this!"

"I will."

"If you don't eat or drink you'll die."

"So be it."

By his grim expression, she knew he meant it. Raj Purohit was never one to make false threats. Just look at her trial.

His death would be on her head.

"Purohitji, don't do this. You don't know the ties that bind me."

"I know only that I've sworn an oath." He pulled a bunched rag from his waist and laid it on the floor. Sitting on it, he rested against the raised earth, his back to her.

She watched him, this priest who'd taught Uda and Bhoj and Vikram. Perhaps this was where they got their stubbornness. "Purohitji, you know that my husband is Krishna. Dwarka is my marital home; my place is here!"

There was a pause and Mira wondered if he'd even heard her.

"I must take you back," he whispered. "I must. You have to forgive us."

"I've already forgiven you."

"Then why is Merwar still punished?"

"I hold no grudges."

"Krishna is angry and the only way to pacify him is through you."

"That's ridiculous."

"I must take you back."

"I won't come!"

"Then I'll die."

She was so furious that one of her tambora's strings snapped. It sprang upwards, nicking her on the chin. She touched the wound and felt blood on her fingers.

Mira drew a deep breath. She stood up, smoothing her hands over her instrument, forgetting that the blood on her fingers was smearing over the wood. "I'll return to my ashram, Purohitji, and bring you refreshments."

"I will take no refreshment until you agree."

She stood there impotently, like a mother with an unruly child.

Turning, she trudged all the way back to the ashram, rubbing her stiff hips. She went into the courtyard and up the stairs to her room where she flung herself on her sleeping mat.

Purohitji doesn't make false threats, she thought. He really will sit out there until I agree. And I will never agree.

If Purohitji dies, it will be the same as if I've taken a katar and stabbed him in the heart myself, she thought.

To kill a Brahmin was one of the worst crimes imaginable.

She'd never escape the repercussions. If he died, Krishna would never accept her.

If she went to Merwar, she was breaking her vow to her guru.

Why was Krishna testing her so? Didn't he know she loved him?

The vedas said that Brahmins were the mouth of Vishnu. They were the knowledge givers, the protectors of scripture, the keepers of law. To kill a Brahmin was as good as suicide.

Mira would be sent to Narak for lifetime upon lifetime with no hope of finding Krishna.

She hugged her tambora. What shall I do?

Her people were dying and they asked for her help. It was her dharma to help them.

But then what of my vow? Gurudev, what shall I do?

Night fell and Mira didn't go down to the courtyard for her meal, not even when her friends called her down to sing in the evening. She remained lying on the floor, thinking about what to do.

The next morning, Mira bathed and dressed, then realized she'd put her clothes on inside out. Before she could fix the problem she heard the bells ringing for the mangal aarti. She was missing it!

She rushed to right her clothes and ran down the lane to the temple, pushing her way through the crowd to get to the front.

Dwarkadish stood before her, his four hands holding the conch, chakra, mace and lotus. He was dressed in deep purple today, just like the purple she'd seen in her meditation.

"Dwarkadish ki jai!" she cried, raising her arms above her head. My husband, she thought, I cannot leave you.

As the aarti finished and the crowd dispersed, Mira went out into the courtyard.

There he was, sitting in the early morning chill, only a rag covering him. He stared at her as she passed.

Mira went back to her ashram, ignoring the calls of the manageress to eat breakfast. In her room, she picked up a shawl and took it down to Purohitji, placing it around his shoulders.

He shook it off. "I've already been offered a shawl and I don't want one." He placed it at her feet, his elderly hands so frail with their knobbly blue veins.

She looked at him, helpless. "But it's so cold!"

"No colder than the dungeon in Chittore." He looked up at her. "I know that you suffered and I didn't send you anything. I don't deserve your kindness."

Miserable, she left the shawl and returned to the ashram.

The morning was cold but the afternoon was hot. Very hot. Hotter than usual, Mira thought. And Purohitji was sitting outside all through the midday hours, when everyone else had retreated to the cool comfort of their homes.

Mira worried her veil to shreds, thinking of him alone and hungry, suffering the sun without a drop of water. She knew what it felt like to be thirsty. At his age, how long would he last?

The women of the ashram came up to her room to find out who the Brahmin was and why neither he nor Mira would eat but she sent them to ask him instead.

Night fell and Mira looked out her window to see him huddled against the dirt, trying to sleep in the cold.

The next day was just the same. And the next.

He looked weak but no matter who offered him food or water, he refused. "Not until my Rani grants my wish," he told them.

The priests of the temple brought him prasad. The sages abandoned their scriptures and the hermits left their meditations to convince him to eat. The women of Mira's ashram sat around him, offering sweet milk and coconut water, for they knew that Mira was suffering hunger with him. Even the children went and pressed his legs, warming his old limbs and pleading with him not to take Mirabai away.

He denied them all.

She awoke the next morning with a rock of dread in her stomach.

If she didn't do something, he was going to die.

She paced the floor of her room, ignoring the calls of the ladies to come downstairs and eat.

The women came up to her room and tried to cheer her with senseless talk. The temple flower girls brought in jasmine which they threaded through Mira's hair, trying to distract her from the old man sitting outside.

By midmorning, she could stand it no longer.

Mira picked up her tambora, covered her hair with her veil and left the ashram.

The manageress called to her but Mira didn't answer.

Head high, she walked down the lane to the courtyard, the wind blowing against her back.

There were holy men around him, grim faced, speaking quietly of the scriptures.

"Purohitji?"

He was dozing but at her voice, he came awake. "Yes, Mirabai?"

"I have a suggestion."

The holy men around him exchanged looks and she could see them wondering if she would surrender.

Purohitji looked hopeful but was so weak he couldn't sit up. "What is it?" he asked.

She swallowed. "I will go and ask my husband. If he gives permission then I'll come with you to Merwar."

His gaze brightened and he nodded. "Yes, yes, of course. Go and ask your Giridar. I will wait for you."

A strange calm came over her. She didn't walk but glided through the arched gateway and down the paved lane. Turning the corner, she entered the temple room. There he stood, her Giridar. Dwarkadish. Ranchor.

He could raise her to Golok, or throw her to Narak.

The holy men had followed her and were now crowding the doorway of the temple with the flower girls and other devotees, straining to see what was happening.

A dark skinned priest was sweeping up the flowers devotees had thrown in offering. He looked up when he saw her standing so close to the altar.

"Bhaiya?" she said.

He came closer, frowning at the crowd in the doorway. "Yes, Mirabai?"

"I must speak with the master alone. I don't want anyone else in the mandir. Is that possible?"

The priest looked around, running his hand over his shaven head. The other priests were serving the deities of Devki, Krishna's mother, and Balaram, his brother. "Let me ask the other sevaks," he said to her.

He caught each of their gazes and gestured to them.

They came and huddled together, breaking off conversation every now and then to look at her.

She caught snatches of their words:

"–we can't say no, it's *Mirabai*–"

"–but we can't leave her alone with the master–"

"–it must be about *him*–"

"–not much time–"

She wasn't anxious or tense. She thought only of what had to be done.

There was further deliberation, then their huddle broke.

The head priest turned to her. "We'll close the temple for you, Mirabai. All you have to do is knock on the door over there," he said, pointing, "and we'll know you're finished."

"I'd be grateful if you locked all the doors so that no one may enter," she said.

The priests looked at each other and nodded.

She waited for them to gather their articles and head for the doors, shooing the curious people outside. Within minutes, Mira heard the sounds of chains being drawn and locked together. Then silence.

She put her tambora on the floor by the altar. From a pouch at her side, she withdrew her ankle bells, fastening them to her feet.

Looking up at Giridar, she chum chummed her foot on the ground.

"All my life, I've danced for you," she told him. "Now I'll dance one last time. And whatever you tell me to do, I'll do it."

Her voice echoed off the marble pillars and she shivered in the silence it left behind. Even the birds above seemed to have stopped singing.

"Tell me what you want," she whispered.

Raising her arms, Mira closed her eyes and began to move.

She danced in a way she never had before. She swayed her hips and arched her back. She flung her arms out and twirled on her toes. She swirled, over and over, the jasmine petals in her hair falling to the ground and crushing beneath her feet. She clapped her hands so hard that her glass bangles broke and the pieces fell to the floor. She danced over them, the shards cutting her feet.

Don't test me anymore, Giridar, she begged him. What must I do?

She swayed and arched, her blood and petals and sweat painting the floor. She jumped and clapped and spun and over and over again, she prayed he wouldn't test her.

I'm yours, Giridar. I'm yours. Tell me what you want!

She wept and her tears ran into her blood and her torn feet.

She danced and danced and her petals fell and her blood flowed.

Giridar, Giridar, how much can I take? Don't test me anymore.

She spun and spun, ankle bells chumming, heart burning.

Mira fell, her body spent, when there was a whisper in her ear.

"Priye."

She looked up into twin moons, blooming lotuses, vast oceans and smiled through her tears.

A pink palm appeared before her.

She placed her golden hand in his.

Dawn light swirled around her as she was lifted. Her feet didn't hurt, her heart didn't burn, and as she followed him up to the altar, Mira could feel the petals on the floor.

# 33

# Gopi

Ravi sat upon the bank of holy Ganga at Panch Ganga Ghat, the mist from the river surrounding him, wetting his skin.

He concentrated on the point between his eyes where a violet chakra spun. His third eye opened and he told it to search.

He saw the tiny island of Bhet Dwarka, where the whole island had waited all day for Mira to emerge. When the moon rose, they broke the locks on the chains to see what had happened.

They found a tambora and a shred of red cotton, both lying at the feet of Dwarkadish. There were petals on the floor and shards of bangles. And there was blood smeared across the ground, except before the lord, where there remained a clear pair of red footprints, small and delicate.

The priests carried the Sisodia Raj Purohit into the temple.

Purohitji knelt at the footprints, weeping, holding the shred of red cotton to his heart. A priest offered him a cup of water, Dwarkadish jal, and he accepted.

Leaving, he took the shred with him for Udai and asked the priests to keep the tambora there. It was Mira's legacy, he told them.

Such love for one he once rejected, Ravi thought.

Ravi looked east, towards southern Merwar, where Udai was building his new city. It would be called Udaipur and its splendor would be yet another Rajput legacy.

Ravi saw Akbar, dining in the halls of the Rajputs, presiding over his rabble of mercenaries. How long could their reign of bloodshed last? Tyrants would rise and fall and still Bharat would live on. Still the holy name would be chanted.

It was for this reason that devotees like Mira took birth. For this reason, Mira had sung, her words touching even a Moghul emperor.

My daughter, Ravi thought, has done well. Her story will not be forgotten.

He opened his eyes and found a cow at his side, nuzzling his shoulder. He reached up his hand and patted its soft black nose.

He wondered when another Gopi would be born, born to sing of the Blue Boy.

Ravi hoped Gopal wouldn't keep him waiting.

And Krishna said to Arjun:

Fix your mind on me, be devoted to me, worship me,
prostrate before me, and you shall come to me only.
Truly, this is my promise to you,
for you are dear to me.

Bhagavad Gita 18.65

# Author's Note

Although I always knew of her name, I first heard the story of Mirabai when I was fifteen years old. To this day, I remember the awe I felt. She was a rebel, a warrior, a devotee, a rockstar.

The historical record of her life, however, is not very complete. In my research for this book, I found that most accounts, though agreeing she lived in the sixteenth century, disagreed on many things, including the date of her birth. Some say around 1500, some say around 1540. I compromised and stuck her in the middle.

Many of the stories about her are legends, folktales that have been passed down through generations. Sometimes she herself gives proof of the myths. Her songs record her trial in the court of Chittore and how she survived drinking poison. She sang of her guru Ravi Das and his mercy upon her. She sang of a Rana, a corrupt king who persecuted her, whom I identified through my research as Vikram.

The other stories, such as meeting Akbar, her guardian serpent, and the mysterious manner of her death are all matters of legend. The historical records only state that she disappeared from Dwarka and for a person as famous as she was, this must have been difficult. For every legend, there is always a seed of truth. The holy ones say that she ascended to her divine abode, and I believe them.

I have woven my story from the historical facts, folktales and legends I could find. You must let me know if my portrayal has been successful. Write to me at P.O.Box 295628, Lewisville, Tx 75029-5628, USA. I would love to hear your comments.

CPSIA information can be obtained
at www.ICGtesting.com
Printed in the USA
FSOW01n1549160715
8940FS